TOLL OF THE GATES

". . . Last of all only the woman Morgaine survived, skilled in *qujalin* witchcraft and bearing still that Sword that casts to death. Much of evil she did in Morija and Baien, rivalling all other evils she has committed . . . but she fled thereafter, taking with her Nhi Vanye i Chya, once of this house, who was ilin to her and therefore bound by his oath."

—Nhi Erij i Myya, in the *Book of Ra-morij*

"Chya Roh i Chya, Lord of Ra-koris, followed the witch Morgaine, for his cousin's sake . . . but Nhi Erij in his writing avows that Chya Roh perished on that journey, and that the Soul that possessed the likeness of Roh thereafter was *qujal*, and hostile to every Godly man . . ."

—the *Book of Baien-an*

SUVOJ

OHTIJ-IN

BARROWS-HOLD

GHADRIN

ANLA'S
CROWN

WELL
OF
SHIUAN

by
C. J. Cherryh

DAW Books, Inc.
Donald A. Wollheim, Publisher
1633 Broadway, New York, N.Y. 10019

Cover art by Michael R. Whelan.

For color prints of Michael Whelan
paintings, please contact:

Glass Onion Graphics
P.O. Box 88
Brookfield, CT 06804

Frontispiece map by the author.

DAW Book Collectors No. 284.

For Andre Norton,
a lady of lovely and gentle
magics

FIRST PRINTING, APRIL 1978

8 9

PRINTED IN THE U.S.A.

PROLOGUE

Whoever first built the Gates that led from time to time and space to space surely gained from them no good thing.

The qhal found the first Gate in the strange ruins of Silen on a dead world of their own sun. They used the pattern, built other Gates, spanned worlds, spanned stars, spanned time itself.

Therein they fell into the trap, and ensnared others—for qhal experimented in time, experimented in worlds, gathered beings and beasts from the whole of Gate-spanned space. They built civilizations, leaped ahead to see their progress, while their subjects, denied access to the Gates, inched through the centuries at real-time.

At the end of time gathered those who had been through all ages, experienced all things, lived most desperately. There were ominous ripplings in reality itself, backtime violated, accelerating disturbance. Some qhal felt it coming; some went mad, recalling truths that were no longer true, or might have been and would not, and were again—matter and time and space undone, ripped loose, finally imploded.

Worlds lay devastated. There were only the remnants of qhalur works and the worlds qhal-tampered; and there were the Gates, flotsam up out of time, untouched by the catastrophe.

And humans arrived on the ruined worlds, in that patch of space that still bore the scars.

Humans were among the victims of the qhal, scattered on the ruined worlds, with other species also qhal-like. For this reason alone humans distrusted the Gates, and feared them.

A hundred men and women passed the qhalur Gates, bound they knew not where, armed to seal the dangerous portals from the far side of space and time, to the very ultimate Gate. There was a weapon devised for that ultimate passage, an end-all force of Gate-drawn power; and until

5

that Gate, it was necessary to seal world after world, age after age—a battle perhaps endless or fatally circular, perhaps limited to qhalur space or cast to Gates the qhal themselves never made.

There were a hundred at the beginning.

The Gates exacted their toll.

BOOK ONE

"... Last of all only the woman Morgaine survived, skilled in qujalin witchcrafts and bearing still that Sword that casts to death. Much of evil she did in Morija and Baien, rivaling all other evils she had committed ... but she fled thereafter, taking with her Nhi Vanye i Chya, once of this house, who was ilin to her and therefore bound by his oath."

— Nhi Erij i Myya, in the Book of Ra-morij

"Chya Roh i Chya, lord of Ra-koris ... followed the witch Morgaine, for his cousin's sake ... but Nhi Erij in his writing avows that Chya Roh perished on that journey, and that the Soul that possessed the likeness of Roh thereafter was qujal, and hostile to every Godly man. ..."

— the Book of Baien-an

Chapter One

||||||||||||||||||||||||||||||||||||||||||||||||||||||||

Seven moons danced across the skies of the world, where there had been one in the days of the ancients. In those days the Wells of the Gods had been open, providing power and abundance to the *khal*-lords who had governed before the time of the Kings. Now the Wells were sealed, beyond the power of men or *khal* to alter. Long ago there had been vast lands on all sides of Shiuan and Hiuaj; but the world now was slowly drowning.

These were the things that Mija Jhirun Ela's-daughter believed for truth.

For all of Jhirun's young life, she had known the waters encroaching relentlessly on the margin of the world, and she had watched Hiuaj diminish by half and the gray sea grow wider. She was seventeen, and looked to see Hiuaj vanish entirely in her lifetime.

When she had been a child, the village of Chadrih had stood near the Barrow-hills of Hiuaj; and beyond that had stood a great levee and a sea wall, securing fields that gave good crops and pasturage for sheep and goats and cattle. Now there was reed-grown waste. The three parcels of land that had supported Chadrih were gone, entirely underwater save for the boundary posts of stacked stone and the useless remnant of the ancient sea wall. The gray stone buildings of the village had become a ruin, with water trickling even at low tide through what had been its streets, and standing window-high at Hnoth, when the moons combined. The roofless houses had become the nesting places of the white birds that wheeled and cried their lonely pipings over the featureless sea.

The people of Chadrih had moved on, those who survived the collapse of the sea wall and the fever and the famine of that winter. They had sought shelter, some among the marsh

9

dwellers at Aren, a determined few vowing to go beyond into Shiuan itself, seeking the security of holds like fabled Abarais of the Wells, or Ohtij-in, among the halfling lords. The Barrows had heard tidings of those that had reached Aren; but what had befallen the few who had gone the long road to Shiuan, none had ever heard.

The breaking of the sea wall had happened in Jhirun's tenth year. Now there was little dry land in all Hiuaj, only a maze of islets separated by marsh, redeemed from the killing salt only by the effluence of the wide Aj, that flowed down from Shiuan and spread its dark, sluggish waters toward the gray sea. In storm the Aj boiled brown with silt, the precious earth washed seaward, in flood that covered all but the hills and greater isles. At high tide, when the moons moved together in Hnoth, the sea pressed inland and killed areas of the marsh, where green grass died and standing pools reeked of decay, and great sea fishes prowled the Aj. Now throughout Hiuaj, there remained only sparse pasturage for goats and for the wild marsh ponies. The sea advanced in the face of the Barrows and the widening marsh ate away at their flank, threatening to sever Hiuaj from Shiuan and utterly doom them. Land that had been sweet and green became a tangle of drowned trees, a series of small hummocks of spongy earth, reed-choked passages that were navigable only by the flat-bottomed skiffs used by marsh folk and Barrowers.

And the Barrow-hills became islands in these last years of the world.

It was Men that had reared these hills, just after the days of the Darkness. They were the burials of the kings and princes of the Kingdoms of Men, in those long-ago days just after the Moon was broken, when the *khal* had declined and Men had driven the *khalin* halflings into their distant mountains. In those days, Men had had the best of the world, had ruled a wide, rich plain, and there had been great wealth in Hiuaj for human folk.

Men had buried their great ones in such towering mounds, in cists of stone: warrior-kings proud with their gold and their gems and their iron weapons, skillful in war and stern in their rule over the farmer-peasantry. They had sought to restore the ancient magics of the Wells, which even the halfling *khal* had feared. But the sea rose and destroyed their plains, and the last Kings of Men fell under the power of the halflings of Shiuan. So the proud age of the Barrow-kings passed, leaving only their burial places clustered about the

great Well called Anla's Crown, that had swallowed up their
wealth and returned them only misery.

In the end there were only scattered villages of Men, farm-
er-folk who cursed the memory of the Barrow-kings. The old
fortresses and burial places were piously avoided by later
generations on the river-plain. Chadrih had been nearer the
Barrows than any other village wished to be; but it had perished last of all the villages in Hiuaj, for all that—which gave
Chadrih folk a certain arrogance, until their own fate took
them. And the Barrow-hills themselves became the last refuge
of all; the Barrow-folk had always lived beyond the pale of
lowland respectability—tomb-robbers now, sometimes herders
and fishermen, accused (while Chadrih stood) of stealing
livestock as well as buried gold. But Chadrih died and the
despised Barrow-folk lived, southernmost of all Men, in a
hold that was a Barrow-king's ruined fortress atop the last
and greatest rock in all Hiuaj, save Anla's Crown itself.

This was Jhirun's world. Sunbrowned and warm, she
guided her flat skiff with practiced thrusts of the pole against
the bottom of the channels that, at this cycle of the tides,
were hardly knee deep. She was barefoot, knowing shoes only
in winter, and she wore her fringe-hemmed skirt tucked
above the knees because there was none to see her. A stop-
pered jar of bread and cheese and another of beer was
nestled in the prow; and there was also a sling and a handful
of smooth stones, for she was skillful with the sling to bring
down the brown marsh fowl.

There had been rain last night and the Aj was up somewhat, enough to fill some of the shallower channels, making
her progress through the hills quicker. There would be rain
again before evening, to judge by the gathering of haze in the
east, across the apricot sun; but high tide, Hnoth, was some
days off. The seven moons danced in order across the watery
sky and the force of the Aj was all that sighed against the
reeds. The Barrows that were almost entirely awash at Hnoth
were bravely evident despite the rains, and the Standing
Stone at Junai was out of the water entirely.

It was a holy place, that hewn stone and its little isle.
Nearby was a finger of the deep marshes, and marsh-folk
came here to Junai's stone to meet on midcycle days with
Barrow-folk to trade—her tall kinsmen with the surly small
men of the deep fens. Meat and shell and metals were their
trade to the marshes; wood and Ohtija grain out of Shiuan
and well-made boats and baskets were what the marshlanders

brought them. But more important than the trade itself was
the treaty that let the trade happen regularly, this seasonal
commerce that brought them together for mutual gain and
removed occasion for feuds, so that any Barrower could
come and go in Barrows-land in safety. There were outlaws,
of course, men either human or halfling, cast out of Ohtij-in
or Aren, and such were always to be feared; but none had
been known this far south for four years. The marshlanders
had hanged the last three on the dead tree near the old *khalin*
ruin at Nia's Hill, and Barrows-men had given them gold for
that good service. Marshlanders served as a barrier to the
folk of Barrows-hold against every evil but the sea, and returned them no trouble. Aren was far into the marsh, and
marshlanders kept to it; they would not even stand in a Barrows-man's shadow when they came to trade, but uttered
loud prayers and huddled together under the open sky as if
they dreaded contamination and feared ambush. They preferred their dying forests and their own observances, that
made no mention of Barrow-kings.

Out here on the edge of the world lay Barrows-land, wide
and empty, with only the conical hills above the flood and the
wide waters beyond, and the flight of the white birds above.
Jhirun knew each major isle, each stone's-throw expanse of
undrowned earth, knew them by the names of kings and
heroes forgotten outside the lore of Barrows-folk, who
claimed the kings for ancestors and could still sing the old
words of the chants in an accent no marshlander could comprehend. Some few of these hills were hollow at their crest,
caps of stone, earth-covered, that had long ago yielded up
their treasure to the plundering of Jhirun's ancestors. Other
mounds still defied efforts to discover the cists buried there,
and so protected their dead against the living. And some
seemed to be true hills, that had no hollow heart of man-
made chambers, with king-treasures and weapons. Such as
did give up treasure sustained the life of Barrows-hold,
providing gold that Barrows-folk remade into rings and sold
anew to marshlanders, who in turn bought grain of Shiuan
and sold it at Junai. Barrows-folk had no fear of the angry
ghosts, their own ancestors, and hammered off the ancient
symbols and melted down the gold, purifying it.

And besides the grain the gold bought, they kept goats and
hunted, and thus secured a small source of food independent
of that trade. Daily Jhirun and her cousins cut grass and
loaded it on skiffs or on the back of the black marsh pony

that they used in the inner hills. By such means they stored
up against the days of Hnoth, and fed their livestock, and
had surplus of cheeses and domestic meat that the marshlanders valued as much as the gold.

The little skiff reached a stretch of faster-moving water,
that place where the current of the Aj reached into the bor-
dering islets, and Jhirun maneuvered into the shallows, holding that margin with care. Afar off she could see the edge of
the world, where the Aj met the devouring sea, and horizon
and sky merged in gray haze. Hereabouts, a great rolling expanse above the flood, was the hill of Anla's Crown.

She did not mean to go near that place, with its ring of
Standing Stones. None ever approached that hill save at
Midyear's Day, when the priests came—her grandfather for
Barrows-hold, and aged Haz for the folk of Aren. Once even
Shiua priests had come to it, down the long road from Ohtij-
in: it was that important, one of the two true Wells. But none
had come since the sea wall broke. The rites were now only
the concern of Hiua, but they were by no means neglected.
And even on that day the priests remained fearful and ventured no closer than a stone's cast, Haz of Aren and her
grandfather approaching separately because of their differ-
ences. In the old days, Barrow-kings had given men to the
Wells there, but that custom had lapsed when the Barrow-
kings fell. The sacrifices had not enlivened the Wells nor
healed the Moon. The Standing Stones stood stark and empty
against the sky, some crazily tilted; and that vast hill that
none dared approach save on the appointed day remained a
place of power and tainted beauty, no refuge for men or halflings. Each priest spoke a prayer and retreated. It was not a
place to be alone; it was such that the senses prickled with
unease even when one was coming with many kinsfolk, and
the two priests and the chanting—a stillness that underlay the
singing and made every noise of man seem a mere echo.
Here was the thing the Barrow-kings had sought to master,
the center of all the eeriness of the Barrows, and if anything
would remain after the waters had risen and covered all
Hiuaj, it would be this hill and those strange stones.

Jhirun skirted widely away from that place, working out of
the current, among other isles. Marks of the Old Ones as well
as the Barrow-kings were frequent here, scattered stones up-
standing in the water and on the crests of hills. Here was her
favorite place when she worked alone, here on the margin of
Anla's Crown, far, far beyond the limit that any marshlander

would dare to come save on Midyear's Day; and out of the convenient limits that her kinsmen cared to work. She enjoyed the silence, the solitude, apart from the brawling chaos of Barrows-hold. Here was nothing but herself and the whisper of reeds, the splash of water, and the lazy song of insects in the morning sun.

The hills glided past, closing in again, and she tended now toward the righthand bank of the winding channel, to the hill called Jiran, after which she was named. It had a Standing Stone at its crest, like others just downstream at water's edge, and Jiran, like the other hills that clustered here, was green with grass fed by the sweet water of the Aj. She stepped out as the skiff came to ground, her bare feet quick and sure on the damp landing. She seized the mooring rope and hauled the skiff well up on the bank so that no capricious play of current could take it. Then she set to work.

The insect-song stopped for a time when she began to swing her sickle, then began again as the place accepted her presence. Whenever she had done sufficient for a sheaf, she gathered the grasses and bound them with a twist of their own stalks, leaving neat rows behind her. She worked higher and higher on the hill in a wheel-pattern of many spokes, converging at the Standing Stone.

From time to time she stopped and straightened her back and stretched in pain from the work, although she was young and well-accustomed to it. At such times she scanned the whole horizon, with an eye more to the haze gathering in the east than to the earth. From the hilltop, as she neared the end of her work, she could see all the way to Anla's Crown and make out the ring of stones atop it, all hazy with the distance and the moisture in the air, but she did not like to look toward the south, where the world stopped. When she looked north, narrowing her eyes in the hope—as sometimes happened on the clearest of days—of imagining a mountain in the distant land of Shiuan, all she could see was gray-blue, and a dark smudge of trees against the horizon along the Aj, and that was the marsh.

She came here often. She had worked alone for four years—since her sister Cil had wed—and she cherished the freedom. For now she had her beauty, still was straight and slim and lithe of muscle; she knew that years and a life such as Cil's would change that. She tempted the gods, venturing to the edge of Anla's hill; she flaunted her choice of solitude even under the eye of heaven. She had been the youngest—

Cil was second-born, and Socha had been eldest—three sisters. Cil was now Ger's wife and always heavy with child, and began to have that leaden-eyed look that her aunts had. Their mother Ewon had died of birth-fever after Jhirun, and their father had drowned himself, so the men said—and therefore the aunts had reared them, added duty, to bow these grim women down with further self-pity. The three sisters had been close, conspirators against their cousins and against the female tyranny of their aunts. Socha had been the leader, conniving at pranks and ventures constantly. But Cil had changed with marriage, and grew old at twenty-two; only Socha remained, in Jhirun's memory, unchanged and beautiful. Socha had been swept away that Hnoth when the great sea wall broke; and Jhirun's last memory of her was of Socha setting out that last morning, standing in that frail, shallow skiff, and the sunlight streaming about her. Jhirun had dreamed ill dreams the night before—Hnoth always gave her nightmares—and she had told her dreams to Socha and wept, in the dark. But Socha had laughed them away, as she laughed at all troubles, and set out the next morning, thus close to Hnoth.

Still happier Socha than Cil, Jhirun thought, when she reckoned Cil's life, and how few her own months of freedom might be. There was no husband left for her in Barrows-hold but her cousins, and the one that wanted her was Fwar, brother of Cil's man Ger and of the same stamp. Fwar was becoming anxious; and so Jhirun was the more insistent on working apart from her cousins, all of them, and never where Fwar might find her alone. Sometimes in bitter fancy she thought of running off into the deep marsh, imagining Fwar's outrage at being robbed of his bride, Ela's fey daughter, the only unwed woman in Barrows-hold. But she had seen the marshlanders' women, that came behind their men to Junai, women as grim and miserable as her aunts, as Cil; and there were Chadrih folk among them, that she feared. Most pleasant imagining of all, and most hopeless, she thought of the great north isle, of Shiuan, where the gold went, where halfling lords and their favored servants lived in wealth and splendor while the world drowned.

She thought of Fwar while she attacked the grass with the sickle, putting the strength of hate into her arm, and wished that she had the same courage against him; but she did not, knowing that there was nothing else. She was doomed to discontent. She was different, as all Ewon's fair children had

been, as Ewon herself had been. The aunts said that there
was some manner of taint in Ewon's blood: it came out most
strongly in her, making her fey and wild. Ewon had dreamed
dreams; so did she. Her grandfather Keln, priest of Barrows-
hold, had given her *sicha* wood and seeds of *azael* to add to
the amulets she wore about her neck, besides the stone Barrow-king's cross, which were said to be effective against
witchery; but it did not stop the dreams. Halfling-taint, her
aunt Jinel insisted, against which no amulets had power,
being as they only availed for human-kind. It was told how
Ewon's mother had met a halfling lord or worse upon the
Road one Midyear's Eve, when the Road was still open and
the world was wider. But Ela's line was of priests; and grandfather Keln had consoled Jhirun once by whispering that her
father as a youth had dreamed wild dreams, assuring her that
the curse faded with age.

She wished that this would be so. Some dreams she
dreamed waking; that of Shiuan was one, in which she sat in
a grand hall, among halflings, claimed by her halfling
kindred, and in which Fwar had perished miserably. Those
were wish-dreams, remote and far different from the sweat-
drenched dreams she suffered of doomed Chadrih and of Socha, drowned faces beneath the waters—Hnoth-dreams that
came when the moons moved close and sky and sea and
earth heaved in convulsions. The tides seemed to move in her
blood as they did in the elements, making her sullen and
prone to wild tempers as Hnoth drew near. During the nights
of Hnoth's height, she feared even to sleep by night, with all
the moons aloft, and she put *azael* sprigs under her pillow, lying sleepless so long as she could.

Her cousins, like all the house, feared her speaking of such
things, saying that they were ill-wishes as much as they were
bad dreams. Only Fwar, who respected nothing, least of all
things to which his own vision did not extend, and liked to
make mock of what others feared, desired her for a wife.
Others had proposed more immediate and less permanent
things, but generally she was left alone. She was unlucky.

And this was another matter that held her to Barrows-hold,
the dread that the marshlanders, who had taken in the
Chadrih folk, might refuse her and leave her outlawed from
every refuge, to die in the marsh. One day she might become
resolved enough to risk it, but that day was not on her yet.
She was free and solitary, and it was, save when she had had
both Socha and Cil, the best time of her life, when she could

roam the isles at will. She was not, whatever the rumors of her gossiping aunts, born of a halfling lord, nor of the little men of Aren, born neither to dine off gold nor to trade in it—but Barrows-born, to dig for it. The sea might have all Hiuaj in her lifetime, drowning the Barrow-hills and all within them; but that was distant and unthreatening on so warm a day.

Perhaps, she thought, with an inward laugh, she was only slightly and sometimes mad, just as mad as living on world's-edge ought to make one. Perhaps when she dreamed her terrible dreams, she was sane; and on such days as this when she felt at peace, then she was truly mad, like the others. The conceit pleased her.

Her hands kept to their work, swinging the sickle and binding the grasses neatly. She was aware of nothing about her but the song of the insects. At early afternoon she carried all her load down to the bank and rested, there on the slope near the water; and she ate her meal, watching the eddies of the water swirling past the opposing hill. It was a place she knew well.

And the while she gazed she realized that a new and curious shadow lay on that other bank, that indeed there was a gaping wound in that hill, opened just beneath that outcrop of rock. Suddenly she swallowed down a great mouthful of her meal and left everything lying—jars, sickle, sheaves of grass—and gathered up the rope and boat-pole.

Cist. A burial chamber, torn open by last night's rain. She found her hands sweating with excitement as she pushed the boat out and poled it across the narrow channel.

The other hill was perfectly conical, showing scars about its top as most such suspicious hills did thereabouts, wounds made by earlier Barrow-folk probing to see whether burial had been made there. Those searchers had found nothing, else they would have plundered it and left it gaping open to the sky.

But the waters, searching near the base, had done what men had failed to do and found what men never had: treasure, gold, the purchase of luxuries here at world's end.

The skiff scraped bottom among the reeds and Jhirun waded ashore up to the knees in water until she could step up on the clay bank. She heaved the skiff onto solid ground, there near the shelf that overshadowed the breach. She trembled with excitement seeing how that apparent rock outcrop was squared on the edge, proving it no work of nature;

the rain had exposed it for the first time to light, for she had been here hardly a hand of days ago and had not seen it. She flung herself down by the opening and peered in.

There was a cold chill of depth about that darkness—no cist at all, but one of the great tombs, the rich ones. Jhirun swallowed hard against the tightness in her throat, wiped her hands on her skirt and worked her shoulders in, turning so that she could fit the narrow opening. For a moment she despaired, reckoning such a find too much for her alone, sure that she must go back and fetch her cousins; and those thieving cousins would leave her only the refuse—if it were still intact when she brought them back. She remembered the haze across the east, and the likelihood of rain.

But as her eyes grew accustomed to the dark, she could see that there was light breaking in from some higher aperture; the top of the tomb must have been breached too, the dome broken. She could not see the interior from this tunnel, but she knew that it must surely be a whole, unrobbed tomb; no ancient robber would have entered a dome-tomb from the top, not without winning himself a broken neck. The probing of some earlier searcher seeking only a cist atop the hill had likely fallen through, creating the wash at the lower level. And that chance had given her such a prize as generations of Barrowers dreamed in vain of finding, a tale to be told over and over in the warm security of Barrows-hold so long as the world lasted.

She clutched the amulets on the cord about her neck, protection against the ghosts. With them, she did not fear the dark of such places, for she had been in and about the tombs from childhood. The dangers she did fear were a weak ceiling or an access tunnel collapsing. She knew better than to climb that slope outside, weakened as it was. She had heard a score of times how great-uncle Lar had fallen to his death among the bones in the opening of the king-hill called Ashrun. She expelled her breath and began to wriggle through where she was, dragging her body through, uncaring for the tender skin of her arms in her eagerness.

Then she lay in what had been the approach to the tomb, a stone-paved access that seemed to slant up and up to a towering door, the opening of which was faintly discernible in the dim light. She rose and felt with her hands the stones she knew would be about her. The first joining was as high as her head, and she could not reach the top of the next block. By this she became certain that it was a tomb of one of the First

Kings after the Darkness, for no other men ever built with such ambition or buried in such wealth.

Such a hill this was, without even the name of a King. It was old and forgotten, among the first to be reared near Anla's hill, in that tradition that ringed the Kings' burials nearest the forces they had wished to master, from which legend said they had come and to which they always sought to return. A forgotten name: but he had been a great one, and powerful, and surely, Jhirun thought with a pounding of her heart, very, very rich.

She walked the access, feeling her way in the dark, and another fear occurred to her, that the opening might have given some wild thing a lair. She did not think such was the case, for the air held no such taint; but all the same she wished that she had brought the boat-pole, or better yet the sickle; and most of all that she had a lamp.

Then she came into the area of the dome, where sunlight shafted down, outlining the edges of things on the floor, the ray itself an outline in golden dust. It fell on stone and mouldering ruin. Her least stirring echoed fearsomely in the soaring height above her head.

Many a tomb had she seen, the little cists often hardly larger than the king buried there, and two great dome-tombs, that of Ashrun and that of Anla, and those long-robbed, Ashrun a mere shell open to the sky. She had been at the opening of one cist-tomb, watching her uncles work, but she had never been alone, the very first to breach the silence and the dark.

The stone-fall from the dome had missed the bier, and the slanting light showed what must have been the king himself, only rags and bones. Against the arching wall were other huddled masses that must once have been his court, bright ladies and brave lords of Men: in her imaginings she saw them as they must have been the day that they followed their king into this place to die, all bedight in their finest clothing, young and beautiful, and the dome rang with their voices. In another place would be the mouldering bones of their horses, great tall beasts that had stamped and whinnied in fear of such a place, less mad than their doomed masters—beasts that had run plains that now were sea; she saw the glint of gilded harness in the dust.

She knew the tales. The fables and the songs in the old language were the life and livelihood of the Barrows, their golden substance the source of the bread she ate, the fabric

of her happier dreams. She knew the names of kings who had
been her ancestors, the proud Mija, knew their manners,
though she could not read the runes; she knew their very
faces from the vase paintings, and loved the beauty of the
golden art they had prized. She was sorry when these precious things must be hammered and melted down; she had
wept much over seeing it when she was a child, not understanding how such beautiful objects were reckoned unholy
and unlucky by marshlanders, and that without that purifying, the gold was useless in trade. The fables were necessary
for the house to teach the children, but there was no value
for beauty in the existence of the Barrows, only for gold and
the value that others set on having it.

She moved, and in doing so, nudged an object beside the
doorway. It fell and shattered, a pottery sound, loud in that
vast emptiness. The nape of her neck prickled, and she was
overwhelmingly aware of the silence after the echo, and of
the impudence of Jhirun Ela's-daughter, who had come to
steal from a king.

She thrust herself out from the security of the wall and
into the main area, where the light streamed down to the bier
of the king and gleamed on dusty metal.

She saw the body of the king, his clothes in spidery tatters
over his age-dark bones. His skeletal hands were folded on
his breast, on mail of rusted rings, and over his face was a
mask of gold such as she had heard was the custom of the
earliest age. She brushed at the dust that covered it, and saw
a fine face, a strong face. The eyes were portrayed shut, the
high cheekbones and delicate moulding of the lips more
khalin than man. The long-dead artist had graven even the
fine lines of the hair of brows and lashes, had made the lips
and nostrils so delicate it was as if they might suddenly draw
breath. It was a young man's face, the stern beauty of him to
haunt her thereafter, she knew, when she slept beside Fwar.
Cruel, cruel, that she had come to rob him, to strip away the
mask and reveal the grisly ruin of him.

At that thought she drew back her hand, and shivered,
touching the amulets at her throat; and retreated from him,
turning to the other hapless dead that lay along the wall. She
plundered them, rummaging fearlessly among their bones for
golden trinkets, callously mingling their bones to be sure the
ghosts were equally muddled and incapable of vengeance on
Midyear's Eve.

Something skittered among them and frightened her so that

she almost dropped her treasure, but it was only a rat, such as sheltered in the isles and fed on wreckage and drowned animals, and sometimes housed in opened tombs.

Cousin, she saluted him in wry humor, her heart still fluttering from panic. His nose twitched in reciprocal anxiety, and when she moved, he fled. She made haste, filling her skirts with as much as she could carry, then returning to the access and laboriously bringing bit after bit down that narrow tunnel and out into daylight. She crawled out after, and loaded the pieces in the skiff, looking all about the while to be sure that she was alone: wealth made her suspect watchers, even where such were impossible. She covered over evrything with grass in the skiff's bottom and hurried again to the entrance, pausing to cast a nervous glance at the sky.

Clouds filled the east. She knew well how swiftly they could come with the wind behind them, and she hurried now doubly, feeling the threat of storm, of flood that would cover the entrance of the tomb.

She wriggled through into the dark again, and felt her way along until her eyes reaccustomed themselves to the dark. She sought this time the bones of the horses, wrenching bits of gold from leather that went to powder in her hands. Their bones she did not disturb, for they were only animals, and she was sorry for them, thinking of the Barrows-hold's pony. If they would haunt anyone, it would be harmless, and she wished them joy of their undersea plains.

What she gained there she took as far as the access and piled in a bit of broken pottery, then returned to the bones of the courtiers. She worked there, gathering up tiny objects while the thunder rumbled in the distance, filling her skirt as she worked slowly around the wall among the bones, into a shadow that grew deeper and colder.

Cold air breathed out of an unseen recess in that shadow, and she stopped with the gold in her lap, peering into that blind dark. She sensed the presence of another, deeper chamber, black and vast.

It fretted at her, luring her. She remembered how at Ashrun's tomb there had been a treasure chamber that yielded more wealth than any buried with king or court. Long moments she hesitated, fingering the amulets that promised her safety. Then she cursed her cowardice and convinced herself; the thunder walked above the hills, reminding her that there was only this one chance, forever.

With a whispered invocation to Arzad, who protected from

ghosts, she edged forward, kneeling, cast a seal-gem into that dark. It struck metal; and thus encouraged, she leaned forward and reached into that darkness.

Her fingers met mouldering cloth, and she recoiled, but in doing so her hand hit metal, and things spilled in a clatter that woke the echoes and almost stopped her heart. Cascading about her knees were dusty gems and plates and cups of gold, treasure that made the objects in her lap seem mere trinkets.

She cursed in anguish for the shortness of the time. She gathered what she could carry and returned to the tunnel to push each piece out into the daylight. Drops of rain spattered the dust as she finally worked her own body out, touched her with chill as she carried the heavy objects to the boat, her steps weaving with exhaustion.

Looking up, she saw the clouds black and boiling. The air had gone cold, and wind sighed noisily through the grasses. Once that storm broke, then the water would rise swiftly; and she had a horror of being shut in that place, water rising over the entrance, to drown her in the dark.

But one piece she had left, a bowl filled with gold objects, itself heavy and solid.

With feverish anxiety she lay down and crawled back into the dark, feeling her way until her eyes cleared and she walked again into the main chamber, where the king lay on his bier.

It was useless to have spared him. She resolved suddenly to make good her theft, for the water would have all in the end, the mask as well. She went to the bier—the only place that the declining light shone, and that dimmed by clouds. A few drops of rain fell on the mask like tears, puddling the dust there, and the wind skirled violently through the double openings, tugging at her skirts, bidding her make urgent haste. But she saw again how fair he had been, and alone now, robbed, his companion ghosts all destroyed, here at the end of time. He had seen the fields wide and green, had ruled holds and villages beside which Chadrih was nothing. To have enjoyed power and never felt hunger, and to have lain down to die amidst all these good things, she thought, was a happy fate.

But at the end he was robbed by a Barrows-girl, his descendant, whose fondest wish was to have a warm cloak and enough to eat; and once to see the green mountains of Shiuan.

Her hand stayed a second time from the mask that covered

him; and a curious object in his skeletal fingers caught her
eye. She moved the bones aside and took it: a bird, such as
she knew today over the marshes—not a lucky symbol to
have been worn by a warrior, who often risked death, nor
had it been part of his armor. She thought rather of some
grieving woman who had laid it there, a death-gift.

And it was strange to think that so homely a creature as a
gull could be common to his age and hers, that he also had
seen the birds above some more distant shore, not knowing
them the heirs of all he possessed. She hesitated at it, for the
white sea birds were a figure of death, that came and went
beyond the world's edge; but, Barrows-bred that she was, she
carried even among the amulets a white gull feather, and
reckoned it lucky, for a Barrows-girl, whose livelihood was
from the dead. The figure was golden, delicate: it warmed in
her hands as it had not done in centuries. She touched the
fine detail of the wings—and thrust it into her bodice when
she saw the dusty jewels beside the king. But they proved
only seal-gems, worthless, for the symbols on them could not
be polished away, and the marshlanders thought them
unlucky.

The rain struck her face, and spotted the dusty bones and
washed upon the mask. Jhirun shivered in the cold wind and
knew by the sound of the water rushing outside that she had
waited dangerously long. Thunder crashed above the hill.

In sudden panic she fled, gathered up what she had come
to fetch, and ran to the exit, wriggled through the tunnel
pushing her treasure out ahead of her, out into the dim light
and the pelting rain. The water in the channel had risen, beginning to lift and pull the boat from its safety on the bank.

Jhirun looked at that swirling, silt-laden water—dared not
burden the boat more. In anguish she set aside her heavy
bowl of trinkets, to wait high upon the bank. Then fearfully
she loosed the mooring rope and climbed aboard, seized up
the pole. The water snatched at the boat, turned it; it wanted
all her skill and strength to drive it where she would, across
the roaring channel to Jiran's Hill—and there she fought it
aground, poured rain-washed treasure into her skirts and
struggled uphill, not to lose a trinket on that slope that
poured with water. She spilled her skirt-full of gold at the
foot of the Standing Stone, made trip after trip to heap up
there what she had won, by a sure marker, where it would be
safe.

Then she tried to launch the skiff again toward the Barrow,

the rain driving along the battered face of the waters in blowing sheets, torn by the wind. The boat almost pulled from her
hands, dragging at the rope; she could not board it—and with
a desperate curse, she hauled back on the rope, dragging the
boat back to land, higher and higher, legs mudstreaked and
scratched and her skirts a sodden weight about them. She
reached a level place, sprawled backward with the rain driving down into her face, the blaze of lightnings blinding her.
The boat was saved: that, at the moment, was more than
gold.

And driven at last by misery, she gathered herself and began to seek relief from the cold. There was a short paddle and
an oiled-leather cover in the skiff. She wrestled the little
boat completely over, heaved the bow up with her shoulder
and wedged the paddle under, making a shelter, however
slight. She crawled within and wrapped her shivering limbs
in the leather, much regretting now the meal she had not
finished, the jars the flood had already claimed.

The rain beat down on the upturned bottom of the boat
with great violence, and Jhirun clenched her chattering teeth,
enduring, while water crept higher up the banks of the hills,
flooded the access of the tomb, covered the treasure she had
been forced to abandon on that other hill.

Of a sudden, a blink of her eyes in the gray-green light of
storm, and the fore part of the Barrow began to slide into the
channel, washed through, the bones and dust of the king gone
sluicing down the flood to a watery rest. She clutched her
amulets and muttered frantic prayers to the six favorable
powers, watching the ruin widen, remembering the stern,
sleeping face of the mask. Tales were told how ghosts went
abroad on Hnoth and Midyear's Eve, how the kings of the
sunken plain hosted drowned souls of Barrow-folk and villagers in their ghostly courts, and lights could be seen above
the marsh—lights that marked their passage. She reckoned
that she had killed some few ghosts by breaking the spells
that held them to earth. They might go where they were
doomed to go hereafter, no longer bound to their king, with
storm to bear them hence.

But about her neck she wore the joined brass links of
Bajen and Sojan the twin kings, that were for prosperity; and
Anla's silver ring, for piety; the bit of shell that was for Sith
the sea lord, a charm against drowning; the Dir-stone for
warding off fevers; the Barrow-king's cross, that was for
safety; and the iron ring of Arzad, favorable mate to the un-

favorable seventh power . . . to Morgen-Angharan of the
white gull feather, a charm that Barrowers wore, though
marshlanders used it only to defend their windows and doorways. By these things Jhirun knew herself protected against
the evils that might be abroad on the winds; she clung to them
and tried to take her mind from her situation.

She waited while the day waned from murky twilight to
starless night, when it became easier to take any fears to
heart. The rain beat down ceaselessly, and she was still
stranded, the waters too violent for the light boat.

Somewhere across the hills, she knew, her cousins and
uncles would be doing the same, sheltering on some high
place, probably in greater comfort. They had gone to gather
wood at the forest's edge, and likely sat by a warm fire at the
ruins on Nia's Hill, not stirring until the rain should cease.
No one would come searching for her; she was a Barrower,
and should have sense enough to do precisely what she had
done. They would reckon correctly that if she had drowned
she was beyond help, and that if she had taken proper pre-
cautions she would not drown.

But it was lonely, and she was afraid, with the thunder
rolling overhead from pole to pole. Finally she collapsed the
shelter entirely, to keep out the prying wind, wrapped in her
leather covering and with the rain beating down above her
with a sound to drive one mad.

Chapter Two

IIIIIIIIIIIIIIIIIIIIIIIIIIIIIIIIIIIIIIIIIIIIIIIIIIIIII

At last the rain ceased, and there was only the rush of water. Jhirun wakened from a brief sleep, numb in her feet, like to smother in the dark. She sneezed violently and heaved up the shelter of her boat and looked about, finding that the clouds had passed, leaving a clear sky and the moons Sith and Añli to light the night.

She turned the boat onto its bottom and staggered to her feet, brushed back her sodden hair. The waters were still running high, and there was still lightning in the north—ominous, for rains came back sometimes, hurled back from the unseen mountains of Shiuan to spread again over Hiuaj.

But there was peace for the moment, satisfaction simply in having survived. Jhirun clenched her gelid hands and warmed them under her arms, and sneezed again. Something pricked her breast, and she felt after it, remembering the gull as her fingers touched warm metal. She drew it forth. The fine traceries of it glittered in the moonlight, immaculate and lovely, reminding her of the beauty that she had not been able to save. She fingered it lovingly and tucked it again into her bodice, grieving over the lost treasure, thinking of all that she had not been able to save. This one piece was hers: her cousins should not take this from her, this beautiful thing, this reward of a night of misery. She felt it lucky for her. She had a collection of such things, pictures on broken pottery, useless seal-gems, things no one wanted, but a gold piece— that she had never dared. They had their right, and she was wrong, she knew, for all the hold had good of the gold that was traded.

But not the gull, never the gull.

There would be a beating instead of a reward, if her kinsmen ever suspected how much of the gold she had failed to rescue from the flood, if ever she breathed to them the tale of the king in the golden mask, that she had let the water have. She knew that she had not done as well as she might, but—

—But, she thought, if she shaped her story so that she seemed to have saved everything there was, then for a few days nothing would be too good for Jhirun Ela's-daughter. Folk might even soften their attitudes toward her, who had been cursed for ill luck and ill-wishing things. At the least she would be due the pick of the next trading at Junai; and she would have—her imagination leaped to the finest thing she had ever desired—a fine leather cloak from Aren in the marshes, a cloak bordered in embroideries and fur, a cloak to wear in hall and about the home island, and never out in the weather, a cloak in which to pretend Barrows-hold was Ohtij-in, and in which she could play the lady. It would be a grand thing, when she must marry, to sit in finery among her aunts at the hearth, with a secret bit of gold next her heart, the memory of a king.

And there would be Fwar.

Jhirun cursed bitterly and wrenched her mind from that dream. The cloak she might well gain, but Fwar spoiled it, spoiled all her dreams. Sharing her bed, he would find the gull and take it, melt it into a ring for trade—and beat her for having concealed it. She did not want to think on it. She sneezed a third time, a quiet, stifled sneeze, for the night was lonely, and she knew that her lot would be fever if she must spend the night sitting still.

She walked, and moved her limbs as much as she could, and finally decided that she might warm herself by gathering up her gold on the hilltop and bringing it down to the boat. She climbed the hill with much slipping on the wet grass, using the tufts of it to pull herself up the steepest part, and found things safe by the Standing Stone.

She flung back her head and scanned all her surroundings under the two moons, the place where the other hill had stood and hardly a third remained. She gazed at the wide-spread waters dancing under the moonlight, the lightning in the south.

And Anla's Crown.

It glowed, a blaze of light like the dead-lights that hovered sometimes over the marsh. She rubbed her eyes, and gazed on it with a cold fear settling into her stomach.

Nothing was atop Anla's hill but the stones and the grass, nothing that the lightning might have set ablaze, and there was no ruddiness of living fire about it. It was ghostly, cold, a play of witchfires about the stones of the Crown.

Almost she had no courage to delay atop the hill, not even for the precious gold. She felt naked and exposed, the Standing Stone that was the sister-stone to those of Anla's Crown looming above her like some watching presence.

But she knelt and gathered up the gold that she could carry, and slid down to the skiff, loaded it aboard, went back for more, again and again. And each time that she looked toward Anla's hill the lights still hovered there.

Jiran's Hill was no longer a refuge from whatever was happening at Anla's Crown: it was altogether too close, on the verge of what strangeness passed there. She dared not wait until morning; the sun itself would seem no comfort, but a glaring eye to mark her presence here too near to Anla.

Better the danger of the currents: against the waters she had some skill, and of them she had less fear. She eased the loaded boat downslope, the long pole and the paddle laid accessible within. Carefully she let it into the edge of the current and felt the pull, judged that she might possibly manage it.

She climbed in; the current seized the skiff, whirled it like a leaf on the flood for an instant before she could bring the pole to bear and take control. She fended herself from impact with the rocks, spun dizzyingly round again, found bottom and almost lost the pole.

It did not hold. She saved the pole and shipped a little water doing it, and suddenly the skiff whipped round the bend of a hill and out, toward the great rolling Aj, toward a current she could in no wise fight.

There was no bottom here. She used the paddle now, desperately, went with the rush and worked to its edge, broke into the shallows again and managed to fight it into the lesser channel between Anla's height and the Barrows. She averted her eyes from the unnatural glow that hovered, that danced upon the waters—used paddle and pole alternately, knowing that she must go this way, that the channels near Anla's great rise would be shallowest, where once the ancient Road had run. The current pulled, trying to take her to the Aj, and thence to the sea, where Socha had died, lost, drowned. But here, while she held to the newly flooded margins, where the skiff whispered over reeds, the waters were almost calm.

She was going home.

Jhirun rested from time to time, drawing up on the shoulder of a Barrow, driving herself further as soon as she had drawn breath. The horror that she had seen at Anla's Crown seemed impossible now, irretrievable to the memory as the interior of the tomb, a thing of the night and the edge of realities. The fear still prickled at the nape of her neck, but more present, more urgent, was the cloud in the north, the fitful flash of lightning.

She feared the hills themselves, that became refuges for small creatures with which she did not care to share the night—rats that skittered shadow-wise over the banks as she passed, serpents that disturbed the grasses as she rested.

And the flood had opened new channels, places not at all familiar, the flooding making even known hills look different. She guided herself by the currents that she fought, by the stars that began to be obscured by clouds. She felt herself carried south, riverward, and ceased to be sure where she was.

But at last before her rose jagged shapes in the water, the ruined buildings of Chadrih. Her heart leaped with joy, for she knew the way from here beyond a doubt, through shallow channels.

The murmur of the water, the frantic song of the frogs and the other creatures of the tall grasses, made counterpoint to the movement of the boat, the slap of water against the bow, the whispers of reeds under the bottom. Jhirun gathered herself to her feet in the skiff, bravely confident now, balanced evenly on her bare feet. The pole touched the sunken stones that she remembered.

Chadrih: she remembered being nine and being thrust out of a house of Chadrih, folk making gestures to avert the evil of a Barrows-child who was known to be fey, to dream dreams. She remembered a sinful satisfaction to see that house deserted, and the windows all naked and empty. The Halmo men had stayed on last, they that had most hated and despised Barrows-folk; and they had drowned when she was twelve. The water had taken them and she could not even remember now what they had looked like.

She swayed her weight and pushed with the pole and sent the skiff down that narrow channel that had once been a cobbled street. The jagged, roofless buildings like eyeless brooding beasts shape-shifted past her. The ruins rustled with wings, the nesting birds disturbed by her passage; and the frogs kept up their mad chorus in the reeds. When she reached the edge of Chadrih she could see the first of the northern Barrows against the lightning-lit sky, and beyond it would lie Barrows Rock and home.

Hills began to pass her again on one side and the other, great conical mounds, shadows that momentarily enfolded her and gave her up again to the clouding sky. And there, just where she knew to look, she first saw the light that would be Barrows-hold tower, a flickering behind wind-tossed trees, a star-like gleam in the murk.

The water was calm here and shallow. Jhirun ventured a glance back between the hills, and could see only empty darkness. She made herself forget that, and looked forward again, keeping her eyes fixed on that friendly beacon, slipping the boat in and out among the hills.

The light flickered the harder, and suddenly the wind began to rise, whipping at her skirts and ruffling the water. There were little whisperings in the reeds and in the brush that overgrew these marshward Barrows. The storm was almost on her, and lightning danced on the black waters. Jhirun drew an aching breath and worked harder as the first heavy drops hit her, unwilling to yield and shelter miserably so close to home.

And alternate with the strokes she made she heard a rippling and splash of water, like a man striding, perhaps just the other side of the hill she was passing.

She stopped for a moment, drifting free, and the sound continued.

Perhaps a stray animal out of the marsh, storm-driven; there were wild ponies there, and occasional deer left. She let the boat glide where it would and listened to the sound, trying to judge just where it was, whether it went four-footed or two, and cold sweat prickled on her ribs.

So close, so close to home: perhaps it was one of her kinsmen, seeking home. But it moved so relentlessly, unregarding of the noise her boat had made, and no voice hailed her. She felt the hair rise on her neck as she thought of outlaws and beasts that came seldom out of the deep fens—things such as might be stirred out of lairs by flood and storm.

A cry came, thin and distorted by the air and the hills.

And then she knew it for the bleating of a silly goat; she was that near home. She felt a wild urge to laugh; some of their own livestock, surely. She hoped so. The boat had begun to move with more rapidity than she liked and she feared the noise she might make using the pole to restrain it. She had let it slip into the main current, where the water curled round the hills; she must stop it. She used the pole carefully, making a rippling despite her efforts to move noiselessly. She was fearfully conscious of the gold that glittered under the lightning, scattered at her feet—treasure to tempt any outlaw, ghost-things and unhallowed as they were. Here in the dark, not alone, she was acutely aware whence the objects had come, and aware too of the gull amulet between her breasts, that made a sharp pain at every push she made, this thing that had last lain between the fingers of a dead king.

She misjudged the channel in her preoccupation; the pole missed purchase and she drifted, helpless, balancing and waiting for the current to take her where she could find bottom again. The skiff whipped round in an eddy and slowed as it rounded the curve of an isle.

And she spun face to face with a rider, a shadowy horseman whose mount went belly-deep in the water—and that rider glittered here and there with linked mail. She thrust for bottom desperately, borne toward him. Strength deserted her hands and she could not hold. The rider loomed close at hand, the face of a young man, pale, beneath the peaked helm. His black horse shied aside, eyes rolling in the lightning flash.

She could not cry out. He reached and shouted at her, a thin voice, lost on the wind as the current pulled her on.

Then she remembered the pole in her nerveless hands and leaned on it, driving the boat to another channel, seeking a way out of this maze.

Water splashed behind her, the black horse—she felt it without looking back. She moved now with more frenzy than skill, her hair blinding her when at last she had to look and know. Through its strands she saw his shape black on the lightning-lit waters behind her.

She whipped her head round again as the skiff passed between two hills, and there, there ahead was the light of Barrows-hold tower, the safety of doors and lights and her own kinsmen ahead. She exerted all her strength and skill, put out of her mind what followed her—the black king under the hill, the king in the mask, whose bones she had let lie undisturbed. She was cold, feeling not her hands nor the balance of her feet, nor anything but her own heart crashing against her ribs and the raw edge of pain on which she breathed.

Barrows-hold filled all her vision, the slope of the landing before her. She drove for it, felt the skiff go aground on mud and reeds, then glide through. She leaped out on shore,

turned to look, saw the black rider still distant; and even then
she thought of the gold and the precious boat that was their
livelihood. She hurled the pole to the ground and gathered up
the rope and pulled and heaved the skiff aground, she skidding and sliding in the mud; a last look at the advancing
rider, the water curling white about the horse's breast as it
came, and she heaped pieces of gold into her skirts.

Then she turned and began to run, bare feet seeking tufts
of grass to aid her climbing. Above her loomed the house, the
cracks of its shuttered windows agleam with light, and the old
tower lit to guide the Barrows' scattered children home. She
dropped a piece of treasure, gathered it again, stumbling.
Rain was falling, the wind hurling the drops into her eyes
with stinging force, and thunder cracked. She heard the suck
of water behind her, the heave of a large body, and looking
back, she saw the black horse and the rider. Lightning glittered coldly off ring-mail, illumined a pale face. The dogs began barking frantically.

She touched her luck amulets with one hand and held the
knotted burden in her skirts with the other and ran, hearing
the rider coming after. The grass was slick. She spilled a
piece of her gold and this time did not stop. Her feet skidded
again on the slick stone paving before the door. She recovered, hurled herself at the closed door.

"Grandfather!" she cried, pounding at the insensate wood.
"Hurry!"

She heard the rider behind her, the wet sound of the animal struggling on the slope, the ring of metal and the panting
whuffs of his breathing.

She cast a look over her shoulder and saw the rider alight
to aid his horse in the climb. His leg gave with him. He
caught his balance and struggled up the slope, holding out his
hand to her. She saw him in the jerking flashes of the lightning.

"Grandfather!" she screamed.

The door came open. She fled into that light and warmth
and turned, expecting the rider to have vanished, as all such
things should. He had not; he was almost at the door. She
seized the door from her grandfather's indecisive hand and
slammed it, helped him drop the bar into place, the gold scattering. Plates and cups clanged against the stones and rattled
to a stop.

Jhirun turned and looked at the others, awe-stricken female faces ringed about the room, women and children, boys

too young to be with the men. There were Cil and aunt Jinel and aunt Zai; but there was no man at all but grandfather Keln.

And she cast a look at him, desperate, fearing that for once her grandfather had no answer. Sprigs of *azael* and Angharan's white feathers hung above doorways of house and stable, above the windows of both floors, wherever there was an access. They jested about them, but they renewed them annually, they that robbed the dead; there were laws, and it was taken for granted that the dead obeyed them.

"The signal," her grandfather breathed; his hands shook more than usual as he waved the women toward the stairs. "Zai, go! All the house, upstairs, and hide."

Plump Zai turned and fled stableward, by the west door, toward the tower—hers to care for the signal-beacons. The others began to herd frightened children toward the stairs to the loft. Some were crying. The dogs were barking furiously; they were shut in the yard, useless.

Old Jinel stayed, her sharp chin set; Cil stayed, her belly swollen with her third child, her other children at her skirts. Cil took off her warm brown shawl and cast it about Jhirun's shoulders, hugged her. Jhirun hugged her back, almost giving way to tears.

Outside came the ring of hooves on stone, circling back and forth before the door, back and forth, to the window. The shutters rattled, ceased.

Then for a long time there was nothing but the shaking of harness and the breathing of the animal outside at the window.

"Ohtija outlaw?" Grandfather asked, looking at Jhirun. "Where did he start trailing you?"

"Out there," she managed to say, clenching her teeth against the impulse to chatter. She tried to gather an explanation.

Steps reached the door, and there was a splintering impact. The children screamed and clung to Cil.

"Go," said Grandfather. "Hurry. Take the children upstairs."

"Hurry," Jhirun echoed, pushing at Cil, who tried to make her come with her, clinging to her. But there was no leaving her grandfather, fragile as he was. Jinel stayed too. Cil fled, her children beside her, for the stairs.

The battering at the door assumed a rhythm, and white wood broke through on the edge of an axe. Jhirun felt her grandfather's arm go about her, and she held to him, trembling, watching the door riven into ruin. It was never meant to withstand attack; no outlaws had ever assaulted the hold.

An entire plank gave way: the door hung ajar, and a man's armored arm reached through, trying to move the bar inside.

"No!" Jhirun cried, tore from her grandfather and ran to seize the great butchering knife from the scullery, her mind only then thinking of tangible defenses; but there was a crash behind her, the bar hitting the floor. She whirled in mid-step, saw the door crash open.

There in the rain stood the warrior-king. He had an axe in his hand and a bow slung at his back, the hilt of a sword riding at his shoulder. The rain sheeted down and made his face look like the drowned dead. He stood there with the black horse behind him and looked about the room as if he were seeking something.

"Take the gold," her grandfather offered him, his old voice stern as it was when he served as priest; but the stranger seemed disinterested in that—reached for the reins and led the tall animal forward, such a horse as had not been seen in Hiuaj since the sea wall broke. It shied at the strange doorway, then came with a rush, and its hindquarters swung round and broke the ruined door farther from its hinges. A golden cup was crushed under its hooves, spurned like a valueless stone.

None of them moved, and the warrior made no move at them. He towered in the center of their little hall and looked about him, he and the horse dripping muddy water onto the stones of the floor; and mingled with that water was blood that flowed from a wound on his leg.

Children were crying upstairs; he looked at the stairs and up toward the loft, while Jhirun's heart pounded. Then he turned his eyes instead to the fireplace. He drew on the reins of the horse and led it forward, toward warmth, himself limping and leaving a trail of blood and water.

And there, his back to that blazing fire, he turned and gazed at them, his eyes wild and anguished. They were dark, those eyes, and dark his hair, when every lord of the north she had heard of was fair. He was tall, armored in plain and ancient style; there was fineness about him that for all his misery made their little hold seem shabby.

She knew what he was; she knew. The gull lay like guilt against her breast, and she longed to thrust it into his hands and bid him go, leave, become what he was. She met his eyes without wanting to, a chill running through her. Here was no wisp of cobweb to fade in firelight: he cast tall shadows across the floor, left tracks of blood and water. Rain dripped from his hair and made him blink, long hair, in a warrior's knot, such as the ancient Kings had worn. His chest rose and fell strongly in ragged breathing; he drew a great breath, and his sigh was audible.

"A woman," he said, his voice nearly gone with hoarseness; and it was a lilting accent she had never heard—save in the songs. "A woman, a rider all—all white—"

"No," Jhirun said at once, touching at the white feather amulet. "No." She did not want him to go on speaking. In her desperation she opened her mouth to bid him gone as she might some trespassing marshlander; but he was not that, he was far from that, and she felt herself coarse and powerless in the face of him. There was no move from her grandfather, a priest, whose warding charms had failed; no word from Jinel, who had never lacked words before. Outside the hall the thunder rolled and the rain sheeted past the ruined door, a surety that the men would be held from returning, barred by risen water.

The visitor stared at them with a strange, lost expression, as if he wanted something; and then with awkwardness and evident pain he turned, and with the axe blade, hooked the kettle that hung over the fire and swung it outward. Steam rolled up from it, fragrant with one of Zai's stews. There was a stack of wooden bowls on the mantel. He filled one with the ladle and sank down where he was, braced his back against the stones. The black horse shook itself of a sudden, spattering the whole room and everyone in it with muddy water.

"Get out!" Grandfather Keln cried, his thin voice cracking with outrage.

The stranger looked at him, no answering rage, only a tired, perplexed look. He did not move, save to lift the steaming bowl to his lips to sip at the broth, still staring at them warily. His hand shook so that he spilled some of it. Even the black horse looked sorrowful, head hanging, legs scored by the passage through the flood. Jhirun hugged her dry shawl about her and forced herself to stop shivering, deciding that they were not all to be murdered forthwith.

Suddenly she moved, went to the shelves across the room and pulled down one of the coarse blankets they used for

rain chill and rough usage. She took it to the invader of their
home, where he sat on their hearthside; and when he, seeing
her intention, leaned forward somewhat, she wrapped it about
him, weapons and all. He looked up, the bowl in one hand,
gathering the blanket with the other. He gestured with the
bowl at the kettle, at her, at all the house, as if graciously
bidding them be free of their own food.

"Thank you," she said, struggling to keep her voice from
shaking. She was hungry, miserably so, and cold. And to
show that she was braver than she was, she pulled the kettle
over to herself and took another bowl, dipped up a generous
helping. "Has everyone else eaten?" she asked in a perfectly
ordinary voice.

"Yes," said Jinel.

She saw by the grease mark on the black iron that this was
so; enough remained for the men. It occurred to her that the
stranger might suspect others yet unfed, might take note by
that how many there were in the house. She pulled the kettle
as far out of his view as she could, sat down on the opposite
side of the hearth and ate, forcing the food down despite the
terror that still knotted her stomach.

*Azae*l sprigs and white feathers: she suspected them nothing, her grandfather's power nothing. She had been where she
should not; and came *this* where he ought not. It was on her
he looked, as if no one else existed for him, as if he cared
nothing for an old man and an old woman who owned the
food and the fire he used.

"I wish you would leave our house," Jhirun declared suddenly, speaking to him as if he were the outlaw her grandfather called him, wishing that this would prove true.

His pale, beard-shadowed face showed no sign of offense.
He looked at her with such weariness in his eyes it seemed he
could hardly keep them open, and the bowl started to tumble
from his hand. He caught it and set it down. "Peace," he
murmured, "peace on this house." And then he leaned his
head against the stone and blinked several times. "A woman,"
he said, taking up that mad illusion of his own, "a woman on
a gray horse. Have you seen her?"

"No," said Grandfather sternly. "None such. Nothing."

The stranger's eyes strayed toward him, to the shattered
door, with such a look that Jhirun followed the direction of
his gaze half expecting to see such a woman there. But there
was only the rain, a cold wind blowing through the open
doorway, a puddle spreading across the stones.

He turned his attention then to the other door, that in the west wall.

"Where does that go?"

"The stable," Grandfather said; and then, carefully: "The horse would be better there."

But the stranger said nothing, and gradually his eyes grew heavy, and he rested his head against the stones of the fireplace, nodding with the weariness that pressed upon him.

Grandfather quietly gathered up the reins of the black horse, the stranger not protesting: he led it toward that door, and aunt Jinel bestirred herself to open it. The beast hesitated, with the goats bleating alarm inside; but perhaps the warm stable smell drew it; it eased its way into that dark place, and Grandfather pulled the door shut after.

And Jinel sat down on a bench amid her abused house and clenched her thin hands and set her jaw and wept. The stranger watched her, a troubled gaze, and Jhirun for once felt pity for her aunt, who was braver than she had known.

A time passed. The stranger's head bowed upon his breast; his eyes closed. Jhirun sat by him, afraid to move. She set her bowl aside, marked suddenly that Jinel rose, walked quietly across the room. Grandfather, who had been by Jinel, went to the center of the room and watched the stranger; and there was a creaking on the stairs.

Jinel reached up to the wall for that great knife they used for butchering, tucked it up in a fold of her skirts. She came back to Grandfather.

A board creaked. Cil was on the stairs; Jhirun could see her now. Her heart beat painfully; the supper lay like a stone in her belly. They were no match for the warrior-king; they could not be. And Cil, brave Cil, a loyal sister, heavy with child: it was for her sake that Cil ventured downstairs.

Jhirun moved suddenly to her knees, touched the stranger. His eyes opened in panic and he clutched the axe that lay across his lap. Behind her in the room she sensed that things had stopped, her house with its furtive movements frozen where matters stood. "I am sorry," Jhirun said, holding his eyes with her own. "The wound—will you let me treat it?"

He looked confused for a moment, his eyes ranging beyond her. Perhaps, she thought in terror, he saw what had been proceeding.

Then he bowed his head in consent, and moved his injured leg to straighten it, moved the blanket aside so that she could see how the leather was rent and the flesh deeply cut. He

drew the bone-handled dagger from his belt and cut the
leather further so that she could reach the wound. The sight
of it made her weak at the stomach.

She gathered herself up and crossed the room to the
shelves, sought clean linen. Jinel met her there and tried to
snatch the cloth from her fingers.

"Let me go," Jhirun hissed.

"Slut," Jinel said, her nails deep in her wrist.

Jhirun tore free and turned, dipped clean water from the
urn in the corner and went back to the stranger. Her hands
were shaking and her eyes blurred as she started to work, but
they soon steadied. She washed the cut, then forced a large
square of cloth through the opening and tied it tightly from
the outside, careful not to pain him. She was intensely aware
of her grandfather and Cil and Jinel watching her, their eyes
on her back—herself touching a strange man.

He laid his hand on hers when she had done; his hands
were fine, long-fingered. She had never imagined that a man
could have such hands. There were scars on them, a fine
tracery of lines. She thought of the sword he carried and
reckoned that he had never wielded tools . . . hands that
knew killing, perhaps, but their touch was like a child's for
gentleness; his eyes were likewise. "Thank you," he said, and
showed no inclination to let her go. His head went back
against the wall. His eyes began to close, exhaustion claiming
him. They opened; he fought against the impulse.

"Your name," he asked.

One should never give a name; it was power to curse. But
she feared not to answer. "Mija Jhirun Ela's-daughter," she
said; and daring much: "What is yours?"

But he did not answer, and unease crept the more upon
her.

"Where were you going?" she asked. "Were you only following me? What were you looking for?"

"To live," he said, with such simple desperation it seized at
her heart. "To stay alive." And he almost slipped from his
senses, the others waiting for his sleep, the whole house
poised and waiting, nearly fifty women and an old man. She
edged closer to him, put her shoulder against him, drew his
head against her. "The woman," she heard him murmur, "the
woman that follows me—"

He was fevered. She felt of his brow, listened to his raving,
that carried the same mad thread throughout. He slipped
away, his head against her heart, his eyes closed.

She stared beyond him, meeting Cil's troubled gaze, none others'.

A time to sleep, a little time for him, and then a chance to escape. He had done nothing to them, nothing of real hurt; and to end slaughtered by a house of women and children, with kitchen knives—she did not want that nightmare to haunt Barrows-hold. She could not live her life and sit by the fire and sew, work at the kitchen making bread, see her children playing by such a hearth. She would always see the blood on those stones.

No wraith, the stranger: his warmth burned fever-hot against her; his weight bruised her shoulder. She had lost herself, lost all sense where her mad dreams ended, no longer tried to reason. She saw the others lose their courage, settle, waiting; she also waited, not knowing for what. She remembered Anla's Crown, and knew that she had passed that edge where human folk ought to stop, had broken ancient warding-spells with as blithe a disdain as the stranger had passed the bits of feather at the door, innocent of fear that would have been wise to feel.

If there had been opportunity she would have begged her grandfather to explain; but he was helpless, his warding spells broken, his authority disregarded. For the first time she doubted the power of her grandfather as a priest—of all priests. She had seen a thing her grandfather had never seen—still could not see; had been where no foot had trod since the Kings.

The hold seemed suddenly a tiny and fragile place amid all the wild waste of Hiuaj, a place where the illusion of law persisted like a light set in the wind. But the reality was the dark, that lay heavy and breathing against her shoulder.

They should not destroy him, they in their mad trust in law and their own sanity. She began to wonder if they even questioned what he was, if they saw only an exhausted and wounded outlaw, and never doubted their conclusion. They were blind, that could not see the manner of him, the ancient armor and the tall black horse, that had no place in this age of the world, let alone in Hiuaj.

Perhaps they did not want to see, for then they would have to realize how fragile their safety was.

And perhaps he would not go away. Perhaps he had come to ruin that peace of theirs—to take Barrows-hold down to the same ruin as Chadrih, to ride one last course across the drowning world, one last glory of the Hiua kings, who had tried to master the Wells and failed, as the halfling Shiua had failed before them.

She had no haste to wake him. She sat frozen in dread while the storm fell away to silence, while the fire began to die in the hearth and none dared approach to tend it.

Chapter Three

||||||||||||||||||||||||||||||||||||||||||||||||||||||

Toward dawn came a stirring outside, soft scuffing on the pavement. Jhirun looked up, waking from half-sleep, her shoulder numb with the stranger's weight.

Came Zai, shivering and wet, stout Zai, who had run to set the beacon. She entered blue-lipped with chill and dripping about the hem of her skirts, and moved as silently as she could.

And behind Zai crept others, out of the mist that had followed the rain: the men came, one after the other, armed with skinning knives and their boat-poles. None spoke. They moved inside, their eyes hard and wary and their weapons ready. Jhirun watched and her heart pounded against her ribs; her lips shaped silent entreaty to them, her cousins, her uncles.

Uncle Naram was first to venture toward the hearth; and Lev after him, with Fwar and Ger beside him. Cil rose up of a sudden from the bench by the door; but Jinel was by her and seized her arm, cautioning her to silence. Jhirun cast a wild look at her grandfather, who stood helplessly at the stable door, and looked back at the men who edged toward her with drawn weapons.

Perhaps her arms tightened the least bit; perhaps there was some warning sound her numbed hearing did not receive; but the stranger wakened of a sudden, and she cried out to feel the push of his arms hurling her at them.

He was on his feet in the same instant, staggering against the mantel, and they rushed on him, rushing over her, who sprawled on the floor. And Fwar, more eager to lay hands on her than on the enemy, seized her and cruelly twisted her arm in hauling her to her feet. In the loft a baby cried, swiftly hushed.

Jhirun looked, dazed by the pain of Fwar's grip, on the

41

stranger who had backed to the corner. She saw his move, quicker than the beat of a bird's wing, that sent his dagger into his hand.

That gave them pause; and in that pause he ripped at the harness at his side and that great sword at his back slid to his hip. He unhooked the sheath of it one-handed.

They panicked, rushed for him in a mass, and of a sudden the sheath flashed across the room loose, and the bright blade was in his two hands, a wheeling arc that scattered blood and hurled her kinsmen back with shrieks of pain and terror.

And he leaned there in his corner a moment, hard-breathing; but the fresh wounds were on his enemies and none had they set on him. The stranger moved, and Fwar gave back, wrenching Jhirun's arm so hard that she cried out, Cil's scream echoing upon her own.

The stranger edged round the room, gathered up his fallen sheath, still with an eye to them; and her kinsmen gave back still further, none of them willing to rush that glittering blade a second time. In the loft were frightened stirrings, back into shadows.

"What will you?" Jhirun heard her grandfather's voice ask from behind her. "Name it and go."

"My horse," he said. "You, old man, fetch all my gear—all of it. I shall kill you otherwise."

And not a muscle did he move, staring at them with the great sword in his hands; nor did they move. Only her grandfather sidled carefully to the stable door and opened it, going to do the stranger's bidding.

"Let her go," the stranger said then to Fwar.

Fwar thrust her free, and she turned and spat at Fwar, shaking with hate. Fwar did nothing, his baleful eyes fixed on the stranger in silent rage, and she walked from him, never so glad to walk away from anything—went from him and to the side of the stranger, who had touched her gently, who had never done her hurt.

She turned there to face them all, these brute, ugly cousins, with thick hands and crass wit and no courage when it was likely to cost them. Her grandfather had been a different man once; but now he had none to rely on but these: brigands, no different at heart than the bandits they paid the marshlanders to catch and hang—save that the bandits preyed on the living.

Jhirun drew a deep breath and tossed her tangled hair from her face and looked on Fwar, hating, seeing the promise of later vengeance for his shame—on her, whom he reckoned already his property. She hated with a depth that left her shaking and short of breath, knowing her hopelessness. She was no more than they; the stranger had taken her part because of his own pride, because it was what a king should have done, but it was not because she was more than her cousins.

He had dropped his dagger to use the sword. She bent, slowly, picked it up, he none objecting; and she walked slowly to the other corner and slashed the strings by which sausages and white cheeses were hung. Jinel squealed with outrage, provoking a child's outcry from the loft; Jinel stifled her cry behind bony hands.

And such prizes Jhirun gathered off the floor and brought back to him. "Here," she said, dropping them at his side on the hearthstones. "Take whatever you can."

This she said to spite them all.

The stableward door opened, and Grandfather Keln led the black horse back in, the beast apprehensive of the room and the men. The warrior gathered the reins into his left hand and tugged at the saddle, testing the girth, but he never stopped watching the men. "I will take the blanket, if you will," he said to Jhirun quietly. "Tie the food into that and tie it on."

She bent down and did this, under her kinsmen's outraged eyes, rolled it all into a neat kit bound with some of the cheese strings and bound it behind the saddle as he showed her. She had to reach high to do this, and she feared the tall horse, but she was glad enough to do this for him.

And then she stood aside while he tugged on the reins and led the black horse through their midst to the open door, none daring to stop him. He paused outside, still on the paving, already greyed by the mist that whitened the morning outside. She saw him rise to the saddle, turn, and the mist took him, and swiftly muffled even the sound of the hooves.

There was nothing left of him, and it was as she had known it would be. She shivered, and shut her eyes, and realized in her hand was still one relic of their meeting, one memory of ancient magics: the hilt of a bone-handled dagger, such as the old Kings had borne to their burials.

She looked on her kinsmen, who were bleeding with wounds and ragged and ill-smelling, which *he* had never been, though he came from the flood, hard-riding; and there was hate in their faces, which he had not given her, though he was set upon and almost killed. She regarded Cil, sallow-faced, with her strength wasted; and Jinel, from whose face all liveliness and love had long since departed.

"Come here," said Fwar, and reached out to jerk her by the arm, his courage regained.

She whipped the knife across his face, struck flesh and heard him scream, blood across his mouth; and she whirled and ran, slashed this way and that among them, saw Cil's face a mask of horror at her madness, her grandfather drawing Cil back for protection. She held her hand then, and ran, free, through their midst, out into the cold and the fog.

The shawl slipped from her shoulders to trail by a corner; she caught it and ran again, through the black brush that appeared out of the mist. The dogs barked madly. She found the corner of the rough stone shelter on the west corner of the hold, and there in the brush she sank down, clutching the knife in bloody fingers and bending over, near to being sick. Her stomach heaved at the memory of Cil's horrified face. Her eyes stung with tears that blurred nothing, for there was only blank mist about her. She heard shouting through the distorting fog, her cousins seeking her, cursing her.

And Cil's voice, full of love and anguish.

Then she did weep, hot tears coursing down her face. She remembered the Cil that had been, when they were three sisters and the world was wider; then Cil could have understood—but Cil had made her choice, for safety, for her children. She was a faithful wife to Ger; and Jhirun knew Ger, who was faithful to nothing, who had laid hands on Jhirun herself in the drunkenness of Midyear, careless of his wife's feelings. Jhirun still had nightmares of that escape; and Ger had a scar to remember it.

And Fwar; she knew she had scarred him badly. He would have revenge for it. She had taken the petty measure of him before them all, and he could not live without revenge for that. She sat trembling in the cold white blankness and clutched against her breast the gull-token of the dead king, and the bloody dagger with it.

"Jhirun!"

That was her grandfather's voice, frantic and angry. Even to him she could not explain what she had done, why she had turned a knife on her own cousins, or what set her shuddering when she looked on her own sister. *Fey*, he must say, which others had always believed; and he would sign holy signs over her, and cleanse the house and renew the broken warding spells.

It was without meaning, she thought suddenly, the chanting and the spells. They lived all their lives in the shadow of world's end; and her children to Fwar or any man would be born to a worse age; and their children to the end of the world. They tried to live as if it were unimportant that the sea was eating away at the marsh and the quakes shaking the stones of the hold. They lived as if gold could buy them years as it bought them grain. They sought safety and warmth and comfort as if it would last, and saw nothing that was real.

There was no peace. The Barrow-king had swept through their lives like a wind out of the dark; and peace was at an end, but they saw nothing.

To accept Fwar, until she had no spirit left; or until she killed him or he killed her, that was the choice she was given.

She drew a great mouthful of air, like one drowning, and stared into the white nothingness and knew that she was not going back. She gathered her limbs under her, and rose and moved quietly through the mist.

Her kinsmen were down by the bank, calling to each other, seeking whether she had left in the boat. Soon they found the gold that was left there, abandoned in the night. Their voices exclaimed in profane greed. Already they were fighting over the prizes she had brought.

She cared nothing for this. She had no more desire for gold or for anything that they valued. She moved quietly round by the stable's outside door, cracked it so that she could see in without being seen. The goats bleated and the birds stirred in the loft, so that her heart froze in her and she knew that the houseward door would be flung open and her presence in the outer stable discovered upon the instant. But there was no stir from the house. She could still hear the shouting down by the boat, distant and angry voices. There would be no better chance than this.

She slipped inside, went to the pony's stall and eased the gate open. Then she took the halter from its peg and slipped it on him, backed him out. He did not want to leave his stable when she reached the outside door, laid back his ears at the weather, but he came when she tugged on the rope—stolid, thick-necked little pony that bore their burdens and amused the children. She grasped the clipped mane and rolled up onto his back, her legs finding pleasant the warmth of his fat sides, and she nudged him with her bare heels and set him moving downslope, having to fight him at first: he thought he knew the trail she wanted, and was mistaken, and had to be persuaded otherwise.

The water had sunk away in the channel this morning, and kept to center. The pony's hooves made deep gouges in the mire, betrayal when the sun should clear the mist away, and the pony had careful work to find a way up the next bank: marshbred, the little beast, that knew his way among the flooded isles, far sturdier for such travelling than the slender-legged horse of the stranger-king. Jhirun patted his neck as they came up safely on the next hill, her legs wet to the knees; and the pony tossed his head and blew a puff of excitement, moving quickly, sensing by now that things were not ordinary this morning, that it was not a workday.

In and out among the Barrow-hills they travelled, in places so treacherous she must often dismount and lead the pony. Her bare feet were muddy and numb with cold, and the mist clung as it could on chill days. She felt the aches of her flight of the night before, the weariness of a night without sleep, but she had no desire to rest. Fwar would find the tracks; Fwar would pursue, if none of the others would. The thought of him coming on her alone, without his father and brother to restrain him, made her sick with fear.

Eventually in the mist she found the way she sought, the stones of the old Road, and solid footing for the pony. She climbed astride again, absorbing the warmth of the pony's sides, her damp shawl wrapped about her. She congratulated herself on having eluded pursuit, began for the first time to believe she might make it away clear. Even the pony moved gladly, his unshod hooves sounding hollowly on the stones and echoing back off unseen hills.

It was the only Road left in all Hiuaj, *khal*-made and more ancient than the Kings. Any who followed her must find her if she delayed; but they must come afoot, and she had the pony's strength under her.

Somewhere ahead, she believed, rode the stranger-king, for a northward track had brought him to Barrows-hold, and there was no way but this for a rider to take. She had no hope of overtaking him on that fine long-legged horse, not once they had both reached the Road itself; but in her deepest hopes she thought he might expect her, wait for her—that he would become her guide through the terror of the wide marsh.

But already he faded in her mind, a vision that belonged to

the dark; and now things were white and gray. Only the gull-image at her heart and the bone-handled dagger in the waistband of her skirt proved that he had ever existed, and that she was most coldly sane, more than all her kinsmen.

In her common sense she knew that she was bound for grief, that she was casting herself into the hands of marshlanders or worse, who would learn, as her cousins knew, that she dreamed dreams, and hate her, as Chadrih-folk hated her, Ewon's fey daughter. But all the terror her nightmares had ever held seemed this morning at her back, hovering about Barrows-hold with a thickness that made it impossible to breathe. Death was there; she felt it, close, close and waiting. Away from Barrows-hold was relief from that pressure; it grew less and less as she rode away . . . not to Aren, to hope for that drab misery, within constant reach of Fwar. She chose to believe that she travelled to Shiuan, where holds sat rich and secure, where folk possessed Hiua gold. It was not so important to reach it as it was to go, now, now, now: the urgency beat in her blood like the heat of fever, beyond all reason.

Socha had smiled the morning she parted from them; Jhirun recalled her wrapped in sunlight, the boat gliding from the landing as it parted into that golden light: Socha had taken such a leave, at Hnoth, when madness swelled as the waters swelled in their channels. Jhirun let herself wonder the darker thoughts that she had always chased from her mind, whether Socha had lived long, swept out into the great gray sea—what night might have been for her, adrift in so much water, what horrid plunging of great monsters sporting near the shell of a boat; and in what mind Socha had come to the end,—whether she had wept for Barrows-hold and a life such as Cil had accepted. Jhirun did not think so.

She drew the gull amulet from between her breasts, safe to see it now in daylight, safe where no one would take it from her; and she thought of the king under the hill, and the stranger—himself driven by a nightmare as her own drove her.

The white rider, the fair rider, the woman behind him: day and white mist, as he was of the dark. In the night she had shuddered at his ravings, thinking of white feathers and of what lay against her heart, that seventh and unfavorable power—that once had prisoned him, before a Barrows-girl had come where she ought not.

The gull glittered coldly in her hand, wings spread, a thing

of ancient and sinister beauty, emblem of the blankness at
the edge of the world, out of which only the white gulls
came, like lost souls: Morgen-Angharan, that the marshlanders cursed, that the Kings had followed to their ruin—the
white Queen, who was Death. A nagging fear urged her to
throw the amulet far into the marsh. Hnoth was coming, as it
had come for Socha, when earth and sea and sky went mad
and the dreams came, driving her where no sane person
would go. But her hand closed firmly about it, possessing it,
and in time she slipped it back into her bodice to stay.

She could not see what lay about her in the mist. The
pony's hooves rang sometimes on bare stone, sometimes
splashed through water or trod on slick mud. The dim shapes
of the hills loomed in the thick air and passed her slowly like
humps of some vast serpent, submerged in the marsh, now on
this side of the Road and now on the other.

Something tall and thin stood beside the roadway. The
pony clopped on toward it, and Jhirun's heart beat faster, her
fingers clenched upon the rein, the while she assured herself
that the pony would not so blithely approach any dangerous
beast. Then it took shape clearly, one of the Standing Stones,
edgewise. She knew it now, and had not realized how far she
had ridden in the mist.

More and more of such stones were about her now. She
well knew where she was: the ruined *khalin* hold of Nia's
Hill was nearby, stones which had stood before the Moon
was broken. She rode now on the border of the marshlands.

The little pony walked stolidly on his way, small hooves
ringing on stone and now muffled by earth; and all that she
could see in the gray world were the nearest stones and the
small patch of earth on which the pony trod, as if creation itself were unravelled before and behind, and only where she
rode remained solid. So it might be if one rode beyond the
edge of the world.

And riding over soft ground, she looked down and saw the
prints of larger hooves.

The Road rose again from that point, so that earth no
longer covered it, and the ancient stone surface lay bare.
Three Standing Stones made a gathering of shadows in the
mist just off the Road. Distantly came an echo off the Stones,
slow and doubling the sound of the pony's hooves. Jhirun
little liked the place, that was old before the Barrows were
reared. Her hands clenched on the pony's short mane as well
as on the rein, for he walked warily now, his head lifted and

with the least uncertainty in his gait. The echoes continued; and of a sudden came the ring of metal on stone, a shod horse.

Jhirun drove her heels into the pony's fat sides, gathering her courage, forcing the unwilling animal ahead.

The black horse took shape before her, horse and rider, awaiting her. The pony balked. Jhirun gave him her heels again and made him go, and the warrior stayed for her, a dark shadow in the fog. His face came clear; he wore a peaked helm, a white scarf about it now. She stopped the pony.

"I came to find you," she said, and his lack of welcome was already sending uncertainties winding about her heart, a sense of something utterly changed.

"Who are you?" he asked, which totally confounded her; and when she stared at him: "Where do you come from? From that hold atop the hill?"

She began to reckon that she was in truth going mad, and pressed her chilled hands to her face and shivered, her shaggy pony standing dwarfed by that tall black horse.

With a gentle ripple of water, a ring of shod hooves on stone, a gray horse appeared out of the mist. Astride him was a woman in a white cloak, and her hair as pale as the day, as white as hoarfrost.

A woman, the warrior had breathed in his nightmare, *a rider all white, the woman that follows me—*

But she came to a halt beside him, white queen and dark king together, and Jhirun reined aside her pony to flee the sight of them.

The black horse overrushed her, the warrior's hand tearing the rein from her fingers. The pony shied off from such treatment, and the short mane failed her exhausted fingers. His body twisted under her and she tumbled down his slick back, seeing blind fog about her, up or down she knew not until she fell on her back and the Dark went over her.

BOOK TWO

Chapter Four

〓〓〓〓〓〓〓〓〓〓〓〓〓〓〓〓〓〓〓〓〓〓〓〓〓〓〓〓〓〓〓

It was not, even within the woods, like Kursh or Andur. Water flowed softly here, a hostile whisper about the hills. The moon that glowed through the fog was too great a moon, a weight upon the sky and upon the soul; and the air was rank with decay.

Vanye was glad to return to the fire, bearing his burden of gathered branches, to kneel by that warmth that drove back the fog and overlay the stench of decay with fragrant smoke.

They had within the ruin a degree of shelter at least, although Vanye's Kurshin soul abhorred the builders of it: ancient stones that seemed once to have been the corner of some vast hall, the remnant of an arch. The gray horse and the black had pasturage on the low hill that lay back of the ruin, and the shaggy pony was tethered apart from the two for its safety's sake. The black animals were shadow-shapes beyond the trees, and gray Siptah seemed a wraith-horse in the fog: three shapes that moved and grazed at leisure behind a screen of moisture-beaded branches.

The girl's brown shawl was drying on a stone by the fire. Vanye turned it to dry the other side, then began to feed branches into the fire, wood so moisture-laden it snapped and hissed furiously and gave off bitter clouds of smoke. But the fire blazed up after a moment, and Vanye rested gratefully in that warmth—took off the white-scarfed helm and pushed back the leather coif, freeing his brown hair, that was cut even with his jaw: no warrior's braid—he had lost that right, along with his honor.

He sat, arms folded across his knees, staring at the girl who lay in Morgaine's white cloak, in Morgaine's care. A warm cloak, a dry bed, a saddlebag for a pillow: this was as much as they could do for the child, who responded little. He thought that the fall might have shaken her forever from her

53

wits, for she shivered intermittently in her silence, and stared
at them both with wild, mad eyes. But she seemed quieter
since he had been sent out for wood—a sign, he thought, either of better or of worse.

When he was warmed through, he arose, returned quietly
to Morgaine's side, from which he had been banished. He
wondered that Morgaine spent so much attention on the
child—little enough good that she could do; and he expected
now that she would bid him go back to the fire and stay
there.

"You speak with her," Morgaine said quietly, to his dismay; and as she gave place for him, rising, he knelt down,
captured at once by the girl's eyes—mad, soft eyes, like a
wild creature's. The girl murmured something in a plaintive
tone and reached for him; he gave his hand, uneasily feeling
the gentle touch of her fingers curling round his.

"She has found you," she said, a mere breath, accented,
difficult to understand. "She has found you, and are you not
afraid? I thought you were enemies."

He knew, then. He was chilled by such words, conscious of
Morgaine's presence at his back. "You have met my cousin,"
he said. "His name is Chya Roh—among others."

Her lips trembled, and she gazed at him with clearing
sense in her dark eyes. "Yes," she said at last. "You are different; I see that you are."

"Where is Roh?" Morgaine asked.

The threat in Morgaine's voice drew the girl's attention.
She tried to move, but Vanye did not loose her hand. Her
eyes turned back to him.

"Who are you?" she asked. "Who are you?"

"Nhi Vanye," he answered in Morgaine's silence, for he
had struck her down, and she was due at least his name for
it: "Nhi Vanye i Chya. Who are you?"

"Jhirun Ela's-daughter," she said, and added: "I am going
north, to Shiuan—"as if this and herself were inseparable.

"And Roh?" Morgaine dropped to her knee and seized her
by the arm. Jhirun's hand left his. For a moment the girl
stared into Morgaine's face, her lips trembling.

"Let be," Vanye asked of his liege. "*Liyo*—let be."

Morgaine thrust the girl's arm free and arose, walked back
to the fireside. For some little time the girl Jhirun stared in
that direction, her face set in shock. "*Dai-khal*," she murmured finally.

Dai-khal: high-clan *qujal*, Vanye understood that much.

He followed Jhirun's glance back to Morgaine, who sat by the fire, slim, clad in black leather, her hair a shining pallor in the firelight. Here too the Old Ones were known, and feared.

He touched the girl's shoulder. She jerked from his fingers. "If you know where Roh is," he said, "tell us."

"I do not."

He withdrew his hand, unease growing in him. Her accents were strange; he hated the place, the ruins—all this haunted land. It was a dream, in which he had entrapped himself; yet he had struck flesh when he rode against her, and she bled, and he did not doubt that he could, that it was well possible to die here, beneath this insane and lowering sky. In the first night, lost, looking about him at the world, he had prayed; increasingly he feared that it was blasphemy to do so in this land, that these barren, drowning hills were Hell, in which all lost souls recognized each other.

"When you took me for him," he said to her, "you said you came to find me. Then he is on this road."

She shut her eyes and turned her face away, dismissing him, weak as she was and with the sweat of shock beading her brow. He was forced to respect such courage—she a peasant and himself once a warrior of clan Nhi. For fear, for very terror in this Hell, he had ridden against her and her little pony with the force he would have used against an armed warrior; and it was only good fortune that her skull was not shattered, that she had fallen on soft earth and not on stone.

"Vanye," said Morgaine from behind him.

He left the girl and went to the side of his liege—sat down, arms folded on his knees, next the fire's warmth. She was frowning at him, displeased, whether at him or at something else, he was not sure. She held in her hand a small object, a gold ornament.

"She has dealt with him," Morgaine said, thin-lipped. "He is somewhere about—with ambush laid, it may well be."

"We cannot go on pushing the horses. *Liyo*, there is no knowing what we may meet."

"She may know. Doubtless she knows."

"She is afraid of you," he objected softly. "*Liyo*, let me try to ask her. We must rest the horses; there is time, there is time."

"What Roh has touched," she said, "is not trustworthy. Remember it. Here. A keepsake."

He held out his hand, thinking she meant the ornament. A blade flashed into her hand, and to his, sending a chill to his heart, for it was an Honor-blade, one for suicide. At first he thought it hers, for it was, like hers, Koris-work. Then he realized it was not.

It was Roh's.

"Keep it," she said, "in place of your own."

He took it unwillingly, slipped it into the long-empty sheath at his belt. "Avert," he murmured, crossing himself.

"Avert," she echoed, paying homage to beliefs he was never sure she shared, and made the pious gesture that sealed it, wishing the omen from him, the ill-luck of such a blade. "Return it to him, if you will. That pure-faced child was carrying it. Remember that when you are moved to gentility with her."

Vanye sank down from his crouch to sit crosslegged by her, oppressed by foreboding. The unaccustomed weight of the blade at his belt was cruel mockery, unintended, surely unintended. He was weaponless; Morgaine thought of practicalities—and of other things.

Kill him, her meaning was: *it is yours to do*. He had taken the blade, lacking the will to object. He had abandoned all right to object. Suddenly he felt everything tightly woven about him: Roh, a strange girl, a lost dagger—a net of ugly complexities.

Morgaine held out her hand a second time, dropped into his the small gold object, a bird on the wing, exquisitely wrought. He closed his hand on it, slipped it into his belt. *Return that to her*, he understood, and consented. *She is yours to deal with.*

Morgaine leaned forward and fed bits of wood into the fire, small pieces that charred rapidly into red-edged black. Firelight gleamed on the edge of silver mail at her shoulder, bathed her tanned face and pale eyes and pale hair in one unnatural light in the gathering dark. *Qujal*-fair she was, although she disclaimed that unhuman blood. He himself was of the distant mountains of Andur-Kursh, of a canton called Morija; but that was not her heritage. Perhaps her birthplace was here, where she had brought him. He did not ask. He smelled the salt wind and the pervading reek of decay, and knew that he was lost, as lost as ever a man could be. His beloved mountains, those walls of his world, were gone. It was as if some power had hurled down the limits of the world and shown him the ugliness beyond. The sun was pale and distant from this land, the stars had shifted in their places, and the moons—the moons defied all reason.

The fire grew higher as Morgaine fed it. "Is that not enough?" he asked, forcing that silence that the alien ruins held, full of age and evil. He felt naked because of that light, exposed to every enemy that might be abroad this night; but Morgaine simply shrugged and tossed a final and larger stick onto the blaze. She had weapons enough. Perhaps she reckoned it was her enemies' lives she risked by that bright fire. She was arrogant in her power, madly arrogant at times—though there were moments when he suspected she did such things not to tempt her enemies, but in some darker contest, to tempt fate.

The heat touched him painfully as a slight breeze stirred, the first hint they had had of any wind that might disperse the mist; but the breeze died and the warmth flowed away again. Vanye shivered and stretched out his hand to the fire until the heat grew unbearable, then clasped that hand to his ribs and warmed the other.

There was a hill beyond the flood, and a Gate among Standing Stones, and this was the way that they had ridden, a dark, unnatural path. Vanye did not like to remember it, that moment of dark dreaming in which he had passed from *there* to *here*, like the fall at the edge of sleep: he steadied himself even in thinking of it.

Likewise Morgaine had come, and Chya Roh before them, into a land that lay at the side of a vast river, under a sky that never appeared over Andur-Kursh.

Morgaine unwrapped their supplies, and they shared food in silence. It was almost the last they had, after which they must somehow live off this bleak land. Vanye ate sparingly, wondering whether he should offer to Jhirun, or whether it was not kinder to let her rest. Most of all he doubted Morgaine would favor it, and at last he decided to let matters be. He washed down the last mouthful with a meager sip of the good wine of Baien, saving some back; and sat staring into the fire, turning over and over in his mind what they were to do with the girl Jhirun. He dreaded knowing. No good name had Morgaine among men; and some of it was deserved.

"Vanye. Is thee regretting?"

He looked up, saw that Morgaine had been staring at him in the ruddy light, eyes that were in daylight sea-gray, world-gray, *qujal*-gray. That gentle, ancient accent had power more than the wind to chill him, reminding him that she had

known more Gates than one, that she had learned his tongue
of men long dead; she forgot, sometimes, what age she lived
in.

He shrugged.

"Roh," she said, "is no longer kin to you. Do not brood on
it."

"When I find him," he said, "I will kill him. I have sworn
that."

"Was it for that," she asked him finally, "that you came?"

He gazed into the fire, unable to speak aloud the unease
that rose in him when she began to encircle him with such
questions. She was not of his blood. He had left his own land,
abandoned everything to follow her. There were some things
that he did not let himself reason to their logical end.

She left the silence on him, a stifling weight; and he
opened his hand, twice scarred across the palm with the
Claiming by blood and ash. By that, he was *ilin* to her, bound
in service, without conscience, honorless save for her honor,
which he served. This parting-gift his clan had bestowed on
him, like the shorn hair that marked him felon and outlaw, a
man fit only for hanging. Brother-slayer, bastard-born: no
other liege would have wanted such a man, only Morgaine,
whose name was a curse wherever she was known. It was
irony that *ilin*-service, penance for murder, had left him far
more blood-guilty than ever he had come to her.

And Roh remained yet to deal with.

"I came," he said, "because I swore it to you."

She thrust at the fire with a stick, sending sparks aloft like
stars on the wind. "Mad," she judged bitterly. "I set thee free,
told thee plainly thee had no possible place outside Kursh,
outside the law and the folk thee knows. I wish thee had believed it."

He acknowledged this truth with a shrug. He knew the
workings of Morgaine's mind better than any living; and he
knew the Claim she had set on him, that had nothing to do
with his scarred hand; and the Claim that someone else had
set on her, crueller than any oath. Her necessity lay sheathed
at her side, that dragon-hilted sword that was no true sword,
but a weapon all the same. It was the only bond that had
ever truly claimed her, and she hated it above all other evils,
qujal or human.

I have no honor, she had warned him once. *It is uncon-
scionable that I should take risks with the burden I carry. I
have no luxury left for virtues.*

Another thing she had told him that he had never doubted: *I would kill you too if it were necessary.*

She hunted *qujal*, she and the named-blade *Changeling*. The *qujal* she hunted now wore the shape of Chya Roh i Chya. She sought Gates, and followed therein a compulsion more than half madness, that gave her neither peace nor happiness. He could understand this in some part: he had held *Changeling* in his own hands, had wielded its alien evil, and there had come such a weight on his soul afterward that no penance of *ilin*-service could ever cleanse him of remembering.

"The law is," he said, "that you may bid me leave your service, but you cannot order it. If I stay, I remain *ilin*, but that is my choice and not yours."

"No one ever refused to leave service."

"Surely," he said, "there have been *ilinin* before me that found no choice. A man is maimed in service, for instance; he might starve elsewhere, but while he stays *ilin*, his *liyo* must at least feed him and his horse, however foul the treatment he may receive in other matters. You cannot make me leave you, and your charity was always more generous than my brother's."

"You are neither halt nor blind," Morgaine retorted; she was not accustomed to being answered with levities.

He made a gesture of dismissal, knowing for once he had touched through her guard. He caught something bewildered in her expression in that instant, something terrified. It destroyed his satisfaction. He would have said something further, but she glanced aside from him with a sudden scowl, removing his opportunity.

"There was at least a time you chose for yourself," she said at last. "I gave you that, Nhi Vanye. Remember it someday."

"Aye," he said carefully. "Only so you give me the same grace, *liyo*, and remember that I chose what I wanted."

She frowned the more deeply. "As you will," she said. "Well enough." And for a time she gazed into the fire, and then the frown grew pensive, and she was gazing toward their prisoner, a look that betrayed some inner war. Vanye began to suspect something ugly in her mind, that was somehow entangled with her questions to him; he wished that he knew what it was.

"*Liyo*," he said, "likely the girl is harmless."

"Thee knows so?"

She mocked him in his ignorance. He shrugged, made a

helpless gesture. "I do not think," he said, "that Roh would have had time to prepare any ambush."

"The time of Gates is not world-time." She hurled a bit of bark into the flames, dusted her hands. "Go, go, we have time now that one of us could be sleeping, and we are wasting it. Go to sleep."

"She?" he asked, with a nod toward Jhirun.

"I will speak with her."

"You rest," he urged her after a moment, inwardly braced against some irrational anger. Morgaine was distraught this night, exhausted—they both were. Her slim hands were tightly laced about her knee, clenched until the strain was evident. Tired as he was, he sensed something greatly amiss. "*Liyo*, let me have first watch."

She sighed, as if at that offer all the weariness came over her at once, the weight of mail that could make a strong man's bones ache, days of riding that wore even upon him, Kurshin and born to the saddle. She bowed her head upon her knee, then flung it back and straightened her shoulders. "Aye," she said hoarsely, "aye, that I will agree to gladly enough."

She gathered herself to her feet, *Changeling* in her hand; but to his amazement she offered it to him, sheathed and crosswise.

It never left her, never. By night she slept with that evil thing; she never walked from where it lay, not more than a room's width before she turned and took it up again. When she rode, it was either under her knee on the gray horse's saddle, or across her shoulders on her sword belt.

He did not want even to touch it, but he took it and gathered it to him carefully; and she left him so, beside the fire. Perhaps, he thought, she was concerned that the warrior who guarded her sleep not do so unarmed; perhaps she had some subtler purpose, reminding him what governed her own choices. He considered this, watching her settle to sleep in that corner of the ruin where the stones still made an arch. She had their saddles for pillow and windbreak, the coarse saddle-blankets, unfolded, for a covering: he had lost his own cloak the same way he had lost his sword, else it would have been his cloak that was lent their injured prisoner, not hers. The consciousness of this vexed him. He had come to her with nothing that would have made their way easier, and borrowed upon what she had.

Yet Morgaine trusted him. He knew how hard it was for

her to allow another hand on *Changeling*, which was obsession with her; she need not have lent it, and did; and he did not know why. He was all too aware, in the long silence after she seemed to have fallen asleep, how clear a target the fire made him.

Roh, if his hands retained any of their former skill, was a bowman of the Korish forests; and a Chya bowman was a shadow, a flitting ghost where there was cover. Likely too the girl Jhirun had kinsmen hereabouts seeking her, if Roh himself did not. And perhaps—Vanye's shoulders prickled at the thought—Morgaine set a trap by means of that bright fire, disregarding his life and hers; she was capable of doing so, lending him her chiefest weapon to ease her conscience, knowing that this, at least, he could use.

He rested the sword between his knees, the dragon-hilt against his heart, daring not so much as to lie down to ease the torment of the mail on his shoulders, for he was unbearably tired, and his eyes were heavy. He listened to the faint sounds of the horses grazing in the dark, reassured constantly by their soft stirrings. Nightsounds had begun, sounds much like home: the creak of frogs, the occasional splash of water as some denizen of the marsh hunted.

And there was the matter of Jhirun, that Morgaine had set upon him.

He tucked a chill hand to his belt, felt the rough surface of the Honor-blade's hilt, wondering how Roh fared, wondering whether he were equally lost, equally afraid. The crackling of the fire at his side brought back other memories, of another fireside, of Ra-koris on a winter's evening, of a refuge once offered him, when no other refuge existed: Roh, who had been willing to acknowledge kinship with an outlawed *ilin*.

He had been moved to love Roh once, Roh alone of all his kinsmen; an honest man and brave, Chya Roh i Chya. But the man he had known in Ra-koris was dead, and what possessed Roh's shape now was *qujal*, ancient and deadly hostile.

The Honor-blade was not for enemies, but the last resort of honor; Roh would have chosen that way, if he had had the chance. He had not. Within Gates, souls could be torn from bodies and man and man confounded, the living with the dying. Such was the evil that had taken Chya Roh; Roh was truly dead, and what survived in him wanted killing, for Roh's sake.

Vanye drew the blade partly from its sheath, touched that

razor edge with gentle fingers, a tightness in his throat, wondering how, of all possessions that Roh might have lost, it had been this, that no warrior would choose to abandon.

She has found you, the girl had said, mistaking them in their kinsmen's resemblance. *Are you not afraid?*

It occurred to him that Roh himself had feared Morgaine, loathed her, who had destroyed his ancestors and the power that had been Koris.

But Roh was dead. Morgaine, who had witnessed it, had said that Roh was dead.

Vanye clenched both hands about *Changeling's* cold sheath, averted his eyes from the fire and saw Jhirun awake and staring at him.

She had knowledge of Roh. Morgaine had left the matter to him, and he loathed what he had asked, realized it for what it truly was—that he did not want the answers.

Suddenly the girl broke contact with his eyes, hurled herself to her feet and for the shadows.

He sprang up and crossed the intervening distance before she could take more than two steps—seized her arm and set her down again on the cloak, *Changeling* safely out of her reach in the bend of his other arm. She struck him, a solid blow across the temple, and he shook her, angered. A second time she hit him, and this time he did hurt her, but she did not cry out—not a sound came from her but gasps for breath, when woman might have appealed to woman—not to Morgaine. He knew whom she feared most; and when she had stopped struggling he relaxed his grip, reckoning that she would not run now. She jerked free and stayed still, breathing hard.

"Be still," he whispered. "I shall not touch you. You will be wiser not to wake my lady."

Jhirun gathered Morgaine's white cloak up about her shoulders, up to her chin. "Give me back my pony and my belongings," she said. Her accent and her shivering together made her very difficult to understand. "Let me go. I swear I will tell no one. No one."

"I cannot," he said. "Not without her leave. But we are not thieves." He searched in his belt and found the gull-ornament, offering it. She snatched it, careful not even to touch his hand, and clenched it with the other hand under her chin. She continued to stare at him, fierce dark eyes glittering in the firelight. The bruised cheek gave the left eye a shadow. "You are his cousin?" she asked. "And his enemy?"

"In my house," he said, "that is nothing unusual."

"He was kind to me."

He gave a sour twist of the lips. "You are fair to look upon, and I would hardly be surprised at that."

She flinched. The look of outrage in her eyes was like a physical rebuff, reminding him that even a peasant girl was born with honor, a distinction that he could not claim. She looked very young, frightened of him and of her circumstances. After a moment it was he that looked aside.

"I beg pardon," he said; and when she kept a long silence, still breathing as if she had been running: "How did you meet him, and when?"

"Last night," she said, words that filled him with relief, on many accounts. "He came to us, hurt, and my folk tried to rob and kill him. He was too quick for us. And he could have killed everyone, but he did not. And he was kind to me." Her voice trembled on the word, insistent this time on being understood. "He went away without stealing anything, even though he was in need of everything. He only took what belonged to him, and what I gave him."

"He is *dai-uyo*," he answered her. "A gentleman."

"A great lord."

"He has been that."

Her eyes reckoned him up and down and seemed perplexed. *And what are you?* he imagined her thoughts in that moment, hoping that she would not ask. The shame of his shorn hair, the meaning of the white scarf of the *ilin*—perhaps she understood, reckoning the difference between him and Chya Roh, highborn, cousin. He could not explain. *Changeling* rested across his knee; he was conscious of it as if it were a living thing: Morgaine's forbidding presence, binding him to silence.

"What will you do with him when you have found him?" Jhirun asked.

"What would you have done?"

She gathered her knees up within the fur and stared at him. She looked as if she were expecting him to strike her, as if she were prepared to bear that—for Roh's sake.

"What were you doing," he asked her, "riding out here with no cloak and no food? You cannot have planned to go far."

"I am going to Shiuan," she said. Her eyes brimmed with tears, but her jaw was set. "I am from the Barrow-hills, and I can hunt and fish and I had my pony—until you took him."

"How did you get the dagger?"

"He left it behind."

"It is an Honor-blade," he said harshly. "A man would not so casually leave that behind."

"There was the fight," she said in a low voice. "I was going to give it back when I found him. I was only going to use it until then."

"To gut fish."

She flinched from the spite in his voice.

"Where is he?" he asked.

"I do not know, I do not know. He said nothing. He only left."

Vanye stared at her, weighing her answers, and she edged back from him as if she did not like his expression. "Go to sleep," he bade her suddenly, and rose and left her there, looking back nevertheless to be sure she did not make some rash bid to escape. She did not. He settled again on his stone by the fire, so that he could watch her. For a time she continued to stare at him through the flames; abruptly she flung herself down and hid herself in the cloak.

He set his hands together on *Changeling*'s pommel, resting against it, all his peace destroyed by the things that she had said.

He understood her loyalty to Roh, even as a stranger; he knew his cousin's manner, that way of reaching for the heart of any who dealt with him—as once Roh had drawn him in spite of Roh's other failings. It was painful to know that this aspect of the man was still intact, that he had his former gentleness, his honesty—all those graces that had been Chya Roh.

But it was illusion. Nothing of Roh's soul or essence could survive. Morgaine had said it, and therefore it was so.

Return it to him, Morgaine bade him, arming him.

He thought of facing Roh at weapons' edge, and another nightmare returned to him, a courtyard in Morija—a flash of blades, a brother's dying. Of that he was guilty. To destroy, to plunge home that blade when it was Roh's face and voice, for this possibly he could prepare himself. . . . *But, o Heaven*, he thought, sickness turning in him, *if it should be more than outward seeming—*

He was kind to me, the girl had said. *He went away without stealing anything, even though he was in need of everything.*

There was no kindness in the *qujal*, who had sought his life and taken Roh's in its place, nothing so simple or so human as kindness, only sweet persuasiveness, the power to convince with seeming logic, to play on a man's worst fears and darkest impulses and promise what he had no intention of giving.

Nor was there honor—the manner of a high-clan warrior, a clan lord, who would not stoop to thievery, not even in great need: that was not the manner of the being who had lied and murdered and stolen through three generations of men, taking what he desired—even the body in which he lived. Generosity was unknown to him.

That was not the *qujal.* It was the manner of Roh himself, Chya and more prideful than practical, the blood they both shared; it was Roh.

"Vanye."

He spun toward the whisper, the tread upon leaves, heart frozen at the sight of the shadowy figure, even when he knew it was only Morgaine. He was embarrassed that he had not heard her moving, though she was herself adopted Chya, and walked silently enough when she chose; but the more he was disturbed for the thoughts in which she had come upon him—that betrayed his oath, while she trusted him.

For a moment he felt that she read him. She shrugged then, and settled beside the fire. "I am not disposed to sleep," she said.

Distress, displeasure—with what, or whom, he could not tell; her eyes met his, disturbing him, striking fear into him. She was capable of irrationality.

Knowing this, still he stayed with her; at such times he remembered that he was not the first who had done so—that she had far more of comrades' blood to her account than that of enemies—that she had slain far more who had shared bread with her than ever she had of those she had wished to harm.

Roh was one such that had crossed her path, and deserved pity for it; Vanye thought of Roh, and of himself, and in that instant there was a distance between himself and Morgaine. He thrust Roh from his mind.

"Do we move on?" he asked her. It was a risk and he knew it, that she might seize upon it in her present mood; he saw that it tempted her sorely—but since he had offered, she was obliged to use reason.

"We will move early," she said. "Go rest."

He was glad of the dismissal, knowing her present mood;

and his eyes burned with fatigue. He took the sword in his hands and gave it to her, anxious to be rid of it, sensing her distress to be parted from it. Perhaps, he thought, this had disturbed her sleep. She folded it into her arms and leaned forward to the fire, as if having it comforted her.

"It has been quiet," he said.

"Good," she answered, and before he could gather himself to his feet: "Vanye?"

"Aye?" He settled back to his place, wanting, and not wanting, to share her thoughts, the things that had robbed her of sleep.

"Did thee trust what she said?"

She had heard then, listening to all that had passed. He was at once guiltily anxious, trying to remember what things he had said aloud and what he had held in his heart; and he glanced at Jhirun, who still slept, or pretended to. "I think it was the truth," he said. "She is ignorant—of us, of everything that concerns us. Best we leave her in the morning."

"She will be safer in our company a time."

"No," he protested. Things came to mind that he dared not say aloud, hurtful things, the reminder that their company had not been fortunate for others.

"And we will be the safer for it," she said, in a still voice that brooked no argument.

"Aye," he said, forcing the word. He felt a hollowness, a sense of foreboding so heavy that it made breath difficult.

"Take your rest," she said.

He departed the warmth of the fire, sought the warm nest that she had quitted. When he lay down amid their gear and drew the coarse blankets over him, every muscle was taut and trembling.

He wished that Ela's-daughter had escaped them when she had run—or better still, that they had missed each other in the fog and never met.

He shifted to his other side, and stared into the blind dark, remembering home, and other forests, knowing that he had entered an exile from which there was no return.

The Gate behind them was sealed. The way lay forward from here, and it occurred to him with increasing unease that he did not know where he was going, that never again would he know where he was going.

Morgaine, his arms, and a stolen Andurin horse: that comprised the world that he knew.

And now there was Roh, and a child who had about her

the foreboding of a world he did not want to know—his own burden, Jhirun Ela's-daughter, for it was his impulse that had laid ambush for her, when by all other chances she might have ridden on her way.

Chapter Five

||||||||||||||||||||||||||||||||||||||||||||||||||||||||

"Vanye."

He wakened to the grip of Morgaine's hand on his arm, startled out of a sleep deeper than he was wont.

"Get the horses," she said. The wind was whipping fiercely at the swaying branches overhead, drawing her fair hair into a stream in the darkness. "It is close to dawn. I let you sleep as long as I could, but the weather is turning on us."

He murmured a response, arose, rubbing at his eyes. When he glanced at the sky he saw the north flashing with lightnings, beyond the restless trees. Wind sighed coldly through the leaves.

Morgaine was already snatching up their blankets and folding them. For his part he left the ring of firelight and felt his way downslope among the stones of the ruins, across the narrow channel and up again to the rise where the horses were tethered. They snorted alarm at his coming, already uneasy at the weather; but Siptah recognized him and called softly—gray Siptah, gentler-mannered than his own Andurin gelding. He took the gray and Jhirun's homely pony together and led them back the way he had come, up again the ruins.

Jhirun was awake. He saw her standing as he came into the firelight, opened his mouth to speak some gentle word to her; but Morgaine intervened, taking the horses. "I will tend them," she said brusquely. "See to your own."

He hesitated, looking beyond her shoulder to Jhirun's frightened face, and felt a deep unease, leaving her to Morgaine's charge; but there was no time for disputes, and there was no privacy for argument. He turned and plunged back into the shadows, making what haste he could, not knowing against what he was racing, the storm or Morgaine's nature.

Dawn was coming. He found the black gelding a shadow in a dark that was less than complete, although the boiling clouds held back the light. He freed the horse, hauled firmly on the cheekstrap as the ungentle beast nipped at him, then in his haste swung up bareback and rode back with halter alone, down across the stream and up again among the trees and the ruins.

He was relieved to find Jhirun calmly sitting by the dying fire, wrapped in her brown shawl, eating a bit of bread. Morgaine was doing as she had said, tending to Siptah's saddling; and she bore *Changeling* on her shoulder harness, as she would when she judged the situation less than secure.

"I have told her that she is coming with us," Morgaine said, as he alighted and flung the blanket up to the gelding's back. He said nothing, unhappy in Morgaine's intention. He bent and heaved the saddle up, settled it and reached under for the girth. "She seemed agreeable in the matter," Morgaine said, seeming determined to draw some word from him on the subject.

He gave attention to his work, avoiding her eyes. "At least," he said, "she might ride double with me. She has a head wound. We might give her that grace—by your leave."

"As you will," said Morgaine after a moment. She rolled her white cloak into its oiled-leather covering and tied it behind her saddle. With a jerk of the thongs she finished, and gathered up Siptah's reins, leading the horse toward the fire, where Jhirun sat.

Jhirun stopped eating, and sat there with the morsel forgotten in her two hands. Like something small and trapped she seemed, with her bruised eyes and bedraggled hair, but there was a hard glitter to those eyes nonetheless. Vanye watched in unease as Morgaine stopped before her.

"We are ready," Morgaine said to her. "Vanye will take you up behind him."

"I can ride my own pony."

"Do as you are told."

Jhirun arose, scowling, started to come toward him. Morgaine reached to the back of her belt, a furtive move. Vanye saw, and dropped the saddlebag he had in hand.

"No!" he cried.

The motion was sudden, the girl walking, the sweep of Morgaine's hand, the streak of red fire. Jhirun shrieked as it touched the tree beside her, and Vanye caught the gelding's bridle as the animal shied up.

Morgaine replaced the weapon at the back of her belt. Vanye drew a shaken breath, his hands calming the frightened horse. But Jhirun did not move at all, her feet braced in the preparation of a step never taken, her arms clenched about her bowed head.

"Tell me again," Morgaine said softly, very audibly, "that you do not know this land, Jhirun Ela's-daughter."

Jhirun sank to her knees, her hands still clenched in her hair. "I have never been further than this down the road," she said in a trembling voice. "I have heard, I have only heard that it leads to Shiuan, and that was before the flood. I do not know."

"Yet you travel it without food, without a cloak, without any preparation. You hunt and you fish. Will that keep you warm of nights? Why do you ride this road at all?"

"Hiuaj is drowning," Jhirun wept. "Since the Wells were closed and the Moon was broken, Hiuaj has been drowning, and it is coming soon. I do not want to drown."

Her mad words hung in the air, quiet amid the rush of wind, the restless stamp and blowing of the horses. Vanye blessed himself, the weight of the very sky pressing on his soul.

"How long ago," asked Morgaine, "did this drowning begin?"

But Jhirun wiped at the tears that spilled onto her cheeks and seemed beyond answering sanely.

"How long?" Morgaine repeated harshly.

"A thousand years," Jhirun said.

Morgaine only stared at her a moment. "These Wells: a ring of stones, is that not your meaning? One overlooks the great river; and there will be yet another, northward, one master Well. Do you know it by name?"

Jhirun nodded, her hands clenched upon the necklace that she wore, bits of sodden feather and metal and stone. She shivered visibly. "Abarais," she answered faintly. "Abarais, in Shiuan. *Dai-khal, dai-khal,* I have told you all the truth, all that I know. I have told everything."

Morgaine frowned, and at last came near the girl, offering her hand to help her rise, but Jhirun shrank from it, weeping. "Come," said Morgaine impatiently, "I will not harm you. Only do not trouble me; I have shown you that . . . and better that you see it now, than that you assume too far with us."

Jhirun would not take her hand. She struggled to her feet unaided, braced herself, her shawl clutched about her. Morgaine turned and gathered up Siptah's reins, rose easily into the saddle.

Vanye drew a whole breath at last, expelled it softly. He left his horse standing and went to the fireside, gathered up his helmet and covered his head, lacing the leather coif at his throat. Last of all he paused to scatter the embers of their campfire.

He heard a horse moving as he turned, recoiled as Siptah plunged across his path, Morgaine taut-reining him to an instant stop. He looked up, dismayed at the rage with which she looked at him.

"Never," she hissed softly, "never cry warning against me again."

"*Liyo*," he said, stricken to remember what he had done, the outcry he had made. "I am sorry; I did not expect—"

"Thee does not know me, *ilin*. Thee does not know me half so well as thee trusts to."

The harshness chilled. For a moment he stared up at her in shock, fixed by that cold as Jhirun had been, unable to answer her.

She spurred Siptah past him. He sought the pony's tether, half blind with shame and anger, ripped it from its branch and tied it to his own horse's saddle. "Come," he bade Jhirun, struggling to keep anger from his voice, with her who had not deserved it. He rose into the saddle, cleared a stirrup for her, suddenly alarmed to see Morgaine leaving the clearing, a pale flash of Siptah's body in the murk.

Jhirun tried for the stirrup and could not reach it; he reached down in an agony of impatience, seized her arm and pulled, dragged her up so that she could throw her leg over and settle behind him.

"Hold to me," he ordered her, jerked her shy hands about his waist and laid spurs to the gelding, that started forward with a suddenness that must have hurt the pony. He pursued Morgaine's path, only dimly aware of branches that raked his face in the passage. He fended them with his right hand and used the spurs a second time. One thing he saw, a pallor through the trees, fast opening a lead on him.

Soul-bound: that was *ilin*-oath, and he had strained the terms between them. Morgaine's loyalty lay elsewhere, to a thing he did not understand or want to know: wars of *qujal*, that had ruined kingdoms and toppled kings and made the name of Morgaine kri Chya a curse in the lands of men.

She sought Gates, the witchfires that were passage between world and world, and sealed them after her, one and another and another. His world had changed, he had been born and

grown to manhood between two beats of her heart, between
two Gate-spanning strides of that gray horse. The day that he
had given her his oath, a part of him had died, that sense of
the commonplace that let ordinary men live, blind and numb
to what terrible things passed about them. He belonged to
Morgaine. He could not stay behind. For a stranger's sake he
had riven what peace had grown between them, and she
would not bear it. It was that way with Morgaine, that he be
with her entirely or be numbered among her enemies.

The trees cut off all view; for a wild moment of terror he
thought that in this wilderness he had lost her. She rode
against time, time that divided her from Roh; from Gates,
that could become a fearful weapon in skilled hands. She
would not be stayed longer than flesh must rest—not for an
hour, an instant. She had forced them through flood and
against storm to bring them this far—all in the obsessive fear
that Roh might be before them at the Master Gate, that ruled
the other Gates of this sad land—when they had not even
known beyond doubt that Roh had come this way.

Now she did know.

Jhirun's arms clenched about him as they slid on the downslope. The pony crashed into them with bruising force, and
the gelding struggled up another ridge and gained the paved
road, the pony laboring to keep the pace.

And there to his relief he saw Morgaine. She had paused, a
dim, pale figure on the road beneath the arch of barren trees.
He raked the gelding with the spurs and rode to close the
gap, reckless in their speed over the uncertain trail.

Morgaine gazed into the shadows, and when he had reined
in by her, she simply turned Siptah's head and rode, sedately,
on her way down the road, giving him her shoulder. He had
expected nothing else; she owed him nothing.

He rode, his face hot with anger, conscious of Jhirun's
witness. Jhirun's arms were clenched about him, her head
against his back. At last he realized how strained was her
hold upon him, and he touched her tightly locked hands. "We
are on safe ground now," he said. "You can let go."

She was shivering. He felt it. "We are going to Shiuan,"
she said.

"Aye," he said. "It seems that we are."

Thunder rolled overhead, making the horses skittish, and
rain began to patter among the sparse leaves. The road lay in
low places for a time, where the horses waded gingerly in
shallow water. Eventually they passed out of the shadow of

the trees and the overcast sun showed them a wide expanse where the road was the highest point and only landmark. Rain-pocked pools and sickly grasses stretched to left and right. In places the water overflowed the road, a fetid sheet of stagnant green, where dead brush had stopped the cleansing current.

"Jhirun," said Morgaine out of a long silence. "What is this land named?"

"Hiuaj," said Jhirun. "All the south is Hiuaj."

"Can men still live here?"

"Some do," said Jhirun.

"Why do we not see them?"

There was long silence. "I do not know," Jhirun said in a subdued voice. "Perhaps they are afraid. Also it is near Hnoth, and they will be moving to higher ground."

"Hnoth."

"It floods here," Jhirun said, hardly audible. Vanye could not see her face. He felt the touch of her fingers on the cantle of the saddle, the shift of her grip, sensed how little she liked to be questioned by Morgaine.

"Shiuan," Vanye said. "What of that place?"

"A wide land. They grow grain there, and there are great holds."

"Well-defended, then."

"They are powerful lords, and rich."

"Then it is well," said Morgaine, "that we have you with us, is it not, Jhirun Ela's-daughter? You do know this land after all."

"No," Jhirun insisted at once. "No, lady. I can only tell you the things I have heard."

"How far does this marsh extend?"

Jhirun's fingers touched Vanye's back, as if seeking help. "It grows," she said. "The land shrinks. I remember the Shiua coming into Hiuaj. I think now it must be days across."

"The Shiua do not come now?"

"I am not sure the road is open," Jhirun said. "They do not come. But marshlanders trade with them."

Morgaine considered that, her gray eyes thoughtful and not entirely pleased. And in all their long riding she had no word save to Jhirun.

By noon they had reached a place where trees grew green at a little distance from the road. The storm had blown over, giving them only a sprinkling of rain as it went, to spend its violence elsewhere. They drew off to rest briefly, on the margin where the current had made a bank at the side of the causeway, and where the grass grew lush and green, a rare spot of beauty in the stagnant desolation about them. The watery sun struggled in vain to pierce the haze, and a small moon was almost invisible in the sky.

They let the horses graze and rest, and Morgaine parcelled out the last of their food, giving Jhirun a third share. But Jhirun took what she was given and drew away from them as far as the narrow strip of grass permitted; she sat gazing out across the marsh, preferring that dismal view, it seemed, and solitude.

And still Morgaine had spoken no word. Vanye ate, sitting cross-legged on the bank beside her, finally having decided within himself that it was not anger that kept her silent now: Morgaine was given to such periods when she was lost in her own thoughts. Something weighed upon her mind, in which he thought he was far from welcome.

"She," Morgaine said suddenly, startling him, softly though she spoke, "was surely desperate to come this road alone. For fear of drowning, says she; Vanye, does it occur to thee to wonder why out of all the years of her life, she suddenly set out, with nothing in preparation?"

"Roh can be persuasive," he said.

"The man is not Roh."

"Aye," he said, disturbed in that lapse, avoiding her eyes.

"And she speaks what we can understand, albeit the accent is thick. I would I knew when she comes, Vanye. She surely did not have her birth from the earth and the fog yesterday noon."

"I think," he said, gazing off in the direction Jhirun stared, ahead, where the forest closed in again, great trees overshadowing the road, "I think her folk are surely in that hold we passed, and Heaven grant they stay there."

"They may be looking for her."

"And we," he said, "may come into trouble on her account, or what is more likely—she will meet it on ours. *Liyo*, I ask you earnestly, send her away—now, while she is near enough home she can find her way back."

"We are not taking her against her will."

"I suppose that we are not," he agreed, not happily. "But we are on a track they cannot mistake."

"The horses do confine us to the roadway," she said, "and this land has shown us one fellow-traveller, and not a breath of others. It occurs to me, Roh being ahead of us, it would be simple for folk hereabouts to choose some place of meeting to their advantage. I do think I saw a shadow move this morning, before you came down the trail."

Cold settled about him—and self-anger; he remembered his reckless ride, how she had turned her back to him and stayed silent when he had joined her. He had taken it for rebuff. "Your sight was clearer than mine," he said. "I was blind to it."

"A trick of the light, perhaps. I was not sure."

"No," he said. "I have never known you prone to visions, *liyo*. I would you could have given me some sign."

"It did not seem good then to discuss it," she said, "nor later, with our guest at your back. Mind, she met us either by design or by chance. If by design, then she has allies—Roh himself, it may be—and if by chance, why, then, she feels herself equal to this ugly land, and she is not delicate. Mind thy back in either case; thee is too good-hearted."

He considered this, which he knew for good sense, and he was ashamed. In all the time that they had ridden this land, he had felt himself lost, had forgotten every lesson of survival he had learned of his own land, as if any place of earth and stone could be utterly different. Blind and deaf he had ridden, like a man shaken from his senses; and little good he had been to her. She had reason for her anger.

"Back there," he said, "this morning: I was startled, or I would not have cried out."

"No more of it."

"*Liyo*, I take oath it was not a thing I would have done; I was surprised; I did not reckon—I could not believe that you would do murder."

"Does that matter?" she asked. "Thee will not appoint thyself my conscience, Nhi Vanye. Thee is not qualified. And thee is not entitled."

The horses moved, quietly grazing. Water sighed under the wind. His pulse dimmed awareness of all else; even the blood seemed dammed up in him, a beating of anger in his veins. He met her pale eyes without intending to; he did not like to look at them when she had this mood on her.

"Aye," he said after a moment.

She said nothing. It was not her custom to argue; and this was the measure of her arrogance, that she disputed with no one, not even with him, who had given her more than his oath. Still one recourse he had with her: he bowed, head upon his hands, to the earth, and sat back, and gave her cold formality, the letter of the *ilin*-oath she had invoked. She hated to be answered back; and he did it so that she was left with nothing to say, and no argument.

Her frown darkened. She cast a stone into the water, and suddenly arose and gathered up Siptah's reins, hurled herself to the saddle. She waited, anger in the set of her jaw.

He stood up and took the reins of his own gelding, the black pony still tethered to the saddle-ring; and he averted his eyes from Morgaine and rose into the saddle, reined over to Jhirun, who waited on the bank.

"Come," he said to her, "either with me or on the pony, whichever pleases you."

Jhirun looked up at him, her poor bruised face haggard with exhaustion, and without a word she held up her hand to be drawn up behind him. He had not thought she would choose so; he had wished that she would not, but he saw that she was nearly spent. He smothered the rage that was still hammering in him, knowing the look on his face must be enough to frighten the girl, and he was gentle in drawing her up to sit behind him. But when she put her arms about him, preparing for their climb to the roadway, he suddenly remembered Morgaine's advice and the Honor-blade that was at his belt. He removed it to the saddle-sheath at his knee, where her hands could not reach it.

Then he turned the horse upslope, where Morgaine awaited him on the road. He expected her to ride ahead, scorning him, but she did not. She set Siptah to walking beside the gelding, knee to knee with him, though she did not look at him.

It was tacit conciliation, he suspected. He gathered this knowledge to himself for comfort, but it was far down the road before there was a word from her, when the cold shadow of the trees began to enfold them again.

"My moods," Morgaine said suddenly. "Forget them."

He looked at her, found nothing easy to say. He nodded, a carefully noncommittal gesture, for the words were painfully forced from her, and he did not think she wanted to discuss the matter. In truth, she owed him nothing, neither apology nor even humane treatment; that was the nature of *ilin* law; but that was not the way between them. Something troubled her, something heart-deep, and he wished that he could put a name to it.

The strangeness of the land was wearing at them both, he

decided; they were tired, and nerves were tautly strung. He felt in his own body the ache, the weight of mail that settled with malevolent cunning into the hollows of a man's body, that galled flesh raw where there was the least fold in garments beneath. Therein lay reason enough of tempers; and she feared—feared Roh, feared ambush, feared things, he suspected uneasily, the like of which he did not imagine.

"Aye," he murmured at last, settling more easily into the saddle. "We are both tired, *liyo*. That is all."

She seemed content with that.

And for many long hours they passed through land that was low and all the same, alternate tracts of cheerless, unhealthy forest and barren marsh, where the road was passable and in most places well above the water. *Qujal*-made, this road, Vanye reckoned to himself—wrought by ancient magics—*qujalin* works lasted, strange, immune to the ages that ate away at the works of men, some seeming ageless, while others crumbled away suddenly as if they had become infected with mortality. There was a time not so long ago when he would have sought any other road than this, that led them so well in the direction Morgaine sought: *qujalin* roads surely led to *qujalin* places—and surely such was this called Abarais, in Shiuan, which Morgaine sought.

And better, far better, could they ride that way alone, unseen, unmarked by men. He felt Jhirun's weight against his back, balancing his own, she seeming to sleep for brief periods. It was a warm and altogether unaccustomed sensation, the nearness of another being: *ilin*, outlaw, bastard motherless from birth, he could recall few moments that any had laid hands on him save in anger. He found it disturbing now, this so harmless burden against him, that weighed against him, and against his mind.

He watched Morgaine, who glanced constantly to this side and that as they rode, searching every shadow; and it came to him what kept his mind so ill at ease: that Morgaine, arrogant as she was, seemed afraid—that she, who had no sane regard for her life or his, was greatly afraid, and that somewhere in that fear rested the child that rode sleeping at his back.

The forest closed in upon the road in the late afternoon and did not yield them up again, a way that grew more and more darksome, where it seemed that evening came premature. The trees here lived, growing in interlaced confusion, thrusting roots out into the channels, reaching branches overhead, powerless against the closely fitted megaliths that were the body of the road. Brush crowded over the margins, making it impossible for two horses to go abreast.

Morgaine, her horse unencumbered, led in this narrow way, a shadow among shadows, riding a pale horse, that pale hair of hers an enemy banner for any hereabouts who did not love *qujal*; and they rode blindly, unable to see beyond that tangle of brush that had found root, seeds and earth piled up against the enduring stones. *Cover your hair*, Vanye wished to tell her, but he felt still that mood in her, that unreason that he did not want to meet yet another time. It was not a time or place for quarrels.

Clouds again began to veil the sky, and that veil grew constantly darker, and plunged the forest into a halflight that destroyed all perspective, that made of the aisles of trees deep caverns hung with moss, and of the roadway a trail without beginning or end.

"I am afraid," Jhirun protested suddenly, the only word she had volunteered all day long. Her fingers clutched Vanye's shoulder-belt as if pleading for his intercession. "The sky is clouding. This is a bad place to be in a storm."

"What is your counsel?" Morgaine asked her.

"Go back. There is known road behind us. Please, lady, let us ride back to higher ground as quickly as we can."

"High ground is too far back."

"We do not know whether the road even goes on," Jhirun urged, desperation in her voice. She wrenched at Vanye's sleeve. "Please."

"And leave ourselves," said Morgaine, "on this side of a flood and Roh safely on the other."

"Roh may drown," Vanye said, set ill at ease by the suspicion that the girl was reasoning more clearly than his liege at the moment. "And if he drowns, all we need do is survive and proceed at leisure. *Liyo*, I think in this the girl is giving us good advice. Let us turn back, now."

Morgaine gave not even the grace of an answer, only laid heels to Siptah and put the gray stud to a quicker pace, that in level places became almost a run.

"Hold on," Vanye bade Jhirun, grim anger in his heart. Her arms went about him, locked tightly as the gelding took a broken stretch of the road and picked up the clear paving again, dragging the exhausted pony after them. A misstep, a

pool deeper than it looked—he feared the reckless pace that
Morgaine chose, and feared equally the prospect of being
caught in this lowest and darkest part of the land when the
storm came down. There was no promise of higher ground as
they went further and further, only of worse, and Morgaine,
blindly insistent on the decision she had made, led them into
it.

The clouds gathered yet more darkly and wind ruffled the
water of the pools. Once something large and dark slid into
the water as Siptah leaped it—vanished beneath the murky
surface. Birds started from cover with a clap of wings and
raucous cries, startling the horses, but they did not slack their
pace more than an instant.

The road parted in a muddy bank, a place riven as if stone
had pulled from stone, a channel flowing between, and Siptah
took it, hooves sliding in the mud, hindquarters bunching as
he drove for the other rise. Vanye sent the gelding in his
wake, and the pony went down on the slide. The gelding
recovered from the impact with a wrench that wrung a cry
from Jhirun—stood still on the upslope, trembling—but the
pony lacked the strength or the inclination to rise. Vanye slid
off and took the pony's halter, hauled against it with his full
weight and brought the animal to its feet, but it simply stood
there and stared at him with ears down and coat standing in
points of mud, its eyes wells of misery.

He slipped the halter from it. "No," Jhirun protested, but
he pushed its head around and slapped it on its muddy rump,
sending it wandering, dazed, back down the bank. He had
dim hope for the animal, but more than he held for their
own fortunes.

He looped the empty rope and halter to the saddle, then
took the reins and led his own horse up the opposing slope.
Morgaine was no longer in sight when he reached the crest.

He swore, rose the awkward way into the saddle, passing
his leg in front, avoiding even so much as a backward glance
at Jhirun. She held to him as he spurred the exhausted animal; he felt her sobbing against his back, whether for grief
over the pony or for terror for herself, he was not sure. Upon
his face now he felt the first drops of rain, and panic rose in
him, the bitter surety of disaster shaping about them.

A moment more brought Morgaine in view—she refused to
hold back now, he thought, because she also had begun to realize that there was no safety, and she sought desperately to

bring them through this place, to find an end of it as there had been an end of all other such forested entanglements.

The pattering fall of rain among the leaves began in earnest, scarring the smooth faces of the pools and chilling the air abruptly.

Soon enough there was no more running. The stone causeway began to be awash in the low places, and the horses picked their way through overgrowth. The rain slanted down, borne on strong wind, blinding, making the horses shy from it.

The gelding stumbled on a root, recovered with an effort that Vanye felt in his own muscles, a failing shudder. He flung his leg over the horn and slid down, beginning to lead the horse, finding its way with his own feet, lest it cripple itself. Ahead of him Siptah walked, slowly now.

"*Liyo,*" he shouted over the roar of the water, that swallowed all lesser sounds. "Let me to the fore."

She heard him and reined back, letting him lead the gelding past. He saw her face when he looked back, haggard and drawn and miserable with weariness—remembered how little she had slept. Now she surely realized that she had chosen amiss in her stubbornness, that she should have heeded Jhirun, who knew this land; but she did not offer even yet to direct them back. Jhirun offered nothing, no word, no objection; she only clung to the saddle, her hair streaming with water, her shawl a soaking rag about her shoulders. She did not even lift her head.

Vanye turned his face into the wind and the rain and led, his feet rapidly numb in the cold water, his boots soaked through. Mud held his feet and wrenched at his joints, and he fought it, moving as rapidly as he could, gasping with exhaustion.

Night was settling about them. The road was lost in twilight. Before them were only hummocks of earth that supported a tree apiece, and the channels between had become torrents. Only an occasional upthrust of rock or the absence of the largest trees in a given line betrayed the presence of the road that underlay the flood.

A vast stele heaved up beside the road, vine-covered and obscured by a tree that had forced it over at an angle and then died, a skeletal ruin. On most such stones the persistent rains had worn away the carvings, but this was harder stone. Here Morgaine paused, leaned in her saddle to seize and pull aside the dead vines, reading the ancient glyphs as if by them she hoped to find their way.

"*Arrhn*," she said. "Here stood a place called Arrhn. There is nothing else."

"Aren," said Jhirun suddenly. "Aren is the marshlanders' hold."

"Where?" Vanye asked. "Where would it lie?"

"I do not know," Jhirun insisted. "But, lady—lady, if it is near—they will shelter us. They must. They will not turn you away. They would not."

"Reasonably," said Morgaine, "if it was *qujalin*, it would have some connection with the road."

Of sound for the moment there was the singing of the wind that tossed the branches, and the mind-numbing roar of the waters that rushed and bubbled about them: elements that had their own argument, that persuaded that even strange shelter was a way to survive.

She set Siptah moving again, and Vanye struggled to keep the lead, the breath tearing in his lungs. He waded up to his knees in some places, and felt the force of the water in his shaking muscles.

"Ride," Morgaine called at him. "Change with me; I will walk a while."

"You could not," he looked back to shout at her—saw her tired face touched with anguish. "*Liyo*," he added, while he had the advantage of her, "I think that you might have used better sense if I were not with you. Only so much can I do." He shook the water from his eyes and swept off the helm that was only added weight, that made his shoulders ache. "Take it for me," he asked of her. The armor too he would have shed if he could have taken the time, but there was none to spare. She took the helm and hung it to her saddlebow by its inside thong.

"You are right," she said, giving him that consolation.

He drew a deep breath and kept moving, laced his fingers in the gelding's cheekstrap and felt his way through the swirling dark waters in a darkness that was almost complete. He walked over his knees now, in a current that almost swept him off his feet. He had feared for the horses' fragile legs. Now he feared for his own. At one moment he went into a hole up to his waist, and thought with increasing panic that he had not much more strength for guiding them: the way ahead looked no better, dark water boiling among the trees.

Something splashed amid the roar of water as he delayed, staring at that prospect before them; he looked back and saw Morgaine waist-deep in the flood, struggling with the current and leading Siptah to reach his side. He cursed tearfully, fought his way to meet her and bid her use good sense, but she caught his arm instantly as he began to object, and drew his attention away to the left, pointing through the murk of night and storm.

The lightning showed a dark mass in that direction, a hill, a heap of stones, massive and dark and crowned with trees, a height that well overtopped any further rise of the waters.

"Aye," he said hoarsely, hope leaping up in him; but he trusted nothing absolutely in this land, and he shook at Jhirun's leg to rouse her and point out the same to her. She stared over his head where he pointed, her eyes shadowed and her face white in the lightning.

"What is that place?" he shouted at her. "What would it be?"

"Aren," she answered, her voice breaking. "It looks to be Aren."

But Morgaine had not delayed. Vanye turned his head and saw her already moving in that direction, their sounds masked from each other by the rush of water—she wading and leading Siptah in that flood. He wiped his eyes and struggled to overtake her, dreading no longer alien ruins or devils or whatever folk might live in this marsh. It was the water he feared, that ripped at his body and strained his knees. It boiled up about them, making a froth on the side facing the current, waist-deep, chest-deep. He saw the course that Morgaine was seeking, indirectly, to go from high point to high point where the trees were; he drew even with her, shook the blinding drops from his eyes and tried to take the reins from Morgaine's hand.

"Go on," he shouted at her, overwhelmed with fear for her. Her lighter weight was more vulnerable to the current that tore at them, her strength perilously burdened by the armor she wore. But she refused vehemently, and he realized then that he was asking something impossible of her: she was too light to dare let go; she clung to the saddle on the other side, Siptah laboring in the strong current. Vanye himself fought the current almost shoulder-deep of a sudden, and the horses began to swim, great desperate efforts of their tired bodies.

"Lord!" Jhirun screamed.

He turned his head to look back at her, turned again in the direction of her gaze to see a great mass coming down on them in the lightning-lit waters, a tree uprooted and coming down the current end toward them.

"*Liyo!*" he cried warning.

It hit, full into the gelding's side, drove against his armor and tore him from the reins, driving him against the gray. Siptah swung under the impact, spilling him under, drove at him with threshing hooves. Roots speared at him, tangled and snagged at his armor. He fought upward against them, had purchase on the jagged mass itself. It rolled with him, spilling him under again, pulling him down with it.

There was a moment of cold, of dark, an impact.

He embraced the obstacle, the tree stabbing at his back with all the force of the current, roots snapping against his armored back. He felt stone against his face. He could breathe for a moment, inhaling air and foaming water. Then the tree tore past, ripping at him, and he slipped, pinned by the force of the current against the rock, breathing the froth boiling about his head. His fingers gripped the rock again, and he hauled himself a painful degree upward and gasped a mouthful of air, saw other stones in the near-dark, the bank close at hand, promising safety.

In desperation he loosed his hold, helpless to swim at the best of times, fighting without skill and weighted by armor and exhaustion. At once he knew it had been a mistake. He could not make it so far against the current. The rush of water dragged him down and whirled him like a leaf around the bend—belly-on to the rock, breath driven from him, skull battered by a second impact as he slipped into yet another stone, numb legs tucked, realizing dully that they were bent because he was aground. He moved, heavy with water and without strength in his limbs, drove again through shallow water and a maze of reeds to sprawl at the bank, to crawl ashore among the stones. For a moment he was numb, the force of the pelting rain painful against his back even through the armor.

There was a time of dark, and at last the rain seemed less violent. He moved, rolled over and stared up, with a sudden clutch of fear as he recognized the cursed stones in the lightning—Standing Stones, *qujalin* ruins that had intercepted his body and saved his life. The monoliths leaned over him like a gathering of giants in the dark and the rain.

"*Liyo!*" he shouted into the roar of waters and the wind. "Morgaine!"

There was no answer.

Chapter Six

||||||||||||||||||||||||||||||||||||||||||||||||||||

The dawn was beginning, the murky clouds picking up indirect light. Vanye splashed across a shallow channel, came up against the bank and rested against a log that had fallen into the water. It might be the same from which he had started this circle of his search, or different. He no longer knew. In the light things began to take on different shapes.

There was only the persistent roar of the flood, the patter of gentle rain on the leaves, always the water, numbing the senses.

"Morgaine!" he cried. How many times he had called, what ground he had covered, he did not remember. He had searched the night long, through ruins and from one islet to another, between moments that he had to sink down and rest. His voice was all but gone. His armor pressed on his shoulders with agonizing weight, and now it would have been far, far easier for his knees to bend, letting him sink down into the cold and the mud and the waters that were likely to have him in the end.

But he would not give way without knowing what had become of his liege. Other trusts in his life he had failed: to kinsmen, to friends, and some of those were dead, but they had had others on whom to rely—Morgaine had no other, none at all.

He leaned forward, elbows tucked against his belly and the log, dragged his feet one and then the other from the mud, that pulled at tendons and muscles and claimed him whenever he rested at all. The rotting trunk became his bridge to higher ground. He climbed it to the bank, used brush for a handhold and struggled to the crest of the hill. Dark gathered about him, his pulse loud in his ears, pressure in his temples. He walked. All that he knew at times was touch, the rough wetness of bark, the stinging slap of leaves and branches he

could not see to avoid, the slickness of wet leaves beneath his
fingers as he fought his way up yet another rise.

He thought himself in Morija once more, Myya archers on
his trail; or something pursued him. He could not remember
where this place was, why he was so cruelly tried, whether he
pursued or was pursued; it was like a thousand other nightmares of his life.

And then he would remember, when the ghosts flitted
mockingly through his memory, so that it was impossible to
sort out image from reality. He knew that he was beyond
Gates, and that he was lost.

That Morgaine was dead occurred to him; he rejected the
possibility not with logic, but with belief. Men died, armies
perished, but Morgaine survived, survived when others could
not, when she herself wished otherwise; she might be lost,
might be hurt, might be stranded alone and afoot in this
land: these images tormented him. Anything else was impossible.

She would have guarded herself first when the mass came
down upon them, would have done that while he tried to
guard her, the girl Jhirun forgotten. Siptah had been between
Morgaine and the impact, and so had the gelding. She
would—his mind began at last to function more clearly on
this track now that he had convinced himself of a means by
which she might have lived—she would instinctively have let
him go down, sought the bank at once, for she carried
Changeling, and therefore she would have fought to live. Such
were the reflexes by which she lived. For her there was one
law: to seek the Gates at whatever cost. Panic would direct
her simply to live, all else forgotten.

And perhaps when that panic passed, she might have
delayed to seek him, as long as she thought it likely he might
have survived. But she knew also that he did not swim, and
she would not search forever. He pictured her shedding a tear
or two—he flattered himself by that—and when morning
came and there was no sign of him, then she would take her
bearings anew and heed the *geas* that drew her.

And that would set her face northward, toward the Master
Gate, and a leavetaking from this sad, drowning earth.

Suddenly he realized that she would have trusted him to
understand her obligations, to trust that she would do the rational, the necessary thing—and make for the one landmark
in all this quaking marsh as soon as possible: the one place
where all travelers met.

The *qujalin* road. She would be there, confident that her *ilin* would be there, would follow if he could, knowing what she would do.

He cursed himself: his driving fear was suddenly that she would have found the road before him, that in the night and the storm she would have gone on—that she might have saved one of the horses, while he was afoot, incapable of overtaking a rider.

He reckoned by the flow of the current which way the road must lie, and walked, tearing his way through the brush on as straight a course as his strength could make him.

He came upon the first stones at midmorning, and everything lay smooth as an unwritten page, no marks at all on the new sheet of mud laid by the flood, only the crooked trail of a serpent and the track of a lizard.

He cast about with all his skill to find any smallest remnant of a track left during the ebb of the flood, and found nothing. Exhausted, he leaned against a low branch and wiped thickly mudded hands on his sodden breeches, trying to think clearly. There was such desperation welling up in him now, his best hope disappointed, that he could have cried his anger and grief aloud to the listening woods. But now that he thought it unlikely that she was nearby to hear, he could not even find the courage to call her name aloud, knowing that there would be silence.

She was moving ahead of him, joining the road further on; or she was yet to come. The other possibility occurred this time with frightening force. He thrust it quickly from his mind.

His one hope, that answered either eventuality, was to be at the place she sought, to reach Abarais as quickly as human strength could carry him and pray—if prayers were heard in this Hell, and for Morgaine—that she would either stay for him or overtake him. He would wait, if he reached Abarais, holding the Gate for her, against men, against Roh, against whatever threat, until she came or until he died.

He gathered himself, fought dizziness as he did at each sudden move, coughed and felt a binding pain in his chest. His throat was raw. Fever burned in him. He had been ill on the run before, and then, with his kinsmen on his trail, it had been possible to sweat the fever out, to keep moving, relying on the horse's strength to carry him.

This time it was his own shaking limbs that must bear him,

and the waters and the inhabitants of them waited for his fall
below that dark surface.

He walked a staggering course down the road, seeking
some sign on the earth—and then he realized that he should
leave one of his own, lest she take his track for Roh's, and
hang back. He tore a branch from a tree, snapped it and
drove its two ends into the mud, a slanting sign that any who
had ranged Andur-Kursh could read like the written word:
Follow! And by it he wrote in the mud the name-glyph of
clan Nhi.

It would last until the waters rose again, which in this
cursed land gave the life of the message to be short indeed;
and with this in mind, he carried a stone from the paving of
the buried road and cut a mark now and again upon a tree
by the road.

Every caution he had learned in two years of outlawry,
fleeing clan Myya, cried out that he guided none but enemies
at his back. Men lived in this land, and they were furtive and
fearful and would not show themselves; and therefore there
were things in this land that men should rightly fear.

Nevertheless he held the center of the road, fearing more
being missed than being found.

And came the time that he ran out of strength, and what
had been a tightness in his chest swelled and took his breath
away. He sank down in his tracks and drew breath carefully,
feeling after ribs that might well be cracked; and at times the
haze came over his mind again. He found a time when he
had not been aware what passed about him, and some moments later he was afoot and walking with no memory of
how he had risen or how far he had come.

There were many such gaps after that, periods when he did
not know where he was going, but his body continued, obedient to necessity and guided by the road.

At last he was faced with a gap in the road where a channel had cut through; he stared at it, and simply sank down on
the slope at water's edge, reckoning how likely he was to
drown attempting it. And strength left him, the exhaustion of
a night without sleep stretching him full-length on the muddy
slope. He was cold. He ceased to care.

A shadow fell over him, a whisper of cloth. He waked violently and struck out, seeing bare feet and a flash of brown
skirt; and in the next moment a staff crashed into his arm—
his head, if his arm had not been quick. He hurled himself at

his attacker, mailed weight and inconsiderable flesh meeting: she went down, still trying for his face, and he backhanded the raking attack hard enough that it struck the side of her face. Jhirun. He realized it as her face came clear out of the shock of the attack.

The blow had dazed her, much as he had restrained it at the last instant; and seeing her, who might know of Morgaine, he was overcome with fear that he had killed her. He gathered her up and shook at her in his desperation.

"Where is she?" he asked, his voice an unrecognizable whisper; and Jhirun sobbed for breath and fought and protested again and again that she did not know.

After a moment he came to his senses and realized the girl was beyond lying; fear was knotted in him so that he found it hard to relax his hands; he was shaking. And when he had let her go she collapsed on the muddy bank sobbing for breath.

"I do not know, I do not know," she kept saying through her tears. "I did not see her or the horses—nothing. I only swam and swam until I came out of the current, that is all."

He clutched this to him, the only hope that he could obtain, that he knew Morgaine could swim, armored though she was; and Jhirun had survived; and he had survived, who could not swim at all. He chose to hope, and stumbled to his feet, gathering up Jhirun's abandoned staff. Then he began to seek the other side of the channel, using the staff to probe the shallowest way. It became waist-deep before it grew shallow again, and he climbed out on the other side, with the staff to help him on the slope.

A splash sounded behind him. He turned, saw Jhirun wading the channel with her skirts a sodden flower about her. Almost the depth became too much for her, but she struggled across the current, panting and exhausted as she reached the bank and began to climb.

"Go back," he said harshly. "I am going on from here. Go home, wherever that is, and count yourself fortunate."

She struggled further up the bank. Her face, already bruised, had a fresh redness across the brow: his arm had done that. Her hair hung in spiritless tangles. She reached the crest and shook the hair back over her shoulders.

"I am going to Shiuan," she said, her chin trembling. "Go where you like. This is my road."

He looked into her tear-glazed eyes, hating her intrusion, half desiring it, for he was lost and desperate, and the silence and the rush of water were like to drive a man mad. "If

Abarais lies in Shiuan," he said, "I am going that way. But I will not wait for you."

"Nor for her?"

"She will come," he said; and was possessed by the need for haste, and turned and began to walk. The staff made walking easier on the broken pavings, and he did not give it up, caring little whether Jhirun needed it or no. She walked barefoot, limping; but the pain of his own feet, rubbed raw by watersoaked boots that were never meant for walking, was likely worse, and somewhere in the night he had wrenched his ankle. He gave her no hand to help her; he was in pain and desperate, and during the long walk he kept thinking that she had no reason whatever to wish him well. If he left her, she could find him in his sleep eventually and succeed at what she had already tried; if he slept in her presence, she could do the same without the trouble of slipping up on him; and as for binding the child to some tree and leaving her in this flood-prone land, the thought shamed him, who had been *dai-uyo*, whose honor forbade dealing so even with a man. At times he looked down on her, wishing her unborn; and when she looked up at him he was unnerved by the distracted look in her eyes. *Mad*, he thought,—*her own folk have cast her out because she is mad. What other manner of girl would be out on this road alone, following after a strange man?*

And came one of those times that he lost awareness, and wakened still walking, with no memory of what had happened. Panic rose in him, exhaustion weakening his legs so that he knew he could as well have fallen senseless in the road. Jhirun herself was weaving in her steps.

"We shall rest," he said in the ragged voice the cold had left him. He flung his arm about her, feeling at once her resistence to him, but he paid it no heed—drew her to the roadside where the roots of a tree provided a place less chill than earth or stone. She tried to thrust free, mistaking his intention; but he shook her, and sank down, holding her tightly against him. She shivered.

"I shall not harm you," he said. "Be still. Rest." And with his arm about her so that he could sense any movement, he leaned his head against a gnarled root and shut his eyes, trying to take a little sleep, still fearing he would sleep too deeply.

She remained quiet against him, the warmth of their bodies giving a welcome relief from the chill of wet garments; and in time she relaxed across him, her head on his shoulder. He slept, and wakened with a start that frightened an outcry from her.

"Quiet," he bade her. "Be still." He had tightened his arm by reflex, relaxed it again, feeling a lassitude that for the moment was healing, in which all things, even terrible ones, seemed distant. She shut her eyes; he did the same, and wakened a second time to find her staring at him, her head on his chest, a regard disturbing in its fixedness. Her body, touching his, was tense, her arm that lay across him stiff, fist clenched. He moved his hand upon her back, more of discomfort than of intent, and felt her shiver.

"Is there none," he asked her, "who knows where you are or cares what becomes of you?"

She did not answer. He realized how the question had sounded.

"We should have sent you back," he said.

"I would not have gone."

He believed her. The determination in that small, hoarse voice was absolute. "Why?" he asked. "You say Hiuaj is drowning; but that is supposition. On this road, you may drown for certain."

"My sister has already drowned," she said. "I am not going to." A tremor passed through her, her eyes focused somewhere beyond him. "Hnoth is coming, and the moons, and the tides, and I do not want to see it again. I do not want to be in Hiuaj when it comes."

Her words disturbed him: he did not understand the sense of them, but they troubled him—this terror of the moons that he likewise shuddered to see aloft. "Is Shiuan better?" he asked. "You do not know. Perhaps it is worse."

"No." Her eyes met his. "Shiuan is where the gold goes, where all the grain is grown; no one starves there, or has to work, like Barrowers do."

He doubted this, having seen Hiuaj, but he did not think it kind to reason with her delusion, when it was likely that neither of them would live to know the truth of it. "Why do not all the Hiua leave, then?" he asked. "Why do not all your folk do what you have done, and go?"

She frowned, her eyes clouded. "I do not think they believe it will come, not to them; or perhaps they do not think it matters, when it is the end. The whole world will die, and the waters will have everything. But she—" The glitter returned to her eyes, a question trembling on her lips; he stayed silent, waiting, fearing a question he could not answer. "She has power over the Wells."

"Yes," he admitted, for surely she had surmised that already.

"And you?"

He shrugged uncomfortably.

"This land," she said, "is strange to you."

"Yes," he said.

"The Barrow-kings came so. They sang that there were great mountains beyond the Wells."

"In my land," he said, remembering with pain, "there were such mountains."

"Take me to that place." Her fist unclenched upon his heart; her eyes filled with such earnestness that it hurt to see it, and she trembled against him. He moved his hand upon her shoulders, wishing that what she asked were possible.

"I am lost myself," he said, "without Morgaine."

"You believe that she will come," she said, "to Abarais, to the Well there."

He gave no reply, only a shrug, wishing that Jhirun knew less of them.

"What has she come to do?" Jhirun asked it all in a breath, and he felt the tension in her body. "Why has she come?"

She held some hope or fear he did not comprehend: he saw it in her eyes, that rested on his in such a gaze he could not break from it. She assumed that safety lay beyond the witchfires of the Gates; and perhaps for her, for all this land, it might seem to.

"Ask Morgaine," he said, "when we meet. As for me, I guard her back, and go where she goes; and I do not ask or answer questions of her."

"We call her Morgen," said Jhirun, "and Angharan. My ancestors knew her—the Barrow-kings—they waited for her."

Cold passed through him. *Witch,* men called Morgaine in his own homeland. She was young, while three generations of men lived and passed to dust; and all that he knew of whence she came was that she had not been born of his kindred, in his land.

When was this? he wanted to ask, and dared not. *Was she alone then?* She had not come alone to Andur-Kursh, but her comrades had perished there. *Qujal,* men called her; she avowed she was not. Legends accounted her immortal; he chose not to believe them all, nor to believe all the evil that was laid to her account, and he asked her no questions.

He had followed her, as others had, now dust. She spoke
of time as an element like water or air, as if she could come
and go within its flow, confounding nature.

Panic coiled about his heart. He was not wont to let his
mind travel in such directions. Morgaine had not known this
land; he held that thought to him for comfort. She had
needed to ask Jhirun the name and nature of the land,
needing a guide.

A guide, the thought ran at the depth of his mind, to this
age, perhaps, as once in Andur she had been confounded by
a forest that had grown since last she had ridden that path.

"Come," he said brusquely to Jhirun, beginning to sit up.
"Come." He used the staff to pull himself to his feet and
drew her up by the hand, trying to shake off the thoughts that
urged upon him.

Jhirun did not let go his hand as they set out again upon
the road; in time he grew weary of that and slipped his arm
about her, aiding her steps, seeking by that human contact to
keep his thoughts at bay.

Jhirun seemed content in that, saying nothing, holding her
own mind private; but there was a difference now in the look
she cast up at him—hope, he realized with a pang of guilt,
hope that he had lent her. She looked up at him often, and
sometimes—unconscious habit, he thought—touched the
necklace that she wore, that bore a cross, and objects that he
did not know; or touched the center of her bodice, where
rested that golden image that he had returned to her—a
peasant girl, who possessed such a thing, a bit of gold
strangely at variance with her rough dress and work-worn
hands.

My ancestors, she had said, *the Barrow-kings*.

"Have you clan?" he asked her suddenly, startling her: her
eyes gazed at him, wide.

"We are Mija," she said. "Ila died out. There is only Mija
left."

Myya. Myya and Yla. His heart seemed to stop and to begin again, painfully. His hand fell from her shoulder, as he
recalled Morija, and that clan that had been his own undoing,
blood-enemy to him; and lost Yla, that had ruled Morija
once, before the Nhi.

"Myya Geraine Ela's-daughter," he murmured, giving her
foreign name the accents of Erd, that lay among mountains
her folk had almost forgotten.

She looked at him, speechless, with her tangled hair and

bruised face, barefoot, in a dress of coarsest wool. She did
not understand him. Whatever anger there was between him
and Myya, it had no part with Jhirun Ela's-daughter; the
blood-feud the Myya had with him carried no force here,
against a woman, in the drowning wastes of Hiuaj.

"Come," he said again, and gathered her the more closely
against his side, beginning to walk again. The clans were
known for their natures: as Chya was impulsive and Nhi was
stubborn, clan Myya was secretive and cold—of cruelty that
had bided close to him all his life, for his half-brothers were
Myya, and she who had mothered them, and not him.

Myya hated well, and waited long for revenge; but he refused to think such things of Jhirun; she was a companion,
on a road that was otherwise alien, and seemed endless, in a
silence that otherwise was filled with the wind and the bub-
bling waters.

There were things worse than an enemy. They lay about
him.

In the evening, with the light fading into streamers of gold
and red, they walked a place where the marsh had widened
and trees were few. Reeds grew beside the road, and great
flocks of white birds flew up in alarmed clouds when they
drew near. Serpents traced a crooked course through the stagnant pools and stirred the reeds.

And Vanye looked at the birds that taunted them and
swore in desire, for hunger was a gnawing pain in his belly.

"Give me a strip of leather," Jhirun asked of him while
they walked; and in curiosity he did so, unlacing one of the
thongs the ring at his belt held for use on harness. He
watched while her strong fingers knotted it this way and that,
and understood as she bent to pick up a stone. He gave her a
second strip to improve her handiwork, and the sling took
shape.

A long time they walked afterward, until the birds began
to wing toward them; and of a sudden she whirled the sling
and cast, a skilled shot. A bird fell from the sky; but it fell
just beyond the reeds, and almost as it hit the water something rose out of the dark waters and snapped it up. Jhirun
simply stood on the bank and looked so wretched that his
heart went out to her.

"Next time," she said.

But there were no more birds. Eventually, with night upon

them, Jhirun pulled up a handful of reeds, and peeled them
to the roots, and ate on this, offering one to him.

It eased the ache in his belly, but it had a bitter taste, and
he did not think a man could live long on such fare. Ahead
stretched a flat and exposed land, the road the only feature in
it; and in the sky the moons began to shine, five in number.

The Broken Moon, Jhirun named them for him as they
walked; and stately Anli, and demon Sith, that danced with
Anli. Only the greatest moon, Li, had not yet risen, but
would appear late in the night, a moon so slow and vast the
fragments of the Broken Moon seemed to race to elude it.

"In the old days," Jhirun said, "there was only one.

> *"Whole Moon and whole land;*
> *and then the Wells gave weal;*
> *came the Three and rived the Moon,*
> *and then the Wells were sealed.*

That is what the children sing."

"Three what?"

"The three moons," she said. "The Demon and the Ladies.
The Moon was broken and then the world began to sink; and
some say when there is only the sea left, then Li will fall into
it and the world will shatter like the Moon. But no man will
be alive to see that."

Vanye looked at the sky, where what she named as Anli
rode, with the tiny orb of Sith beside it. By night there was a
cloud in which the moons moved: moondust, Morgaine had
called it. He thought that apt, a sorcery of the perishing
world, that it perish at least in beauty, a bow of light to form
the path of the moons. He remembered Li, that hung as a
vast light above the clouds two nights past, and shuddered to
think of it falling, for it looked as if it truly might.

"Soon," said Jhirun, "will be Hnoth, when Li overtakes the
others, and then the waters rise. It is close—and then this
road will be all underwater."

He considered this, brooding upon it. Of Morgaine there
had been no sign, no track, no trace; Jhirun's warning added
new anxiety. But Morgaine would not delay on low ground;
she might at the moment be no farther behind them than the
trees that lay on the horizon.

He marked how wearily Jhirun walked, still striving to
match his stride, never once complaining, though she
breathed hard in her effort. He felt his own legs unsteady

with exhaustion, the armor he wore a torment that set his
back afire.

And Morgaine might be only a little distance behind them.

He stopped, where a grassy bank faced the shallowest tract
of marsh; he took Jhirun by the arm and brought her there,
and cast himself down, glad only to have the weight of mail
distributed off his back and shoulders. Jhirun settled with
him, her head on his chest, and spread her bedraggled shawl
wide to cover as much of them both as might be.

"We will walk again before sunrise," he said.

"Yes," she agreed.

He closed his eyes, and the cessation of pain was such that
sleep came quickly, a weight that bore his mind away.

Jhirun screamed.

He jerked awake, hurling her back from him; and looked
about, realizing that they were alone. Jhirun wept, and the
forlorn sound of it oppressed him. He touched her, finding
her shaking, and gathered her to him, his own heart still laboring.

She had dreamed, he thought; the girl had seen enough in
their journey that she had substance enough for nightmares.
"Go back to sleep," he urged her, holding her as he might
have held a frightened child. He settled back again, his arms
tightly about her, and his mind oppressed by a dread of his
own, that he was not going to find Morgaine. She had not
come; she had not overtaken them; he began to think of
delaying a day in this place, giving her surely enough time to
overtake him.

And thereby he might kill himself and Jhirun, being out
upon this flat stretch of road when next a storm came down
and the water rose. For Jhirun's sake, he thought that he
should keep moving until they found safety, if safety existed
anywhere in this land.

Then, without Jhirun, he could settle himself to wait,
watching the road, to wait and to hope.

Morgaine was not immortal; she, like Roh, could drown.
And if she were gone—the thought began to take root in
him—then there was no use in his having survived at all—to
become again what he had been before she claimed him.

Hunted now, it might well be, by other Myya, for Jhirun's
sake.

Morgaine had seen a forest grow; against his side breathed
something as terrible.

Jhirun still wept, her body racked by long shudders, whatever had terrified her still powerful in her mind. He tried to rest, and so to comfort her by his example, but she would not relax. Her whole body was stiff.

Sleep weighed him into darkness again, and discomfort brought him back, aware first that the land was bright with moonlight and then that Jhirun was still awake, her eyes fixed, staring off across the marsh. He turned his head, and saw the risen disc of Li, vast, like a plague-ridden countenance; he did not like to look upon it.

It lit all the land, bright enough to cast a shadow.

"Can you not sleep?" he asked Jhirun.

"No," she said, not looking at him. Her body was still tense, after so long a time. He felt the fear in her.

"Let us use the light," he said, "and walk some more."

She made no objection.

By noon, wisps of cloud began to roll in, that darkened and grew and spread across the sky. By afternoon there was cloud from horizon to horizon, and the tops of the occasional trees tossed in a wind that boded storm.

There were no more rests, no stopping. Jhirun's steps dragged, and she struggled, gasping in her efforts, to hold the pace. Vanye gave her what help he could, knowing that, if she ever could not go on, he could not carry her, not on a road that stretched endlessly before them.

In his mind constantly was Morgaine; hope began to desert him utterly as the clouds darkened. And beside him, on short, painful breaths, Jhirun began nervously to talk to him, chattering hoarsely of her own hopes, of that refuge to which others of her land had fled, those that dared the road. Here lay wealth, she insisted, here lay plenty and safety from the floods. She spoke as if to gather her own courage, but her voice distracted him, gave him something to occupy him but his own despair.

And of a sudden her step lagged, and she fell silent, dragging on his arm. He stopped, cast her a glance to know what had so alarmed her, saw her staring with vague and frightened eyes at nothing in particular.

There was a sound, that suddenly shuddered through the earth. He felt it, caught at Jhirun and sprawled, the both of them nothing amid such violence. He pulled at her arms, drawing her from the water's edge, and then it was past and quiet. They lay facing each other, Jhirun's face pale and set in terror. Her nails were clenched into his wrists, his fingers clenched on hers, enough to bruise. He found his limbs trembling, and felt a shudder in her arms also. Tears filled her eyes. She shook her tangled hair and caught her breath. He felt the terror under which Jhirun lived her whole life, who claimed her world was dying, whose very land was as unstable as the storm-wracked heavens.

He gathered her up, rising, held her to him, no longer ashamed by his own fright. He understood. He brushed mud from her scraped elbows, from her tear-stained cheek, realizing how desperately she was trying to be brave.

"Only little shakings, usually," she said, "except when the sea wall broke and half of Hiuaj flooded; this one was like that." She gave a desperate and bitter laugh, an attempt at humor. "We are only a hand's breadth closer to the sea now, that is what we say."

He could not laugh, but he pressed her close against his side in appreciation of her spirit, and shivered as the wind bore down on them, bringing heavy drops of rain.

They started walking, together. In places even the road was buckled, the vast paving-blocks pulled awry. Vanye found himself still shaken, in his mind unconvinced that the earth would stay still; and the crack of thunder that rolled from pole to pole as if the sky were tearing made them both start.

The rain began in earnest, the sky darkened to a sickly greenish cast, and the sound of it drowned all other sounds, the sheeting downpour separating them from all the world save the area of the causeway they walked. In places the surface of the road was ankle-deep in rapid water, and Vanye probed the stones with the staff lest they fall into a wash and drown.

It became evening, the rain coming with less violence, but steadily; and hills enfolded them as if by magic, as if they had materialized out of the gray-green murk and the curtains of rain. Of a sudden they were there, in the west, brought into dream-like relief by the sinking light; and quickly more took shape ahead of them, gray and vague as illusion.

"Shiuan," breathed Jhirun; and her hand tightened on his arm. "We have come through; we have reached Shiuan."

Vanye answered nothing, for at once he thought of Morgaine, and that destroyed any joy he had in his own survival. He thought of Morgaine, and reckoned with a last stubborn hope that the flooding had not been impassable or without warning: some little chance yet remained. But Jhirun's hap-

piness was good to see; he answered the pressure of her hand
with a touch of his own.

The hills began to enfold them closely as they walked,
while the day waned. The road clung to the side of one and
then the other, and never again sank below the water. Beside
it, water poured, and spilled down ridges and between hills in
its haste to reach the marsh.

Vanye stopped, for something strange topped the highest
hill in their sight: a hulk that itself took shape out of the
rain—gray towers, a little lighter than the clouds that boiled
above them in the storm-drowned twilight.

"It is Ohtij-in," Jhirun shouted up at him through the roar
of the rain. "It is Ohtij-in, the first of the holds of Shiuan."

Joy filled her voice at the sight of that grim place; she
started forward, but he stood fast, and she stopped, holding
her shawl about her, beginning to shiver in the chill that
came rapidly when they stopped moving.

"They are well-fortified," he said, "and perhaps—perhaps
we should pass them by in the night."

"No," she argued. "No." There were tears in her voice. He
would gladly have dismissed her, bidden her do as it pleased
her; and almost he did so, reckoning that for her it might be
safety enough.

Then he remembered how much she knew of Morgaine,
and where Morgaine might be sought; of him, too, and where
he was bound.

"I would not trust it," he said to her.

"Marshlands and Ohtij-in trade," she pleaded with him,
shaking as she hugged her shawl about her, drenched as it
was. "We are safe here, we are safe; o lord, they must give us
food and shelter or we will die of this cold. This is a safe
place. They will give us food."

Her light clothing clung to her skin. She was suffering cruelly, while he had the several layers of his armor, burden
though it was; their bellies were empty, racked sometimes
with cramps; his own legs were weak with exhaustion, and
she could scarcely walk. It was reason that she offered him,
she who knew this land and its people; and in his exhaustion
he began to mistrust his own instincts, the beast-panic that
urged him to avoid this place, all places that might hem him
in. He knew outlawry, the desperate flights and sometime
luck that had let him live—supplied with weapons, with a
horse, with knowledge of the land equal to that of his enemies. There had been game to hunt, and customs that he

knew. Here he knew not what lay down the road, was lost apart from that track, vulnerable on it; and any enemies in this land could find him easily.

He yielded to the tug of her hand. They walked nearer, and he could see that the whole of the place called Ohtij-in was one hold, a barrel within a great wall that followed the shape of the hill on which it sat. Many towers rose about the central keep, part of the wall, each crazily buttressed, as if each support had been an affair of ingenuity and desperation never amended by later effort. Brush grew up about the walls; black trees that supported leaves only at the extremities of their branches, already inclined southward, inclined still further in the force of the storm wind, reaching fingers toward the lichen-blotched walls. The whole place seemed time-worn, a place without sharp edges, where decay was far advanced, dreaming away to death.

He rubbed at his eyes in the rain and tried to focus on it.

"Come," Jhirun was urging him, her teeth chattering with cold.

Perhaps, he thought confusedly, Morgaine would pass this way; she must; there was no other.

Jhirun drew at his arm and he went; he saw, as they left the road on the short spur that led toward the hill, that there was a solid wooden gate in the arch facing them, younger by far than the stones that framed it, the first thing in all this waste that looked new and strong.

Best, he thought, to assume confidence in his bearing, to approach as innocent folk that feared nothing and brought no threat with them.

"Hai!" he shouted up at the frowning walls, trying to out-shout the wind, and he found his voice a weary and strangled sound that lacked all the confidence he attempted. "Hai! Open your gates!"

A light soon winked in the tower nearest the gate; a shuttered window opened to see them in that almost-darkness, and a bell began to ring, high-pitched and urgent. From that open shutter it was certain that they suffered the scrutiny of more than one observer, a series of black shapes that appeared there and vanished.

Then the shutter was closed again, and there was silence from the bell, no sound but the rush of water that sluiced off the walls and gathered on the stone paving before the gate. Jhirun shivered miserably.

Came the creak of a door yielding; the sally-port beside the

main gate opened, veiled in the rain, and one man put his
head forth to look at them. Black-robed he was, with a cloak
about him so that only his face and hands were visible.
Timidly he crept forward, opening the gate wider, holding his
rain-spattered cloak about him and standing where a backward step would put him within reach of the gateway.

"Come," he said. "Come closer."

Chapter Seven

||||||||||||||||||||||||||||||||||||||||||||||||||||||||

"A priest," said Jhirun. "A Shiua priest."

Vanye let go a careful breath, relieved. The black robes were of no order that he knew, not in his homeland, where vesper and matin bells were a familiar and beloved sound; but a priest, indeed, and in all this gray and dying land there was no sight so welcome, the assurance that even here were human and godly men. He was still cautious in coming forward as they were summoned, for there were likely archers in the shadows atop the wall, bows drawn and arrows well-aimed. So would many a border hold in Kursh and Andur receive night-coming travellers, using the sally port for fear of a concealed force, keeping the archers ready if things went amiss.

But throughout all Andur-Kursh, even in the hardest years, there was hospitality, there was hearth-law, and halls were obliged to afford charity to wayfarers, a night's shelter, be it in hall, be it in a lowly guest-house without the walls. Vanye kept his hands in sight, and stopped and stood to be seen clearly by the priest, who gazed at them both in wonder, face white and astonished within the cowl, a white spot in the descending night.

"Father," said Vanye, his voice almost failing him in his hoarseness and his anxiety, "Father, there is a woman, on a gray horse or a black or, it might be, afoot. You have not seen her?"

"None such," said the priest. "None. But if any other traveler passes Ohtij-in, we will know it. Come in, come in and be welcome."

Jhirun stepped forward; Vanye felt an instant's mistrust and then ascribed it to exhaustion and the strangeness of the place. It was too late. If he would run, they could hunt him down easily; and if they would not, then here was shelter and

102

food and he was mad to reject it. He hesitated, Jhirun tugging at his hand, and then he came, by the sally port, into a
space between two walls, where torches flared and rain
steamed on their copper shieldings.

A second priest closed the sally port and barred it; and
Vanye scanned with renewed misgivings the strength of the
gates, both inner and outer: a double wall defended this approach to Ohtij-in. The second priest pulled a cord, ringing
the bell, and ponderously the inner gates swung open, upon
torchlight, rain, and armed men.

There was no flourish of weapons, no rush at them, only
an over-sufficient escort—pikemen standing beneath the wind-
blown glare of torches, light gleaming wetly on bronze half-
face helms that bore on the brow the likeness of grotesque
faces—on armor that was long-skirted scale and plate, with
intricate embellishment—on pikes with elaborate and cruel
barbs.

It was a force far stronger than any hold at peace would
keep under arms on a rainy night. The sense of something utterly amiss wound coldly through Vanye's belly: the terror of
the strange armor, the excessive preparation for defense in an
unpeopled land. Even Jhirun seemed to have lost all her trust
in the place, and kept close to his side.

A priest tugged at the staff he yet held; he tightened his
grip on it, trying to make sense of such a welcome, to know
whether there might be more profit in resisting or in ap-
pealing to their lord. He let the staff go, thinking as he did so
that it was small defense in any case.

Weapons were turned, and their escort opened ranks to receive them into their midst. The priests stayed by them, the
pikemen on all sides; and beyond them, even in the rain,
stood a horde of silent men and women, folk wrapped in
ragged cloaks. A moment of peace lasted, then an outcry began among them, a wild shriek from one that rushed forward; others moved, and cries filled the courtyard. Hands
reached through the protective screen of pikes to touch them.
Jhirun cried out and Vanye held her tightly, glad now to go
where the grotesquely armored guards bade them; he stared
at mad eyes and open mouths that shouted words that he
could not understand, and felt their hands on his back, his
shoulders. A pikeshaft slammed out into hysterical faces,
bringing blood: their own people they treated so. Vanye
gazed at that act in horror, and cursed himself for ever having come toward this place.

It was to the keep that they were being taken, that vast
central barrel that supported all the rest of the structure.
Above the wild faces and reaching hands Vanye saw those li-
chen-covered walls; and against them was a miserable tangle
of buildings huddled under the crazy buttresses. The cobbled
yard was buckled and cracked, splits filled with water, and
rain-scarred puddles filled the aisle between the rough shelters
that leaned against wall and towers. Next to the keep also were
pent livestock, cattle and goats; and soil from those pens and
the stables joined the corruption that flowed through the
courtyard and through the shelters. Against the corner of the
steps as they drew near the keep was a sodden mass of fur,
dead rat or some other vermin lying drowned, an ugliness
flushed out by the rains.

Men lived in such wretchedness. No lord of repute in Andur-Kursh would have kept his people so—would have even
permitted such squalor, not even under conditions of war.
Madness reigned in this place, and misery; and the guards
used their weapons more than once as they cleared the steps.

A gate, barred and chained and guarded within, confronted
them; a gatekeeper unlocked and ran back the chain to admit
them all. Surely, Vanye thought, a lord must needs live behind chains and bars, who dwelled amid such misery of his
people; and it promised no mercy for strangers, when a man
had none for his own folk. Vanye wished now never to have
seen this place; but the bars gaped for them, swallowed them
up and clanged shut again. Jhirun looked back; so did he,
seeing the keeper replacing the chain and lock at once, while
the mob pressed at the gate, hands beginning to reach
through the bars, voices shouting at them.

The inner doors opened to admit them, thundered shut after. They faced a spiral ramp, and with the priest and four of
the escort bearing torches from the doorway, they began their
ascent. The ramp led slowly about a central core with doors
on this side and that, and echoes rang hollowly from the
heights above. The whole of the place had a dank and musty
smell, a quality of wet stone and age and standing water. The
corridor floor was uneven, split in not a few places, with
cracks in the walls repaired with insets of mortared rubble.
The guards kept close about them the while, two torchbearers
behind and three before, shadows running the walls in chaos.
Behind them was the fading sound of voices from the gate;
and softly, softly as they climbed, began to come the strains
of music, strange and wild.

The music grew clearer, uncanny accompaniment to the iron tread of armed men about them; and the air grew warmer, closer, tainted with sweet incense. Jhirun was breathing as if she had been running, and Vanye also felt the dizziness of exhaustion and hunger and sudden heat; he lost awareness of what passed about him, and cleared his senses only slowly as the guards shifted about and encountered others, as soft voices spoke, and doors opened in sequence before them.

The music died, wailing: golden, glittering figures of men and women paused in mid-movement, tall and slim and silver-haired.

Qujal.

Jhirun's touch held him, else he would have hurled himself at guards and doors and died; her presence, frightened, at his side, kept him still as the foremost of the tall, pale men walked toward him, surveyed him casually with calm, gray eyes.

An order was given, a language he did not know; the guards laid hand on his arms and turned him to the left, where was another door; and certain of the other pale lords left their places and came, quietly, as they were withdrawn from that bright hall and into an adjoining room.

It was a smaller hall, with a fire blazing in the fireplace, a white dog lying at the hearth. The dog sprang up and began to bark frantically, sending mad echoes rolling through the halls, drowning the music that had begun again next door, until one of the guards whipped her yelping into silence. Vanye stared at the act, jarred by that mistreatment of a beast, and looked about him, at wealth, luxury, carved woods, carpets, bronze lamps—and the *qujal*-lords gathered by the door, resplendent in brocades and jewels, talking together in soft, astonished accents.

Three moved to the fore, to seat themselves at the chairs of the long table: an old man, in green and silver, he it was who had come first to look at them—and because he was first and because of his years, Vanye reckoned him for lord in the hall. At his right sat a youth in black and silver; at his left, another youth in blue and green of fantastical design, whose eyes were vague and strange, and rested in distant speculation on Vanye's when he looked him in the face. Vanye flinched from that one, and felt Jhirun step back. His impulse even now was to run, deserting her, though guards and chains and double gates lay between him and freedom: nothing that could befall Jhirun in this place seemed half so terrible as the chance that they would realize what he was, and how he had come.

Morgaine's enemies: he had come her road, and set himself against her enemies, and this was the end of it. They stood studying him, talking together in whispers, in a language he could not understand. A black-robed figure edged through that pale and glittering company, past the scale-armored guards, and deferentially whispered to the seated lords: the priest, who deferred to *qujalin* powers.

They have lost their gods, Morgaine had told him once; yet here was a priest among them. Vanye stood still, listening to that whispered debate, watching: a priest of demons, of *qujal*—this he had trusted, and delivered himself into their hands. The room grew distant from him, and the buzz of their soft voices as they discussed him was like that of bees over a Kurshin meadow, the hum of flies above corruption, the persistent rush of rain against the shuttered windows. He grew dizzy, lost in the sound, struggling only to keep his senses from sliding away.

"Who are you?" the old man asked sharply, looking directly at him; he realized then it was the second asking.

And had it been a human lord in his own hall, he would have felt obliged to bow in reverence: *ilin* that he was, he should bow upon his face, offering respect to a clan lord.

He stood still and hardened his face. "Lord," he said in the whisper that remained of his voice, "I am Nhi Vanye i Chya." He touched the hand of Jhirun, which rested on his arm. "She is Myya Jhirun i Myya Ela's-daughter, of a hold in Hiuaj. She calls this an honorable hold, and says," he added in grim insolence, "that your honor will compel you to give us a night's shelter and send us on our way in the morning with provisions."

There was a silence after that, and the lesser lords looked at each other, and the old lord smiled a wolf-smile, his eyes pale and cold as Morgaine's.

"I am Bydarra," said the old lord, "master of Ohtij-in." A gesture of his hand to left and right indicated the youth in black and him in blue, whose vague, chill eyes were those of one dreaming awake. "My sons," said Bydarra, "Hetharu and Kithan." He drew a long breath and let it go again, a smile frozen upon his face. "Out of Hiuaj," he murmured at last. "Does the quake and the flood scour out more lostlings to plague us? You are of the Barrow-hills," he said to Jhirun; and to Vanye, "and you are not."

"No," Vanye agreed, having nothing else to say; his very accent betrayed him.

"From the far south," said Bydarra.

There was a hush in the room. Vanye knew what the lord implied, for in the far south were only waters, and a great hill crowned with a ring of Standing Stones.

He said nothing.

"What is he?" Bydarra asked suddenly of Jhirun. Vanye felt her hand clench: a peasant girl, barefoot, among these glittering unhuman lords.

And then it occurred to him that she was, though human, *of* them: of their priest, their gods, their sovereignty.

"He is a great lord," she answered in a faint, breathless voice, with a touch of witlessness that for a moment seemed dangerous irony; but he knew her, and they did not. Bydarra looked on her a moment longer, distastefully, and Vanye inwardly blessed her subtlety.

"Stranger," said Hetharu suddenly, he in black brocade: Vanye looked toward him, realizing something that had troubled him—that this one's eyes were human-dark, despite the frost-white hair, but there was no gentleness in voice or look. "You mentioned a woman," Hetharu said, "on a gray horse or a black, or afoot, it might be. And who is she?"

His heart constricted; he sought an answer, cursing his rashness, and at last simply shrugged, refusing the question, hoping that Jhirun too would refuse it; but she did not owe them the courage it would take to keep up her pretense of ignorance. There would come a time, and quickly, when they would not ask with words. And Jhirun—Jhirun knew enough to ruin them.

"Why are you here?" asked Hetharu.

For shelter from the rain, he almost answered, insolent and unwise; but that might advise them how Jhirun had subtly mocked them. He held his peace.

"You are not *khal,*" said Kithan from the other side, his dreaming eyes half-lidded, his voice soft as a woman's. "You are not even halfling. You style yourself like the southern kings. This is a charade. Some find it impressive. But if you are expert with the Wells, o traveller—then why are you at our gate, begging charity? Power—ought to be better fed and better clothed."

"My lord," the priest objected.

"Out," said Kithan, in that same soft tone. "Go impress the rabble in the courtyard, . . . *man.*"

Bydarra stirred, rose stiffly to his feet, leaning on one arm of the chair. He looked at the priest, pursed his lips as if he would speak, and refrained. His gaze swept the other lords, and the guards, and lastly returned to Kithan and Hetharu.

Hetharu glowered; Kithan leaned back, eyes distant, moved a languid hand in a gesture of inconsequence.

The priest remained, silent and unhappy, and slowly Bydarra turned to Vanye, an old man in his movements, the seams of years and bitterness outlining his pale eyes and making hard his mouth. "Nhi Vanye," he said quietly. "Do you wish to answer any of the questions my sons have posed you?"

"No," said Vanye, conscious of the men at his back, the demon-helms that doubtless masked more of their folk. In Andur-Kursh, *qujal* had been fugitives, fearing to be known; but here *qujal* ruled. He recalled the courtyard where men lived, true men, who had cried out and reached for them, and instead they had trusted to *qujal*.

"If it is shelter you seek," said Bydarra, "you shall have it. Food, clothing—whatever your needs be. Ohtij-in will give you your night's hospitality."

"And an open gate in the morning?"

Bydarra's lined face was impassive, neither appreciating the barb nor angered by it. "We are perplexed," said Bydarra. "While we are thus perplexed, our gates remain closed. Doubtless these matters can be quickly resolved. We will watch the roads for the lady you mention, and for you—a night's hospitality."

Vanye bowed the least degree. "My lord Bydarra," he said, the words almost soundless.

They walked the winding corridor again, still ascending. Vanye kept Jhirun against his side, lest the guards think to separate them without resistance; and Jhirun hung her head dispiritedly, seeming undone, hardly caring where they were taken. About them a flurry of brown-clad servants bore trays and linens, some racing ahead, others rushing back again, shrinking against the walls motionless as they and their armored escort passed, averting their faces in terror unheard of in the worst bandit holds of Andur-Kursh.

Each bore a dark scar on the right cheek; Vanye noticed it on servant after servant they passed in the dim light, realized at last that it was a mark burned into the flesh, distinguishing the house servants from the horde outside. Outrage struck him, that the lords of Ohtij-in should mark men, to know their faces, as if this were the sole distinguishing of those who served them in their own hall.

And that men accepted this—to escape, perhaps, the misery outside—frightened him, as nothing human in this land had yet done.

The spiral branched, and they turned down that corridor, entered yet another spiral that wound upward yet a little distance, so that they seemed to have entered one of the outer towers. An open door welcomed them, and they were together admitted to a modest hall that was cheerful with a fire in the hearth, carpeted, with food and linens set on the long table in the midst of the room.

The servants who yet remained in the room bowed their heads and fled on slippered feet, pursued by the harsh commands of the chief of the escort. The guards who had entered withdrew; the door was closed.

A bar dropped down outside, echoing, the truth of *qujalin* hospitality. Vanye stared at the strength of that wooden door, anger and fear moiling within him, and forebore the oath that rose in him; instead he hugged Jhirun's frail shoulders, and brought her to the hearth, where it was warmest in the room, that still bore a chill—settled her where she might rest against the stones. She held her shawl tightly about her, head bowed, shivering.

Gladly enough he would have cast himself down there to rest, but the urge of hunger was by a small degree greater, the sight of food and drink too much to resist.

He brought the platter of meat and cheese to the hearth and set it by Jhirun; he gathered up the bottle of drink, and cups, his hands shaking with exhaustion and reaction, and set them on the stones between them as he knelt down. He poured two foaming cups and urged one into Jhirun's passive hand.

"Drink," he said bitterly. "We have paid enough for it, and of all things else, they have no need to poison us."

She lifted it in her two hands and swallowed a great draught of it; he sipped the brew and grimaced, loathing the sour taste, but it was wet and eased his throat. Jhirun emptied hers, and he gave her more.

"O lord Vanye," she said at last, her voice almost as hoarse as his. "It is ugly, it is ugly; it is worse than Barrows-hold ever was. The ones that came here would have been better dead."

The refuge toward which the Hiua had fled . . . he recalled all her hopes of sanctuary, the bright land in which they would escape the dying of Hiuaj. It was a cruel end for her, no less than for him.

"If you find the chance," he said, "go, make yourself one of those in the yard outside."

"No," she said in horror.

"Outside, there is some hope left. Look at the ones that serve here—did you not see? Better the courtyard: listen to me—the gates may be opened during the day; they must open sometime. You came by the road; you can return by it. Go back to Hiuaj, go back to your own folk. You have no place among *qujal*."

"Halflings," she said, and spat dryly. She tossed her tangled hair and set her jaw, that tended to quiver. "They are half-blood or less, and doubtless I can say the same, if the gossip about my grandmother is true. We were the Barrow-kings, and halflings were the beggars then; they were no better than the lowlanders. Now, now we rob our ancestors for gold and sell it to halflings. But I will not crawl in the mud outside. These lords—only the high lords, like Bydarra—they are—they are of the Old Ones, Bydarra and his one son—" She shivered. "They have the blood—like *her*. But the priest—" The shiver became a sniff, a shrug of disdain. "The priest's eyes are dark. The hair is bleached. So with many of the others. They are no more than I am. I am not afraid of them. I am not going back."

All that she said he absorbed in silence, cold to the heart; that even a Myya could prize a claim to *qujalin* blood—he did not comprehend. He swore suddenly, half a prayer, and leaned against the lintel of the fireplace, forehead against his arm, staring into the fire and tried to think what he could do for himself.

Her hand touched his shoulder, gently, timidly; he turned his head and looked at her, finding only a frightened girl. The heat at his side became painful; he suffered it deliberately, not willing to think clearly in the directions that opened before him.

"I am not going back," she repeated.

"We shall leave here," he said, which he knew for a lie, but he thought that she wanted some promise, something on which to build her courage. He said it out of his own fear, knowing how easily she could tell the lords of Ohtij-in all that she knew: with this promise he meant to purchase her silence. "Only continue to say nothing, and we shall find a way to leave this foul place."

"For Abarais," she said. Her voice, hoarse as it was, came alive. The light danced in her eyes. "For the Well, for your land, and the mountains."

He lied this time by keeping silent. They were the greatest lies he had ever told, he who had once been a *dai-uyo* of Morija, who had fought to possess honor. He felt unclean, remembering her courage in the hall, and swore to himself that she would not come to hurt for it, not that he could prevent. But the true likelihood was that she would come to hurt, and that he could do nothing.

He was *ilin*, bound to a service; and this one essential truth he did not think she understood, else she would not trust her life to him. This also he did not say, and was ashamed and miserable.

She offered him food, and a second cup of the drink, attacking the food herself with an appetite he lacked. He ate because he knew that he must, that if there was hope in strength, it must be his; he forced each mouthful down, hardly tasting it, and followed it with a heavy draught of the sour drink.

Then he rested his back against the fireplace, his shoulders over-warm and his legs numb from the stones, and began to take account of himself, his water-soaked armor and ruined boots. He began to work at the laces at his throat, having to break some of them, then at the buckles at his side and shoulder, working sodden leather through.

Jhirun moved to help him, tugging to free the straps, helping him as he slipped off first the leather surcoat and then the agonizing weight of the mail. Freed of it, he groaned with relief, content only to breathe for a moment. Then came the sleeveless linen haqueton, and that sodden and soiled, and bloody in patches.

"O my lord," Jhirun murmured in pity, and numbly he looked at himself and saw how the armor had galled his water-soaked skin, his linen shirt a soaked rag, rubbing raw sores where there had been folds. He rose, wincing, stripped it off and dropped it to the floor, shivering in the cold air.

Among the clothes on the table he found several shirts, soft and thin, that came of no fabric he knew; he disliked the feel of the too-soft weaving, but when he drew one on, it lay easily upon his galled shoulders, and he was grateful for the touch of something clean and dry.

Jhirun came, timidly searching among the *qujalin* gifts for her own sake. She found the proper stack, unfolded the brown garment uppermost, stood staring at it as if it were alive and hostile—a brown smock such as the servants wore.

He saw, and swore—snatched it from her hands and hurled it to the floor. She looked frightened, and small and miserable in her wet garments.

He picked up one of the shirts and a pair of breeches. "Wear these," he said. "Yours will dry."

"Lord," she said, a tremor in her voice. She hugged the offered clothing to her breast. "Please do not leave me in this place."

"Go dress," he said, and looked away from her deliberately, hating the appeal and the distress of her—who looked to him, who doubtless would concede to anything to be reassured of his lies.

Who might the more believe him if she were thus reassured.

Unwed girls of the countryside of Andur and of Kursh were a casual matter for the *uyin* of the high clans—peasant girls hoping to bear an *uyo's* bastard, to be kept in comfort thereafter: an obligation to the *uyo*, a matter of honor. But therein both parties knew the way of things. Such a thing was not founded in lies or in fear.

"Lord," she said, across the room.

He turned and looked at her, who still stood in her coarse peasant skirts, the garments held against her.

The tread of men approached the door outside, an ominous and warlike sound. Vanye heard it, and heard them pause. Jhirun started to hurry to his side.

The bar of the door crashed back. Vanye looked about as it opened, whirling a chill draft into the room and fluttering the fire; and there in the doorway stood a man in green and brown, who leaned on a sheathed longsword—fronted him with a look of sincere bewilderment.

"Cousin," said Roh.

Chapter Eight

||||||||||||||||||||||||||||||||||||||||||||||||||||||||||

"Roh," Vanye answered, and heard a rustle of cloth at his left: Jhirun, who drew closer to him. He did not turn his head to see, only hoping that she would stay neutral. He himself stood in shirt and breeches; and Roh was armored. He was weaponless, and Roh carried a longsword, sheathed, in his hand.

There had been no weapons in the room, neither knife with the food nor iron by the fire. In desperation Vanye reckoned what his own skill could avail, a weaponless swordsman against a swordsman whose primary weapon had been the bow.

Roh leaned more heavily on the sword's pommel and shouted over his shoulder a casual dismissal of the guards in the corridor, then stood upright, cast wide his arm in a gesture of peace.

Vanye did not move. Roh tossed his sword and caught it midsheath in one hand; and with a mocking flourish discarded it on the table by the door. Then he came forward several paces, limping slightly, bearing that sober, slightly worried expression that was Roh's very self.

And his glance swept from Vanye to Jhirun, utterly puzzled.

"Girl," he said wonderingly, and then shook his head and walked to a chair and sat down, elbows upon the chair's arms. He gave a silent and humorless laugh. "I thought it would be Morgaine. Where is she?"

The plain question shot through other confusions, making sense—Roh's presence making sense of many matters in Ohtij-in. Vanye set his face against him, grateful to understand at least one enemy, and wished Jhirun to silence.

"She *is*," Roh said, "hereabouts."

It was bait he was desired to take: he burned to ask what

Roh knew, and yet he knew better—shifted his weight and let go his breath, realizing that he had been holding it. "You seem to have found welcome enough here," he answered Roh coldly, "among your own kind."

"I have found them agreeable," said Roh. "So might you, if you are willing to listen to reason."

Vanye thrust Jhirun away, toward the far corner of the room. "Get back," he told her. "Whatever happens here, you do not want to be part of it."

But she did not go, only retreated from his roughness, and stood watching, rubbing her arm.

Vanye ignored her, walked to the table where the sword lay, wondering when Roh would move to stop him; he did not. He gathered it into his hands, watching Roh the while. He drew it part of the way from the sheath, waiting still for Roh to react; Roh did not move. There was only a flicker of apprehension in his brown eyes.

"You are a lie," Vanye said. "An illusion."

"You do not know what I am," Roh answered him.

"Zri . . . Liell . . . Roh . . . How many names have you worn before that?"

Liell, sardonic master of Leth, whose mocking humor and soft lies he well knew: he watched sharply for that, waited for the arrogant and incalculably ancient self to look out at him through Roh's human eyes—for that familiar and grandiose movement of the hands, some gesture that would betray the alien resident within his cousin's body.

There was nothing of the like. Roh sat still, watching him, his quick eyes following each move: afraid, that was evident. Reckless: that was like Roh, utterly.

He drew the sword entirely. *Now,* he thought. *Now, if ever—before conscience, before pity.* His arm tensed. But Roh simply stared at him, a little flinching when he moved.

"No!" Jhirun cried from across the room. It came near loosing his arm before he had consciously willed it; he stayed the blow—jolted to remember a courtyard in Morija, and blood, and sickness that knotted in him, robbing him suddenly of strength.

With a curse he rammed the sword into sheath, knowing himself, as Roh had known him.

Coward, his shorn hair marked him. He saw the narrow satisfaction in Roh's eyes.

"It is good to see you," Roh said in a hollow, careful voice. "Nhi Vanye, it is good to see any kindred soul in this for-

saken land. But I am sorry for your sake. I had thought that
you would have used good sense and ridden home. I never
thought that you would have come with her, even if she ordered it. Nhi honor: it is a compulsion. I am sorry for it. But
the sight of you is very welcome."

"Liar," Vanye said between his teeth; but the words, like a
Chya shaft, flew accurately to the mark. He felt the wound,
the desperation of exile, in which Roh—anyone who could
prove that the things he remembered had ever existed—was a
presence infinitely precious. The accents of home even on an
enemy's lips were beautiful.

"There is no point in quarreling before witnesses," said
Roh.

"There is no point in talking to you."

"Nhi Vanye," said Roh softly, "come with me. Outside. I
have sent the guards elsewhere. Come." He rose from the
chair, moved carefully to the door, looking back at him.
"Alone."

Vanye hesitated. That door was what he most earnestly
desired, but he knew no reason that Roh should wish him
well. He tried to think what entrapment Roh needed use, and
that was none at all.

"Come," Roh urged him.

Vanye shrugged, went to the fireside, where his armor lay
discarded—slung his swordbelt over his shoulder and hung
the sword from it, ready to his hand: thus he challenged Roh.

"As you will," Roh said. "But it is mine; and I will ask it
back eventually."

Jhirun came to the fireside, her eyes frightened, looking
from one to the other of them: many, many things she had
not said; Vanye felt the reminder in her glance.

"I would not leave her alone," he said to Roh.

"She is safe," Roh said. He looked directly at Jhirun, took
her unresisting hand, and gone in him was every guardedness
and ungentle tone. "Do not fear anything in Ohtij-in. I
remember a kindness and return it doubled if I can, as I return other things. No harm will come to you. None."

She stayed still, seeming to trust nothing. Vanye delayed,
fearing to leave her, fearing that might be Roh's purpose: to
separate them; and in another mind, fearing what evil he
might do her by holding to her, linking her with him, when
he had only enemies in Ohtij-in.

"I do not think I have a choice," he said to her, and did
not know whether she understood. He turned his back on her,

feeling her stare as he walked to the door. Roh opened it, brought him out into the dim corridor, where a cold wind hit his light clothing and set him shivering.

There were no guards in sight, not a stir anywhere in the corridor.

Roh closed the door and dropped the bar. "Come," he said then, motioned to the left, toward the ascent of the spiral ramp.

Turn after turn they climbed, Roh slightly in the lead; and Vanye found his exhaustion such that he must put a hand on the core wall to steady his step. Roh climbed, limping only slightly, and Vanye glared at his back, his hand on the sword, waiting for Roh to show sensible fear of him and glance back only once; but Roh did not. *Arrogant,* Vanye thought, raging in his heart; but it was very like Roh.

At last they arrived at a level floor, and a doorway, up low steps. Roh opened that door, admitting a gust of wind that skirled violently into the tower, chilling the very bones. Outside was night, and the scent of recent rain.

He followed Roh outside, atop the very crest of the outermost tower of Ohtij-in, where the moons' wan light streamed through the ragged clouds: Anli and Sith were overhead, and hard behind them hurtled the fragments of the Broken Moon, while on the horizon was the vast white face of Li, pocked and scarred. The wind swept freely across the open space. Vanye hung back, in the shelter of the tower core, but Roh walked to the edge, his cloak held closely about him in the blast of the wind.

"Come," Roh urged him, and Vanye came, knowing himself mad even to have come this far, alone with this *qujal* in man's guise. He reached the edge and looked down, dizzied at the view down the tower walls to the stones below; he caught at the solidity of the battlement with one hand and at the sword's hilt with the other.

If Roh meant to destroy him, he thought, there was ample means for that. He ignored Roh for an instant, cast a look at all the country round about, the glint of moonlight on black floodwaters that wove a spider's web about the drowning hills. Through those hills lanced the road that he could not reach, subtle torment.

Roh's hand touched his shoulder, drawing his attention back. His other hand described the circuit of the land, the hold itself.

"I wanted you to see this," Roh said above the howl of

wind. "I wanted you to know the compass of this place. And *she* will finish it, end all hope for them. That is what she has come to do."

He turned a hard look on Roh, leaned against the stonework, for he had begun to shiver convulsively in the wind. "It is impossible for you to persuade me," he said, and held up his scarred hand to the moonlight. "Roh or Liell, you should remember what I am, at least."

"You doubt me," said Roh.

"I doubt everything about you."

Roh's face, hair torn by the wind, assumed a pained earnestness. "I knew that she would hunt me. She was always our enemy. But from you, Nhi Vanye i Chya, I hoped for better. You took shelter from me. You slept at my hearth. Is that nothing to you?"

Vanye flexed his fingers on the corded hilt of the sword, for they were growing numb with cold. "You are supposing," he said hoarsely, "what passed between Roh and me—what was surely common knowledge throughout Chya—and I do not doubt you had your spies. If you want me to believe you, then tell me again what Roh told me last in Ra-koris, when there was none to hear."

Roh hesitated. "To come back," he said, "free of her."

It was truth. The unexpectedness of it numbed him. He leaned against the stonework, ceasing even to shiver, and abruptly turned his face from Roh. "And it might be that Roh counseled with others before saying that to me."

Roh pulled him about by the shoulder, grimacing into the wind.

"So you could say, Vanye, for any other thing you might devise to try me. You cannot be sure, and you know it."

"There is one thing you cannot answer," Vanye said. "You cannot tell me why you are here in this land. Roh would not have fled the road we took; he had no reason to—but Liell had every reason. Liell would have run for his life; and Roh had no reason to."

"He is here," Roh said, a hand upon his heart. "Here. So also am I. My memories—all are Roh's—they are both."

"No," he said. "No. Morgaine said that would not happen; and I would rather take her word than yours—in any matter."

"I am your cousin. I could have taken your life; but I am your cousin. You have the sword. There is no witness here to say it was no fair fight—if the Shiua lords cared. You are al-

ready known for a kinslayer many times over. Use it. Or listen to me."

He flung off Roh's hand, blind as a turn of his head
brought his own shorn hair into his eyes. He shook it free,
stalked off across the battlements, stood staring down into the
squalor of that courtyard, the wind pushing at his back, fit to
tear him from the edge and cast him over.

"Nhi Vanye!" Roh called him. He turned and looked, saw
Roh had followed him. He stubbornly turned his head toward
the view downward, toward the paving and the poor shelters
huddled against the keep walls. He felt the breaking of the
force of the wind as Roh stepped between it and him.

"If you are kinsman to me," Vanye said, "free me from
this place. Then I will believe your kinship."

"Me? And care you nothing for that child that came with
you?"

He looked back, stung, unable to argue. He affected a
shrug. "Jhirun? Here is where she wanted to be, in Shiuan, in
Ohtij-in. This is the land she wished for. What is she to me?"

"I had thought better of you," Roh said after a moment.
"So, surely, had she."

"I am *ilin*. Nothing else. There are human folk here, men,
and so she can survive. They have."

"*There* are men," said Roh, and pointed at the squalid
court, where beasts and men shared neighboring quarters.
"That is the lot of men in Ohtij-in. That is their life, from
birth to death. Men now. Tomorrow the rest that survives in
this land will live in that poverty, and the *qujal*-lords know it.
Of their charity, of their *charity*, Nhi Vanye, these lords have
let men shelter within their walls; of their *charity* they have
fed them and clothed them. They owed them nothing; but
they have let them live within their gates. You—you are not
so charitable—you would let them die, that girl and all the
rest. That is what you would do to me. The sword's edge is
kinder, cousin, than what is waiting for all this land. Murder—is kinder."

"I have nothing to do with what is happening to these
people. I cannot help them or harm them."

"Can you not? The Wells are their hope, Vanye. For all
that live and will live in this world, the Wells are all the hope
there is. They had no skill to use them; but by them, these
folk could live. I could do it. Morgaine surely could, but she
will not, and you know that she will not. Vanye, if that an-

cient power were used as it once was used, their lot would be different. Look on this, look, and remember it, cousin."

He looked, perforce. He did not wish to remember the sight, and the faces that had raged wildly beyond the guards' pikes, the desperate hands that had reached through the grate. "All this is a lie," he said. "As you are a lie."

"The sword's edge," Roh invited him, "if you believe that beyond doubt."

He lifted his face toward Roh, wishing to see truth, wishing something that he could hate, finding nothing to attack—only Roh, mirror-image of himself, more alike him than his own brothers.

"Send me from here," he challenged him who wore the shape of Roh, "if you believe that you can convince me. At least you know that I keep my sworn word. If you have a message for Morgaine herself, then give it to me and I will deliver it faithfully—if I can find her, of which I have doubts."

"I will not ask you where she is," Roh said. "I know where she is going; and I know that you would not tell me more than that. But others might ask you. Others might ask you."

Vanye shivered, remembering the gathering in the hall, the pale lords and ladies who owed nothing to humanity. A fall to the paving below was easier than that. He stepped forward to the very edge, inwardly trying whether he had the courage.

"Vanye," Roh cried, compelling his attention. "Vanye, she will have little difficulty destroying these folk. They will see her, they will flock to her, trusting, because she is fair to see—and she will kill them. It has happened before. Do you think that there is compassion in her?"

"There has been," he said, the words hanging half soundless in his throat.

"You know its limits," said Roh. "You have seen that, too."

Vanye cursed aloud, flung himself back from the battlements and sought the door, sought warmth, fought to open it against the force of the wind. He tore it open, and Roh held it, came in after him. The torches in the hall fluttered wildly until the door slammed. Roh dropped the latch. They remained on opposite sides of the little corridor, facing one another.

"Say to them that you could not persuade me," Vanye said. "Perhaps your hosts will forgive you."

"Listen to me," said Roh.

Vanye unhooked the sheathed sword and cast it across the
corridor; Roh caught it, mid-sheath, and looked at him in
perplexity.

"God forgive me," Vanye said.

"For not committing murder?" Roh said. "That is incongruous."

He stared at Roh, then tore his eyes from him and began
to walk rapidly down the corridor, descending the ramp.
There were guards below. He stopped when their weapons
levelled toward him.

Roh overtook him and set his hand on his arm. "Do not be
rash. Listen to me, cousin. Messengers are going out, have already sped, despite the storm, bearing warnings of her
throughout the whole countryside, to every hold and village.
She will find no welcome among these folk."

Vanye jerked free, but Roh caught his arm again. "No,"
said Roh. The guards stood waiting, helmed, faceless,
weapons ready. "Will you be handled like a peasant for the
hanging?" Roh whispered in his ear, "or will you walk peace-
ably with me?"

Roh's hand tightened, urged. Vanye suffered the grip upon
his arm, and Roh led him through the midst of the guards,
walked with him down the windings of the corridors; and
they did not stop at the door of the room that confined
Jhirun, but went farther, into a branching corridor, that
seemed to lead back to the main tower. The guards walked at
their backs, two bearing torches.

"Jhirun," Vanye reminded Roh, as they entered that other
corridor.

"I thought that was a matter of no concern to you."

"She is a chance meeting," he said. "And no more than
that. She set out looking for you, hoping better from you
than she had where she was: the measure of that, you may
know better than I. You were kind to her, she said."

"She will be safe," said Roh. "I also keep my word."

Vanye frowned, glanced away. Roh said nothing further.
They entered a third corridor, that came to an end in a blind
wall; and in a narrow place on the right was a deeply
recessed doorway. Shadows ran the walls as the guards overtook them, while Roh opened the door.

It was a plain room, with a fire blazing in the hearth, a
wooden bench by the fire, table, chairs. And Hetharu waited
there, Bydarra's dark-eyed son, seated, with a handful of others likewise seated about him—pale-haired men, although

only Hetharu seemed so by nature, his long locks white and
silken about his shoulders. He leaned elbows upon his knees,
warming his hands at the fire; and by the fire stood a priest,
whose brittle, bleached hair described a nimbus about his
balding head.

Vanye stopped in the doorway, confused by the situation
of things, so important a man, so strangely assorted the company. Roh set his hand on his shoulder and urged him gently
forward. The guards took up stations inside and out as the
doors were closed and the gathering became a private one.
Helms were removed, revealing faces thin and pale as those
of the higher lords, eyes as dark as Hetharu's: young men, all
that were gathered here, save the priest, furtive in their quiet.
There was the brocaded finery of the lords, the martial plate-
and-scale of the men-at-arms, the plainness of the furnishings.
Guards had been posted outside as well as within the room.
These things touched uneasily at Vanye's mind, warning of
something other than mere games of terror with him. The
gathering breathed of something ugly, that concerned the
qujal themselves, powers and alliances within their ranks.

And he was seized into the midst of it.

"You won nothing of him?" Hetharu asked of Roh. Roh
left Vanye's side and took the vacant bench beside the fire,
one booted foot tucked up, disposing himself comfortably
and at his ease, leaving Vanye as if he were harmless.

In peevish insolence Vanye shifted his weight suddenly,
and hands reached for daggers and swords all about the
room; he tautened his lips, a smile that rage made slight and
mocking, and slowly, amid their indecision, moved to take his
place beside Roh on the bench, near the fire's warmth. Roh
straightened slightly, both feet on the floor; and the look in
Hetharu's eyes was angry. Vanye met that stare with a stubborn frown, though within, he felt less than easy: here was,
he thought, a man who would gladly resort to force, who
would enjoy it.

"My cousin," said Roh, "is a man of his word, and reckons
that word otherwise bestowed . . . although this may change.
As matters stand now, he does not recognize reason, only the
orders of his liege: that is the kind of man he is."

"A dangerous man," said Hetharu, and his dark, startling
eyes rested full on Vanye's. "Are you dangerous, Man?"

"I thought," said Vanye slowly, with deliberation, "that
Bydarra was lord in Ohtij-in. What is this?"

"You see how he is," said Roh. And on faces round about

there was consternation: guilt, fear. Hetharu glowered. Vanye read the tale writ therein and liked it less and less.

"And his liege?" asked Hetharu. "What has he to say of her?"

"Nothing," said Roh. And in their long silence, Vanye's heart beat rapidly. "It is of little profit," said Roh, "to question him on that account. I will not have him harmed, my lord."

Vanye heard, not understanding, not believing Roh's defense of him; but he saw in that moment that a hint of caution appeared in Hetharu's manner—uncertainty that held him from commanding Roh.

"You," said Hetharu suddenly, looking at Vanye, "do you claim to have come by the Wells?"

"Yes," Vanye answered, for he knew that there was no denying it.

"And can you manage them?" the priest asked, a husky, quiet voice. Vanye looked up into the priest's face, reading desire there, not knowing how to deal with the desires that gathered thickly in this room, centered upon him and upon Roh. He did not want to die; abundantly, he did not want to die, butchered by *qujal*, for causes he did not understand, that had nothing to do with him.

He did not answer.

"You are a Man," said the priest.

"Yes," he said, and noticed that the priest carried a knife at his belt, curious accoutrement for a priest; and that all the others were armed. The priest wore a chain of objects about his neck, stone and shell and bone—familiar—Vanye realized all at once where he had seen such, daily, along with a small stone cross, profaned by nearness to such things. He stared at the priest, the rage that he could maintain against armed threat ebbing coldly in the consideration of devils, and those that served them—and the state of his soul, who served Morgaine, and who companied with a human girl who wore such objects about her neck.

Only let them keep the priest from him. He tore his gaze away from that one, lest the fear show, lest he give them a weapon.

"Man," said Hetharu, looking on him with that same fixed stare, "is this truly your cousin?"

"Half of him was my cousin," Vanye said, to confound them all.

"You see how he tells the truth," Roh said softly, silk-

over-metal. "It does not always profit him, but he is forward
with it: an honest man, my cousin Vanye. He confuses many
people with that trait, but he is Nhi; you would not understand that, but he is Nhi, and he cannot help this over-nice
devotion to honor. He tells the truth. He makes himself enemies with it. But in your honesty, cousin, tell them why your
liege has come to this land. What has she come to do?"

He saw the reason for his presence among them now, how
he had been, in his cleverness, guided to this. He knew that
he should have held his peace from the beginning. Now
silence itself would accuse, persuasive as admission. His
muscles tautened, mind numbed when he most needed it. He
had no answer.

"To seal the Wells forever," Roh said. "Tell me, my honest, my honorable cousin—is that or is that not the truth?"

Still he held his peace, searching desperately for a lie, not
practiced in the art. There was none he could shape that
could not be at once unravelled.

"Deny it, then," said Roh. "Can you do that?"

"I deny it," he said, reacting as Roh thrust at him what he
most wanted; and even as it slipped his lips he knew he had
been maneuvered.

"Swear to it," Roh said; and as he began to say that also:
"On your oath to her," Roh said.

By your soul: that was the oath; and their eyes were all on
him, like wolves in a circle. His lips shaped the words, knowing the effort for useless, utterly useless; on his soul too was
his duty to Morgaine, that bade him try.

But Roh set his hand on his arm, mercifully stopping him,
leaving him trembling with sickness. "No," Roh said. "Spare
yourself the guilt, Vanye; you do not wear it well. You see
how it is, lord Hetharu. I have shown you the truth. My
cousin is an honest man. And you, my lord, will swear to me
that you will set no hand on him. I bear him some affection,
this cousin of mine."

Heat mounted steadily to Vanye's face. There seemed no
profit in protesting this baiting defense. He met Hetharu's
dark and resentful eyes. "Granted," Hetharu said after a moment, and glanced at Roh. "He is yours. But I cannot answer
for my father."

"No one," said Roh, "will set hand on him."

Hetharu glanced down, and aside, and frowned and rose.
"No one," he echoed sullenly.

"My lords," said Roh, likewise rising. "A safe sleep to you."

There was a moment of silence, of seething anger on the part of the young lord. Surely it was not accustomed that Bydarra's son receive his dismissal from a dark-haired guest. But fear hovered thickly in the room when Roh looked at them all in their turn: eyes averted from his, to one side and the other, pretending to find interest in the stones of the floor or the guarded door.

Hetharu shrugged, a false insouciance. "My lords," he said to his companions. "Priest."

They filed out with rustling brocade and the clash of metal, those slim fair lords with their attendant guard, half-human—until there was only Roh, who quietly closed the door, making the room again private.

"Give me the sword again," Vanye said, "cousin."

Roh regarded him warily, hand on the hilt. He shook his head and showed no inclination to come near him now. "You do not seem to understand," Roh said. "I have secured your life, and your person, from some considerable danger. I have a certain authority here—while they fear me. It does not serve your own cause to fight against me."

"It is your own life you have secured," Vanye said, and arose to stand with his back to the fire, "so that they will not try me too severely and find your kinsman is only human."

"That too," said Roh. He started to open the door, and hesitated, looking back. "I wish that I could persuade you to common sense."

"I will go back to the room where I was," Vanye said. "I found it more comfortable."

Roh grinned. "Doubtless."

"Do not touch her," Vanye said. Roh's grin faded; he faced him entirely, regarded him with an earnest look.

"I have said," Roh said, "that she would be safe. And she will be safer—apart from you. I think you understand this."

"Yes," Vanye said after a moment.

"I would help you if you would give me the means."

"Good night," Vanye said.

Roh delayed, a frown twisting his face. He extended his hand, dropped it in a helpless gesture. "Nhi Vanye—my life will end if your liege destroys the Wells—not suddenly, but surely, all the same. So will everything in this land . . . die. But that is nothing to her. Perhaps she cannot help what she is or what she does. I suspect that she cannot. But you at least have a choice. These folk—will die, and they need not."

"I have an oath to keep. I have no choice at all."

"If you had sworn to the devil," Roh said, "would it be a pious act to keep your word?"

Unthought, his hand moved to bless himself, and he stopped, then with deliberation completed the gesture, in this place of *qujal*, where priests worshipped devils. He was cold, inside.

"Can she do as you have done?" asked Roh. "Vanye, is there any land where she has traveled where she is not cursed, and justly? Do you even know whether you serve the side of Men in this war? You have an oath; you have made yourself blind and deaf because of it; you have left kinsmen dead because of it. But to what have you sworn it? Do you wonder what was left in Andur-Kursh? You will never know what you wrought there, and perhaps that is well for your conscience. But here you can see what you do, and you will live in it. Do you think the Wells have kept these folk in misery? Do you think the Wells are the evil? It was the loss of them that ruined this land. And this is the likeness of Morgaine's work. This is what she does, what she leaves behind her wherever she passes. There is nothing more terrible that could befall you than to stay behind where she has passed. You and I know it; we were born in the chaos she wrought in our own Andur-Kursh. Kingdoms fell and clans died under her guidance. She is disaster where she passes, Nhi Vanye. She kills. That is her function, and you cannot prevent her. To destroy is her whole purpose for being."

Vanye turned his face aside and gazed at the barren walls, at the single slit of a window, slatted with a wooden shutter.

"You are determined not to listen," said Roh. "Perhaps you are growing like her."

Vanye glanced back, face set in anger. "Liell," he named Roh, the name that had been his last self, that had destroyed Roh. "Murderer of children. You offered me haven too, in Ra-leth; and I saw what a gift *that* was, what prosperity you brought those that came under your hand."

"I am not Liell any longer."

I.

Vanye felt a tightness about his heart, himself caught and held by that level gaze. "Who is talking to me?" he asked in a still voice. "Who are you, *qujal?* Who were you?"

"Roh."

Bile rose into his throat. He turned his face away. "Get out of here. Get away from me. Do me that grace at least. Let me alone."

"Cousin," said Roh softly. "Have you never wondered who Morgaine was?"

The question left silence after it, a numbness in which he could be aware of the sounds of the fire, the wind outside the narrow window. He found it an effort to draw breath in that silence.

"You have wondered, then," said Roh. "You are not entirely blind. Ask yourself why she is *qujal* to the eye and not to the heart. Ask whether she always tells the truth . . . and believe me, that she does not, not where it is most essential, not where it threatens the thing she seeks. Ask how much of me is Roh, and I will tell you that the essence of me is Roh; ask why you are kept safe, hostile to me as you are, and I will tell you it is because we are—truly—cousins. I feel that burden; I act upon it because I must. But ask yourself what *she* became, this liege of yours. My impulses are human. Ask yourself how human she is. Less than any here—whose blood is only halfling. Ask yourself what you are sworn to, Nhi Vanye."

"Out!" he cried, so that the door burst open and armed guards were instant with lowered weapons. But Roh lifted his hand and stopped them.

"Give you good night," Roh murmured, and withdrew.

The door closed. A bolt shot into place outside.

Vanye swore under his breath, cast himself down on the bench by the fire.

A log crashed, glowing ruin, stirring a momentary flame that ran the length of the charred edge and died. He watched the shifting patterns in the embers, heart pounding, for it seemed to his blurring senses that the floor had shifted minutely, a fall like the Between of Gates.

Animals bleated outside. He heard the distant murmur of troubled voices. The realization that it had been no illusion sent sweat coursing over his limbs, but the earth stayed still thereafter.

He let go his pent breath, stared at the fire until the light and heat wearied his eyes and made him close them.

Chapter Nine

||||||||||||||||||||||||||||||||||||||||||||||||||||

Guards intruded in the morning, servants bringing food and water, a sudden flurry of footsteps, crashing of bolts and doors; savory smells came with the dishes that rattled in the servants' hands.

Vanye rose to his feet by the dying fire. He ached; the pain of his swollen, chafed feet made him stagger violently, brace himself against the stonework. The pikes in the hands of the guards lowered toward him a threatening degree. The servants stared at him, soft-footed men, marked on the faces by the sign of a slashed circle—marked too in the eyes by a fear that was biding and constant.

"Roh," he asked of the servants, of the guards, his voice still hoarse. "Send for Roh. I want to see him." For this morning he recalled a lost dagger, lost with Morgaine, and a thing that he had sworn to do; and things he had said in the night, and not said.

None answered him now. The servants looked away, terrified. The demon-helms shadowed the eyes of the halfling guards, making their faces alike and expressionless toward him.

"I need a change of clothing," he said to the servants; they flinched from him as if he had a devil, and made haste to put themselves in the shadow of the guards, beginning to withdraw.

"The firewood is almost gone," he shouted at them, irrational panic taking him at the thought of dark and cold in the room thereafter. "It will not last the day."

The servants fled; the guards withdrew, closing the door. The bolt went home.

He was trembling, raging at what he knew not: Roh, the lords of this place—at himself, who had walked willingly into it. He stood now and stared at the door, knowing that no

127

force would avail against it, and that no shouting would bring
him freedom. He limped over to the table and sat down on
the end of the bench, reckoning coldly, remembering every
door, every turning, every detail of the hold inside and out.
And somewhere within Ohtij-in——he tried to remember that
room too——was Jhirun, whom he could not help.

He drank of what the servants had left——sparingly, reckoning that if his hosts were unwilling to give him firewood to
keep him warm they would likely bring him nothing else for
the day; he ate, likewise sparingly, and turned constantly in
his mind the image he could shape of the hold, its corridors,
its gates, the number of the men who guarded it, coming
again and again to the same conclusion: that he could not
pass so many barriers and remain a fugitive across a land
that he did not know, afoot, knowing no landmark but the
road——on which his enemies could swiftly find him.

Only Roh came and went where he would.

Roh might set him upon that road. There would be a cost
for that freedom. The food went tasteless in his mouth the
while he considered what it might cost him, to be set at
Abarais, to obtain Roh's trust.

To destroy Roh: this was the thing she had set him last to
do, a matter as simple as his given word, from which there
was no release and no appeal, be it an act honorable or dis-
honorable: honor was not in question between *ilin* and *liyo*.

It was not necessary to wonder what would befall him
thereafter; it did not matter thereafter to what he had
sworn——it was a weight no longer on his conscience, a last
discharge of obligations.

He became strangely comfortable then, knowing the limits
of his existence, knowing that it was not necessary any longer
to struggle against Roh's reasoning. He had, for the first time
in his life, accounted for all possibilities and understood all
that was necessary to understand.

None came near the room. The long day passed. Vanye
went earliest to the window, that he thought a mercy of his
jailers, narrow though it was, a kindness to allow him access
to the sky——until he eased back the wooden slat that covered
it. There was nothing beyond but a stone wall that he could
almost touch with outstretched arm; and when he leaned
against the sill and tried to see downward, there was a ledge
below. On the left was a buttress of the tower, that cut off his

view; on the right was another wall, likewise near enough to
touch.

He left the window unshuttered, despite the blindness of it
and despite the occasional chill draft. So long accustomed to
the sky above him, he found the closeness of walls unbearable. He watched the daylight grow until the sun shone
straight down the shaft, and watched it fade into shadow
again as the sun declined in the sky. He listened to the
wailing of children, the sounds of livestock, the squealing of
wheels, as if the gates of Ohtij-in were open and some manner of normal traffic had begun. Men shouted, accented
words that he did not recognize, but he was glad to hear the
voices, which seemed coarsely ordinary and human.

A shadow began to fall, more swiftly than the decline of
the day; thunder rumbled. Drops of rain spattered the tiny
area of ledge visible beneath the window—drops that ceased,
began again, pattering with increasing force as the sprinkling
became a shower.

And the last of the wood burned out, despite his careful
hoarding of the last small logs and pieces. The room chilled.
Outside, the rain whispered steadily down the shaft.

Metal clattered up the hall, the sound of armed men. It
was not the first time in the day: occasionally there had come
sounds from within the tower, distant and meaning nothing.
Vanye only stirred when he realized they were growing
nearer—rose to his feet in the almost-darkness, hoping for
such petty and precious things as firewood and food and
drink, and fearing that their business might be something
else.

Let it be Roh, he thought, trembling with anxiety, the an-
ticipation of all things at an end, only so the chance
presented itself.

The bolt went back. He blinked in the flare of torches that
filled the opening door, that made shadows of the guards and
the men until they were within the room: light glittered on
brocade, gleamed on bronze helms and on pale hair.

Bydarra, he recognized the elder man; and with him,
Hetharu. The combination jolted against the memory of the
night—of furtive meetings within this prison of his, of young
lordlings and secrecies.

Vanye stood still by the fireplace, while the guards set their
torches in place of the stubs in the brackets. The room outside those interlocked circles of light was dark by compari-
son, the rainy daylight a faint glow in the recess, less bright

than the torches. The character of the room seemed changed,
a place unfamiliar, where *qujal* intervened, contrary to all his
own intentions. He looked at the guards that waited in the
doorway, the light limning demon-faces and outlandish scale.
He looked on them with a slowly growing terror, the consciousness of things outside the compass of himself and Roh.

"Nhi Vanye," Bydarra hailed him, not ungently.

"Lord Bydarra," he answered. He bowed his head slightly,
responding to the soft courtesy, though the guards about
them denied that any courtesy was meant, though Hetharu's
thin, wolfish face beside his father's held nothing of good
will. Vanye looked up again, met the old lord's pale eyes
directly. "I had thought that you would have sent for me to
come to you."

Bydarra smiled tautly, and answered nothing to that
insolence. Of a sudden there was about this gathering too the
hint of secrecies, the lord of Ohtij-in intriguing within his
own hold, not wishing a prisoner moved about the halls with
what noise and notice would attend such moving. Bydarra
asked no questions, proposed nothing immediate, only waited
on his prisoner, with what purpose Vanye felt hovering
shapeless and ominous among the lords of Ohtij-in.

And in that realization came a horrid suspicion of hope:
that of ruining Roh, there was a chance here present. It was
not the act of a warrior: he felt shame for it, but he did not
think that he could reject whatever means offered itself. He
made himself numb to what he did.

"Have you come," Vanye asked of the *qujal*, "to learn of
me what things Roh would not tell you?"

"And what might those things be?" Bydarra asked softly.

"That you cannot trust him."

Again Bydarra smiled, this time with more satisfaction. His
features were an aged mirror of Hetharu's, who was close
beside him—a face lean and fine-boned, but Bydarra's eyes
were pale: Morgaine's features, he thought with an inward
shudder, horrified to see that familiar face reflected in her enemies. No pure *qujal* had been left in Andur-Kursh. He saw
one for the first time, and thought, unwillingly, of Morgaine.

Ask yourself, Roh had said, taunting him, *what you are
sworn to.*

"Go," Bydarra bade the guards, and they went, closing the
door; but Hetharu stayed, at which Bydarra frowned.

"Dutiful," Bydarra murmured at him distastefully; and he
looked at Vanye with a mocking twist of his fine lips. "My

son," he said with a nod at Hetharu. "A man of indiscriminate taste and energetic ambitions. A man of sudden and sweeping ambitions."

Vanye glanced beyond Bydarra's shoulder, at Hetharu's still face, sensing the pride of this man, who stood at his father's shoulder and heard himself insulted to a prisoner. For an irrational instant Vanye felt a deep impulse of sympathy toward Hetharu—himself bastard, half-blood, spurned by his own father. Then a suspicion came to him that it was not casual, that Bydarra knew that he had reason to distrust this son, that Bydarra had reason to come to a prisoner's cell and ask questions.

And Hetharu had urgent reason to cling close to his father's side, lest the old lord learn of meetings and movements that occurred in the night within the walls of Ohtij-in. Vanye met Hetharu's eyes without intending it, and Hetharu returned his gaze, his dark and human eyes promising violence, seething with ill will.

"Roh urges us," said Bydarra, "to treat you gently. Yet he calls you his enemy."

"I am his cousin," Vanye countered quietly, falling back upon Roh's own stated reasoning.

"Roh," said Bydarra, "makes vast and impossible promises—of limitless arrogance. One would think that he could reshape the Moon and turn back the waters. So suddenly arrived, so strangely earnest in his concern for us—he styles himself like the ancient Kings of Men, and claims to have power over the Wells. He seeks our records, pores over maps and old accounts of only curious interest. And what would you, Nhi Vanye i Chya? Will you likewise bid for the good will of Ohtij-in? What shall we offer you for your good pleasure if you will save us all? Worship, as a god?"

The sting of sarcasm fell on numbness, a chill, to think of Roh, a Chya bowman, a lord of forested Koris, searching musty *qujalin* records, through runic writings that Men did not read—save only Morgaine. "Roh," Vanye said, "lies to you. He does not know everything; but you are teaching it to him. Keep him from those books."

Bydarra's silvery brow arched, as if he found the answer different from his expectation. He shot a look at Hetharu, and walked a distance to the far recess of the room, by the window slit, where wan daylight painted his hair and robes with an edge of white. He looked out that viewless window for a moment as if he pondered something that did not need sight, and then looked back, and slowly returned to the circle of torchlight.

"We," said Bydarra, "we are the heirs of the true *khal*. Mixed-blood we all are, but we are their heirs, nonetheless. And none of us has the skill. It is not in those books. The maps are no longer valid. The land is gone. There is nothing to be had there."

"Hope," said Vanye, "that that is so."

"You are human," Bydarra said contemptuously.

"Yes."

"Those books," Bydarra said, "contain nothing. The Old Ones were flesh and bone, and if men will worship them, that is their choice. Priests—" The old lord made a shrug of contempt, nodding toward the wall, by implication toward the court that lay below. "Parasites. The lowest of our halfling blood. They venerate a lie, mumbling nonsense, believing that they once ruled the Wells, that they are doing some special service by tending them. Even the oldest records do not go back into the time of the Wells. The books are worthless. The Hiua kings were a plague the Wells spilled forth, and they tampered with the forces of them, they hurled sacrifices into them, but they had no more power than the Shiua priests. They never ruled the Wells. They were only brought here. Then the sea began to take Hiuaj. And lately—there is Roh; there is yourself. You claim that you have arrived by the Wells. Is that so?"

"Yes," Vanye answered in a faint voice. The things that Bydarra said began to accord with too much. Once in Andur a man had questioned Morgaine; the words had long rested, in a corner of his mind, awaiting some reasoned explanation: *The world went wide*, she had answered that man, *around the bending of the path. I went through*. And suddenly he began to perceive the *qujal*-lord's anxiety, the sense that in him, in Roh, things met that never should have met at all . . . that somewhere in Ohtij-in was a Myya girl, far, far from the mountains of Erd and Morija.

"And the woman," asked Bydarra, "she on the gray horse?"

He said nothing.

"Roh spoke of her," Bydarra said. "You spoke of her; the Hiua girl confirms it. Rumor is running the courtyard: talk, careless talk, before the servants. Roh hints darkly of her intentions; the Hiua girl confounds her with Hiua legend."

Vanye shrugged lest he seem concerned, his heart beating

hard against his ribs. "The Hiua set herself on my trail; I think her folk had cast her out. Sometimes she talks wildly. She may be mad. I would put no great trust in what she says."

"Angharan," Bydarra said. "Morgen-Angharan. The seventh and unfavorable power: Hiua kings and Aren superstition are always tangled. The white queen. But of course if you are not Hiua, this would not be familiar to you."

Vanye shook his head, clenched his hand over his wrist behind his back. "It is not familiar to me," he said.

"What is her true name?"

Again he shrugged.

"Roh," said Bydarra, "calls her a threat to all life—says that she has come to destroy the Wells and ruin the land. He offers his own skill to save us—whatever that skill may prove to be. Some," Bydarra added, with a look that made Hetharu avoid his eyes sullenly, "some of us are willing to fall at his feet. Not all of us are gullible."

There was silence, in which Vanye did not want to look at Hetharu, nor at Bydarra, who deliberately baited his son.

"Perhaps," Bydarra continued softly, "there is no such woman, and you and the Hiua girl are allied with this Roh. Or perhaps you have some purposes we in Ohtij-in do not know yet. Humankind drove us from Hiuaj. The Hiua kings were never concerned with our welfare, and they never held the power that Roh claims for himself."

Vanye stared at him, calculating, weighing matters, desperately. "Her name is Morgaine," he said. "And you would be better advised to offer her hospitality rather than Roh."

"Ah," said Bydarra. "And what bid would she make us? What would she offer?"

"A warning," he said, forcing the words, knowing they would not be favored. "And I give you one: to dismiss him and me and have nothing to do with any of us. That is your safety. That is all the safety you have."

The mockery left Bydarra's seamed face. He came closer, his lean countenance utterly sober, pale eyes intense: tall, the halflings, so that Vanye found himself meeting the old lord eye to eye. Light fingers touched the side of his arm, urging confidentiality, the while from the edge of his vision Vanye saw Hetharu leaning against the table, arms folded, regarding him coldly. "Hnoth is upon us," Bydarra said, "when the floods rise and no traveling is possible. This Chya Roh is anxious to set out for Abarais now, this day, before the road is

closed. He seems likewise anxious that you be sent to him
when he is there, directly as it becomes possible; and what
say you to this, Nhi Vanye i Chya?"

"That you are as lost as I am if ever you let him reach
Abarais," Vanye said. The pulse roared in him as he stared
into that aged *qujalin* face, and thought of Roh in possession
of that Master Gate, with all its power to harm, to enliven
the other Gates, to reach out and destroy. "Let him ever
reach it and you will find yourself a master of whom you will
never free yourself, not in this generation or the next or the
next. I know that for the truth."

"Then he can do the things he claims," said Hetharu suddenly.

Vanye glanced toward Hetharu, who left the table and advanced to his father's side.

"His power would be such," Vanye said, "that the whole of
Shiuan and Hiuaj would become whatever pleased him—
pleased *him,* my lord. You do not look like a man that would
relish having a master."

Bydarra smiled grimly and looked at Hetharu. "It may be,"
said Bydarra, "that you have been well answered."

"By another with something to win," said Hetharu, and
seized Vanye's arm with such insolent violence that anger
blinded him for the moment: he thrust his arm free, one
clear thread of reason still holding him from the princeling's
throat. He drew a ragged breath and looked to Bydarra, to
authority.

"I would not see Roh set at Abarais," Vanye said, "and
once your own experience shows you that I was right, my
lord, I fear it will be much too late to change your mind."

"Can you master the Wells yourself?" Bydarra asked.

"Set me at Abarais, until my own liege comes. Then—ask
what you will in payment, and it will go better with this
land."

"Can you," asked Hetharu, seizing him a second time by
the arm, "manage the Wells yourself?"

Vanye glared into that handsome wolf-face, the white-
edged nostrils, the dark eyes smoldering with violence, the
lank white hair that was not, like the lesser lords', the work
of artifice.

"Take your hands from me," he managed to say, and cast
his appeal still to Bydarra. "My lord," he said with a desperate, deliberate calm, "my lord, in this room, there was some

bargain struck—your son and Roh and other young lords together. Look to the nature of it."

Bydarra's face went rigid with some emotion; he thrust
Hetharu aside, looked terribly on Vanye, then turned that
same look toward his son, beginning a word that was not finished. A blade flashed, and Bydarra choked, turned again under Hetharu's second blow, the bright blood starting from
mouth and throat. Bydarra fell forward, and Vanye staggered
back under the dying weight of him—let him fall, in horror,
with the hot blood flooding his own arms.

And he stared across weapon's edge at a son who could
murder father and show nothing of remorse. There was fear
in that white face: hate. Vanye met Hetharu's eyes and knew
the depth of what had been prepared for him.

"Hail me lord," said Hetharu softly, "lord in Ohtij-in and
in all Shiuan."

Panic burst in him. "Guard!" he cried, as Hetharu lifted
the bloody dagger and slashed his own arm, a second foun-
tain of blood. The dagger flew, struck at Vanye's feet, in the
spreading dark pool from Bydarra's body. Vanye stumbled
back from the dagger as the door opened, and there were
armed men there in force, pikes lowered toward him.
Hetharu leaned against the fireplace in unfeigned shock, leaking blood through his fingers that clasped his wounded arm to
his breast.

"He—" Vanye cried, and staggered back under the blow of
a pikeshaft that sent him sprawling and drove the wind from
him. He scrambled for his feet and hurled himself for the
door, barred from it by others—thrown aside, seized up the
dagger that lay in the pool of blood, and drove for Hetharu's
throat.

An armored body turned the blade, a face before him
grimacing in pain and shock: more blood flooded his hands,
hot, before the others dragged him back and crashed with
him over a bench. The blows of pikestaves and boots overwhelmed him and he lay half-sensible in a pool of blood, his
own or Bydarra's, he no longer knew. They moved his battered arms and cords bit into his wrists.

Shouts echoed. Throughout the halls there began a shriek
of alarm, the sounds of women's voices and the deeper
mourning of men. He listened to this, on the edge of consciousness, the shrieks part of the torment of chaos that raged
about him.

He remained on the floor, untouched. Men came for

Bydarra's body, and they carried it forth on a litter in grim
silence; and another corpse they carried out too, that of a
man-at-arms, that Vanye dimly realized was to his charge.
And thereafter, when the room was clear and more torches
had been brought, men gathered him up by the hair and the
arms, and bowed him at Hetharu's feet.

Hetharu sat, while a priest wound his arm about with clean
linen soaked in oils; and there was in Hetharu's shock-pale
face a taut and wary look. Armed men were about him, and
one, bare-faced, his coarse bleached hair gathered back in a
knot, handed Hetharu a cup of which he drank deeply. In a
moment Hetharu sighed, and returned the cup, and leaned
back in the chair while the priest tied the bandage.

A number of other lords came, elegant and jewelled, in
delicate fabrics. There was silence in the room, and the constant flow of whispers in the corridor outside. As each lord
came forward to meet Hetharu there was a slight bow, an
obeisance, some only scant. It was the passing of power, there
in that bloody cell—many an older lord whose obeisance was
cold and hesitant, with looks about at the armed guards that
stood grimly evident; and younger men, who did not restrain
their smiles, wolf-smiles and no evidence of mourning.

And lastly came Kithan, waxen-pale and languid, attended
by a trio of guards. He bowed to kiss his brother's hand, and
suffered his brother's kiss upon his cheek, his face cold and
distant the while. He stumbled when he attempted to rise and
turn, steadied by the guards, and blinked dazedly, and stared
down at Vanye.

Slowly the distance vanished in those dilated pale eyes, and
something came into them of recognition, a mad hatred, distraught and violent.

"I had no weapon," Vanye said to him, fearing the youth's
grief as much as Hetharu's calculation. "The only weapon—"

An armored hand smashed across his mouth, dazing him;
and no one was interested in listening not even Kithan, who
simply stared at him, empty-eyed, unasking what he would
have said. After a moment someone took Kithan by the arm
and led him out, like a confused child.

Women had come, pale-haired and cold, who bowed and
kissed Hetharu's hand and returned on silent feet to the corridor, a whisper of brocade and a lingering of perfume amid
the oil and armor of the guards.

Then, a stir among the departing mourners, brusque and
sudden, came Roh, himself attended by guards, one on either

side. Roh was armored, and cloaked, and bore his bow and his longsword slung on his back for travel.

Vanye's heart leaped up in an instant's forlorn hope that died when he reminded himself of the illusion that was Roh, when Roh ignored him, and addressed himself to the patricide, Bydarra's newly powerful son.

"My lord," Roh murmured, and bowed, but he did not kiss Hetharu's hand or make any other courtesy, at which faces clouded, not least of them Hetharu's. "The horses are saddled," Roh said. "The tide is due at sunset, I am told; and we had best make some small haste."

"There will be no delay," said Hetharu.

Again Roh bowed, only as much as need be; and turned his head and for the first time looked down on Vanye, who knelt between his guards. "Cousin," Roh said sorrowfully, as a man would reproach a too-innocent youth. Heat stung Vanye's face; and something in him responded to the voice, all the same. He looked up into Roh's brown eyes and lean, tanned face, seeking Liell, struggling to summon hate. It only came to him that they two had known Andur-Kursh, and that he would not see it again; and that when Roh had left, he would be alone among *qujal*.

"I do not envy you," Vanye said, "your company on the road."

Roh's eyes slid warily to Hetharu, back again; and Roh bent then, and took Vanye's arm, drawing him to his feet in spite of the guards. His hand lingered, kindly as a brother's.

"Swear to my service," Roh said in a low voice, for him alone. "Leave hers, and I will take you with me, out of here."

Vanye jerked his head in refusal, setting his jaw lest he show how much he desired it.

"They will not harm you," Roh said, which he needed not have said.

"What you will is not law for them," Vanye said. "I did not kill Bydarra: on my oath, I did not. They have done this to spite you; I am nothing to them but a means of touching you."

Roh frowned. "I will see you at Abarais. With *her*, I will not compromise—I cannot—but with you—"

"Take me with you now if you hope for that. Do not ask an oath of me; you know I cannot give it. But will you rather trust them at your back? You will be alone with them, and when they have what they want—"

"No," Roh said after a moment that trust and doubt had

seemed closely balanced. "No. That would not be wise of me."

"At least take Jhirun out of this place."

Again Roh hesitated, seeming almost to agree. "No," he said. "Nothing to please you: I do not think you hope for my long life. She stays here."

"To be murdered. As I will be."

"No," said Roh. "I have made an understanding for your welfare. And I will see it kept; we have bargained, they and I. I will see you at Abarais."

"No," said Vanye. "I do not think you will."

"Cousin," said Roh softly.

Vanye swore and turned away, bile rising in his throat. He shouldered through his guards, who lacked orders and stood like cattle, confused. None checked him. He went to the window slit and looked out at the rain-glistening stones, ignoring all of them as they made their arrangements to leave, with much clattering of arms and shouting up and down the corridors.

Group by group, to their various purposes, the gathering dispersed. Roh was among the first to leave. Vanye did not turn his head to see. He heard the room deserted, and the door heavily sealed, and distantly in the halls echoed the tramp of armed men.

Out in the yard there began a tumult among the people, and the clatter of horses on the pavings. Voices of men and women pierced the commotion, for a moment clear and then subdued again.

One lord was leaving Ohtij-in; the former could not possibly have been buried yet. Such was Hetharu's haste, to ride with Roh, seeking power; and such Roh had doubtless promised him, with promises and threats and direct warnings to bring him quickly to Abarais, before flood should come, before the way should be closed. Perhaps Bydarra had opposed such a journey, inventing delays, but Bydarra would no more oppose anything—perhaps at Roh's urging; it was Hetharu's cruel humor that had placed the blame where Roh least wanted it.

Vanye heard the number of horses in the yard and reckoned that most of the force of Ohtij-in must be going.

And if Morgaine lived, she would have to contend with *that* upon the road—if she had not already, more wary and more wise than her *ilin*, skirted round Ohtij-in and passed toward Abarais.

It was the only hope that remained to him. If Morgaine had done so, Roh was finished, powerless. This was surely the fear in Roh's mind, that drove him to create chaos of Ohtij-in, that drove him to accept allies that would turn on him when first they could. If Roh came too late, if Morgaine had passed, and the Wells were dead and sealed against him, then those same allies would surely kill him; and then would be another bitter reckoning, at Ohtij-in, for the hostage for a dead enemy.

But if Roh was not too late, if Morgaine was in truth lost, then there were other certainties: himself bidden to Abarais, to serve Roh—masterless *ilin*, to be Claimed to another service.

There was nothing else, no other choice for him—but to seek Roh's life; and the end of that, too, he knew.

A door closed elsewhere, echoing in the depths; a scuff on stone sounded outside, steps in the corridor. He thought until the last that they were bound elsewhere: but the bolt of the door crashed back.

He looked back, the blood chilling in his veins as he saw Kithan, with armed men about him.

Kithan walked to the end of the table, steady in his bearing; his delicate features were composed and cold.

"They are leaving," Kithan said softly.

"I did not," Vanye protested, "kill your father. It was Hetharu."

There was no reaction, none. Kithan stood still and stared at him, and outside there was the sound of horses clattering out the gates. Then those gates closed, booming, inner and outer.

Kithan drew a long, shuddering breath, expelled it slowly, as if savoring the air. He had shut his eyes, and opened them again with the same chill calm. "In a little time we shall have buried my father. We do not make overmuch ceremony of our interments. Then I will see to you."

"I did not kill him."

"Did you not?" Kithan's cloud-gray eyes assumed that dreaming languor that formerly possessed them, but now it seemed ironical, a pose. "Hetharu would have more than Ohtij-in to rule. Do you think that Roh of the Chya will give it to him?"

Vanye answered nothing, not knowing where this was tending, and liking it little. Kithan smiled.

"Would this cousin of yours take vengeance for you?" asked Kithan.

"It might be," Vanye answered, and Kithan still smiled.

"Hetharu was always tedious," Kithan said.

Vanye drew in a breath, finally reading him. "If you aim at your brother—free me. I am not Roh's ally."

"No," said Kithan softly. "Nor care I. It may be that you are guilty; or perhaps not. And that is nothing to me. I see no future for any of us, and I trust you no more than Hetharu should have trusted your kinsman."

"Hetharu," Vanye said, "killed your father."

Kithan smiled and shrugged, turned his shoulder to him. He made a signal to one of the men with him, toward the door. That man summoned others, who held between them a small and tattered shadow.

Jhirun.

He could not help her. She recognized him as he moved a little into the torchlight. Her shadowed face assumed a look of anguish. But she said nothing, seeing him, nor cried out. Vanye lowered his eyes, apology for all things between them, lifted them again. There was nothing that he could say to ease her plight, and much that he could say to make it worse, making clear his regard for her.

He turned from the sight of her and of them, and walked back to stare out the window.

"Make a fire in the west tower hall," Kithan bade one of the guards.

And they withdrew, and the door closed.

Chapter Ten

||||||||||||||||||||||||||||||||||||||||||||||||||||||

The thunder rumbled almost constantly, and in time the torches, whipped by the wind that had free play through the small cell, went out, one by one, leaving dark. Vanye sat by the window, leaning against the stones, letting the cold wind and spattering rain numb his face as his hands long since were numb. The cold eased the pain of bruises; he reckoned that if it also made him fevered, if they delayed long enough, then that was only gain. He blinked the water from his eyes and watched the pattern of lightning on the raindrops that crawled down the stones opposite the narrow window. So far as it was possible, he concentrated entirely on that slow progress, lost in it.

Somewhere by the gate a bell began to ring, monotone and urgent. Voices shouted, lost in the thunder. The burial party had returned, he thought, and sharper fear began to gather in him; he fought it with anger, but the taste of it was only the more bitter, for he was angry most of all that he was without purpose in his misery, that he was seized into others' purposes, to die that way: child-innocent, child-ignorant—he had trusted, had expected, had assumed.

Likewise Roh was being slowly ensnared, carefully maneuvered, having taken to himself allies without law, adept in treacheries of a breed unimagined in Andur-Kursh. Best that Roh perish—and yet he did not entirely wish it: rather that Hetharu would find himself surprised, that Roh would repay them—bitterly.

There was nothing else.

The bell still rang. And now there came the tread of many men in the corridors, echoing up and down the winding halls—a scrape of stone in the hall outside, the bolt crashing back.

There were guards, rain still glistening on their demon-

141

faced helms and the scale of their armor in the torchlight
they brought with them. Vanye gathered himself to his feet
on the second try, came with them of his own accord as far
as the hall, where he might reckon their number.

There were eight, ten, twelve of them. *So many?* he wondered bitterly, astonished that they could so fear him, reckoning how his hands were tied and his legs, numb with cold,
unsteady under him.

They seized him roughly and brought him down the corridor, and down and down the spirals, past the staring white
faces of delicate *qujalin* ladies, the averted eyes of servants.
Cold air struck him as the door at the bottom of the spiral
opened, and there before them was the barred iron gate, the
keeper running back the chain to let them out.

Outside was rain and torchlight, and a confused rabble, a
mass of faces shouting, drowning the noise of the bell.

Vanye set his feet, resisted desperately being brought out
into that; but the guards formed about him with pikes levelled, and others forced him down the steps. Mad faces surrounded them, rocks flew: Vanye felt an impact on his
shoulder and jerked back as fingers seized on his shirt and
tried to pull him away from the guards. A man went down
then with a pike through his belly, writhing and screaming,
and the men-at-arms hurried, broke through the mass: Vanye
no longer resisted the guards, fearing the mob's violence
more.

And the bell at the gate still tolled, adding its own mad
voice to the chaos. A door in the barbican tower opened,
more guards ready to take them into that refuge, a serried
line of weapons to defend it.

A pikeman went down, stone-struck. The mob surged inward. Vanye recoiled into the hands of his guards as the
rabble seized on him, almost succeeding this time in taking
him. There was a skirmish, sharp and bloody, peasants
against armored pikemen, and the guards moved forward
over wounded and dying.

The insanity of it was beyond comprehension, the attack,
the hatred, whether they aimed it at him or at their own lords
. . . knowing that Bydarra was slain, that the greater force of
the hold had departed. The guards seemed suddenly fearfully
few; the power that Kithan held was stretched thin in Ohtij-in
amid this violence that surged within the court, outside its
doors. The madness cared no longer what it attacked.

There was a sound, deep and rumbling, that shook the

walls, that wrung horrified screams from the surging mob—
that stopped the guards in their tracks.

And the gate vanished in a second rumbling of stones: the
arch that had spanned it collapsed, the stones whirling away
like leaves into darkness, so that little rubble remained. It was
gone. The mob shrieked and scattered, abandoned improvised
weapons, a scatter of staves and stones on the cobbles; and
the guards levelled futile weapons at that incredible sight.

In that darkness where the gate had been was a shimmer,
and a rider, white-cloaked, on a gray horse, a shining of
white hair under the remaining torches; and the glimmering
was a drawn sword.

The blade stayed unsheathed. It held darkness entrapped at
its tip, darkness that eclipsed the light of torches where it was
lifted. The gray horse moved forward a pace; the crowd
shrieked and fled back.

Morgaine.

She had come to this place, come after him. Vanye
struggled to be free, feeling a wild urge to laughter, and in
that moment his guards cast him sprawling and fled.

He lay still, for a moment dazed by his impact on the wet
paving. He saw Siptah's muddy hooves not far from his head
as she rode to cover him, and he did not fear the horse; but
above him he saw Morgaine's outstretched hand, and
Changeling unsheathed, shimmering opal fires and carrying
that lethal void at its tip: oblivion uncleaner than any the
qujal could deal.

He feared to move while that hovered over him. "Roh—"
he tried to warn her; but his hoarse voice was lost in the
storm and the shouting.

"Dai-khal," he heard cry from the distance. *"Angharan
. . . Angharan!"* He heard the cry repeated, echoed off the
walls, warning carried strangely by the wind; and thereafter
quiet settled in the courtyard, among humans and *qujal* alike.

Siptah swung aside; Vanye struggled to reach his knees, did
so with a tearing pain in his side that for a moment took his
breath away. When his sight cleared, he saw Kithan and the
other lords in the unbarred doorway of the keep, abandoned
by the guards. There was no sound, no movement from the
qujal. Their faces, their white hair whipping on the wind,
made a pale cluster in the torchlight.

"This is my companion," Morgaine said softly, above the
rush of rain; and it was likely that there was no place in the

courtyard that could not hear her. "Poor welcome have you given him."

There was for a moment only the steady beat of the rain into the puddles, the restless stamp of Siptah's feet, and came the sound of hooves behind, another rider coming through the ruined gate: the black gelding, ridden by a stranger, who swung down from the saddle and waited.

Vanye gathered his feet under him, careful of the fire of *Changeling*, that gleamed perilously near him. "*Liyo*," he said, forcing sound into his raw throat, trying to shout. "Roh, by the north road, before the sun set. He has not that much start—"

She whipped her Honor blade from her belt left-handed, letting Siptah stand. "Turn," she said, and leaned from the saddle behind him, slashed the cords that held his hands. His arms fell, leaden and painful; he looked at her, turning, and she gestured toward his horse, and the man that held it.

Vanye drew a deep breath and made what effort he could to run, reached the waiting horse and hauled himself into the saddle, head reeling and hands too stiff to feel the reins that the man thrust into his possession. He looked down into that stranger's scarred face, stung with irrational resentment, rage that this man had been given his belongings, had ridden at her side: he saw that resentment answered in the peasant's dark eyes, the grim set of scarred lips.

Stone rattled. Dark shapes moved in the misting rain, creeping over the massive stones of the shattered gateway, the ruined double walls: men—or less than men. Vanye saw, and felt a prickling at his neck, beholding the dark shapes that moved like vermin amid the vast, tumbled stones.

With a sudden shout at him, Morgaine reined about and rode for that broken gateway, sending the invaders scrambling aside; and Vanye jerked feebly at the reins, the black gelding already turning, accustomed to run with the gray. He caught his balance in the saddle as the horses cleared the ruined gate and hit even stride again, down the rain-washed stones, passing a horde of those small, dark men. Downhill they rode, clattering along the paving, faster and faster as the horses found clear road ahead. Morgaine led, and never yet had she sheathed the sword, that was danger to all about it; Vanye had no wish to ride beside her while she bore that naked and shimmering in her hand.

Stonework yielded to mud, to brush, to stonework again, and the jolting drove pain into belly and lungs, and the rain

blinded and the lightning redoubled: Vanye ceased to be
aware of where he rode, only that he must follow. Pain ate at
his side, a misery that clutched at muscle and spread over all
his mind, blotting out everything but the sense that kept his
hand on the rein and his body in the saddle.

The horses spent their first wind, and slowed: Vanye was
aware when *Changeling* winked out, going into sheath—and
Morgaine asked things to which he gave unclear answer, not
knowing the land or the tides. She laid heels to Siptah and
the gray leaned into renewed effort, the gelding following.
Vanye used his heels mercilessly when the animal began to
flag, fearful of being left behind, knowing that Morgaine
would not stop. They rounded blind turns, downslope and up
again, through shallow water and over higher ground.

And as they mounted a crest where the hills opened up, a
wide valley spread before them, black waters as far as the eye
could see, froth roaring and crashing about the rocks and the
stonework, swallowing up the road.

Morgaine reined in with a curse, and Vanye let the gelding
stop, both horses standing with sides heaving. It was over,
lost. Vanye bowed upon the saddlehorn with the rain beating
at his thinly clad back, until the pain of his side ebbed and he
could straighten.

"Send he drowns," Morgaine said, and her voice trembled.

"Aye," he answered without passion, coughed and leaned
again over the saddle until the spasm had left him.

Siptah's warmth shifted against his leg, and he felt Morgaine's touch on his shoulder. He lifted his head. The lightning showed her face to him, frozen in a look of concern, the
rain like jewels on her brow.

"I thought," he said, "that you would have left, or that you
were lost."

"I had my own difficulties," she said; and with anguish she
slammed her fist against her leg. "Would you could have found
a chance to kill him."

The accusation shot home. "When the rain stops—" he offered in his guilt.

"This is the Suvoj," she said fiercely, "by the name that I
have heard, and that is not river-flood: it is the sea, the tide.
After Hnoth, after the moons—"

She drew breath. Vanye became aware of the malefic force
of the vast light that hung above the lightning, that lent the
boiling clouds strange definition. And when next the flashes
showed him Morgaine clearly, she had turned her head and

was gazing at the flood with an expression like a hunting wolf. "Perhaps," she said, "perhaps there are barriers that will hold him, even past the Suvoj."

"It may be, *liyo*," he said. "I do not know."

"If not, we will learn it in a few days." Her shoulders fell, a sigh of exhaustion; she bowed her head and threw it back, scattering rain from her hair. She drew Siptah full about.

And perhaps the lightning showed him clearly for the first time, for her face took on a sudden look of concern. "Vanye?" she asked, reaching for him. Her voice reached him thinly, distantly.

"I can ride," he said, although for very little he would have denied it. The prospect of another such mad course was almost more then he could bear; the pain in his ribs rode every breath. But the gentleness fed strength into him. He began to shiver, feeling the cold, where before he had had the warmth of movement. She unclasped the cloak from about her throat and flung it about his shoulders. He put up his hand to refuse it.

"Put it on," she said. "Do not be stubborn." And gratefully he gathered it about him, taking warmth from the horse and from the cloak that she had worn. It made him shiver the more for a moment, his body beginning to fight the cold. She took a flask from her saddle and handed it across to him; he drank a mouthful of that foul local brew that stung his cut lip and almost made him gag, but it eased his throat after it had burned its way down, and the taste faded.

"Keep it," she said when he offered to return it.

"Where are we going?"

"Back," she said, "to Ohtij-in."

"No," he objected, the reflex of fear; it leapt out in his voice, and made her look at him strangely for a moment. In shame he jerked the gelding's head about toward Ohtij-in, started him moving, Siptah falling in beside at a gentle walk. He said nothing, wished not even to look at her, but pressed his hand to his bruised ribs beneath the cloak and tried to ignore the panic that lay like ice in his belly—Roh safely sped toward Abarais, and themselves, themselves returning into the grasp of Ohtij-in, within the reach of treachery.

And then, a second impulse of shame for himself, he remembered the Hiua girl whom he had abandoned there without a thought toward her. It was his oath, and that was as it must be, but he was ashamed not even to have thought of her.

"Jhirun," he said, "was with me, a prisoner too."

"Forget her. What passed with Roh?"

The question stung; guilt commingled with dread in him. He looked ahead, between the gelding's ears. "Lord Hetharu of Ohtij-in," he said, "went with Roh northward, to reach Abarais before the weather turned. I walked into this place, thinking to claim shelter. It is not Andur-Kursh. I have not managed well, *liyo*. I am sorry."

"Which first—Roh's leaving or your coming?"

He had deliberately obscured that in his telling; her harsh question cut to the center of the matter. "My coming," he said. *"Liyo—"*

"He let you live."

He did look at her, tried to compose his face, though all his blood seemed gathered in his belly. "Did I seem to be comfortable there? What do you think that I could have done? I had no chance at him." The words came, and immediately he wished he had said nothing, for there was suddenly a lie between them.

And more than that: for he saw suspicion in her look, a quiet and horrid mistrust. In the long silence that followed, their horses side by side, he wished that she would rebuke him, quarrel, remind him how little caution he had used and what duty he owed her, anything against which he could argue. She said nothing.

"What would you?" he cried finally, against that silence. "That you had come later?"

"No," she said in a voice strangely subdued.

"It was not for me," he surmised suddenly. "It was Roh you wanted."

"I did not," she said very quietly, "know where you were. Only that Roh had sheltered in Ohtij-in: that I did hear. Other word did not reach me."

She fell silent again, and in the long time that they rode in the rain he clutched her warm cloak about him and reckoned that she had only given him the truth that he had insisted on knowing—more honest with him than he had been with her. Roh had named her liar, and she did not lie, even when a small untruth would have been kinder; he held that thought for comfort, scant though it was.

"Liyo," he asked finally, "where were you? I tried to find you."

"At Aren," she replied, and he cursed himself bitterly. "They are rough folk," she said. "Easily impressed. They feared me, and that was convenient. I waited there for you. They said that there was no sign of you."

"Then they were blind," he said bitterly. "I held to the road; I never left it. I thought only that you would leave me and keep going, and trust me to follow."

"They knew it, then," she said, a frown settling on her face. "They did know."

"It may be," he said, "that they feared you too much."

She swore in her own tongue, at least that was the tone of it, and shook her head, and what bided in her face then, lightning-lit, was not good to see.

"Jhirun and I together," he said, "walked the road; and it brought us to Ohtij-in, out of food, out of any hope. I did not know what I would find; Roh was the last that I expected. *Liyo*, it is a *qujal*-ruled hold, and there are records there, in which Roh spent his time."

The oath hissed between her teeth. She opened her lips to say something; and then, for they were rounding the turn of a hill, from the distance came a sound carried on the wind, the sound of distress, of riot; and she stopped, gazing at a sullen glow among the hills.

"Ohtij-in," she said, and set heels to Siptah, flying down the road. The gelding dipped his head and hurled himself after; Vanye bent, ignoring the pain of his side, and rode, round the remembered bendings of the road, turn after turn as the shouting came nearer.

And suddenly the height of Ohtij-in hove into view, where the inner court blazed with light and roiling smoke through the riven gates, where black, diminutive figures struggled amid the fires.

Shadow-shapes huddled beside the road, that became women and ragged children, bundles and baggage. The gray horse thundered near them, sent the wretched folk shrieking aside, and the black plunged after.

Into the chaos of the inner court they rode, where fire had ravaged the shelters, rolling clouds of bitter smoke up into the rainy sky, where dead animals lay and many a corpse besides, among them both dark-haired and white, both men and halflings. At the keep gate, against the wall, a remnant of the guard was embattled with the peasants, and heaped up dead there thicker than anywhere else.

Men scattered from the hooves of the gray horse, shrieks and screams as the witch-sword left its sheath and flared into opal light more terrible than the fires, with that darkness howling at its tip. A weapon flew; the darkness drank it, and it vanished.

And the guard who had cast it fled, dying on the spears of the ragged attackers. It was the last resistance. The others threw down their arms and were cast to their faces by their captors, down in the mire and blood of the yard.

"Morgen!" the ragged army hailed her, raising their weapons. *"Angharan! Angharan!"* Vanye sat the gelding beside her as folk crowded round them with awed hysteria in their faces, he and his nervous horse touched by scores of trembling hands as they touched Siptah, rashly coming too near the unsheathed blade; shying from it, they massed the more closely about him, her companion. He endured it, realizing that he had been absorbed into the fabric of legends that surrounded Morgaine kri Chya—that he himself had become a thing to frighten children and cause honest men to shudder—that they had condemned him to all he had suffered, refusing to tell to his liege what they surely had known; and that those of Ohtij-in would lately have killed him.

He did not strike, though he trembled with the urge to do so. He still feared them, who for the hour hailed him and surrounded him with their insane adoration.

"Angharan!" they shouted. "Morgaine! Morgaine! Morgaine!"

Morgaine carefully sheathed *Changeling*, extinguishing its fire, and slid to the ground amid that press, men pushing at each other to make way for her. "Take the horses," she bade a man who approached her with less fear than the others, and then she turned her attention to the keep. There was silence made in the courtyard at last, an exhausted hush. She walked through their midst to the steps of the keep, *Changeling* crosswise in her hands, that it could be drawn in an instant. There she stood, visible to them all, and ragged and bloody men came and paid her shy, awkward courtesies.

Vanye dismounted, took up her saddle kit, that she would never leave behind her, and fended off those that offered help, no difficult matter. Men fled his displeasure, terrified.

Morgaine stayed for him, her foot on the next step until he had begun to ascend them, then passed inside. Vanye slung the saddlebag over his shoulder and walked after, up the steps and into the open gateway, past the staring dead face of the gatekeeper, who lay sprawled in the shadows inside.

Men took up torches, leading their way. Vanye shuddered

at what he saw in the spiral halls, the dead both male and female, both *qujal* and guiltless human servants, the ravaged
treasures of Ohtij-in that littered the halls. He kept walking,
up the spiralling core that would figure thereafter in his
nightmares, limping after Morgaine, who walked sword in
hand.

She will finish it, Roh had prophesied of her, *end all hope
for them. That is what she has come to do.*

Chapter Eleven

||||||||||||||||||||||||||||||||||||||||||||||||||

In the lord's hall too there was chaos, bodies lying where they had fallen. Even the white dog was dead by the hearth, in a pool of blood that stained the carpets and the stones, and flowed to mingle with that of its master and mistress. A knot of servants huddled in the corner for protection, kneeling.

And in the other corner men were gathered, rough and ragged folk, who held prisoner three of the house guard, white-haired halflings, stripped of their masking helms, bound, and surrounded by peasant weapons.

Vanye stopped, seeing that, and the sudden warmth of the fire hit him, making breath difficult; he caught for balance against the door frame as Morgaine strode within the room and looked about.

"Get the dead out of the hold," she said to the ragged men who awaited her orders. "Dispose of them. Is their lord among them?"

The eldest man made a helpless gesture. "No knowing," he said, in an accent difficult to penetrate.

"*Liyo*," Vanye offered, from the doorway, "a man named Kithan is in charge of Ohtij-in, Hetharu's brother. I know him by sight."

"Stay by me," she ordered curtly; and to the others: "Make search for him. Save all writings, wherever found, and bring them to me."

"Aye," said one of that company at whom she looked.

"What of the rest?" asked the eldest, a stooped and fragile man. "What of the other things? Be there else, lady?"

Morgaine frowned and looked about her, a warlike and evil figure amid their poor leather and rags; she looked on prisoners, on dead men, at the small rough-clad folk who depended on her for orders in this tumult, and shrugged. "What matter to me?" she asked. "What you do here is your own af-

fair, only so it does not cross me. A guard at our door, servants to attend us—" Her eyes swept to the corner where the
house servants cowered, marked men in brown livery who
had served the *qujal*. "Those three will suffice. And Haz, give
me three of your sons for guards at my quarters, and no
more will I ask of you tonight."

"Aye," said the old man, bowed in awkward imitation of a
lord's courtesy; he gestured to certain of the young men—
small folk, all of them, who approached Morgaine with lowered eyes, the tallest of them only as high as her shoulder,
but broad, powerful young men, for all that.

Marshlanders, Vanye reckoned them: *men of Aren.* They
spoke among themselves in a language he could not comprehend: men, but not of any kind that his land had known,
small and furtive and, he suddenly suspected, without any
law common to men that he knew. They were many, swarm-
ing the corridors, wreaking havoc; they had failed deliberately to find him for Morgaine—and yet she came back
among them as if she utterly trusted them. He became conscious that he was not armed, that he, who guarded her back,
had no weapon, and their lives were in the hands of these
small, elusive men, who could speak secrets among themselves.

A body brushed past, taller than the others, black-robed;
Vanye recoiled in surprise, then recognized the priest, who
was making for Morgaine. In panic he moved and seized the
priest, jerked at the robes, thrust him sprawling to the floor.

Morgaine looked down on the balding, white-haired priest,
whose lean face was rigid with terror, who shook and
trembled in Vanye's grip. In a sudden access of panic as
Morgaine stepped closer, the priest sought to rise, perhaps to
run, but Vanye held him firmly.

"Banish him to the court," Vanye said, remembering how
this same priest had lured him into Ohtij-in, promising safety;
how this priest had stood at Bydarra's elbow. "Let him try his
fortunes out there, among men."

"What is your name?" Morgaine asked of the priest.

"Ginun," the slight halfling breathed. He twisted to look up
at Vanye, dark-eyed, an aging man—and perhaps more man
than *qujal*. Fear trembled on his lips. "Great lord, many
would have helped you, many, many—*I* would have helped
you. Our lords were mistaken."

"Where were you?" Vanye asked, bitterness so choking him
he could hardly speak; he thrust the man free. "You knew

your lord, you knew what would happen when you led me to him."

"Take us with you," Ginun wept. "Take us with you. Do not leave us behind."

"Where," asked Morgaine in a chill voice, "do you suppose that we will go from here?"

"Through the Wells—to that other land."

The hope in the priest's eyes was terrible to see as he looked from one to the other of them, chin trembling, eyes suffused with tears. He lifted his hand to touch Morgaine, lost courage and touched Vanye's hand instead, a finger-touch, no more. "Please," he asked of them.

"Who has told you this thing?" Morgaine asked. "Who?"

"We have waited," the priest whispered hoarsely. "We have tended the Wells and we have waited. Take us through. Take us with you."

Morgaine turned her face away, not willing more to talk with him. The priest's shoulders fell and he began to shake with sobs; at Vanye's touch he looked up, his face that of a man under death sentence. "We have served the *khal,*" he protested, as if that should win favor of the conqueror of Ohtij-in. "We have waited, we have waited. Lord, speak to her. Lord, we would have helped you."

"Go away," said Vanye, drawing him to his feet. Unease moved in his heart when he looked on this priest who served devils, whose prayers were to the works of *qujal.* The priest drew back from his hands, still staring at him, still pleading with his eyes. "She has nothing to do with you and your kind," Vanye told the priest. "Nor do I."

"The Barrow-kings knew her," the priest whispered, his eyes darting past him and back again. He clutched convulsively at the amulets that hung among his robes. "The lord Roh came with the truth. It was the truth."

And the priest fled for the door, but Vanye seized him, hauled him about, others in the room giving back from him. The priest struggled vainly, frail, desperate man. *"Liyo,"* Vanye said in a quiet voice, fearful of those listening about them; prepared to strike the priest silent upon the instant. *"Liyo,* do not let him go. This priest will do you harm if he can. I beg you listen to me."

Morgaine looked on him, and on the priest. "Brave priest," she said in a voice still and clear, in the hush that had fallen in the room. "Fwar!"

A man came from the corner where the house guards were

held, a taller man than most, near Morgaine's height.
Square-faced he was, with a healing slash that ran from right
cheek to left chin, across both lips. Vanye knew him at once,
him that had ridden the gelding into the courtyard—the face
that had glared sullenly up at him. Such a look he received
now; the man seemed to have no other manner.

"Aye, lady?" Fwar said. His accent was plainer than that
of the others, and he bore himself boldly, standing straight.

"Have your kinsmen together," Morgaine said, "and find
the *khal* that survive. I want no killing of them, Fwar. I want
them set in one room, under guard. And you know by now
that I mean what I say."

"Aye," Fwar answered, and frowned. The face might have
been ordinary once. No more; it was a mask in which one
most saw the eyes, and they were hot and violent. "For some
we are too late."

"I care not who is to blame," Morgaine said. "I hold you,
alone, accountable to me."

Fwar hesitated, then bowed, started to leave.

"And, Fwar—"

"Lady?"

"Ohtij-in is a human hold now. I have kept my word.
Whoever steals and plunders now—steals from you."

This thought went visibly through Fwar's reckoning, and
other men in the room stood attentive and sobered.

"Aye," Fwar said.

"Lady," said another, in a voice heavy with accent, "what
of the stores of grain? Are we to distribute—?"

"Is not Haz your priest?" she asked. "Let your priest divide
the stores. It is your grain, your people. Ask me no further
on such matters. Nothing here concerns me. Leave me."

There was silence, dismay.

One of the marshlanders pushed at the *qujalin* guards,
directing them to the door. In their wake went others, Fwar,
Haz; there were left only Haz's three sons, claimed as guards,
and the weeping priest, Ginun, and the three servants, who
knelt cowering in the far corner.

"Show me," said Morgaine to the servants, "where are the
best lodgings with a solid door and some secure room nearby
where we can lodge this priest for his own protection."

She spoke softly with them. One moved, and the others
gathered courage, kneeling facing her, eyes downcast.
"There," said the oldest of them, himself no more than a

youth, and pointed toward the door that led inward, away
from the central corridor.

There was a small, windowless storeroom opposite a lordly
hall. Here Morgaine bade the priest disposed, with a bar
across that door, and that chained, and the door visible by
those who would guard their own quarters. It was Vanye's to
put the priest inside, and he did so, not ungently.

He hated the look of the priest's eyes as he was set within
that dark place, forbidden a light lest he do himself and others harm with it. The priest's terror fingered at nightmares of
his own, and he hesitated at closing the door.

Priest of devils, who would have worshipped at Morgaine's
feet, an uncleanness that attached itself to them, saying things
it was not good to hear, Vanye loathed the man, but that a
man should fear the dark, and being shut within, alone—this
he understood.

"Keep still," he warned Ginun last, the guards out of hearing. "You are safer here, and you will be safe so long as you
do keep still."

The priest was still staring at him when he closed the door,
his thin face white and terrified in the shadow. Vanye
dropped the bar and locked the chain through it—made haste
to turn his back on it, as on a private nightmare, remembering the roof of the tower of his prison—Roh's words, stored
up in this priest, waiting to break forth. He thought in agony
that he should see to it that the priest never spoke—that he,
ilin, should take that foulness on his own soul and never tell
Morgaine, never burden her honor with knowing it.

He was not such a man; he could not do it. And he did
not know whether this in him was virtue or cowardice.

The sons of Haz had taken up their posts at the door.
Morgaine awaited him in the hall beyond. He went to her,
into the chambers that had been some great lord's, and
dropped the saddlebags that he had carried onto the stones of
the hearth, staring about him.

More bodies awaited them: tapestries rent, bodies of men-
at-arms and the one-time lords lying amid shattered crystal
and overturned chairs. Vanye knew them. One was the body
of an old woman; another was that of one of the elder lords,
he that had made most grudging obeisance to Hetharu.

"See to it," Morgaine said sharply to the servants. "Re-
move them."

And while this was being attended, she righted a heavy chair and put it near the fire that still blazed in the hearth for its former owners, extended her legs to it, booted ankles crossed, paying no attention to the grisly task that went on among the servants. *Changeling* she set point against the floor and leaning by her side, and gave a long sigh.

Vanye averted his eyes from what passed in the room. Too much, too many of such pathetic dead: he had been of the warriors, but of a land where men fought men who chose to fight, who went armed, in notice of such intention. He did not want to remember the things that he had seen in Ohtij-in, alone or in her company.

And somewhere in Ohtij-in was Myya Jhirun, lost in this chaos, hidden or dead or the possession of some rough-handed marshlander. He thought of that, sick at heart, weighed his own exhaustion, the hazard of the mob outside, who spoke a language he could not understand, but he was obliged. For other wretched folk within the hold, for other women as unfortunate, he had no power to stop what happened—only for Jhirun, who had done him kindness, who had believed him when he said he would take her from Ohtij-in.

"*Liyo*," he said, and dropped to his knees at the fireside, by Morgaine. His voice shook, reaction to things already past, but he had no shame for that; they were both tired. "*Liyo*, Jhirun is here somewhere. By your leave I am going to go and do what I can to find her. I owe her."

"No."

"*Liyo*—"

She stared into the fire, her tanned face set, her white hair still wet from the rain outside. "Thee will go out in the courtyard and some Shiua will put a knife in thy back. No. Enough."

He thrust himself to his feet, vexed by her protection of him, exhausted beyond willingness to debate his feelings with her. He started for the door, reckoning that she had expressed her objection and that was the sum of it. He was going, nonetheless. He had seen to her welfare, and she knew it.

"*Ilin*," her voice rang out after him. "I gave thee an order."

He stopped, looked at her: it was a stranger's voice, cold and foreign to him. She was surrounded by men he did not know, by intentions he no longer understood. He stared at her, a tightness closing about his heart. It was as if she, like the land, had changed.

"I do not need to reason with you," she said.

"Someone," he said, "should reason with you."

There was long silence. She sat and stared at him while he felt the cold grow in her.

"I will have your belongings searched for," she said, "and you may take the horse, and the Hiua girl, if she is still alive, and you may go where you will after that."

She meant it. Outrage trembled through him. Almost, almost he spun on his heel and defied her—but there was not even anger in her voice, nothing against which he could argue later, no hope that it was unthought or unmeant. There was only utter weariness, a hollowness that was beyond reaching, and if he left, there would be none to reach her, none.

"I do not know," he said, "to what I have taken oath. I do not recognize you."

Her eyes remained focused somewhere past him, as if she had already dismissed him.

"You cannot send me away," he cried at her, and his hoarse voice broke, robbing him of dignity.

"No," she agreed without looking at him. "But while you stay, you do not dispute my orders."

He let go a shaking breath, and came to where she sat, knelt down on the hearthstones and ripped off the cloak she had lent him, laid it aside and stared elsewhere himself until he thought that he could speak without losing his self-control.

She needed him. He convinced himself that this was still true; and her need was desperate and unfair in its extent and therefore she would not order him to stay, not on her terms. Jhirun, he thought, would be on his conscience so long as he lived; but Morgaine—Morgaine he could not leave.

"May I," he asked finally, quietly, "send one of the servants to see if he can find her?"

"No."

He gave a desperate breath of a laugh, hoping that it was an unthought reaction in her, that she would relent in an instant, but laugh and hope died together when he looked at her directly and saw the coldness still in her face. "I do not understand," he said. "I do not understand."

"When you took oath to me," she said in a thin, hushed voice, "one grace you asked of me that I have always granted so far as I could: to remain untouched by the things I use

and the things I do. Will you not grant that same grace to
this girl?"

"You do not understand. *Liyo,* she was a prisoner; they
took her elsewhere. She may be hurt. The women out
there—they are a prey to the marshlanders and the mob in
the court. Whatever else, you are a woman. Can you not find
the means to help her?"

"She may be hurt. If you would heal her, leave my service
and see to it. If not, have mercy on her and leave her alone."
She lapsed into silence for a moment, and her gray eyes
roamed the room, with its torn tapestries and shattered
treasures. From the courtyard there was still shouting and
screaming, and her glance wandered to the windows before
she looked back to him. "I have done what I had to do," she
said in an absent, deathly voice. "I have loosed the Barrows
and the marshlands on Shiuan because it was a means to
reach this land most expediently, with force to survive. I do
not lead them. I only came among them. I take shelter here
only until it is possible to move on. I do not look at what I
leave behind me."

He listened, and something inside him shuddered, not at
the words, which deserved it, but at the tone of them. She
was lying; he hoped with all his heart that in this one thing
he understood her, or he understood nothing at all. And to
rise now, to walk out that door and leave her, took something
he did not possess. In this, too, he did not know whether it
was courage or cowardice.

"I will stay," he said.

She stared at him, saying nothing. He grew afraid, so
strange and troubled her look was. There were shadows
beneath her eyes. He reckoned that she had not slept well,
had rested little in recent days, with no companion to guard
her sleep among strangers, with no one to fill the silence with
which she surrounded herself, implacable in her purpose and
disinterested in others' desires.

"I will make discreet inquiry," she said at last. "It may be
that I can do something to have her found without finding
her . . . only so you know clearly what the conditions are."

He heard the brittleness in her voice, knew what it masked,
and bowed, in shaken gratitude, touched his brow to the
hearthstones, sat up again.

"There is surely a bed to be had," she said, "and an hour
or more before I shall be inclined to need it."

He looked beyond her, to the open arch of the shadowed next room, where the servants had begun stirring about, the removal of the former owners completed. There was a light somewhere within, the opening and closing of cabinets, the rustle of fabrics. A warm bed: he longed toward it, exhausted—luxury that he seldom knew, and far different from the things he had expected at the end of this ugly day.

It was far different, he thought, from what many others knew this night: Jhirun, if she still lived, Kithan, bereft of power, Roh—fled into the storm and the flood this night, in his private nightmare that centered upon Morgaine—Roh, with Abarais before him and the chance of defeating them.

But Morgaine gazed down on him now with a face that at last he knew, tired, inexpressibly tired, and sane.

"You take first rest," he said. "I shall sit by the fire and keep an eye on the servants."

She regarded him from half-lidded eyes, shook her head. "Go as I told you," she said. "I have eased your conscience, so far as I can. Go on. You have given me matters to attend yet; now let me attend them."

He gathered himself up, almost fell in doing it, his feet asleep, and he steadied himself against the mantel, looked at her apologetically. Her gaze, troubled and thoughtful, gave him benediction; and he bowed his head in gratitude.

Nightmares surrounded her at times. There was one proceeding in the courtyard and elsewhere in the hold this night. *Stop it,* he wanted to plead with her. *Take command of them and stop it. You can do it, and will not.*

She had led an army once; ten thousand men had followed her before his age, and had been swept away into oblivion, lost. Clans and kingdoms had perished, dynasties ended, Andur-Kursh plunged into a hundred years of poverty and ruin.

So clan Yla had perished in her service, to the last man, lost in the void of Gates; so passed much of Chya, and many a man of Nhi and Myya and Ris. Horrid suspicion nagged at him.

He looked back at her, where she sat, a lonely figure before the fire. He opened his mouth to speak to her, to go back and tell her what things he had begun to fear of this land, to hear her say that they were not so.

There were the servants, who would overhear and repeat things elsewhere. He dared not speak, not before them. He turned away toward the other room.

There was the softness of a down mattress, the comfort of fabrics smooth and soft; of cleanliness, that most of all.

She would call him, he reckoned, in only a little while; there was not that much of the night remaining. He slept mostly dressed, in clean clothing that he had discovered in a chest, the former lord as tall as he and no whit slighter, save in the length of arm and breadth of shoulder. The fine cloth rested easily on his hurts; it was good to feel it, to have stripped away the stubble of days without a razor, and to rest with his hair damp from a thorough scrubbing, . . . in a place warm and soft, fragrant with a woman's care, be she servant or murdered *qujalin* lady.

He wrested his mind from such morbid thoughts, determined not to remember where he was, or what things he had seen outside. He was safe. Morgaine watched his sleep, as he would watch hers in turn. He cast himself into trusting oblivion, determined that nothing would rob him of this rest that he had won.

Small sounds disturbed him now and then; once the opening of the outer door alarmed him, until he heard Morgaine's soft voice speaking calmly with someone, and that door then close, and her light tread safely in the room next his. Once he heard her in the room with him, searching the closets and chests, and knew that soon enough she would call him to his watch; he headed himself back into a few treasured moments of sleep. He heard the splash of water in the bath, the room mostly dark save for a single lamp there and the fireplace in the next room; grateful for the small remaining time, pleased to know she also took the leisure for such comforts as he had enjoyed, he shut his eyes again.

And the rustle of cloth woke him, the sight of a woman, *qujal*, in a white gown, ghost-pale in the darkness. He did not know her for an instant, and his heart crashed against his ribs in panic, thinking murder, and of the dead. But Morgaine drew back the coverlet on her side of the great bed, and he, with some embarrassment, prepared to quit the other before she must bid him do so.

"Go back to sleep," she said, confounding him. "The servants are out and the door is bolted on our side. There is no need for either of us to stay awake, unless thee is overnice. I am not."

And in her hand was *Changeling*, that always slept with her; she laid it atop the coverlet, a thing fell and dangerous, in the valley that would be between them. Vanye rested very

still, felt the mattress give as she settled beside him and drew
the covers over her, heard the gentle sigh of her breath.

And felt the weight of *Changeling*, that rested between.

He held no more urge to sleep, his heart still beating rapidly. It was that she had startled him, he told himself at
first—he found it disturbing that for that single instant he
had not known her—*frost-fair, frost-fair*, an old ballad sang
of her, and like frost, burning to the touch. It was kindness
that she had not displaced him to the hearthside; it was like
her that she was considerate in small things. Perhaps she
would not have rested, having sent him to a pallet on the
hard stone. Perhaps it was amends for the harsh words she
had used earlier.

But it was not the same as campfires they had shared,
when they had shared warmth, both armored, companions in
the dark, one always waking in dread of ambush. He listened
to her breathing, felt the small movements that she made,
and tried to distract his mind to other thoughts, staring at the
dark rafters. He cursed silently, half a pious prayer, wondering how she would understand it if he did withdraw to the
hearthside.

Woman that she was, she might not have thought overmuch of the gesture; perhaps she did not understand.

Or perhaps, he thought in misery, she wished him inclined
to defy that barrier, and tormented him deliberately.

She had asked him why he came with her. *Your charity*,
he had told her lightly, *was always more generous than my
brother's.* The remark had stung her; he wished to this day
that he had asked why, that he understood why it had angered her, or why in all that bitter day it had seemed to set
her at odds with him.

He was human; he was not sure that she was. He had been
a godfearing man; and he was not sure what she was. Logic
did not avail, thus close to her. All Roh's arguments collapsed, thus close to her; and he knew clearly what had
drawn him this side of Gates, although he still shuddered to
look into her gray and alien eyes, or to lie thus close to her;
the shudder melded into quite another feeling, and he was
horrified at himself, who could be moved by her, his liege,
and thousandfold murderer, and *qujal*, at least to the eye.

He was lost, he thought, and possessed only this resolve,
that he tried to remember that he was Kurshin, and Nhi, and
that she was cursed in his land. Half that men told of her
were lies; but much that was as terrible he had seen himself.

And that logic likewise was powerless.

He knew finally that it was neither reason nor virtue that stood in his way, but that did he once attempt that cold barrier between, she might lose all trust for him. *Ilin*, she had said once, hurtfully, *thee has a place—Ilin*, she had said this night, *I have given thee an order*.

Pride forbade. He could not be treated thus; he dreaded to think what torment he could create for them, she trying to deal with him as a man, he trying to be both man and servant. She had a companion older than he, a demanding thing, and evil, that lay as a weight against his side; no other could be closer than that.

And if she had regard for him, he thought, she surely sensed the misery that she could cause him, and kept him at a distance, until this night, that she, over-practical, over-kindly, omitted to send him to his place.

He wondered for whose sake she had placed the sword between, for her peace of mind or for his.

Chapter Twelve

||||||||||||||||||||||||||||||||||||||||||||||||||||

Something fell, a weight upon the floor.

Vanye wakened, flung an arm wide, to the realization that Morgaine's place beside him was vacant and cold. White daylight shone in the next room.

He sprang up, still half-blind, fighting clear of the sheets, and stumbled to the doorway. He blinked at Morgaine, who was dressed in her accustomed black armor and standing by the open outer door. A mass of gear—armor—rested on the hearthside; it had not been there the night before. Books and charts were heaped on the floor in a flood of daylight from the window, most of them open and in disorder. Servants were even then bringing in food, dishes steaming and savory, setting gold plates and cups on the long table.

And just outside the door, in conversation with Morgaine, stood a different set of guards: taller, slimmer men than the run of marshlanders. She was speaking with them quietly, giving orders or receiving reports.

Vanye ran a hand through his hair, let go his breath, deciding that there was nothing amiss. He ached; his lacerated wrists hurt to bend after a night's rest, and his feet—he looked down, grimacing at the ugly sores. He limped back into the bedroom and sought a fresh shirt from the supply in the wardrobe, and found a pair of boots that he had set aside the night before, likewise from the wardrobe. He sat in the shadow, on the bed, working the overly tight boots onto his sore feet, and listened to Morgaine's voice in the next room, and those of the men with whom she spoke. He did not make sense of it; the distance was too great and their accent was difficult for him. It seemed awkward to go into the other room, breaking in upon her business. He waited until he had heard Morgaine dismiss them, and heard the servants finish their arranging of breakfast and leave. Only then he arose

and ventured out to see what matters were between them in
cold daylight.

"Sit," she offered him, bidding him to the table; and with a
downcast expression and a shrug: "It is noon; it is still rain-
ing occasionally, and the scouts report that there is no
abating of the flood at the crossing. They give some hope that
matters will improve tonight, or perhaps tomorrow. This they
have from the Shiua themselves."

Vanye began to take the chair that she offered, but when
he drew it back to sit down, he saw the stain on the carpet
and stopped. She looked at him. He pushed the chair in
again, then walked round the table and took the opposite one,
not looking down, trying to forget the memory of the night.
Quietly he moved his plate across the narrow table.

She was seated. He helped himself after her, spooned food
onto gold plates and sipped at the hot and unfamiliar drink
that eased his sore throat. He ate without a word, finding it
wildly incongruous to be sharing table with Morgaine,
stranger than to have shared a bed. He felt it improper to sit
at table in her presence: to do so belonged to another life,
when he had been a lord's son, and knew hall manners and
not the ashes of the hearthside or the campfire of an outlaw.

She also maintained silence. She was not given to much
conversation, but there was too much strangeness about them
in Ohtij-in that he could find that silence comfortable.

"They do not seem to have fed you well," she remarked,
when he had disposed of a third helping, and she had only
then finished her first plate.

"No," he said, "they did not."

"You slept more soundly than ever I have seen you."

"You might have waked me," he said, "when you wakened."

"You seemed to need the rest."

He shrugged. "I am grateful," he said.

"I understand that your lodging here was not altogether
comfortable."

"No," he agreed, and took up his cup, pushing the plate
away. He was uneasy in this strange humor of hers, that discussed him with such persistence.

"I understand," Morgaine said, "that you killed two
men—one of them the lord of Ohtij-in."

He set the cup down in startlement, held it in his fingers
and turned it, swirling the amber liquid inside, his heart
beating as if he had been running. "No," he said. "That is not

so. One man I killed, yes. But the lord Bydarra—Hetharu murdered him: his own son—murdered him, alone in that room with me; and I would have been hanged for it last night, that at the least. The other son, Kithan—he may know the truth or not; I am not sure. But it was very neatly done, *liyo*. There is none but Hetharu and myself that know for certain what happened in that room."

She pushed her chair back, turning it so that she faced him at the corner of the table; and she leaned back, regarding him with a frowning speculation that made him the more uncomfortable. "Then," she said, "Hetharu left in Roh's company, and took with him the main strength of Ohtij-in. Why? Why such a force?"

"I do not know."

"This time must have been terrible for you."

"Yes," he said at last, because she left a silence to be filled.

"I did not find Jhirun Ela's-daughter. But while I searched for her, Vanye, I heard a strange thing."

He thought that the color must long since have fled his face. He took a drink to ease the tightness in his throat. "Ask," he said.

"It is said," she continued, "that she, like yourself, was under Roh's personal protection. That his orders kept you both in fair comfort and safety until Bydarra was murdered."

He set the cup down again and looked at her, remembering that any suspicion for her was sufficient motive to kill. But she sat at breakfast with him, sharing food and drink, while she had known these things perhaps as early as last night, before she lay down to sleep beside him.

"If you thought that you could not trust me," he said, "you would be rid of me at once. You would not have waited."

"Is thee going to answer, Vanye? Or is thee going to go on evading me? Thee has omitted many things in the telling. On thy oath—on thy oath, Nhi Vanye, no more of it."

"He—Roh—found welcome here, at least with one faction of the house. He saw to it that I was safe, yes; but not so comfortable, not so comfortable as you imagine, *liyo*. And later—when Hetharu seized power—then, too—Roh intervened."

"Do you know why?"

He shook his head and said nothing. Suppositions led in many directions that he did not want to explore with her.

"Did you speak with him directly?"

"Yes." There was long silence. He felt out of place even to

be sitting in a chair, staring at her eye to eye, when that was
not the situation between them and never had been.

"Then thee has some idea."

"He said—it was for kinship's sake."

She said nothing.

"He said," he continued with difficulty, "that if you—if
you were lost, then—I think he would have sought a Claiming . . ."

"Did you suggest it?" she asked; and perhaps the revulsion
showed on his face, for her look softened at once to pity.
"No," she judged. "No, thee would not." And for a moment
she gazed on him with fearsome intentness, as if she prepared
something from which she had long refrained. "Thee is ignorant," she said, "and in that ignorance, valuable to him."

"I would not help him against you."

"You are without defense. You are ignorant, and without
defense."

Heat rose to his face, anger. "Doubtless," he said.

"I could remedy that, Vanye."

*Become what I am, accept what I serve, bear what I bear
. . .*

The heat fled, leaving chill behind. "No," he said. "No."

"Vanye—for your own sake, listen to me."

Hope was in her eyes, utterly intense: never before had she
pleaded with him for anything. He had come with her: perhaps then she had begun to hope for this thing that she had
never won of him. He remembered then what he had for a
time forgotten, the difference there was between Morgaine
and what possessed Chya Roh: that Morgaine, having the
right to order, had always refrained.

It was the thing she wanted most, that alone might give her
some measure of peace; and she refrained.

"Liyo," he whispered, "I would do anything, anything you
set me to do. Ask me things that I can do."

"Except this," she concluded, in a tone that pierced his
heart.

"Liyo—anything else."

She lowered her eyes, like a curtain drawn finally between
them, lifted them again. There was no bitterness, only a deep
sorrow.

"Be honest with me," he said, stung. "You nearly died in
the flood. You nearly died, with whatever you seek to do left
undone; and this preys on your mind. It is not for my sake
that you want this. It is for yourself."

Again the lowering of the eyes; and she looked up again. "Yes," she said, without a trace of shame. "But know too, Vanye, that my enemies will never leave you in peace. Ignorance cannot save you from that. So long as you are accessible to them, you will never be safe."

"It is what you said: that one grace you always gave me, that you never burdened me with your *qujalin* arts; and for that, for that I gave you more than ever my oath demanded of me. Do you want everything now? You can order. I am only *ilin*. Order, and I will do what you say."

There was warfare in the depths of her eyes, yea and nay equally balanced, desperately poised. "O Vanye," she said softly, "thee is asking me for virtue, which thee well knows I lack."

"Then order," he said.

She frowned darkly, and stared elsewhere.

"I tried," he said in that long silence, "to reach Abarais, to wait for you. And if I could have used Roh to set me there—I would have gone with him—to stop him."

"With what?" she asked, a derisive laugh; but she turned toward him again, and even yet her look pleaded with him. "If I were lost, what could you have done?"

He shrugged, searched up the most terrible thing that he could envision. "Casting *Changeling* within a Gate: that would suffice, would it not?"

"If you could set hands on it. And that would destroy you; and destroy only one Gate." She took *Changeling* from her side and laid it across the arms of her chair. "It was made for other use."

"Let be," he asked of her, for she eased the blade fractionally from its sheath. He edged back, for he trusted her mind, but not that witch-blade; and it was not her habit to draw it ever unless she must. She stopped; it lay half-exposed, no metal, but very like a shard of crystal, its magics restrained until it should be wholly unsheathed.

She held it so, the blade's face toward him, while opal fires swirled softly in the *qujalin* runes on its surface. "For anyone who can read this," she said, "here is the making and unmaking of Gates. And I think thee begins to know what this is worth, and what there is to fear should Roh take it. To bring this within his reach would be the most dangerous thing you could do."

"Put it away," he asked of her.

"Vanye: to read the runes—would thee learn simply that?

Only that much—simply to read the *qujalin* tongue and speak it. Is that too much to ask?"

"Do you ask it for yourself?"

"Yes," she said.

He averted his eyes from it, and nodded consent.

"It is necessary," she said. "Vanye, I will show you; and take up *Changeling* if ever I am lost. Knowing what you will know, the sword will teach you after—until you have no choice, as I have none." And after a moment: "*If* I am lost. I do not mean that it should happen."

"I will do this," he answered, and thereafter sat a cold hardness in him, like a stone where his heart had been. It was the end of what he had begun when he had followed her; he realized that he had always known it.

She rammed the dragon sword back into its sheath and took it in the curve of her arm—nodded toward the fireside, where armor lay, bundled in a cloak. "Yours," she said. "Some of the servants worked through the night on it. Go dress. I do not trust this place. We will settle the other matter later. We will talk of it."

"Aye," he agreed, glad of that priority in things, for as she was, she might win yet more of him, piece by piece: perhaps she knew it.

And there was an ease in her manner that had not been there in many a day, something that had settled at peace with her. He was glad for that, at least. He took it for enough; and arose from the table and went to the fireside—heard her rise and knew her standing near him as he knelt and unfolded the cloak that wrapped his recovered belongings.

His armor, familiar helm that had been in her keeping: he was surprised and pleased that she had kept it, as if sentiment had moved her, as if she had hoped to find him again. There was his mail, cleaned and saved from rust, leather replaced: he received that back with great relief, for it was all he owned in the world save the black horse and his saddle. He gathered it up, knowing the weight of it as he knew that of his own body.

And out of it fell a bone-handled dagger: Roh's—an ill dream recurring. It lay on the stones, accusing him. For one terrible instant he wondered how much in truth she knew of what had passed.

"Next time," she said from behind him, "resolve to use it."

His hand went to his brow, to bless himself in dismay; he hesitated, then sketchily completed the gesture, and was the more disquieted afterward. He gathered up the bundle, dagger and all, and carried it into the other room where he might have privacy, where he might both dress and breathe in peace.

He would die in this forsaken land the other side of Gates, he thought, jerking with trembling fingers at the laces of his clothing; that much had been certain from the beginning— but that became less terrible than what prospect opened before him, that little by little he would lose himself, that she would have all. Murder had sent him to her, brother-killing; *ilin*-service was just condemnation. But he reckoned himself, what he had been, and what he had become; and the man that he was now was no longer capable of the crime that he had done. It was not just, what lay before him.

He set himself into his armor, leather and metal links in which he had lived the most part of his youth; and though it was newly fitted and most of the leather replaced, it settled about his body familiar as his own skin, a weight that surrounded him with safety, with habits that had kept him alive where his living had not been likely. It no longer seemed protection.

Until you have no choice, Morgaine had warned him, *as I have none.*

He slipped Roh's dagger into the sheath at his belt, a weight that settled on his heart likewise: this time it was with full intent to use it.

A shadow fell across the door. He looked up. Morgaine came with yet another gift for him, a longsword in its sheath.

He turned and took it from her offering hands—bowed and touched it to his brow as a man should when accepting such a gift from his liege. It was *qujalin,* he did not doubt it: *qujalin* more than *Changeling* itself, which at least had been made by men. But with it in his hands, for the first time in their journey through this land, he felt a stir of pride, the sense that he had skill that was of some value to her. He drew the blade half from the sheath, and saw that it was a good double-edged blade, clean of *qujalin* runes. The length was a little more than that of a Kurshin longsword, and the blade was a little thinner; but it was a weapon he knew how to use.

"I thank you," he said.

"Stay armed. I want none of these folk drawing for your naked back; and it would be the back, with them. They are wolves, allies of chance and mutual profit."

He hooked it to his belt, pulled the ring on his shoulder belt and hooked that, settling it to a more comfortable position at his shoulder. Her words touched at something in him, a sudden, unbearable foreboding, that even she would say what she had said. He looked up at her. *"Liyo,"* he said in a low voice. "Let us go. Let us two, together . . . leave this place. Forget these men; be rid of them. Let us be out of here."

She nodded back toward the other room. "It is still misting rain out. We will go, tonight, when there is a chance the flood will ebb."

"Now," he insisted, and when he saw her hesitate: *"Liyo,* what you asked, I gave; give me this. I will go, now, I will find us a packhorse and some manner of tent for our comfort. . . . Better the cold and the rain than this place over our heads tonight."

She looked tempted, urgently tempted, struggling with reason. He knew the restlessness that chafed at her, pent here, behind rock and risen water. And for once he felt that urge himself, an instinct overwhelming, a dark that pressed at their heels.

She gestured again toward the room beyond. "The books . . . I have only begun to make sense of them . . ."

"Do not trust these men." Of a sudden all things settled together in his mind, taking form; and some were in those books; and more were pent in the shape of a priest, locked in the dark down the hall. She could be harmed by these things, these men. The human tide that lapped about the walls of Ohtij-in threatened her, no less than the *qujal*-lords.

"Go," she bade him suddenly. "Go. See to it. Quietly."

He snatched up his cloak, caught up his helm, and then paused, looking back at her.

Still he was uneasy—parted from her in this place; but he forebore to warn her more of these men, of opening the door to them: it was not his place to order her. He drew up the coif and settled his helm on, and did not stay to put on the cloak. He passed the door, between the new guards, and looked at those three with sullen misgivings—looked too down the hall, where the priest Ginun was imprisoned, without drink or food yet provided.

That too wanted tending. He dared not have the guards wait on that man, a priest of their own folk, treated thus. Something had to be done with the priest; he knew not what.

In haste he slung the heavy cloak about him and fastened

it as he passed the door out of the corridor, uneasy as he walked these rooms that were familiar to him under other circumstances—as he passed marshlanders, who turned and stared at him and made a sign he did not know. He entered the spiral at the core of the keep, passed others, feeling their stares at his back as he walked that downward corridor. Even armed, he did not feel safe or free here. Torches lit the place, a bracket at every doorway, profligate waste of them; and the smallish men of Aren came and went freely up and down the ramp, no few of them drunken, decked in finery incongruous among their peasant clothes. Here and there passed other men, tall and grim of manner, who did not mix with the marshlanders: Fwar's kindred, a hard-eyed lot; something wrathful abode in them, that touched at familiarity.

The Barrows and the marshlands, Morgaine had said, naming them that followed her; *Barrow-folk,* Vanye realized suddenly.

Myya.

Jhirun's kinsmen.

He hastened his pace, descending the core, the terror that breathed thickly in the air of this place now possessing a name.

The courtyard was quieter than the keep, a dazed quiet, the misting rain glistening on the paving stones, a few folk that might be Shiua or marshlanders moving about wrapped in cloaks and shawls. There was a woman with two children at her skirts: it struck him strangely that nowhere had there been children among the *qujal,* none that he had seen; and he did not know why.

The woman, the children, the others—stopped and looked at him. He was afraid for a moment, remembering the violence that had surged across these stones; but they showed no disposition to threaten him. They only watched.

He turned toward the pens and the stables, where their horses waited. Cattle lowed in the pens to his right, beasts well cared-for, better than the Shiua. The roofs of the shelters on his left were blackened, the windows eaten by fire. Folk still lived there; they watched him from doorways, furtively.

He looked behind him when he reached the stable doors, fearful that more might have gathered at his back; the same few stood in the distance, still watching him. He dismissed them from his concern and eased open the stable door, entered into that dark place, that smelled pleasantly of hay and horses.

It was a large, rambling structure, seeming to wind irregularly about the keep wall, with most of the stalls empty, save those in the first row. On the right side he counted nine, ten horses, mostly bay; and on the left, apart from the others, he saw Siptah's pale head, ears pricked, nostrils flaring at the presence of one he knew; in an empty stall farther stood a shadow that was his own Andurin gelding.

Racks at the end of the aisle held what harness remained: he saw what belonged to Siptah, and reckoned his own horse's gear would be near it. He delayed at the stalls, offered his hand to Siptah's questing nose, patted that great plate of a cheek, went further to assure himself his own horse was fit. The black lipped at his sleeve; he caught the animal by the mane and slapped it gently on the neck, finding that someone had been horseman enough to have rubbed both animals down, when he had not. He was glad of this: Kurshin that he was, he was not accustomed to leave his horse to another man's care. He checked feet and found them sound: a shoe had been reset, not of his doing; it had been well-done, and he found nothing of which to complain, though he searched for it.

And then he set himself to prepare them. There would be need of grain, that as much as the supplies they would need for themselves: their way was always too uncertain to travel without it. He searched the likely places until he had located the storage bins, and then cast about to see whether there was, amid all the gear remaining, a packsaddle. There was nothing convenient. At last he filled his own saddlebags with what he could, and took Morgaine's gear and his own, and slung it over the rails of the respective stalls, ready to saddle.

Something moved in the straw, in the shadows. At first he took it for one of the other horses, but it was close. The sudden set of the gelding's ears and the sound at once alarmed him: he whirled, reaching for the Honor-blade, wondering how many there were, and where.

"Lord," said a small voice out of the dark, a female voice, that trembled.

He stood still, set his back against the rails of the stall, though he knew the voice. In a moment she moved, and he saw a bit of white in the darkness at the racks, where the windows were closed.

"Jhirun," he hailed her softly.

She came, treading carefully, as if she were yet uncertain of him. She still wore her tattered skirt and blouse; her hair showed wisps of straw. She held to the rail nearest with one hand and kept yet some distance from him, standing as if her legs had difficulty in bearing her weight.

He slid the blade back into sheath, stepped under the uppermost rail and into the aisle. "We looked for you," he said.

"I stayed by the horses," she said in a thin voice. "I knew *she* had come. I did not know whether you were alive."

He let go a long breath, relieved to find this one nightmare an empty one. "You are safe. They are Hiua that have this place now: your own people."

She stayed silent for a long moment; her eyes went to the saddles on the rails, back again. "You are leaving."

He took her meaning, shook his head in distress. "Matters are different. There is no safety for you with us. I cannot take you."

She stared at him. Tears flooded her eyes; but suddenly there was such a look of violence there that he recalled how she had set out the marshland road, alone.

And that he must, having saddled the horses, go back to Morgaine and leave the animals in Jhirun's care, or deal with her in some fashion.

"At least," she said, "get me out of Ohtij-in."

He could not face her. He started to take up one of the saddles, to attend his business with the horses.

"Please," she said.

He looked back at her, eased the saddle back onto the rail. "I am not free," he said, "to give and take promises. You are Myya; you have forgotten a great deal in Hiuaj, or you would have understood by looking at me that I am no longer *uyo* and that I have no honor. You were mistaken to have believed me. I said what I had to say, because you left me no choice. I cannot take you with me."

She turned her back, and walked away; he thought for a moment that she was going back into the shadows to sit and weep for a while, and he would allow her that, before he decided what he must do with her.

But she did not return into the dark. She went to the harness rack and took bridle and saddle, tugging the gear into her arms and staggering with the weight of it. He swore, watching her come down the aisle toward him, dangling the girth in the foul straw and near to tripping on it, hard-breathing with the effort and with her tears.

He blocked her path and jerked it from her hands, cast it into the straw and cursed at her, and she stood empty-handed and stared up at him, her eyes blind with tears.

"At least when you go," she said, "you could give me help as far as the road. Or at least do not stop me. You have no right to do that."

He stood still. She bent, trying to pick up the saddle from the ground, and was shaking so that she had no strength in her hands.

He swore and took it from her, slung it up to the nearest rail. "Well enough," he conceded. "I will saddle a horse for you. And what you do then, that is your business. Choose one."

She stared at him, thin-lipped, and then walked to the stall halfway down, laid a hand on that rail that enclosed a bay mare. "I will take her."

He came and looked at the mare, that was deep enough of chest, but smallish. "There might be better," he said.

"This one."

He shook his head, reckoning that she would have what she wished, and that perhaps a girl whose experience of horses extended most to a small black pony judged her limits well enough. He did as she wished.

And with Jhirun's mare saddled, he returned to his own horse, and to Siptah—took meticulous pains with their own gear, that might have to stand a hard ride and few rests: he appropriated a coil of harness leather, and a braided leather rope as well; and at last he closed the stalls and prepared to leave.

"I have to go advise my lady," he told Jhirun, who waited by her mare. "We will come as quickly as possible. Something might delay us a little time, but not for long."

Anguish crossed her face: he frowned at it, turned all the same to leave, reckoning at least that the horses were safe while Jhirun had some gain from aiding them.

"No," Jhirun whispered after him, ran suddenly and caught his arm; he looked back, chilled at the terror in her face: a sense of ambush prickled about him.

"Lord," she whispered, "there is a man hiding here. Do not leave, do not leave me here."

He seized her arm so hard that she winced. "How many more? What have you arranged for me?"

"No," she breathed. "One. He—" With her head she gestured far off across the stalls, into the dark. "He is there. Do not leave me with him, not now, with the horses—Kithan. It is Kithan."

She stifled a cry; he opened his hand, realizing he had wrenched her arm, and she rubbed the injured wrist, making no attempt to run.

"When the attack came," she said, "he came here and could not get out. He has slept—I took a hayfork, and I came on him to kill him, but I was afraid. Now he will have heard us moving—he will come here when he thinks it safe, when you are gone."

He slipped the ring of his sword, drew it carefully from sheath. "You show me where," he said. "And if you are mistaken, Myya Jhirun i Myya—"

She shook her head. "I thought we were leaving," she whispered, through tears. "I thought it would be all right, no need, no need for killing—I do not want to—"

"Quiet," he said, and seized her wrist, pushing her forward. She began to lead him, as silently as possible, into the dark.

Small, square windows gave light within the stable, shafts of dusty light, and a maze of aisles and stalls, sheaves of straw, empty racks for harness. The building curved, irregularly, following the keep wall, and the aisles were likewise crooked, row upon row of box stalls, empty—a hay loft, a nesting-place for birds that fluttered wings and stirred restlessly.

Jhirun's hand touched his, cautioning. She pointed down a row of stalls, where the shadow was darkest. He began to go that way, drawing her with him, watching the stalls on either side of him, aware how easily it could prove ambush.

A white shape bolted at the end of the stalls, running. Vanye jerked at Jhirun's wrist, darted into a cross-aisle, into the next row.

The man raced—white hair flying—for a farther aisle. Vanye let Jhirun go, and ran, pursuing him, in time to see him scale a rail barrier and scramble for open windows. The lead was too great. The *qujal* disappeared outside, hurling himself through, as Vanye reached the stall railing.

He stood, cursing inwardly, whirled about on guard as a sound reached his ears; Jhirun came running to him. He let fall his sword arm.

And outside he heard the hue and cry, human hounds a-hunt, and Kithan loose for their quarry, the whole of Ohtij-in astir: they would not be long in taking him.

He swore, an oath that he had never used, and shook

Jhirun's fingers roughly from his arm and started back toward the front of the stable, she struggling along beside him, hard-breathing.

"Stay here," he said. "Mind the horses. I am going to Morgaine. We are leaving here as quickly as may be."

Chapter Thirteen

|||||||||||||||||||||||||||||||||||||||||||||||||||||||

There was chaos in the courtyard, men raced from doorways. Vanye walked through it, shouldered his way through a press that was coming out of the keep, folk giving back from him in fright when they saw him. He kept his sword, sheathed, in his left hand, and entered the halls of the keep, moving as quickly as he could without running. He would not run: there was panic enough ready to break loose, and he was known as Morgaine's servant.

He reached the lords' halls, high in the tower, crossed through to the inner chambers and startled the guards that were on watch there, who snatched at weapons and then confusedly moved out of his path, recognizing his right to pass. He flung the door open and slammed it behind him, for the first time daring draw the breath he needed.

Morgaine faced him—she standing by the window, her hand upon the sill. Distress was in her look. Distantly the cries of men could be heard from the courtyard below.

"Thee's stirred something?" she asked him.

"Kithan," he said. "*Liyo,* the horses are saddled, and we only need go—now, quickly. Someone will come into that stable and see things prepared if we wait overlong, and I do not think long farewells are fit for this place."

A cry went up, outside. She turned and leaned upon the sill, gazing down into the yard. "They have taken him," she said quietly.

"Let us go, *liyo.* Let us go from here, while there is time."

She turned toward him a second time, and there was a curious expression in her eyes: doubt. Panic rose in him. In one thing he had lied to her, and the lie gathered force, troubling all the peace that had grown between them.

"I do not think that it would be graceful of us," she said, "to try to pass them in the hall. They are bringing him into

177

the hold. Doubtless they are bringing him here. —So short a
time from my sight, Vanye, and so much difficulty. . . . Was
it a chance meeting?"

He drew breath, let it go quickly. "I swear to you. Listen
to me. There are things the lord Kithan can say that do not
bear saying, not before these men of yours. Do not question
him. Be rid of him, and quickly."

"What should I not ask him?"

He felt the edge in that question, and shook his head. "No.
Liyo, listen to me. Unless you would have all that Roh said
made common knowledge in Ohtij-in—avoid this. There can
be questions raised that you do not want asked. There is a
priest down the hall . . . and Shiua out in the court, and servants, and whatever *qujal* are still alive . . . that would raise
questions if they lost all care of their lives. Kithan will do
you no good. There is nothing he can say that you want to
hear."

"And was it a chance meeting, Vanye?"

"Yes," he cried, in a tone that shocked the silence after.

"That may be," she said after a moment. "But if you are
correct—then it would be well to know what he has said already."

"Are you ready," he asked her, "to leave upon the instant?"

"Yes," she said, and indicated the fireside, where her belongings were neatly placed; he had none.

Outside, in the halls, there was commotion. It was not long
in reaching them—the sounds of shouting, the heavy sound
of steps approaching.

A heavy hand rapped at the door. "Lady?" one asked from
outside.

"Let them in," Morgaine said.

Vanye opened it, and in his other hand only his thumb
held the sheath upon the longsword: a shake would free it.

Men were massed outside, a few of the marshlanders; but
chief among them was the scarred Barrows-man, Fwar, with
his kinsmen. Vanye met that sullen face with utter coldness,
and stepped back because Morgaine had bidden it, because
they were hers—violent men unlike the Aren-folk: he surmised seeing them now who had done most of the slaughter
in Ohtij-in, that were murder to be ordered, they would enjoy
it.

And among them, from their midst, they thrust the dishev-
eled figure of the *qujal*-lord, thin and fragile-seeming in their

rough hands. Blood dabbled the satin front of Kithan's brocade garment, and his white hair was loose and wild, matted
with blood from a cut on his brow.

Fwar cast the dazed halfling to the floor. Morgaine settled
herself in a chair, leaned back, *Changeling* balanced on her
knee, under her hand; she watched calmly as the former lord
of Ohtij-in gathered himself to rise, but they kept him on his
knees. Vanye, moving to his proper place at Morgaine's
shoulder, saw the force of the *qujal's* gray eyes, no longer full
of dreams, no longer distant, but filled with heat and hate.

"He is Kithan," said Fwar, his scarred lips smiling.

"Let him up," Morgaine said; and such hate there was in
Kithan that Vanye extended his sheathed sword between,
cautioning him; but the captured halfling had some sense. He
stumbled to his feet and made a slight bow of the head, homage to realities.

"I shall have you put with the others," Morgaine said
softly. "Certain others of your folk do survive, in the higher
part of this tower."

"For what?" Kithan asked, with a glance about him.

Morgaine shrugged. "For whatever these men allow."

The elegant young lordling stood trembling, wiped a bloody
strand of hair from his cheek. His eyes strayed to Vanye's,
who returned him no gentleness, and back again. "I do not
understand what is happening," he said. "Why have you done
these things to us?"

"You were unfortunate," said Morgaine.

The arrogance of that answer seemed to take Kithan's
breath away. He laughed after a moment, aloud and bitterly.
"Indeed. And what do you gain of such allies as you have?
What when you have won?"

Morgaine frowned, gazing at him. "Fwar," she said, "I do
not think it any profit to hold him or his people."

"We can deal with them," said Fwar.

"No," she said. "You have Ohtij-in; and you have my order, Fwar. Will you abide by it, and not kill them?"

"If that is your order," said Fwar after a moment, but
there was no pleasure in it.

"So," said Morgaine. "Fwar's kindred and Haz of Aren
rule in Ohtij-in, and you rule your own kind. As for me, I
am leaving when the flood permits, and you have seen the
last of me, my lord Kithan."

"They will kill us."

"They may not. But if I were you, my lord, I would seek shelter elsewhere—perhaps in Hiuaj."

There was laughter at that, and color flooded Kithan's white cheeks.

"Why?" Kithan asked when the coarse laughter had died. "Why have you done this to us? This is excessive revenge."

Again Morgaine shrugged. "I only opened your gates," she said. "What was waiting outside was not of my shaping. I do not lead them. I go my own way."

"Not looking to what you have destroyed. Here is the last place where civilization survives. Here—" Kithan glanced about at the fine tapestries that hung slashed and wantonly ruined. "Here is the wealth, the art of thousands of years, destroyed by these human animals."

"Out there," said Morgaine, "is the flood. Barrows-hold has gone; Aren is going; there is nothing left for them but to come north. It is your time; and you chose your way of meeting it, with such delicate works. It was your choice."

The *qujal* clenched his arms across him as at a chill. "The world is going under; but this time was ours, tedious as it was, and this land was ours, to enjoy it. The Wells ruined the world once, and spilled this Barrows-spawn into our lands— that drove other humans into ruin, that plundered and stole and ruined and left of us only halfbreeds, the survivors of their occupations. They tampered with the Wells and ruined their own lands; they ruined the land they took and now they come to us. Perhaps *he* is of that kind," he said, with a burning look at Vanye, "and came through the Wells; perhaps the one named Roh came likewise. The Barrow-kings are upon us again, no different than they ever were. But someone did this thing to us—someone of knowledge more than theirs. Someone did this, who had the power to open what was sealed."

Morgaine frowned, straightened, drawing *Changeling* into her lap; and of a sudden Vanye moved, seized the slight halfling to silence him, to take him from the room: but Morgaine's sharp command checked him. None moved, not he nor the startled peasants, and Morgaine arose, a distraught look on her face. She withdrew a space from them, looked back at him, and to Fwar, and seemed for a moment dazed.

"The Barrow-kings," she said then: there was a haunted expression in her eyes. . . . Vanye saw it and remembered Irien, ghosts that followed her, an army, lost in that great valley: ten thousand men, of which not even corpses remained.

His ancestors, that were to her but a few months dead.

"Liyo," he said quietly, his heart pounding. "We are wasting time with him. Set the halfling free or put him with the others, but there are other matters that want attention. Now."

Sanity returned sharply to Morgaine's gaze, a harsh look bestowed on Kithan. "How long ago?"

"Liyo," Vanye objected. "It is pointless."

"How long ago?"

Kithan gathered himself with an intake of breath, assumed that pose of arrogance that had been his while he ruled, despite that Vanye's fingers bit into his arm. "A very long time ago.—Long enough for this land to become what it is. And surely," he shot after that, pressing his advantage, "you are about to bid equally with the man Roh: life, wealth, restoration of the ancient powers. Lie to me, ancient enemy. Offer to buy my favor. It is—considering the situation—purchasable."

"Kill him," Fwar muttered.

"Your enemy has gone," Kithan said, "to Abarais—to possess the Wells; to take all the north. Hetharu is with him, with all our forces; and eventually they will come back."

Fear was thick in the room. Morgaine stood still. The Barrows-men seemed hardly to breathe.

"The Shiua spoke the same," said one of the marshlanders.

"When the flood subsides," said Morgaine, "then there will be a settling with Roh; and he will not return to Ohtij-in. But that is my business, and it need not concern you."

"Lady," said Fwar, fear distorting his face, "when you have done that—when you have reached the Wells—what will you do then?"

Vanye heard, mind frozen, the halfling held with one hand, the other hand sweating on the grip of his sword. It was not his to answer: with his eyes he tried to warn her.

"We have followed you," a Barrows-man said. "We are yours, we Barrowers—We will follow you."

"Take them," Kithan laughed, a bitter and mocking laugh; and of a sudden the foremost of the Aren-folk fled, his fellows with him, thrusting their way through the tall Barrows-men, running.

Still Kithan laughed, and Vanye cursed and hurled him aside, into the midst of the Barrows-men, who hurled him clear again; Vanye unsheathed the sword, and Kithan halted, within striking distance of him, and knowing it.

"No," Morgaine forbade him. "No." And to the Barrowers: "Fwar, stop the Aren-folk. Find me Haz."

But the Barrowers too remained as if dazed, pale of face, staring at her. One of them touched a luck-piece that he wore hanging from a cord about his neck. Fwar bit at his lip.

And Kithan smiled a wolf-smile and laughed yet again. "World's-end, world's-end, o ye blind, ye Barrows-rabble. She has followed you through the Wells to repay you for all you have done . . . your own, your personal curse. An eyeblink for her, from there til now, but there is no time in the Wells, nor distance. We are avenged."

A knife whipped from sheath: a Barrows-man drew—for Morgaine, for Kithan, unknown which: Vanye looked toward it, and that man backed away, whey-faced and sweating.

There was silence in the room, heavy and oppressive; and of a sudden there was a stir outside, as the animals in the pens began bawling all at once. Furniture quivered, and the surface in the wine pitcher on the table shimmered and then men sprang one way and the other as chairs danced and the floor heaved sickeningly underfoot, masonry parting in a great crack down the wall that admitted dusty daylight. The fire crashed, a burning log rolled across the carpet, and there were echoing crashes and screams throughout the hold.

A rumbling shook the floor, deafening, sudden impact jolting the very stones of the hold.

Then it was done, and anguished screams resounded outside and throughout the keep. Vanye stood clinging to the back of a chair, Kithan to the table, the laughter shaken from him, and the Barrows-men stood white and trembling against the riven wall.

"Out," Morgaine shouted at them. "Out of here, clear the hold. Out!"

There was panic. The Hiua rushed the doorway in a mass, pushing and cursing at each other in their haste; but Vanye, sword's point levelled at Kithan, saw Morgaine delay to gather her belongings from the fireside.

"Go," he told her, reaching for her burden. She did not yield it, but left, quickly. Vanye abandoned Kithan, intent on staying with Morgaine; and the halfling darted from the door, raced the other way down the hall, a way that led upward.

"His people," said Morgaine; and Vanye felt an instant's respect for the *qujal*-lord, realizing what he was about.

And as he looked he saw another thing—broken timbers, a doorframe riven and shattered, and a door ajar.

The priest.

"Go!" he shouted at Morgaine; and turned back, running,

slid to a stop and pulled that jammed door wide, splintering
wood as he did so.

The storeroom was empty. The priest was a slight man, the
opening he had forced sufficient for the body of so slender a
man, and the priest was gone.

He turned and ran, back the way Morgaine should have
gone, past a cabinet that was overturned and shattered, a wall
that leaned perilously. He saw her, redoubled his effort and
overtook her just as she reached the main corridor.

Terror reigned in that long spiral: few had torches, and the
fall of some in the corridor had darkened areas of the passage. Servants gained courage to push and shove like free
men: screaming women and children of the Aren-folk fought
with hold servants for passage, and men pushed ruthlessly
where strength would avail in their haste. One of the sons of
Haz fought his way to Morgaine's side, pleading for comfort,
babbling words almost impossible to understand. Morgaine
tried to answer, caught for balance on his arm as they came
to the riven place that had always been in the corridor. It was
the width of a man's body now. A child fell, screaming, and
Vanye seized it by its clothing and deposited it safely across,
hearing a stone crumble. It hit water far below.

And Morgaine, with the marshlander to make way for her,
had kept moving. Vanye saw her gone and fought his own way
through, ruthless as the others, desperate.

The gate at the bottom was not barred: it had not been
since the attack. He saw Morgaine step clear, onto the steps,
in the drizzling rain, and caught his own breath as he overtook her, dazed, dimly conscious that they were still being
jostled by those that poured out behind.

But his eyes, like hers, fixed in shock on the gate, for the
barbican tower had fallen, leaving a wider gap beside the
ruined gates; and pitiful folk clambered over the rubble in
the falling rain, where the uppermost stones had fallen among
the shelters, crushing them, crushing flesh and timbers alike
under megaliths the size of two men.

Shiua saw Morgaine standing there, and there went up a
cry, a wailing. They came, dazed and fearfully; and Vanye
gripped his sword tightly in his fist, but he realized then that
they came for pity, pleading with their gestures and their outcries. There gathered a crowd, both marshlanders and folk of
the shelters, Hiua and Shiua mingled in their desolation.
None reached her: she stepped off the last step and walked
among them, they giving back to give her place, pressing at

each other in their zeal to avoid her. Vanye went at her back,
sword in hand, fearful, seeing the mob that once had
threatened him now pleading desperately with them both.
Hands touched him as they would not touch Morgaine, but
they were pleas for help, for explanation, and he could not
give it.

Morgaine slung her cloak about her and put up the hood
as she walked across the yard, and there, in the clear of
threatening stones, she turned and looked back at the keep.

Vanye looked, a quickly stolen glance, for fear of those
about them, and saw that the tower that had fallen had taken
one of the buttresses too, riving it away from the keep. There
was a crack in that vast tower, opening it widely to the elements and promising further ruin.

"I would give nothing for its chance of standing the hour,"
Morgaine said. "There will be other shocks." And for the instant she gazed about the yard, seemed herself in a state of
shock. Over the babble of prayers and panicked questions
rose the steady keening of men and women over their dead.

And suddenly she flung back her head and shouted to
those of the Aren-folk near her: "There is no staying here. It
will all collapse. Gather what you must have to live, and go,
get out of here!"

Panic spread at that dismissal; she did not regard the questions others shouted at her, but seized at Vanye's sleeve. "The
horses. Get our horses out before that wall goes."

"Aye," he agreed, and then realized it meant leaving her;
half a step he hesitated, and saw her face with that unreason-
ing fixedness, saw the folk that crowded frantically about her,
that in their fear would cling to her: she could not get away.
He fled, steps quickening, avoiding this man and that, racing
across the puddled yard to the stable, remembering Jhirun,
left to her own devices, panicked horses and the damage of
the quake.

The stable door was ajar. He pushed it open. Chaos
awaited him inside that warm darkness, planks down where
horses had panicked and broken their barriers. There was a
wild-eyed bay that had had the worst of it: it bolted when he
flung the stable door wide. Other horses were still in stalls.

"Jhirun," he called aloud, seeing with relief Siptah and his
own horse and Jhirun's mare still safe.

No voice responded. There was a rustling of straw—many
bodies in the darkness.

Fwar stepped into the light, his kinsmen emerging likewise

from the shadows, from within a stall, over the bars of another: armed men, carrying knives. Vanye spun half about,
caught a quick glimpse of others behind him.

He slung the sheath from his sword and sent it at them,
whirled upon the man at his left and toppled him writhing in
the straw, bent under a whistling staff and took that man too:
his comrade fled, wounded.

A crash attended those behind, Siptah's shrill scream. Vanye
turned into a knife attack, ducked under the clumsy move
and used the man's arm to guide his blade, whipped it free
and came on guard again, springing back from the man that
sprawled at his feet.

The others scattered, what of them survived, save Fwar,
who tried to stand his ground: a shadow moved, a flash of a
bare ankle—Fwar started to turn, knife in hand, and Vanye
sprang for him, but the swing of harness in Jhirun's hands
was quicker. Chain whipped across Fwar's head, brought him
down screaming: and in blind rage he tried to scramble up
again.

Vanye reversed the blade, smashed the hilt into Fwar's
skull, sprawled the man face-down in the straw. Jhirun stood
hard-breathing, still clenching the chain-and-leather mass in
her two hands; tears streamed down her face.

"The quake," she murmured, choking, "the rains, and the
quake—oh, the dreams, the dreams, my lord, I dreamed . . ."

He snatched the harness from her hands, hurting her as he
did so, and seized her by the arm. "Go," he said. "Get to
horse."

It was in his mind to kill Fwar: of all others that had perished, this one he would have wished to kill, but now it was
murder. He cursed Jhirun's help, knowing that he could have
taken this man in clean fight, that after killing kin of his, this
was the wrong man to leave alive.

Jhirun came back to his side, leading the bay mare. "Kill
him," she insisted, her voice trembling.

"This is kin of yours," he said angrily—minded as the
words left his mouth that she had once said something of the
same to him. "Go!" he shouted at her, and jerked her horse's
head about, pushed her up as she set foot in the stirrup.
When she landed astride he struck the mare on the rump and
sent it hence.

Then he flung open the stalls of Siptah and his own horse,
dragged at their reins and led the horses down the aisle, past
the bodies. His sword sheath lay atop the straw; he snatched

it up and kept moving, paused only in the light of the doorway to settle his sword at his side and mount up.

The gelding surged forward: he fought to control the viletempered animal with the Baien stud in tow; and overtook Jhirun, who was having difficulty with the little mare in the press of the yard. Vanye shouted, cursing, spurred brutally, and the crowd parted in terror as the three horses broke through. About them, folk already streamed toward the shattered gates, their backs laden with packs, some leading animals or pulling carts. Women carried children, older children carried younger; and men struggled under unwieldy burdens that would never permit them long flight.

And from the keep itself folk came streaming out, bearing gold and all such things as were useless hereafter—men who had come to possess the treasures of Ohtij-in and stubbornly clung to them in its fall.

Morgaine stood safely by the ruin of the tower, a stationary figure amid the chaos, waiting, with solid stone at her back and *Changeling,* sheathed, in her two hands.

She saw them: and suddenly her face set in anger, such that Vanye felt the force of it to the depth of him; but when he rode to her side, ready to swear that Jhirun's presence was no planning of his, she said not a word, only caught Siptah's reins from his hand and set her foot into the stirrup, settling herself into the saddle and at once checking the gray's forward motion. A cry went up from the crowd. A loose cow darted this way and that in bovine panic through the crowd, and the horses shied and stamped.

"Give me time," Vanye shouted at Morgaine, "to go back and free the horses in the stalls."

And of a sudden the earth heaved again, a little shudder, and a portion of the keep wall slid into ruin, another tower toppling, with terrible carnage. The horses plunged, fighting restraint. The wails of frightened people rose above the sound that faded.

From the shaken keep poured other fugitives, the *qujal-*folk, and the black robes of a priest among them—pale folk and conspicuous in the crowd, dazed, ill-clothed for the cold, save for a few house guards in their armor.

"No," Morgaine answered Vanye's appeal to her. "No. There is no lingering here. Let us go."

He did not dispute it, not with the threat of further ruin about them: his Kurshin soul agonized over the trapped horses, and over another ugliness that he had left, half-finished. The collapse of the keep would end it, he thought, burying the dead and the living, ending a thing that should have ended long ago, however the Myya had come through into this land: he took it upon his own conscience, never to tell Morgaine what was pointless to know, never to regret those several lives, that had betrayed her and tried to murder him.

The horses moved, Morgaine riding in the lead, seeking their way through the slow-moving crowd more gently than the war-trained gray would have it. Vanye kept close at Morgaine's back, watching the crowd, and once, that a sound first drew his attention in that direction, looking at Jhirun, who rode knee to knee with him. He met her eyes, shadowed and fierce, minding him how she had lately urged him to murder—this the frightened child that he had taken back with them, Myya, and living, when he would gladly have known the last of her kind dead.

With all his heart he would have ridden from her now, and with Morgaine have sought some other, unknown way from Ohtij-in; but there was none other, and the Suvoj barred their way within a few leagues. There was no haste, no need of hurrying, only sufficient to clear the walls, where yet a few desperate folk still searched for bodies beneath the massive stones, beyond help and hope.

A line of march stretched out northward from Ohtij-in; and this they joined, moving more quickly than the miserable souls that walked.

And when they were well out on the road came another rumble and shudder of the earth. Vanye turned in his saddle and others turned and looked, seeing the third tower fallen: and even as he gazed, the center of Ohtij-in sank down into ruin. The sound of it reached them a moment later, growing and dying. Jhirun cried out softly, and a wail arose from the people, a sound terrible and desolate.

"It has gone," Vanye said, sickened to the heart to think of the lives that surely were extinguished there, an unconscious enemy, and the wretched, the innocent, who would not leave off their searching.

Morgaine alone had not turned to see, but rode with her face set toward the north. "Doubtless," she said after they had ridden some distance further, "the breach at the gate removed stability for the barbican tower; and the fall of the barbican prepared the fall of the next, and so it began—else it might have gone on standing."

Her doing, who had breached the gate. Vanye heard the
hollowness in her voice, and understood what misery lay
beneath it. *I do not look,* she had said, *at what I leave behind
me.*

He wished that he had not looked either.

The rain whispered down into the grass on the hills and
into the puddles on the road, and a stream ran the course between the hills, frothing and racing over brush and obstacles.
Now and again they rode past a man with his family that had
wearied and sat down on the slope to rest. Sometimes they
passed abandoned bundles of goods, where some man had
cast them down, unable to carry them farther. And once
there was an old man lying by the roadside. Vanye dismounted to see to him, but he was dead.

Jhirun hugged her shawl about her and wept. Morgaine
shrugged helplessly, nodded for him to get back to horse and
forget the matter.

"Doubtless others will die," she said, and that was all—no
tears, no remorse.

He climbed back into the saddle and they kept moving.

Overhead the clouds had begun to show ragged rents, and
one of the moons shone through in daylight, wan and white,
a piece of the Broken Moon, that passed more quickly than
the others; the vast terror that was Li had yet to come.

The hills cut them off from view of what lay behind, gray-
green hills that opened constantly before them and closed behind; and gradually their steady pace brought them to the
head of the long line of weary folk. They rode slowly there,
for there was nowhere to go but where the column went, and
no profit in opening a wide lead.

They were first to reach the hillside that overlooked the
lately flooded plain, the rift of the Suvoj, where still great
pools showed pewter faces to the clouded sky, small lakes,
rocks that upthrust strange shapes, stone more solid than the
water had yet availed to wear away; it was a bleak and dead
place, stretching far to the other hills, but the road went
through it until the river, and there the stones made only a
ripple under the surface of the flood.

A stench went up from the rotting land, the smell of the
sea mingled with dying things. Vanye swore in disgust when
the wind carried it to them, and when he looked toward the
horizon he saw that the hills ended and melted into gray, that
was the edge of the world.

"The tide comes in here," murmured Jhirun. "It overcomes the river, as it does the Aj."

"And goes out again," said Morgaine, "tonight."

"It may be," said Jhirun, "it may be. Already it is on the ebb."

The noise of others intruded on them, the advance of the column that came blindly in their wake. Morgaine glanced over her shoulder, reined Siptah about, yet holding him.

"This hill is ours," she said fiercely. "And company will not be comfortable for us. Vanye—come, let us stop them."

She led Siptah forward, toward the van of the column, that were strong men, Aren-folk, who had fled early and marched most strongly: and Vanye slung his sword across the saddle-bow and kept pace with her, a shadow by her side as she gave orders, directed sullen, confused men to one side and the other of the road, bidding them set up shelters and make a camp.

Two of the Barrows-men were there, grim, tall men: Vanye noticed them standing together and cast them a second, anxious look, wondering had they been two of the number with Fwar—or whether they were innocent of that ambush and did not yet know the bloodfeud that was between them. They gave no evidence of it.

But there was yet another matter astir among them, sullen looks toward the hill where Jhirun waited, standing by the bay mare, her shawl clutched about her in the cold, damp wind.

"She is ours," one of the two Barrowers said to Morgaine.

Morgaine said nothing, only looked at him from the height of Siptah's back, and that man fell silent.

Only Vanye, who rode at her back, heard the murmuring that followed when Morgaine turned away; and it was ugly. He turned his horse again and faced them, the two Barrows-men, and a handful of marshlanders.

"Say it louder," he challenged them.

"The girl is fey," said one of the marshlanders. "Ela's-daughter. She cursed Chadrih, and it fell. The quake and the flood took it."

"And Barrows-hold," said one of the Barrows-men. "Now Ohtij-in."

"She brought the enemy into Barrows-hold," said the other of the Barrowers. "She is fey. She cursed the hold, killed all that were in it, the old, the women and the children, her own sister. Give her to us."

Vanye hesitated, the gelding restless under him, misgivings gathering in him, remembering the dream upon the road, the mad-eyed vagaries, the tense body pressed against his.

Oh, the dreams, the dreams, my lord, I dreamed. . . .

He jerked the gelding's head about, spurred him past their reaching hands, sought Morgaine, who moved alone among the crowds, giving orders. He joined her, saying nothing; she asked nothing.

A camp began to take shape, makeshift huddles of stitched skins and brush and sodden blankets tied between trees or supported on hewn saplings. Some had brought fire, and one borrowed to the next, wet wood smoking and hissing in the mist, but sufficient to stay alight.

The column was still straggling in at dusk, finding a camp, finding their places in it, seeking relatives.

Morgaine turned back to the hill that she had chosen, where she had permitted no intrusion; and there Jhirun waited, shivering, with wood she had gathered for a fire. Vanye dismounted, already searching out with his eye this and that tree that might be cut for shelter. But Morgaine slid down from Siptah's back and stared balefully at the flood that raged between them and the other side, dark waters streaked with white in the dusk.

"It is lower," she said, pointing to the place where the road made a white-frothing ridge in the flood. "We might try it after we have rested a bit."

The thought chilled him. "The horses cannot force that. Wait. Wait. It cannot be much longer."

She stood looking at it still, as if she would disregard all his advice, staring toward that far bank, where mountains rose, where was Roh, and Abarais, and a halfling army.

The flood would not be sufficient to have delayed Roh this long; Vanye reckoned that for himself, and did not torment her with asking or saying it. She was desperate, exhausted; she had spent herself in answering questions among the frightened folk behind them, in providing advice, in settling disputes for space and wood. She had distracted herself with these things, gentle when he sensed in her a dark and furious violence, that loathed the clinging, terrified appeals to her, the faces that looked to her with desperate hope.

"Take us with you," they wept, surrounding her.

"Where is my child?" a mother kept asking her, clinging to

the rein until the nervous, war-trained gray came near to breaking control.

"I do not know," she had said. But it had not stopped the questions.

"Will my daughter be there?" asked a father, and she had looked at him, distracted, and murmured *yes*, and spurred the gray roughly through the press.

Now she stood holding her cloak about her against the chill and staring at the river as at a living enemy. Vanye watched her, not moving, dreading that mood of hers that slipped nearer and nearer to irrationality.

"We camp," she said after a time.

Chapter Fourteen

||||||||||||||||||||||||||||||||||||||||||||||||||||||||||||

There was one mercy shown them that evening. The rain stopped. The sky tore to rags and cleared, though it remained damp everywhere, and the smoke of hundreds of fires rolled up and hung like an ugly mist over the camp. Scarred Li rose, vast and horrid, companionless now. The other moons had fled; and Anli and demon Sith lagged behind.

They rested, filled with food that Morgaine had put in her saddlebags. They sat in a shelter of saplings and brush, with a good fire before them; and Jhirun sat beside them, eating her share of the provisions with such evident hunger that Morgaine tapped her on the arm and put another bit of bread into her lap, charity that amazed Jhirun and Vanye alike.

"I have not lacked," Morgaine said with a shrug—for it must come from someone's share.

"She hid in the stable," Vanye said quietly, for Morgaine had never asked: and that lack of questions worried at him, implying anger, a mood in which Morgaine herself was unwilling to discuss the matter. "That was why your searchers could not find her."

Morgaine only looked at him, with that impenetrable stare, so that he wondered for a moment had there been searchers at all, or only inquiry.

But Morgaine had promised him; he thrust the doubt from his mind, effort though it needed.

"Jhirun," Morgaine said suddenly. Jhirun swallowed a bit of bread as if it had gone dry, and only slightly turned her head, responding to her. "Jhirun, there are kinsmen of yours here."

Jhirun nodded, and her eyes slid uneasily toward Morgaine, wary and desperate.

"They came to Aren," Morgaine said, "hunting you. And you are known there. There are some Aren-folk who know

your name and say that you are halfling yourself, and in
some fashion they blame you for some words you spoke
against their village."

"Lord," Jhirun said in a thin voice, and edged against
Vanye, as if he could prevent such questions. He sat stiffly,
uncomfortable in the touch of her.

"A quake," said Morgaine, "struck Hiuaj after we three
parted company. There was heavy damage at Aren, where I
was; and the Barrows-folk came then. They said there was
nothing left of Barrows-hold."

Jhirun shivered.

"I know," said Morgaine, "that you cannot seek safety
among your own kinsmen . . . or with the Aren-folk. Better
that you had remained lost, Jhirun Ela's-daughter. They have
asked me for you, and I have refused; but that is for now.
Vanye knows—he will tell you—that I am not generous. I
am not at all generous. And there will come a time when we
cannot shelter you. I do not care what quarrel drove you out
of Barrows-hold in the first place; it does not concern me. I
do not think that you are dangerous; but your enemies are.
And for that reason you are not welcome with us. You have
a horse. You have half our food, if you wish it; Vanye and I
can manage. And you would be wise to take that offer and
try some other route through these hills, be it to hide and live
in some cave for the rest of your days. Go. Seek some place
after the Ohtija have dispersed. Go into those mountains and
look for some place that has no knowledge of you. That is
my advice to you."

Jhirun's hand crept to Vanye's arm. "Lord," she said
faintly, plaintively.

"There was a time," Vanye said, hardly above a breath,
"when Jhirun did not say what she might have said, when she
did not say all that she knew of you, and stayed by me when
it was not convenient. And I will admit to you that I gave
her a promise . . . I know—that I had no right to give any
promise, and she should not have believed me, but she did
not know that. I have told her that she should not have believed me; but would it be so wrong, *liyo*, to let her go where
we go? I do not know what other hope she has."

Morgaine stared at him fixedly, and for a long, intermina-
bly long moment, said nothing. "Thee says correctly," she
breathed at last. "Thee had no right."

"All the same," he said, very quietly, "I ask it, because I
told her that I would take her to safety."

Morgaine turned that gaze on Jhirun. "Run away," she said. "I give you a better gift than he gave. But on his word, stay, if you have not the sense to take it. Unlike Vanye, I bind myself to nothing. Come with us as long as you can, and for as long as it pleases me."

"Thank you," Jhirun said almost soundlessly, and Vanye pressed her arm, disengaging it from his. "Go aside," he said to her. "Rest. Let matters alone now."

Jhirun drew away from them, stood up, left the shelter for the brush, beyond the firelight. They were alone. Across the camp sounded the wail of an infant, the lowing of an animal, the sounds that had been constant all the evening.

"I am sorry," Vanye said, bowed himself to the ground, expected even then her anger, or worse, her silence.

"I was not there," Morgaine said quietly. "I take your word for what you did, and why. I will try. She will stay our pace or she will not; I cannot help her. *That*—" She gestured with a glance toward the camp. "That also has its desires, that are Jhirun's."

"They believe," he said, "that there is a way out for them. That it lies through the Wells. That they will find a land on the other side."

She said nothing to that.

"*Liyo*—" he said carefully, "you could do that—you could give them what they believe—could you not?"

A tumult had arisen, as others had arisen throughout the evening, on the far side of the camp, distant shouts carrying to them: disputes, dissents, among terrified people.

Morgaine set her face and shook her head abruptly. "I could, yes, but I will not."

"You know why they have followed you. You know that."

"I care nothing for their beliefs. I will not."

He thought of the falling towers of Ohtij-in: *only a hand's breadth closer to the sea*. Jhirun had laughed, attempting humor. Somewhere the child was still crying. Among the rabble there were the innocent, the harmless.

"Their land," he said, "is dying. It will come in the lifetime of some that are now alive. And to open the Gates for them—would that not—?"

"Their time is finished, that is all. It comes to all worlds."

"In Heaven's good name, *liyo*,—"

"Vanye. Where should we take them?"

He shook his head helplessly. "Are we not to leave this land?"

"There are no sureties beyond any Gate."

"But if there is no other hope for them——"

Morgaine set *Changeling* across her knees. The dragon eyes of the hilt winked gold in the firelight, and she traced the scales with her fingers. "Two months ago, Vanye, where were you?"

He blinked, mind thrust back across Gates, across mountains: a road to Aenor, a winter storm. "I was an outlaw," he said, uncertain what he was bidden remember, "and the Myya were close on my trail."

"And four?"

"The same." He laughed uneasily. "My life was much of the same, just then."

"I was in Koris," she said. "Think of it."

Laughter perished in him, in a dizzying gap of a hundred years. Irien: massacre—ancestors of his had served Morgaine's cause in Koris, and they were dust. "But it *was* a hundred years, all the same," he said. "You slept; however you remember it, it was still a hundred years, and what you remember cannot change that."

"No. Gates are outside time. Nothing is fixed. And in this land—once—an unused Gate was flung wide open, uncontrolled, and poured men through into a land that was not theirs. That was not *theirs*, Vanye. And they took that land . . . men that speak a common tongue with Andur-Kursh; that remember *me*."

He sat very still, the pulse beating in his temples until he was aware of little else. "I knew," he said at last, "that it might be; that Jhirun and her kindred are Myya."

"You did not tell me this."

"I did not know how. I did not know how to put it together; I thought how things would stray the Gate into Andur-Kursh, lost—to die there; and could not men——"

"Who remember *me*, Vanye."

He could not answer; he saw her fold her arms about her knees, hands locked, and bow her head, heard her murmur something in that tongue that was hers, shaking her head in despair.

"It was a thousand years," he objected.

"There is no time between Gates," she answered him with an angry frown; and saw his puzzlement, his shake of the head, and relented. "It makes no difference. They have had their time, both those that were born to this land and those that invaded it. It is gone. For all of them, it is gone."

Vanye frowned, found a stick in his hands, and broke it, once, twice, a third time, measured cracks. He cast the bits into the fire. "They will starve before they drown. The mountains will give them ground whereon to stand, but the stones will not feed them. Would it be wrong, *liyo*, would it be wrong—once, to help them?"

"As once before it happened here? Whose land shall I give them, Vanye?"

He did not have an answer. He drew a breath and in it was the stench of the rotting land. Down in the camp the tumult had never ceased. Shrieks suddenly pierced the heavier sounds, seeming closer.

Morgaine looked in that direction and frowned. "Jhirun has been gone overlong."

His thoughts leaped in the same direction. "She would have had more sense," he said, gathering himself to his feet; but in his mind was the girl's distraught mood, Morgaine's words to her, his dismissal of her. The horses grazed, the bay mare with them, still saddled, although the girths were loosened.

Morgaine arose, touched his arm. "Stay. If she has gone, well sped; she survives too well to fear she would have gone that way."

The shouting drew nearer: there was the sound of horses on the road, of wild voices attending. Vanye swore, and started of a sudden for their own horses. There was no time left: riders were coming up their very hill, horses struggling on the wet slope.

And Jhirun raced into the firelight, a wild flash of limbs and ragged skirts. The riders came up after, white-haired lord and two white-haired house guards.

Jhirun raced for the shelter, as Vanye slipped the ring of his longsword and took it in hand: but Morgaine was before him. Red fire leaped from her hand, touching smoke in the drenched grass. Horses shied: Kithan—first of the three—flung up his arm against the sight and reined back, stopping his men.

And at that distance he faced Morgaine. He shouted a word in his own tongue at her, in an ugly voice, and then in a shriek of desperation: "Stop them, stop them!"

"From what," she asked, "Kithan?"

"They have murdered us," the *qujal* cried, his voice shaking. "The others—stop them; you have the power to stop them if you will."

There was ugly murmuring in the camp; they could hear it even here: it grew nearer—men, coming toward the slope.

"Get the horses," Morgaine said.

Two lights appeared behind the screen of young trees, lights that moved; and a dark mass moved behind them. The halflings turned to look, terror in their faces. Vanye spun about, encountered Jhirun, seized her and thrust her again toward the shelter. "Pick up everything!" he shouted into her dazed face.

She moved, seized up blankets, everything that lay scattered, while he ran for the horses, adjusted harness, that of their own horses and Jhirun's bay mare as well. The stubborn gelding shied as he started to mount: he seized the saddle-horn and swung up in a maneuver he had hardly used since he was a boy, armored as he was: and he saw to his horror that Morgaine had made herself a shield for the three *qujal*, they at her back, the mob advancing not rapidly, but with mindless force.

He grasped Siptah's reins, leaning from the saddle, and spurred forward, through the *qujal*, reined in with Siptah just behind Morgaine.

She stood still, with him at her back; and faced the oncoming men afoot. Vanye stared at what came, panic surging in him, memory of the courtyard—of a beast without reason in it.

And in the torchlight at the head of them he saw Barrows-folk, and Fwar . . . Fwar, his scarred face no better for a dark slash across it. They came with knives and with staves; and with them, panting in his haste, came the priest Ginun.

"*Liyo!*" Vanye said, with all the force in him. "To horse!"

She moved, nothing questioning, turned and sprang to the saddle in a single move. He kept his eye on Fwar in that instant, and saw murder there. In the next moment Morgaine had swung Siptah around to face them, curbing him hard, so that he shied up a little. She unhooked *Changeling*, held it across the saddlebow.

"Halflings!" someone shouted, like a curse; but from other quarters within the mob there were outcries of terror.

Morgaine rode Siptah a little distance across the face of the crowd, and paced him back again, a gesture of arrogance; and still they feared her, and gave back, keeping the line she drew.

"Fwar!" she cried aloud. "Fwar! What is it you want?"

"Him!" cried Fwar, a beast-shout of rage. "Him, who killed Ger and Awan and Efwy."

"You led us here," shouted one of the sons of Haz. "You have no intention of helping us. It was a lie. You will ruin the Wells and ruin us. If this is not so, tell us."

And there arose a bawling of fear from the crowd, a voice as from one throat, frightening in its intensity. They began to press forward.

A rider broke through the *qujal* from the rear: Vanye jerked his head about, saw Jhirun, a great untidy bundle on the saddle before her, saw the dark arm of the mob that had broken through the woods attempting to encircle them; Jhirun cried warning of it.

In blind instinct Vanye whirled in the other direction—saw a knife leave Fwar's hand. He flung up his arm: it hit the leather and fell in the mud, under his horse's hooves. Jhirun's cry of warning still rang in his ears.

The mob surged forward and Morgaine retreated. Vanye ripped out his sword, and fire burned from Morgaine's hand, felling one of the Barrowers. The front rank wavered with an outcry of horror.

"Angharan!" someone cried; and some tried to flee, abandoning their weapons and their courage; but weapons were hurled from another quarter, stones. Siptah shied and screamed shrilly.

"Lord!" Jhirun cried; Vanye reined about as Shiua came at them, seeking to attack the horses. The gelding shied back, and Vanye laid about him with desperate blows, the *qujal* striking what barehanded blows they could.

Vanye did not turn to see what had befallen his liege; he had enemies of hers enough before him. He wielded the longsword with frenzied strength, spurred the gelding recklessly into the attackers and scattered their undisciplined ranks, only then daring turn, hearing screams behind him.

Bodies lay thickly on the slope; fires burned here and there in the brush; the mob broke in flight, scattering down the hillside in advance of Siptah's charge.

And Morgaine did not cease: Vanye spurred the gelding and followed her, blind to tactic and strategy save the realization that she wanted the road, wanted the hill clear of them.

Folk screamed and scattered before them, and Vanye felt the gelding avoid a body that had fallen before him, then recover and stretch out running as they gained the level ground, the *qujalin* road. Morgaine turned, heading out for

the causeway across the Suvoj, scattering screaming enemies
that had turned the wrong way.

On either side stretched flooded land, a vast expanse of
shallow water, and the road ran as a narrow thread across it,
toward the flooded crossing, where water swirled darkly over
the stones. Here, well out upon that roadway, Morgaine
stopped, and he with her, reining about as four riders came
after them to the same desperate refuge—three terrified *qujal*
and a Barrows-girl, this all their strength, and the roar of the
Suvoj at their backs.

On the hillside that they had left, the Hiua regrouped,
gathering their forces and their courage, and there was much
of shouting and crying. Torches were waved. The glow of fire
lit the center of their rallying place, and on that hillside was
a tree, from which dangled objects—the aspect of which filled
Vanye with apprehension.

"They have hanged them!" Kithan cried in anguish.

But neither Kithan nor his two men ventured forward
against those odds. *His people,* Vanye understood, reckoning
the number of dangling corpses against his memory of the
band of *qujal* that had fled crumbling Ohtij-in, a pitiable
group, among them women and old ones. *Qujal* they might
be, but bile rose in his throat as he gazed on that sight.

And of a sudden came a shout from that gathering by the
tree, and the wave of a torch, exhorting a new attack against
them.

"Get back," Morgaine bade their companions; and the rush
came, a dark surge of bodies pouring out onto the causeway.
Changeling came free of its sheath, opal color flickering up
and down its blade, that ominous darkness howling at its tip,
and the first attacker mad enough to fling himself at Morgaine entered that dark and whirled shrieking away within it,
sucked into that oblivion.

The mob did not retreat. Others swept against them, wild-
eyed and howling their desperation. Vanye laid about him
with his sword, reining tightly to keep the gelding from being
pushed over the brink.

And suddenly those men that attacked him were alone.
Morgaine spurred Siptah into that oncoming horde, swept the
terrible blade in an arc that became vacant of enemies and
corpses, a crescent that widened.

With a shout she rode farther, driving them in retreat before her, taking any man that delayed, the blade flickering

with the cold opal fire, slow and leisurely as it took man after man into that void, dealing no wound, sparing none.

"*Liyo!*" Vanye cried, and spurred after her, shouldering a screaming marshlander over the brink. "*Liyo!*" He rode to land's edge; and there perhaps his voice first reached her. She reined about, and he saw the arc of the sword, the sudden eclipse of the light as it swung toward him. He reined over, hard, and the gelding slid on the wet stones, skidding. He recovered. The horse trembled and fretted under him, Morgaine's wild face staring at him in the balefire of *Changeling*.

"Put it up," he urged her in what of a voice remained to him. "No more. No more."

"Get back."

"No!" he cried at her. But she would not listen to him: she turned Siptah's head toward the people that gathered on the hillside, and spurred forward onto the muddy earth. Women and children cried out and ran, and men held their ground desperately, but she came no farther, circling back and forth, back and forth.

"*Liyo!*" Vanye screamed at her; and when she would not come, he rode forward, carefully, reining in a few paces behind, where he was safe from her as well as from the enemy.

She stopped, sat her horse facing the great empty space that she had made between the causeway and their attackers. There was, after that confusion and madness, a terrible silence made. And she kept the sword unsheathed, waiting, while time passed and the silence continued.

A voice broke the stillness, distant and its owner well hidden in the darkness. There were curses spoken against her, who had deceived them; there were viler things shouted. She did not move, nor seem provoked, although at some of the words Vanye trembled with rage and wished the man within reach. Almost he answered back himself; but something there was about Morgaine's silence and waiting against which such words, either attacking or defending, were empty. He had held *Changeling*: he knew the agony that grew in one's arm after long wielding of it, the drain upon one's very soul. She did not move, and the voice grew still.

And at last Vanye gathered his resolve and toed the gelding forward. "*Liyo*," he said, so that she would know that it was he. She did not protest his approach now; nor did she turn her head from the darkness she was watching.

"It is enough," he urged her quietly. "*Liyo*—put it away."

She gave no answer, nor moved for a time. Then she lifted

Changeling so that the darkness at its tip aimed toward the huddle of tents and shelters, and that one great tree, whereon corpses dangled and twisted above a dying fire.

And then she lowered her arm, as if the weight of the sword suddenly grew too much. "Take it," she said hoarsely.

He eased close to her, stretched out both his hands and gently disengaged her rigid fingers from the dragon grip, taking it into his own hand. The evil of it ran through his bones and into his brain, so that his eyes blurred and his senses wavered.

She did not offer him the sheath, which was all that might damp its fires and render it harmless. She did not speak.

"Go back," he said. "I will watch them now."

But she did not answer or offer to move. She sat, straight and silent, beside him—believing, he was sure, that did it come to using the sword he had less willingness than she; lives and nations were on her conscience. His crimes were on a human scale.

And they sat their horses side by side, the two of them, until he found the sword making his arm ache, until the pain of it was hard to bear. He counted only his breaths, and watched the slow passage of Li's descent; and the horses grew weary and restless under them.

From the camp there was no stirring.

"Give it back," Morgaine said at last; he did so, terrified in the passing of it, the least touch of it fatal. But her hand was strong and sure as she received it.

He looked behind him, at the rift of the Suvoj, where the others waited. "The waters are lower," he said. And after a moment: "The Hiua will not dare come. They have given up. Put it away."

"Go," she said; and harshly: *"Go back!"*

He drew his horse's head about and rode back to the others, the *qujal* at one side of the roadway, Jhirun at the other, holding the mare's reins as she sat on the stone edge.

And the girl gathered herself up as she saw him coming, staggered with exhaustion as she went forward to meet him. "Lord," she said, holding the gelding's reins to claim his attention, "lord, the halflings say we might perhaps cross. They are talking of trying it." There was a wild, desperate grief in her face, like something graven there, incapable of changing. "Lord—will she let us go?"

"Go, now," he bade her on his own, for there was no reasoning with Morgaine; and as he sat watching them mount up and begin to take their horses out onto that dangerous passage, he was dismayed at his own callousness, that he could send men and a woman ahead to probe the way for his liege—in his place, because she valued him and not them.

Such he began to be, obedient to Morgaine. He made his heart cold, though his throat was tight with shame for himself, watching those four lorn figures struggling across that dangerous flooded stonework.

And when he saw that they were well past the halfway point and still able to proceed, he turned and rode back to Morgaine's side.

"Now," he said hoarsely. "Now, *liyo*. We can cross."

Chapter Fifteen

||||||||||||||||||||||||||||||||||||||||||||||||||||||||||

Vanye set himself in the lead, riding the skittish gelding toward the rift that thundered and echoed with flood. The retreating water had left the land glittering with water under the moon. A number of uprooted trees lay about the pool-studded plain, several having rammed the causeway, creating heaps of brush that loomed up on the side where the current had been, skeletal masses festooned with strings of dead grasses and leaves.

Then the causeway arched higher above the rocky shelf, pierced by spans above the water: a bridge that extended in vast arches out across the rift.

Please Heaven, Vanye thought, contemplating what lay before them, *let the earth stay still now.* The horse slowed, side-stepping; he touched it with his heels gently and kept it moving.

The current thundered and boiled through the spans that had lately been entirely submerged. Vast megaliths formed that structure, that as yet neither quake had dislodged nor flood eroded. A tree hung on the edge of the roadway, itself dwarfed by the spans, so that it seemed only some dangling bit of brush, but its roots thrust up taller than horse and rider. Vanye avoided looking directly down into the current, that dizzied the senses—save once: saw the waters sweeping down on the one side and through into endless water on the other, an expanse that seemed to embrace all creation. In the midst of it hung the thread of the bridge, and themselves small and lost amid the crash and roar that flung up spray as a mist about them.

He turned his head—suddenly, unreasoningly anxious about Morgaine, at once comforted to know her close behind him. She bore *Changeling* sheathed at her shoulders; her pale hair seemed to glow in the half-light, whipped on the wind as she also turned to look back.

Torches massed at the beginning of the causeway, like so many stars flickering there, beginning to stream out onto it.

What they had loosed on Ohtij-in was still following them, violent and desperate. Morgaine turned forward again; so did he, anxious for their safety on the bridge. The roadway was wide: it would have been possible to run, but the roar of the water and the sight of it had the animals wild-eyed with distress. It was not a place to let them go.

Yet ahead the small party with Jhirun had left the bridge, even now riding the security of the farther causeway and climbing the slope of the far-side road.

Dawn grew as they traversed that last, agonizingly slow distance; light showed them the way ahead more clearly, and the river had sunk yet more, so that it was worse to look down, where white froth rumbled and boiled about the arches of *qujalin* design and vast size, the water slipping down into a chasm as the Suvoj became a river and no longer a sea.

The brink of the far cliff came within reach. Vanye spurred his horse and it began to gather speed, sending a scatter of water from an occasional puddle. At the last he cast a look over his shoulder, obsessed with the dread that Morgaine might decide to turn and finish on that dizzying bridge what she had begun—for safety's sake.

She did not. Siptah likewise leaned into a run, following, and Vanye turned his face again, seeing the safety of the mountains ahead, a rise in the stone road that bore them upward to the hills.

To Abarais.

The dawn, breaking over the long slash of the Suvoj, showed a road well-kept that ascended steadily among the hills. For a time they rode hard, until they were within a stone's cast of the *qujal* and of Jhirun, and found leisure to walk their horses, until they had caught their breath.

Jhirun, riding somewhat apart from the halflings, looked back as if she might rein back and join them ... but she did not; nor did the halflings.

Then of a sudden Morgaine laid heels to Siptah and rode through, startling the weary party and starting the horses to running again, along the ascending road among the hills. Vanye, staying with her, felt the fading strength of the Andurin gelding and the unsureness in his stride, the animal's shoulders slick with sweat and froth; and by now the others were dropping behind, their horses spent.

"For pity," he shouted across at Morgaine, when the gelding's bravest effort could not keep stride, burdened with a man's weight; and the Baien gray was drenched with sweat. "*Liyo,* the horses—enough."

She yielded, slowed; the horses walked again, their breath coming in great lung-tearing puffs, and Morgaine turned in the saddle to look back—not, it was likely, at the *qujal,* who struggled to stay with them, but dreading the appearance of others on the road behind them.

The light grew, flung misty peaks into outline, a central body of mountains rounded and clustered together, a last refuge. There was a desolation about them that struck to the heart. Vanye recalled the vast chains of his own mountains, reaching sharp ridges at the sky, stretching as far as the eye could see and the heart could imagine. Of these there was immediate beginning and end, and they had a blurred, aged quality, weathering that was of many ages, a yielding likewise toward the sea.

Yet on the hillsides began to be signs of habitations, fields under cultivation, protected by terraces, and stonework to carry away the flooding: recent works, the hand of farmers, small fields and orchards that were flooded in many areas, but a sign that here lay the true strength of Shiuan, a still-solid wealth that had supported the glittering lords and the humanity that had crowded within their walls.

And on the crest of a long hill, from which it was possible to see the road in all directions, Morgaine reined in, leaned on the saddlebow a moment, then dismounted. Vanye did likewise, himself aching in all his bones, and took Siptah's reins from her nerveless hand.

She stared past him, down the long road where the halflings were only beginning that hill. "A time to rest," she said.

"Aye," he agreed gladly enough, and busied himself loosening girths and slipping bits to ease the horses, tending to them while Morgaine withdrew a little to that rocky upthrust that was the cap of the hill, where flat stones afforded a place to sit other than the damp earth.

He finished his task, and brought the flask of Hiua liquor and a wrapped bit of food, and offered them to her, hoping against expectation to the contrary that she would accept them. She sat with *Changeling* unhooked and leaning against her shoulder, her right arm cradled in her lap in an attitude of evident pain; but she lifted her head and bestirred herself to take a share of what he offered, as much to avoid dispute with him, he thought, as because she had appetite for anything. He drank and ate a few mouthfuls himself; and by this time the halflings were drawing near them, with Jhirun lagging far behind.

"*Liyo*," Vanye said carefully, "we would do well to take what chance we have to rest now. We have pushed the horses almost as far as possible. We are climbing; there looks to be more of it, and there may be a time ahead that speed will serve us better than it does now."

She nodded, mutely accepting his argument, whether or not it coincided with her own reasons. Her eyes were void of interest in what passed about her. He heard the approach of the halflings with a private anguish, not wanting strangers near her when this mood was on her. He had seen it before, that soulless energy that seized her and kept her moving, responding only to the necessity that drove her. At the moment she was lost . . . knew him, perhaps, or confused him with men long since dust; the time was short for her, who had passed Gate and Gate and Gate in her course, and confounded then and now, who but months ago had ridden into a war in which his ancestors had died.

A hundred years lay in that gap for him. For Jhirun. . . . He gazed upon her distant figure with a sudden and terrible understanding. A thousand years. He could not conceive of a thousand years. A hundred were sufficient to bring a man to dust; five hundred reached into a time when nothing had stood in Morija.

Morgaine had ridden across a century to enter his age, had gathered him to her, and together they had crossed into a place a thousand years removed from Jhirun's beginnings, whose ancestors lay entombed in the Barrows . . . men that Morgaine might have known, young, and powerful in that age of the world.

He had crossed such a gap, not alone of place, but of time.

O God, his lips shaped.

Nothing that he had known existed. Men, kinsmen, all that he had ever known was aged, decayed, gone to sifting dust. He knew then what he had done, passing the Gate. It was irrevocable. He wanted to pour out questions to Morgaine, to have them answered, to know beyond doubt what things she had never told him, for pity.

But the *qujal* were with them. Horses drew up on the

margin. Lord Kithan, armorless, bareheaded, swung down from his saddle and walked toward them with one of his men, while the other attended the horses.

Vanye rose and slipped the ring that held his sword at his shoulder, setting himself between Kithan and Morgaine; and Kithan stopped—no longer the elegant lord, Kithan: his thin face was weary; his shoulders sagged. Kithan lifted a hand, gestured no wish to contend, then sank down on a flat stone some distance from Morgaine; his men likewise settled to the ground, pale heads bowed, exhausted.

Jhirun rode in among the *qujal*'s horses, slid from the saddle and held to it. In a moment she made the effort to loosen the girth of her horse, then led the animal to a patch of grass, too unsure of it to let it go. She sat down, holding the reins in her lap, and stayed apart from them all, tired, seeming terrified of everything and everyone about her.

"Let go the reins," Vanye advised her. "The mare will likely stand, with other horses about; she has run too far to be interested in running."

And he held out his hand, bidding her to them; Jhirun came, and sank down on the bare ground, arms wrapped about her knees and her head bowed. Morgaine took note of her presence, a stare she might have given one of the animals, disinterested. Vanye settled his back against a rock, his own head throbbing with lack of sleep and the conviction that the earth still lurched and swayed with the motion of the horse.

He dared not sleep. He watched the halflings from slitted eyes until the rest had at least given him space to breathe, and until thirst became an overwhelming discomfort.

He rose, went back to his horse and took the waterflask that hung from the saddlebow, drank, keeping an eye to the *qujal*, who did not stir. Then he slung it over his shoulder and returned, pausing to take from Jhirun's saddle the awkward bundle she had made of their blankets.

He cast the bundle down where he had been sitting, to remake it properly; and he offered the flask to Morgaine, who took it gratefully, drank and passed it to Jhirun.

One of the *qujal* moved; Vanye turned, hand on his sword, and saw one of the house guards on his feet. The *qujal* came toward them, grim of face and careful in his movements; and he addressed himself to Jhirun, who had the waterflask. He held out his hand toward it, demanding, insolent.

Jhirun hesitated, looking for direction; and Vanye sullenly

nodded consent, watching as the halfling took the flask and
brought it back to Kithan. The halfling lord drank sparingly,
then gave it to his men, who likewise drank in their turn.

Then the same man brought it back, offered it to Vanye's
hand. Vanye stood, jaw set in a scowl, and nodded toward
Jhirun, from whom the man had taken it. He gave it back to
her, looked again to Vanye with a guarded expression.

And inclined his head—courtesy, from a *qujal*. Vanye
stiffly returned the gesture, with no grace in it.

The man returned to his lord. Vanye grasped the ring at
his shoulder, drew it down to hook it, then settled again at
Morgaine's feet.

"Rest," he bade her. "I will watch."

Morgaine wrapped herself in her cloak and leaned against
the rocks, closing her eyes. Quietly Jhirun curled up to sleep;
and likewise Kithan and his men, the frail *qujal*-lord pillow-
ing his head on his arms, and in all likelihood suffering somewhat from the wind, in his thin hall garments.

It grew still, in all the world only the occasional sound of
the horses, and the wind that sighed through the leaves.
Vanye gathered himself to his feet and stood with his back
against a massive rock, so that he might not yield to sleep un-
knowing. Once he did catch himself with his eyes closed, and
paced, his knees weak with exhaustion, so long as he could
bear it: he was, Kurshin-fashion, able to sleep in the saddle,
far better than Morgaine.

But there was a limit. "*Liyo*," he said after a time, in desperation, and she wakened. "We might move on," he said;
and she gazed at him, who was unsteady with weariness, and
shook her head. "Rest," she said, and he cast himself down
on the cold earth, the world still seeming to move with the
endless motion of the horse. It was not long that he needed,
only a time to let the misery leave his back and arm, and the
throbbing leave his skull.

Someone moved. Vanye wakened with the sun on him,
found the *qujal* awake and the day declined to afternoon.
Morgaine sat as she had been, with *Changeling* cradled
against her shoulder. When he looked up at her, there was a
clarity to her gray eyes that had been lacking before, a clear
and quiet sense that comforted him.

"We will be moving," Morgaine said, and Jhirun stirred
from her sleep, holding her head in her hands. Morgaine

passed him the flask; he sipped at it enough to clear his mouth, and swallowed with a grimace, gave it back to her.

"Draw breath," she bade him, when he would have risen at once to see to the horses. Such patience was unlike her. He saw the look of concentration in her gaze, that rested elsewhere, and followed it to the halflings.

He watched Kithan, who with trembling hands had taken an embroidered handkerchief from his pocket, and extracted from it a small white object that he placed in his mouth.

For a moment Kithan leaned forward, head in hands, white hair falling to hide his face; then with a movement more graceful, he flung his head back and restored his handkerchief to its place within his garment.

"*Akil*," Morgaine murmured privately.

"*Liyo?*"

"A vice evidently not confined to the marshlands. Another matter of trade, I do suppose . . . the marshlands' further revenge on Ohtij-in. He should be placid and communicative for hours."

Vanye watched the halfling lord, whose manner soon began to take on that languid abstraction he had seen in hall, that haze-eyed distance from the world. Here was Bydarra's true, his *qujalin* son, the heir that surely the old lord would have preferred above Hetharu; but Kithan had arranged otherwise, a silent abdication, not alone from the defense he might have been to his father and his house, but from all else that surrounded him. Vanye regarded the man with disgust.

But neither, he thought suddenly, had Kithan resorted to it last night, when a mob had murdered his people before his eyes; not then nor, he much suspected, despite what he had seen in that cell—had Kithan taken to it the hour that Bydarra was murdered, when he had been compelled to pay homage to his brother, stumbling when he tried to rise: his recovery after Hetharu's departure from Ohtij-in had been instant, as if it were a different man.

The *akil* was real enough; but it was also a convenient pose, a means of camouflage and survival: Vanye well understood the intrigues of a divided house. It might have begun in boredom, in the jaded tastes and narrow limits of Ohtij-in; or otherwise.

I dreamed, Jhirun had wept, who looked further than the day, and could not bear what she saw. She had fled to Shiuan in hope; for the Shiua lord, there was nowhere to flee.

Vanye stared at him, trying to penetrate that calm that in-

sulated him, trying to reckon how much was the man and
how much the *akil*—and which it was that had stood within
his cell that night in Ohtij-in, coldly planning his murder only
to spite Hetharu, by means doubtless lingering and painful.

And Morgaine took them, Kithan and his men, who had
no reason to wish her well: she delayed for them, while the
halfling lord retreated into his dreams: he chafed at this,
vexed even in their company.

"This road," Morgaine said suddenly, addressing Kithan,
"goes most directly to Abarais."

Kithan agreed with a languorous nod of his head.

"There is none other," said Morgaine, "unmapped in your
books."

"None horses might use," said Kithan. "The mountains are
twisted, full of stonefalls and the like; and of lakes; of
chasms. There is only this way, save for men afoot, and no
quicker than we go. You do not have to worry for the rabble
behind us, but," he added with a heavy-lidded smile of
amusement, "you have the true lord of Ohtij-in ahead of you,
with the main part of our strength, a-horse and armed, a
mark less easy than I was in Ohtij-in. And they may afford
you some little inconvenience."

"To be sure," said Morgaine.

Kithan smiled, resting his elbows on the shelf of rock at his
back; his pale eyes fixed upon her with that accustomed distance, unreachable. The men that were with him were alike
as brothers, pale hair drawn back at the nape, the same
profile, men dark-eyed, alike in armor, alike in attitude, one
to his right, one to his left.

"Why are you with us?" Vanye asked. "Misplaced trust?"

Kithan's composure suffered the least disturbance; a frown
passed over his face. His eyes fixed on Vanye's with obscure
challenge, and a languid pale hand, cuffed in delicate lace,
gestured toward his heart. "On your pleasure, Barrows-lord."

"You are mistaken," Vanye said.

"Why," asked Morgaine very softly, "*are* you with us, my
lord Kithan, once of Ohtij-in?"

Kithan tossed his head back and gave a silent and mirthless
laugh, moved his wrist in the direction of the Suvoj. "We
have little choice, do we not?"

"And when we do meet with Roh and with Hetharu's
forces, you will be at our backs."

Kithan frowned. "But I am your man, Morgaine-
Angharan." He extended his long legs, crossed, before him,

easy as a man in his own hall. "I am your most devoted servant."

"Indeed," said Morgaine.

"Doubtless," said Kithan, regarding her with that same distant smile, you will serve me as you served those who followed you to Ohtij-in."

"It is more than possible," said Morgaine.

"They were your own," Kithan exclaimed with sudden, plaintive force, as if he pleaded something; and Jhirun, flinching, edged against the rocks at Vanye's side.

"They may have been once," Morgaine said. "But those that I knew are long buried. Their children are not mine."

Kithan's face recovered its placidity; laughter returned to his half-lidded eyes. "But they followed you," he said. "I find that ironical. They knew you, knew what you had done to their ancestors, and still they followed you, because they thought you would make an exception of them; and you served them exactly as you are. Even the Aren-folk, who hate you, and tie up white feathers at their doorways—" He smiled widely and laughed, a mere breath. "A reality. A fixed point in all this reasonless universe. I am *khal*. I have never found a point on which to stand or a shrine at which to worship—til now. You *are* Angharan; you come to destroy the Wells and all that exists. You are the only rational being in the world. So I also follow you, Morgaine-Angharan. I am your faithful worshipper."

Vanye thrust himself to his feet, hand to his belt, loathing the *qujal*'s insolence, his mockery, his elaborate fancies: Morgaine should not have to suffer this, and did, for it was not her habit to avenge herself for words, or for other wrongs.

"At your pleasure," he said to Kithan.

Kithan, weaponless, indicated so with an outward gesture, a slight hardness to his eyes.

"Let be," Morgaine said. "Prepare the horses. Let us be moving, Vanye."

"I might cut their reins and their girths for them," said Vanye, scowling at the halfling lord and his two men, reckoning them, several, a moderately fair contest. "They could test their horsemanship with that, and we would not have to give them further patience."

Morgaine hesitated, regarding Kithan. "Let him be," she said. "His courage comes from the *akil*. It will pass."

The insouciance of Kithan seemed stung by that. He

frowned, and leaned against the rock staring at her, no longer
capable of distance.

"Prepare the horses," she said. "If he can hold our pace,
well; and if not—the Hiua will remember that he companied
with me."

There was unease in the guards' faces, a flicker of the same
in Kithan's; and then, with a bow, a taut smile: *"Arrhthein,"*
he said to her. *"Sharron a thrissn nthinn."*

"Arrhtheis," Morgaine echoed softly, and Kithan settled
back with an estimating look in his eyes, as if something had
passed between them of irony and bitter humor.

It was the language of the Stones. *I am not qujal,* Morgaine had insisted to him once, which he believed, which he
still insisted on believing.

But when he had gone, at Morgaine's impatient gesture, to
attend the horses, he looked back at them, his pale-haired
liege and the pale-haired *qujal* together, tall and slender, in
all points similar; a chill ran through him.

Jhirun, human-dark, a wraith in brown, scrambled up and
quitted that company and ran to him, as he gathered up the
reins of her mare and brought it to the roadside. He threw
down there the bundle she had made of their supplies and began rerolling the blankets, on his knees at the side of the
stone road. She knelt down with him and began with feverish
earnestness to help him, in this and when he began to tie the
separate rolls to their three saddles, redistributing supplies
and tightening harness.

Her mare's girth too he attended, seeing that it was well
done, on which her life depended. She waited, hovering at his
side.

"Please," she said at last, touching at his elbow. "Let me
ride with you; let me stay with you."

"I cannot promise that." He avoided her eyes, and brushed
past her to attend the matter of his own horse. "If the mare
cannot hold our pace, still she is steady and she will manage
to keep you ahead of the Hiua. I have other obligations. I
cannot think of anything else just now."

"These men—lord, I am afraid of them. They—"

She did not finish. It ended in tears. He looked at her and
remembered her the night that Kithan had visited his cell,
small and wretched as she had been in the hands of the
guards, men half-masked and anonymous in their demon-
helms. Her they had seized, and not him.

"Do you know these men?" he asked of her harshly.

She did not answer, only stared at him helplessly with the
flush of shame staining her cheeks; and he looked askance at
Kithan's man, who was likewise caring for his lord's horse.
Privately he thought of what justice Kursh reserved for such
as they: her ancestors had been, though she had forgotten it,
tan-uyin, and honorable, and proud.

He was not free to take up her quarrel. He had a service.

He set his hand on hers; it was small, but rough, a
peasant's hand, that knew hard labor. "Your ancestors," he
said, "were high-born men. My father's wife was Myya, who
gave him his legitimate sons. They are a hard-minded clan,
the Myya; they 'my lord' only those that they respect."

Her hand, leaving his, went to her breast, where he remembered a small gold amulet that once he had returned to her.
The pain her eyes had held departed, leaving something clear
and far from fragile.

"The mare," he said, "will not run that far behind, Myya
Jhirun."

She left him. He watched her, at the roadside, bend and
gather a handful of smooth stones, and drop them, as she
straightened, into her bodice. Then she gathered up the
mare's reins and set herself into the saddle.

And suddenly he saw something beyond her, at the bottom
of the long hill, a dark mass on the road beyond the knoll
that rose like a barrow-mound at the turning.

"Liyo," he called out, appalled at the desperate endurance
of those that followed them, afoot. Not for revenge: for revenge they surely could not follow so far or so determinedly
. . . but for hope, a last hope, that rested not with Morgaine,
but with Roh.

There were Shiua and the priest, who knew what Roh had
promised in Ohtij-in; and there was Fwar: for Fwar, it would
be revenge.

Morgaine stood at his side, looked down the road. "They
cannot keep our pace," she said.

"They need not," said Kithan; and gone now was the slur-
ring of his speech; fear glittered through the haze of his eyes.
"There are forces between us and Abarais, my lady Morgaine, and one of them is my brother's. Hetharu will have
ridden over whatever opposition he meets: he is not loved by
the mountain lords. But so much the more will forces be on
the move in this land. Your enemy has sent couriers
abroad: folk here will know you; they will be waiting for

you; and being mad, they are, of course, interested in living.
We may find our way quite difficult."

Morgaine gave him a baleful look, took *Changeling* from
her shoulder and hooked it to her saddle before she set foot
in the stirrup. Vanye mounted, and drew close to her, thinking no longer of what followed them or of Myya Jhirun i
Myya; it was Morgaine he protected, and if that should entail
turning on three of their companions, he would be nothing
loath.

The land opened before them, rich with crops and dark
earth; and closed again and opened, small pockets of culti-
vated earth hardly wider than a field or two between opposing
heights, and occasionally a small marsh and a reed-rimmed
lake.

Crags rose towering on all sides of them, a limit to the sky
that in other days Vanye would have found comfortable, a
view much like home; but it was not his land, and nowhere
was there indication what might lie ahead. He looked into the
deep places of the weathered rocks, the recesses that were often overgrown with trees and man-tall weeds, and knew that
in one thing at least Kithan had told the truth: that there was
no passage for a horseman off this road; and if there were
trails in the hills, as surely there were, even a runner must
needs be born to this land to make much speed.

They did not press the horses, that like themselves had
gone without sleep and rest; Kithan rode with them, his two
men trailing, and last rode Jhirun, whose bay mare was content to lag by several lengths.

And at dusk, as they came through one of the many nar-
rows, there appeared stones by the road, set by men; and
against the forested cliffs beyond was a stone village, a
sprawling and untidy huddle next the road.

"Whose?" Morgaine asked of Kithan. "It was not on the
maps."

Kithan shrugged. "There are many such. The land hereabouts is Sotharra land; but I do not know the name of the
village. There will be others. They are human places."

Vanye looked incredulously at the halfling lord, and judged
that it was likely the truth, that a lord of Shiuan did not trouble to learn the names of the villages that lay within reach of
his own land.

Morgaine swore, and came to a slow stop on the road,
where they were last screened by the trees and the rocks. A

spring flowed at the roadside, next the trees. She let Siptah drink, and herself dismounted and knelt upcurrent, drinking from her hand. The *qujal* followed her example, even Kithan drinking from the stream like any peasant; and Jhirun overtook them and cast herself down from her mare to the cool bank.

"We shall rest a moment," Morgaine said. "Vanye—"

He nodded, stepped down from the saddle, and filled their waterflasks the while Morgaine watched his back.

And constantly, while they let the horses breathe and took a little of their small supply of food, Morgaine's eye was on their companions or his was, while the dusk settled and became night.

Jhirun held close, by Morgaine's side or his. She sat quietly, for the most part, and braided her long hair in a single plait down the back, tied it with a bit of yarn from her fringed skirt. And there was something different in her bearing, a set to her jaw, a directness to her eyes that had not been there before.

She set herself with them as if she belonged: Vanye met her eye, remembered how she had intervened in Fwar's ambush in the stable, and reckoned that were he an enemy of Myya Jhirun i Myya, he would well guard his back. A warrior of clan Myya, restrained by codes and honor, was still a bad enemy. Jhirun, he remembered, knew nothing of such restraints.

It was at the men of Kithan that she stared in the darkness, and they would not look toward her.

And when they remounted, Jhirun rode insolently across the path of Kithan and his men, turned and glared at Kithan himself.

The *qujal*-lord brought up short, and seemed not offended, but perplexed at such arrogance in a Hiua peasant. Then, with elaborate irony, he reined his horse aside to give her place.

"We are going through," said Morgaine; "and from now on I do not trust we will be able to rest for more than a few moments at any stopping. We are near Sotharrn, it seems; and we are, from Sotharrn, within reach of Abarais."

"By tomorrow, *liyo?*" Vanye asked.

"By tomorrow night," she said, "or not at all."

Chapter Sixteen

|||||||||||||||||||||||||||||||||||||||||||||||||||||

The village sprawled at the left of the road, silent in the dark, beneath a forested upthrust of rock that shadowed it from Anli's wan light: a motley gathering of stone houses, surrounded by a wall as high as a rider's head.

The horses' hooves rang unevenly off the walls as they rode by. There was no stirring within, no light, no opening of the shuttered windows that overtopped the wall, no sound even of livestock. The gate was shut, a white object affixed to its center.

It was the wing of a white bird, nailed there, the boards smeared blackly with the blood.

Jhirun touched the necklace that she wore and murmured something in a low voice. Vanye crossed himself fervently and scanned the shuttered windows and overshadowing crags for any sign of the folk that lived there.

"You are expected," Kithan said, "as I warned you."

Vanye glanced at him, and at Morgaine—met her eyes and saw the shadow there, as it had been at the bridge.

And she shivered, a quick and strange gesture, full of weariness, and set Siptah to a quicker pace, to leave the village behind them.

The pass closed about them, a place where rock had tumbled to the very edge of the road, boulders man-large. Vanye gazed up at the dark heights, and with a shiver of his own, used the spurs. They came through the throat of that place at a pace that set the echoes flying, and there was no fall of stones, no stir of life from the cliffs.

But when, halfway across the next small valley, he turned and looked back, he saw a red glow of fire atop those cliffs.

"*Liyo*," he said.

Morgaine looked, and said nothing. The Baien gray had struck that pace that, on level ground, he could hold for

some space; and the gelding could match him stride for
stride, but not forever.

The alarm was given: henceforth there was no stopping.
What Roh had not known was spread now throughout the
countryside.

Soon enough there was another, answering fire among the
hills to their left.

The towers appeared unexpectedly in the morning light,
half-hidden in forested crags: walls many-turreted and more
regular than those of Ohtij-in, but surely as old. They domi-
nated the widest of the valleys that they had seen; and culti-
vated fields lay round about.

Morgaine reined back briefly, scanning that hold, that
guarded the pass before them.

And far behind them, horses unable to stay their pace,
rode the three *qujal,* and last of all, Jhirun.

Vanye unhooked his sword and secured the sheath, mark-
ing the smoke that hung above those walls. He laid the naked
blade across the saddlebow. Morgaine took *Changeling* from
its place beneath her knee, and laid it, still sheathed, across
her own.

"*Liyo,*" Vanye said softly. "When you will."

"Carefully," she said.

She let Siptah go; and the gelding matched pace with him,
at an easy gait, toward the towers and the pass.

Smoke rose there steadily, as it had from many a point
about the valleys, fire after fire passing the alarm.

But it was not, as the others had been, white brush-smoke;
it spread darkly on the sky, and as they rode near enough to
see the walls distinctly, they could see in that stain upon the
heavens the wheeling flight of birds, that hovered above the
hold.

The gates stood agape, battered from their hinges: they
could see that clearly from the main road. A dead horse lay
in the ravine beside the spur of road that diverged toward
those gates; birds flapped up from it, disturbed in their
feeding.

And curiously, across that empty gateway were cords,
knotted with bits of white feather.

Morgaine reined in—suddenly turned off toward that gate;
and Vanye protested, but no word did she speak, only rode
warily, slowly toward that gateway, and he made haste to

overtake her, falling in at her side the while she approached that strange barrier. The only sound was the ring of hooves on stone and the hollow echo off the walls—that, and the wind, that blew strongly at the cords.

Ruin lay inside. A cloud of black birds, startled, fluttered up from the stripped carcass of an ox that lay amid the court. On the steps of the keep sprawled a dead man; another lay in the shadow of the wall, prey to the birds. He had been *qujal*. His white hair proclaimed it.

And some three, hanged, twisted slowly on the fire-blackened tree that had grown in the center of the courtyard.

Morgaine reached for the lesser of her weapons, and fire parted the strands of the feathered cords. She urged Siptah slowly forward. The walls echoed to the sound of the horses and to the alarmed flutter of the carrion birds. Smoke still boiled up from the smouldering core of the central keep, from the wreckage of human shelters that had clustered about it.

Riders clattered up the stones outside. Morgaine wheeled Siptah about as Kithan's party came within the gates and reined to a dazed halt.

Kithan looked slowly about him, his thin face set in horror; there was horror too in the face of Jhirun, who arrived last within the gateway, her mare stepping skittishly past the blowing strands of cords and feathers. Jhirun held tightly to the charms about her neck and stopped just inside the gates.

"Let us leave this place," Vanye said; and Morgaine took up the reins, about to heed him.

But Kithan suddenly hailed the place, a loud cry that echoed in the emptiness; and again he called, and finally turned his horse full circle to survey all the ruined keep, the dead that hung from the tree and that lay within the yard, while the two men with him looked about them too, their faces white and drawn.

"Sotharrn," Kithan exclaimed in anguish. "There were better than seven hundred of our folk here, besides the Shiua." He gestured at the fluttering cords. "Shiua belief. Those are for fear of you."

"Would Hetharu have gathered forces here," Morgaine asked him, "or lost them? Was this riot, or was it war?"

"He follows Roh," Kithan said. "And Roh has promised him his heart's desires—as he doubtless would promise others, halfling and human." He gazed about him at the shelters that had housed men, that were empty now, as—Vanye realized suddenly—the village in the night had lain silent, as the valleys and hills between had been vacant, with only the alarm fires to break the peace.

And of a sudden one of the guards reined about, and spurred through the gates. The other hesitated, his pale face a mask of anguish and indecision.

Then he too rode, whipping his tired horse in his frenzy, and vanished from sight, deserting his lord, seeking safety elsewhere.

"No!" cried Morgaine, checking Vanye's impulse to pursue them; and when he reined back: "No. There are already the fires: they are enough to have warned our enemies. Let them go." And to Kithan, who sat his horse staring after his departed men: "Do you wish to follow them?"

"Shiuan is finished," Kithan said in a trembling voice, and looked back at her. "If Sotharrn has fallen, then no other hold will stand long against Hetharu, against Chya Roh, against the rabble that they have stirred to arms. What you will do—do. Or let me stay with you."

There was no arrogance left him. His voice broke, and he bowed his head, leaning against the saddlebow. When he lifted his face again, the look of tears was in his eyes.

Morgaine regarded him long and narrowly.

Then without a word she rode past him, for the gate where the feathered cords fluttered uselessly in the wind. Vanye delayed, letting Jhirun turn, letting Kithan go before him. Constantly he felt a prickling between his own shoulders, a consciousness that there might well be watchers somewhere within the ruins—for someone had strung the cords and tried to seal the gate from harm, someone frightened, and human.

No attack came, nothing but the panic flight of birds, a whispering of wind through the ruins. They passed the gate on the downward road, riding slowly, listening.

And Vanye watched the *qujal*-lord, who rode before him, pale head bowed, yielding to the motion of the horse. Without choices, Kithan—without skill to survive in the wilderness that Shiuan had become, helpless without his servants to attend him and his peasants to feed him . . . and now without refuge to shelter him.

Better the sword's edge, Vanye thought, echoing something that Roh had said to him, and then dismayed to remember who had said it, and that it had been true.

At the road's joining, Morgaine increased the pace. "Move!" Vanye shouted at the halfling, spurring forward, and

struck Kithan's horse with the flat of his blade, startling it
into a brief burst of speed. They turned northward onto the
main road, slowing again as they came beyond arrowflight of
the walls.

On sudden impulse Vanye looked back, saw on the walls
of Sotharrn a brown, bent figure, and another and another—
ragged, furtive watchers that vanished the instant they realized they had been seen.

Old ones, deserted, while the young had been carried away
with the tide that swept toward Abarais: the young, who
looked to live, who would kill to live, like the horde that followed still behind them.

The land beyond Sotharrn bore more signs of violence,
fields and land along the roadway churned to mire, as if the
road itself could no longer contain what poured toward the
north. Tracks of men and horses were sharply defined beside
the road and in mud yet unwashed from the paving stones.

"They passed," Vanye said to Morgaine, as they rode knee
to knee behind Jhirun and Kithan, "since the rain stopped."

He tried to lend her hope; she frowned over it, shook her
head.

"Hetharu delayed here, perhaps," she said in a low voice.
"He would be enough to deal with Sotharrn. But were I Roh,
I would not have delayed for such an untidy matter if there
were a choice: I would have gone for Abarais. And once
there, then no hold will stand. I would be glad to know where
Hetharu's force is; but I fear I know where Roh is."

Vanye considered that; it was not good to think on. He
turned his mind instead to forces that he understood.
"Hetharu's force," he said, "looks to have gathered considerable number; perhaps two, three thousand by now."

"There are also the outlying villages," she said. "—Kithan."

The halfling reined back somewhat, and Jhirun's mare,
never one to take the lead, lagged too, coming alongside so
that they were four abreast on the road. Kithan regarded
them placidly, his eyes again vague and hazed.

"He is only half sensible," Vanye said in disgust. "Perhaps
he and that store of his were best parted."

"No," said Kithan at once, straightening in his saddle. He
made effort to look at them directly, and his eyes were
possessed of a distant, tearless sadness. "I have listened to
your reckoning; I hear you well . . . Leave me my consolation, Man. I shall answer your questions."

"Then say," said Morgaine, "what we must expect. Will Hetharu gain the support of the other holds? Will they move to join him?"

"Hetharu—" Kithan's mouth twisted in a grimace of contempt. "Sotharrn always feared him . . . that did he succeed to power in Ohtij-in, then attack would come. And they were right, of course. Some of our fields flooded this season; and more would have gone the next; and the next. It was inevitable that the more ambitious of us would reach across the Suvoj."

"Will the other holds follow him or fight him now?"

Kithan shrugged. "What difference to the Shiua; and to us—Even we bowed and kissed his hand in Ohtij-in. We who wanted nothing but to live undisturbed . . . have no power against whoever does not. Yes, most will be with him: to what purpose anything else? My guards have gone over to him: that is where they are going. There is no question of it. They saw my prospects, and they know defeat when they smell it. So they went to him. The lesser holds will flock to do the same."

"You may go too if you like," Morgaine said.

Kithan regarded her, disturbed.

"Be quite free to do so," she said.

The horses walked along together some little distance; and Kithan looked at Morgaine with less and less assurance, as if she and the drug together confused him. He looked at Jhirun, whose regard of him was hard; and at Vanye, who stared back at him expressionless, giving him nothing, neither of hatred nor of comfort. Once more he glanced the circuit of them, and last of all at Vanye, as if he expected that some terrible game were being made of him.

For a moment Vanye thought that he would go; his body was tense in the saddle, his eyes, through their haze, distracted.

"No," Kithan said then, and his shoulders fell. He rode beside them sunk in his own misery.

None spoke, Vanye rode content enough in Morgaine's presence by him, a nearness of mind in which words were needless; he knew her, that had they been alone she would have had nothing to say. Her eyes scanned the trail as they rode, but her mind was elsewhere, desperately occupied.

At last she drew from her boot top a folded and age-yellowed bit of parchment, a map cut from a book; and silently, leaning from the saddle, she indicated to him the road. It

wound up from the Suvoj, that great rift clearly recognizable;
but the lands of Ohtij-in were shown as wide, plotted fields,
that no longer existed. There were fields mapped on this side
also, along the road and within the hills; and holds besides
that which seemed to be Sotharrn, scattered here and there
about the central mountains.

And amid those mountains, a circular mark, lay Abarais:
Vanye could not read the runes, but her finger indicated it,
and she named it aloud.

He lifted his eyes from the brown ink and yellowed page,
to the mountains that now loomed before them. Greenish-
black evergreen covered their flanks. Their rounded peaks
were bald and smooth and their slopes were a tumble of great
stones, aged, weather-worn—a ruin of mountains in a dying
land.

Above them passed the Broken Moon, in a clear sky; the
weather held for them, warm as the sun reached its zenith;
but when the sun declined toward afternoon, the hills seemed
overlain with a foul haze.

It was not cloud; none wreathed these low hills. It was the
smoke of fires, from some far place within the mountains,
where other holds had been marked on the map.

"I think that would be Domen," said Kithan, when they
questioned him on it. "That is next, after Sotharrn. On the
far side of the mountains lie Marom and Arisith; and
Hetharu's forces will have reached for those also."

"Still increasing in number," said Morgaine.

"Yes," said Kithan. "The whole of Shiuan is within his
hands—or will be, within days. He is burning the shelters, I
would judge: that is the way to move the humanfolk, to draw
them with him. And perhaps he burns the holds themselves.
He may want no lords to rival him."

Morgaine said nothing.

"It will do him no good," Vanye said, to dispossess Kithan
of any hopes he might still hold. "Hetharu may have Shiuan—but Roh has Hetharu, whether or not Hetharu has yet
realized it."

Stones rose beside the road, Standing Stones, that called to
mind that cluster beside the road in Hiuaj, near the marsh;
but these stood straight and powerful in the evening light.

And beyond those Stones moved a white-haired figure,
leaning on a staff, who struggled to walk the road.

They gained upon that man rapidly; and surely by now the

traveler must have heard them coming, and might have looked around; but he did not. He moved at the same steady pace, painfully awkward.

There was an eeriness about that deaf persistence; Vanye laid his sword across the saddlebow as they came alongside the man, fearing some plan concealed in this bizarre attitude—a ruse to put a man near Morgaine. He moved his horse between, reining back to match his pace.

Still the man did not look up at them, but walked with eyes downcast, step by agonized step with the staff to support him. He was young, wearing hall-garments; he bore a knife at his belt, and the staff on which he leaned was the broken remnant of a pike. His white hair was tangled, his cheek cut and bruised, blood soaked the rough bandages on his leg. Vanye hailed him, and yet the youth kept walking; he cursed, and thrust his sheathed sword across the man's chest.

The *qujal* stopped, downcast eyes fixed on something other and elsewhere; but when Vanye let fall the sword, he began to walk again, struggling in his lameness.

"He is mad," Jhirun said.

"No," said Kithan. "He does not wish to see you."

Their horses moved along with the youth, slowly, by halting paces; and softly Kithan began to question him, in his own tongue—received an anguished glance of him, and an answer, spoken on hard-drawn breaths, the while he walked. Names were named that touched keenly Vanye's interest, but no other word of it could he grasp. The youth exhausted his supply of breath and fell silent, walked on, as he had been before.

Morgaine touched Siptah and moved on, Vanye at her side; and Jhirun with them. Kithan followed. Vanye looked back, at the youth who still doggedly, painfully, struggled behind them.

"What did he say?" Vanye asked of Morgaine. She shrugged, not in a mood to answer.

"He is Allyvy," said Kithan in her silence. "He is of Sotharrn; and he has the same madness as took the villagers: he says that he is bound for Abarais, as all are going, believing this Chya Roh."

Vanye looked at Morgaine, found her face grim and set; and she shrugged. "So we are too late," she said, "as I feared."

"He has promised them," said Kithan, "another and better land: a hope to live; and they are going to take it. They are gathering an army, to march toward it; holds are burned: they say there is no need of them now."

He looked again at Morgaine, expecting some answer of her. There was none. She rode with her eyes fixed, no more slowly, no more quickly, passing the ruined fields. He saw in her a tautness that trembled beneath that placid surface, something thin-strung and fragile.

Violence, terror: it flowed to his own taut nerves.

Let us retreat, a thing in him wanted to say. *Let us find a place, lost in the hills, when all of them have passed, when the Wells are sealed. There is life enough for us, peace—once you have lost and can no longer hope to follow him. We could live. We might grow old before the waters rose to take these mountains. We would be alone, and sealed, safe, from all our enemies.*

She knew her choices, he reckoned to himself, and chose what she would; but he began to think, in deep guilt, what it would be did they find Roh gone: that that was earnestly to be hoped, else she would hurl herself against an army, taking all with her.

It was a traitorous thought; he realized it, and crossed himself fervently, wishing it away—met her eyes and feared suddenly that she understood his fear.

"*Liyo*," he said in a quiet voice, "whatever wants doing, I will do."

It seemed to reassure her. She turned her attention back to the way they rode, and to the hills.

Night began to fall, streaks of twilight that shaded into dark among the smokes across the hills, a murky and ugly color. They rode among stones that gathered more and more thickly about the road, until it became clear that here had been some massive structure, foundations that lay naked and exposed in great intersecting rectangles and circles and bits of arches. Constantly the earth bore signs that vast numbers had traveled this way, and lately.

And there was a dead man by the road. The black birds rose up from his body like shadows into the dark, a heavy flapping of wings.

Violence within the army's own ranks attended them, Vanye reckoned: desperate men, frightened men; and men and halflings massed together. They were not long in coming upon other dead, and one was a woman, and one was a black-robed priest, frail and elderly.

"They are beasts," Kithan exclaimed in anguish.

None disputed him.

"What shall we do," asked Jhirun, who had remained silent most of the day, "what shall we do when we reach Abarais, if they are all gathered there?"

It was not a witless question; it was a desperate one . . . Jhirun, who knew less than they what must be done, and who endured all things patiently in her hope. Vanye looked at her and shook his head helplessly, foreseeing what he thought Jhirun herself began to foresee, what Morgaine had tried earnestly to warn her, weaponless as the Barrows-girl was, and without defenses.

"You also," said Morgaine, "are still free to leave us."

"No," Jhirun said quietly. "Like my lord Kithan, I have nothing to hope for from what follows us; and if I cannot get through where you are going, at least—" She made a helpless gesture, as if it were too difficult a thing to speak. "Let me try," she said then.

Morgaine considered her a moment as they rode, and finally nodded in confirmation.

The dark fell more and more heavily about them, until there was only the light of the lesser moons and the bow in the sky in which the moons traveled, a cloudy arc across the stars. From one wall of the wide valley to the other were the dark shapes of vast ruins, no longer Standing Stones, but spires, straight on their inner, roadward faces, with a curving slant on their outer. They were aligned with the road on either side, and began to set inward to enclose it.

Their way became an aisle, so that they no longer had clear view of the hills; the stone spires began to set against the very edge of the paving, like ribs along the spine of the road.

The horses' hooves echoed loudly down that passage, and the shifting perspectives of that vast aisle, lit only by the moons, provided ample cover for ambush. Vanye rode with his sword across the saddlebow, wishing that they might make faster passage through this cursed place, and knowing at the same time the unwisdom of racing blindly through the dark. The road became entirely blind at some points, as it turned and the spires cut off their view on all sides.

And thereafter the road began to climb as well as wind, in long terraced steps that led ultimately to a darkness—a starless shadow that as they neared it began to take on the detail of black stonework, that lay as a wall before them: a vast cube of a building that overtopped the spires, that diverged to form an aisle before it.

"An-Abarais," murmured Kithan. "Gateway to the Well."

Vanye gazed at it with foreboding as they rode: for once before he had seen the like; and beside him Morgaine took *Changeling* into her hand. The gray horse blew nervously, side-stepping, then started forward again, taking the narrowing terraces; Vanye spurred the gelding to make him keep pace, put from his mind their two companions that trailed them.

It was no Gate, but a fortress that could master the Gates; *qujal,* and full of power. It was a place that Roh would not have neglected.

There was no other way through.

Chapter Seventeen

||||||||||||||||||||||||||||||||||||||||||||||||||||||

The road met the fortress of An-Abarais: and it vanished into a long archway, black and cheerless, with night and open sky at its other end. But the slanted spires shaped another road, fronting the fortress; and in that crossing of ways Morgaine reined in, scanning all directions.

"Kithan," she said, as their two companions overtook them. "You watch the road from here. Jhirun: come. Come with us."

Jhirun cast an apprehensive look at all of them, left and right; but Morgaine was already on her way down that righthand aisle, a pale-haired ghost on a pale horse, almost lost in shadow.

Vanye reined aside and rode after, heard Jhirun clattering along behind him in haste. What Kithan would do, whether he would stay or whether he would flee to their enemies—Vanye refused to reckon: Morgaine surely tempted him, dismissed him for good or for ill; but her thoughts would be set desperately elsewhere at the moment, and she needed her *ilin* at her back.

He overtook her as she stopped in that dark aisle, where she had found the deep shadow of a doorway; she dismounted, pushed at that door with her left hand, bearing *Changeling* in her right.

It yielded easily, on silent hinges. Cold breathed forth from that darkness, wherein the moonlight from the doorway showed level, polished stone. She led Siptah forward, within the door, and Vanye bent his head and rode carefully after, shod hooves ringing irreverently in that deep silence. Jhirun followed, afoot, tugging at the reluctant mare, a third clatter of hooves on the stone. When she was still, there was no sound but the restless shift of leather and the animals' hard breathing.

Vanye slid his sword from its sheath and carried it naked in his hand; and suddenly light glimmered from Morgaine's hands as she began to do the same, baring *Changeling's* rune-written blade. The opal shimmer grew, flared into brilliance enough to light the room, casting strange shadows of slanting spires, a circular chamber, a stairway that wound its way among the spires.

From *Changeling* came a pulsing sound, soft at first, then painful to the senses, that filled all the air and made the horses shy. The light brightened when Morgaine swept its tip up and leftward; and by this they both knew the way they must go, reading the seeking of the blade toward its own power.

And did they meet, unsheathed blade and living source, it would end both: whatever madness had made *Changeling* had made it indestructible save by Gates.

Morgaine sheathed it as quickly as might be; and the horses stood trembling after. Vanye patted the gelding's sweating neck and slid down.

"Come," Morgaine said, looking at him. "Jhirun—watch the horses. Cry out at once if something goes in the least amiss; put your back against solid stone and stay there. Above all else do not trust Kithan. If he comes, warn us."

"Yes," she agreed in a thin voice; and half a breath Vanye hesitated, thinking to lend her a weapon—but she could not use it.

He turned, overtook Morgaine, emptied his mind of all else—watching her back, watching the shadows on whatever side she was not watching. Right hand and left the shadows passed them, and as soon as the darkness became absolute, a light flared in Morgaine's hand, a harmless, cold magic, for it only guided them: little as he liked such things, he trusted the hand that held it. Nothing she might do could fright him here, in the presence of powers eldritch and *qujalin*: the sword of metal that he bore was a useless thing in such a place, all his arts and skills valueless—save against ambush.

A door faced them; it yielded noisily to Morgaine's skilled touch, startling him; and light blazed suddenly in their faces, a garish burst of color, of pulsing radiance. Sound gibbered at them; he heard the echo of his own shameful outcry, roll-ing through the halls.

It was the heart of the Gates, the Wells, the thing that ruled them: and though he had seen the like before and knew that no mere noise or light could harm him, he could not

shame away the clutch of fear at his heart, his traitor limbs
that reacted to the madness that assailed them.

"Come," Morgaine urged him: the suspicion of pity in her
voice stung him; and he gripped his sword and stayed close at
her heels, walking as briskly as she down that long aisle of
light. Light redder than the sunset dyed her hair and her skin,
glittered bloodily off mail and stained *Changeling's* golden
hilt: the sound that roared about them drowned their foot-
falls so that she and he seemed to drift soundlessly in the
glow. Morgaine spared not a glance for the madness on either
side of them: *she belongs here,* he thought, watching her—
who in Andurin armor, of a manner a hundred years older
than his own, paused before the center of those blazing pan-
els. She laid hands on them with skill, called forth flurries of
lights and sound that drowned all the rest and set him trembling.

Qujal, he thought, *as they were.*
As they would wish to be.

She looked sharply back at him, beckoned him; he came,
with one backward look, for in that flood of sound anyone
might steal upon them from the doorway unawares. But she
touched his arm and commanded his attention upon the instant.

"It is locked," she said, speaking above the roar, "wide
open. There is a hold upon it that cannot be broken: Roh's
work. I knew that this would be the case if he reached it
first."

"You can do nothing?" he asked of her; and beyond her
shoulder saw the pulsing lights that were the power and life
of the Gates. He had borne as much as he wished to bear,
and more than he wanted to remember; but he knew too
what she was telling him—that here was all the hope they
had, and that Roh's hand had sealed it from them. He tried
to gather his thoughts amid the noise: sight and sound
muddled together, chaos he knew he would not remember, as
he could not remember the between of Gates: he did not
know how to call what he saw, and his thoughts would not
hold it. Once before he had walked such a hall; and he
remembered now a patch of blood on the floor, a corridor, a
stairway that was different—as if elsewhere in this building a
door lay in ruins and at his side stood a brother he had lost.

Who was dust now, long dead, nine hundred years ago.

The confusion became too much, too painful. He watched
Morgaine turn and touch the panel again, doing battle with

something he did not understand nor want to know. He understood it for hopeless.

"*Morgaine!*"

Roh's voice, louder than the noise about them.

Vanye looked up, the sword clenched in his fist; and Roh's
shape drifted amid the light and the sound, pervisible, larger
than life.

It spoke: it whispered words in the *qujalin* tongue, a whisper that outshouted the sounds from the walls. Vanye heard
his own name on its insubstantial lips, and crossed himself,
loathing this thing that taunted him, that whispered his name
to Morgaine, whispered things he could in no wise understand: his cousin Roh. He saw the face that was so nearly his
own, alike as a brother's—the brown eyes, the small scar at
the cheek that he remembered. It was utterly Roh.

"*Are you there, cousin?*" the image asked suddenly, sending cold to his heart. "*Perhaps not. Perhaps you remain safe
at Ohtij-in. Perhaps only your liege has come, and has forgotten you. But if you are beside her, remember what we spoke
of on the rooftop, and know that my warning was true: she
is pitiless. I seal the Wells to seal her out, and hope that it
may suffice; but, Nhi Vanye, kinsman, you may come to me.
Leave her. Her, I will not let pass; I dare not. But you I will
accept. For you, there is a way out of this world, as I give it
to others, if she would permit it. Come and meet me at
Abarais: so long as you can hear this message, there is still a
chance. Take it, and come.*"

The image and the voice faded together. Vanye stood
stricken for a moment; and then he dared look at Morgaine,
to find question in the look that she returned him—a deadly
mistrust.

"I shall not go," he insisted. "There was nothing agreed between us, *liyo*—ever. On my life, I would not go to him."

Her hand, that had slipped to the weapon at the back of
her belt, returned to her side; and of a sudden she reached
out and took his arm, drew him to the counter and set his
hand there, atop the cold lights.

"I shall show you," she told him. "I shall show you; and on
your life, *ilin*, on your *soul*, do you not forget it."

Her fingers moved, instructing his; he banished to a far refuge in him his threatened soul, that shuddered at the touch of
these cold things. She bade him thus and thus and thus, a
patterned touch on the colors, upon one and the other and
the next; he forced it into his memory, branded it there,

knowing the purpose of what he was given, little as it might avail here, with Roh's touch to seal the power against their tampering.

Again and again she bade him repeat for her the things that she had taught; mindlessly Roh's ghost overhung them, repeating things that mocked them, endlessly, blind, void of sense. Vanye's hands shook when that began again, but he did not falter in the pattern. Sweat prickled on him in his concentration; yet more times she bade him do what she had shown him.

He finished yet again, and looked at her, pleading with his look that it be enough, that they quit this place. She gazed at him, face and hair dyed with the bloody light, as if searching him for any fault; and above her yet again Roh's face began to mouth its words into the throbbing air.

And suddenly she nodded that it was enough, and turned toward that door by which they had come.

They walked the long aisle of the room. Vanye's nerves screamed at him to take flight, to run; but she did not, and he would not. His nape prickled as Roh's voice pursued them; he knew that did he turn and look there would be Roh's face hovering in the air—urging at him with reasonings that no longer had allure: better to sit helpless while the seas rose, than to surrender to that, which had lied to him from the beginning, which for a time had made him believe that a kinsman lived in this forsaken Hell, in this endless exile.

The darkness of the stairway lay before them; Morgaine shut the door and sealed it, shook him from his bewilderment to show him how it was done. He nodded blank, heartless understanding, his senses still filled with the sound and the light, and the terror of knowing what she had fed into his mind.

He held what men and *qujal* had murdered to possess; and he did not want it, with all his heart he did not. He put out his hand to the wall, still blind, save for the beam that Morgaine carried; he felt rough stone under his fingertips, felt the steps under his feet; and still his mind was dazed with what he had seen and felt. He wished it all undone; and he knew that it was too late, that he had been Claimed in a way that had no release, no freedom.

Down and down the curving stair they went, until he could hear the stamp and blowing of the horses—friendly, familiar sound, native to the man who had ascended the stairs; it was as if a different man had come down, who could not for a moment realize that the things he knew outside that terrible room could still exist, untouched, unshaken by what had shaken him.

Morgaine put out the light she bore as they stepped off the last step, and Jhirun came to them, full of whispered questions—her tearful voice and frightened manner reminding him that she also had endured the terror of this place—and knew nothing of what it held. He envied her that ignorance—touched her hand as she gave the reins of his horse to him.

"Go back," he told her. "Myya Jhirun, ride back the way we came and hide somewhere."

"No," said Morgaine suddenly.

He looked toward her, startled, dismayed; he could not read her face in the darkness.

"Come outside," she said; and she led Siptah through the doorway, waiting for them in the moonlight. Vanye did not look at Jhirun, having no answers for her; he led the gelding out, and heard Jhirun behind him.

"Jhirun," said Morgaine, "go watch the road with Kithan."

Jhirun looked from one to the other of them, but ventured no word in objection: she started away, leading her horse down the long aisle of slanting spires to the place where Kithan sat, a shadow among shadows.

"Vanye," said Morgaine softly, "would thee go to him? Would thee take what he offers?"

"No," he protested upon the instant. "No, upon my oath, I would not."

"Do not swear too quickly," she said; and when he would have disputed her: "Listen to me: this one order—go to him, surrender—go with him."

He could not answer for a moment; the words were dammed in his throat, refusing utterance.

"My order," she said.

"This is a deception of yours," he said, indignant that she did not take him into her trust, that she thus played games with him. "You are full of them. I do not think that I deserve it, *liyo.*"

"Vanye—if I cannot get through, one of us must. I am well known; I am disaster to you. But you—go with him, swear to his service; learn what he can teach you that I have not. And kill him, and go on as I would do."

"*Liyo,*" he protested. A shiver set into his limbs; he wound his cold fingers into the black horse's mane, for all that he had trusted dropped away beneath him, as the mountains had vanished that morning beyond the Gate, leaving all about him naked and ugly.

"You are *ilin*," she said. "And you take no guilt for it."

"To take bread and warmth and then kill a man?"

"Did I ever promise thee I had honor? It was otherwise, I think."

"Oath-breaking . . . *Liyo*, even to him—"

"One of us," she said between her teeth, *"one* of us must get through. Remain sworn to me in your mind, but let your mouth say whatever it must. Live. He will not suspect you; he will come to trust you. And this is the service I set on you: kill him, and carry out what I have shown you, without end—without end, *ilin*. Will you do this for me?"

"Aye," he said at last; and in his bitterness: "I must."

"Take Kithan and Jhirun; make some tale that Roh will believe, how Ohtij-in has fallen, of your release by Kithan— omitting my part in it. Let him believe you desperate. Bow at his feet and beg shelter of him. Do whatever you must, but stay alive, and pass the Gate, and carry out my orders—to the end of your life, Nhi Vanye, and beyond if thee can contrive it."

For a long moment he said nothing; he would have wept if he had tried to speak, and in his anger he did not want that further shame. Then he saw a trail of moisture shine on her cheek, and it shook him more than all else that she had said.

"Be rid of the Honor-blade," she said. "It will raise a question with him you cannot answer."

He drew it and gave it to her. "Avert," he murmured, the word almost catching in his throat; she echoed the wish, and slipped it through her belt.

"Beware your companions," she said.

"Aye," he answered.

"Go. Make haste."

He would have bowed himself at her feet, an *ilin* taking final, unwilling leave; but she prevented him with a hand on his arm. The touch numbed: for a moment he hesitated with a thing spilling over in him that wanted saying, and she, all unexpected, leaned forward and touched her lips to his, a light touch, quickly gone. It robbed him of speech; the moment passed, and she turned to take up the reins of her horse. What he would have said seemed suddenly a plea for himself, and she would not hear it; there would be dispute, and that was not the parting he wanted.

He hurled himself into the saddle, and she did likewise,

and rode with him as far as the crossing of the road and the aisle, the arch that led through into Abarais, where Jhirun and Kithan awaited them.

"We are going on," he said to them, the words strange and ugly to him, "we three."

They looked puzzled, dismayed. They said nothing, asked nothing; perhaps the look of the two of them, *ilin* and *liyo*, made a barrier against them. He turned his horse into the passage, into the dark, and they went with him. Suddenly he looked back, in dread that Morgaine would already be gone.

She was not. She was a shadow, she and Siptah, against the light behind them, waiting.

Fwar and his kind, whatever remained of them, would be coming. Suddenly he realized the set of her mind: the Barrows-folk, that she once had led—ages hence. There was a bond between them, an ill dream that was recent in her mind, a *geas* apart from *Changeling*. He remembered her at the Suvoj, sweeping man after man away into oblivion—and the thing that he had seen in her eyes.

They were your own, Kithan had protested, even a *qujal* appalled at what she had done. They followed her; she waited for them this time, as time after time he had feared she might turn and face them, her peculiar nightmare, that would not let her go.

She waited, while the Gate prepared to seal. Here she stopped running; and laid all her burden upon him. Tears blurred his eyes; he thought wildly of riding back, refusing what she had set him to do.

And that she would not forgive.

They exited the passage into the light of rising Li, saw the valley of Abarais before them, the jagged spires of ruins, and in the far distance—campfires scattered like stars across the mountains: the host of all Shiuan.

He looked back; he could not see Morgaine any longer.

He rammed the spurs into the gelding's flanks and led his companions toward the fires.

Chapter Eighteen

||||||||||||||||||||||||||||||||||||||||||||||||||

The vast disc of Li inclined toward the horizon. There was a stain of cloud at that limit of the sky, and wisps of cloud drifted across the moon-track overhead.

The sinking moon yet gave them light enough for quick traveling—light enough too for their enemies. They were exposed, in constant view from the cliffs that towered on either side of the road, above the ruins. Ambush was a constant possibility: Vanye feared it with a distant fear, not for himself, but for the orders he had been given—the only thing he had left, he thought, that was worth concern. That at some moment a shaft aimed from those cliffs should come bursting leather and mail links and bone—the pain would be the less for it, and quickly done, unlike the other, that was forever.

Until you have no choice, her words echoed back to him, a persistent misery, a fact that would not be denied. *Until you have no choice—as I have none.*

Once Jhirun spoke to him; he did not know what she had said, nor care—only stared at her, and she fell silent; and Kithan likewise stared at him, pale eyes sober and present, purged of the *akil* that had clouded them.

And the watchfires grew nearer, spreading before them like a field of stars, red and angry constellations across their way, that began to dim at last like those in the heavens, with the first edge of day showing.

"There is nothing left," Vanye told his companions, realizing that their time grew short, "only to surrender to my cousin and hope for his forbearance."

They were silent, Jhirun next to him and Kithan beyond. Their faces held that same restrained fear that had possessed them since they had been hastened, without explanation, from An-Abarais. They still did not ask, nor demand assurances of him. Perhaps they already knew he had none to give.

"At An-Abarais," he continued while they rode, walking the horses, "we learned that there was no choice. My liege has released me." He suppressed the tremor that would come to his voice, set the muscles of his jaw and continued, beginning to weave the lie that he would use for Roh. "There is more kindness in her than is apparent—for my sake, if not for yours. She knows the case of things, that Roh might accept me, but never her. You are nothing to her; she simply does not care. But Roh hates her above all other enemies; and the less he knows of what truly passed at Ohtij-in, the more readily he will take me—and you. If he knows that I have come directly from her, and you likewise from her company—he will surely kill me; and for me, he has some affection. I leave it to you how much he would hesitate in your case."

Still they said nothing, but the apprehension was no less in their eyes.

"Say that Ohtij-in fell in the quake," he asked of them, "and say that the marshlanders attacked when Aren fell—say whatever you like of the truth; but do not let him know that we entered An-Abarais. Only she could have passed its doors and learned what she learned. Forget altogether that she was with us, or I shall die; and I do not think that I will be alone in that."

Of Jhirun he was sure; there was a debt between them. But there was one of a different nature between himself and Kithan: it was the *qujal* that he feared, and the *qujal* that he most needed to confirm his lie as truth.

And Kithan knew it: those unhuman eyes took on a consciousness of power, and a smug amusement.

"And if it is not Roh who gives the orders," Kithan said, "if it is Hetharu, what shall I say, Man?"

"I do not know," Vanye said. "But a father-slayer will hardly stick at brother-killing; and he will share nothing with you . . . not unless he loves you well. Do you think that is so, Kithan Bydarra's-son?"

Kithan considered it, and the smugness faded rapidly.

"How well," Kithan asked, scowling, "does your cousin love you?"

"I will serve him," Vanye answered, finding the words strange to his lips. "I am an *ilin* now without a master; and we are of Andur-Kursh, he and I . . . you do not under-

stand, but it means that Roh will take me with him, and I
will serve him as his right hand; and that is something he
cannot find elsewhere. I need you, my lord Kithan, and you
know it; I need you to set myself at Roh's side, and you
know that you can destroy me with an ill-placed word. But
likewise you need me—else you will have to deal with
Hetharu; and you know that I bear Hetharu a grudge. You
do not love him. Stand by me; and I will give you Hetharu,
even if it takes time."

Kithan considered, his lips a thin line. "Aye," he said, "I
do follow your reasoning. But, Nhi Vanye, there are two men
of mine that may undo it all."

Vanye recalled that, the house guards that had fled, that
added a fresh weight of apprehension to his mind; he
shrugged. "We cannot amend that. It is a large camp. If I
were in the place of such men, I would not rush to authority
and boast that I had deserted my lord."

"Are you not doing so now?" Kithan asked.

Heat flamed in his face. "Yes," he admitted hoarsely. "By
her leave; but those are details Roh need not know . . . only
that Ohtij-in has fallen, and that we are escaped from it."

Kithan considered that a moment. "I will help you," he
said. "Perhaps my word can bring you to your cousin. Seeing
Hetharu discomfited will be pleasure enough to reward me."

Vanye stared at him, weighing the truth behind that cyni-
cal gaze, and looked questioningly also at Jhirun, past whom
they had been talking. She looked afraid in that reckoning, as
if she, a peasant, knew her worth in the affairs of lords who
strove for power.

"Jhirun?" he questioned her.

"I want to live," she said. He looked into the fierceness of
that determination and doubted, suddenly; perhaps she saw it,
for her lips tightened. "I will stay with you," she said then.

Tears shone in her eyes, of pain or fear or what other
cause he did not know, nor spare further thought to wonder.
He had no care for either of them, Myya nor halfling lord,
only so they did not ruin him. His mind was already racing
apace, to the encamped thousands that lay ahead, beginning
to plot what approach they might make so that none would
slay them out of hand.

Whatever their need for haste, it could be measured by the
fact that none of the horde that followed Roh had yet begun
to move: the watchfires still glowed in the murky beginnings
of dawn. It was best, he thought, to ride in slowly, as many a

party must have done, come to join the movement that
flowed toward the Well: anxiously he measured the rising
light against the distance to the far edge of the fires, and
liked not the reckoning. They could not make it all before the
light showed them for the ill-assorted companions they were.

But there was no other course that promised better.

Soon they rode out of the ruin altogether, and among the
stumps of young trees, saplings that had been hewn off the
beginning slope of the mountain—for shelters, or to feed the
fires of the camp. And soon enough they rode within scent of
cookfires, and the sound of voices.

Sentries started from their posts, seizing up spears and advancing on them. Vanye kept riding at a steady pace, the others with him; and when they had come close in the dim light,
the sentries—dark-haired Men—stood confused by the sight
of them and backed away, making no challenge. Perhaps it
was the presence of Kithan, Vanye thought, resisting the
temptation to look back; or perhaps—the thought came to
him with peculiar irony—it was himself, cousin to Roh, similar in arms and even in mount, for the two horses, Roh's
mare and his gelding, were of the same hold and breeding.

They entered the camp, that sprawled in disorder on either
side of the paved road. At a leisurely pace they rode past the
wretched Shiua, who huddled drowsing by their fires, or
looked up and stared with furtive curiosity at what passed
them in the dawning.

"We must find the Well," Vanye observed softly; "I trust
that is where we will find Roh."

"Road's-end," answered Kithan, and nodded toward the
way ahead, that began to wind up to the shoulder of the
mountains. "The Old Ones built high."

Somewhere a horn sounded, thin and far, a lonely sound
off the mountain-slopes. Over and over it sounded, sending
the echoes tumbling off the valley walls; and about them the
camp began to stir. Voices began to be heard, strained with
excitement; fires began to be extinguished, sending up plumes
of smoke.

Jhirun looked from one side to the other in apprehension.
"They are beginning to move," she said. "Lord, surely the
Well is open, and they are beginning to move."

It was true: everywhere men were stripping shelters and
gathering their meager belongings; children were crying and
animals were bawling in alarm and disturbance. In moments,

those lightest burdened had begun to seek the road, pouring out onto that way that led them to the Well.

Roh's gift, Vanye thought, his heart pained for the treason he felt, his human soul torn by the sight of the overburdened folk about him, that edged from the path of their horses. Morgaine would have doomed them; but they were going to live.

He came, to bow at Roh's feet—and one day to kill him; and by that, to betray these folk: he saw himself, an evil presence gently threading his way among them, whose faces were set in a delirious and desperate hope.

He served Morgaine.

There was at least a time you chose for yourself, she had said.

Thee will not appoint thyself my conscience, Nhi Vanye. Thee is not qualified.

He began to know.

With a grimace of pain he laid spurs and the reins' ends to the black gelding, startling Shiua peasants from his path, frightened folk yielding to him and his two companions, that held close behind him. Faces tore away in the dim light before him, stark with fear and dismay.

The road wound steeply upward. An archway rose athwart it, massive and strange. They passed beneath, passed through the vanguard of the human masses that toiled up the heights, and suddenly rode upon forces of *qujal*, demon-helmed and bristling with lances, whose women rode with them, pale-haired ladies in glittering cloaks, and, very few among them, a cluster of pale, grave-eyed children, who stared at the intrusion with the sober mien of their elders.

A band of *qujal* amid that mass reined themselves across the road, where its turning made passage difficult, with a dizzying plunge into depths on the right hand. Authority was among them, bare-headed, white hair streaming in the wind; and his men ranged themselves before him.

Vanye reined back and reached for his sword. "No," Kithan said at once. "They are Sotharra. They will not stop us."

Uneasily Vanye conceded the approach to Kithan, rode at his shoulder and with Jhirun at his own rein hand, as they drew to a slow halt before the halflings, with levelled pikes all about them.

Little Kithan had to say to them: a handful of words, of which one was Ohtij-in and another was Roh and another

was Kithan's own name; and the Sotharra lord straightened
in his saddle, and reined aside, the pikes of his men-at-arms
flourishing up and away.

But when they had ridden through, the Sotharra rode behind them at their pace; and Vanye ill-liked it, though it gave
them passage through the other masses of halflings that rode
the winding ascent. Hereafter was no retreat: he was committed to the hands of *qujal,* to trust Kithan, who could say
what he wished to them.

And if Roh had already passed, and if it were Hetharu
who must approve his passage: Vanye drove that thought
from his mind.

A turning of the road brought them suddenly into sight of
a round hill, ringed about by throngs of halfling folk: the
horses slowed of their own accord, snorting, walking skittishly, weary as they were.

It grew upon the senses, that oppression that Vanye knew
of Gates, that nerve-prickling unease that made the skin feel
raw and the senses over-weighted. It was almost sound, and
not. It was almost touch, and not.

He saw the place to which they went, in a day that yet had
a murkiness in its pastel clouds: there were tents; there were
horses; and the road came to an end in a place shadowed by
slanted spires.

And the Well.

It was a circle of Standing Stones, like that of Hiuaj: not a
single Gate, but a gathering of them, and they were alive.
Opal colors streamed within them, like illusion in the daylight, a constant interplay of powers that filled the air with
uneasiness; but one Gate held the azure blue of sky, that was
terrible with depth, that made the eyes ache with beholding
it.

Kithan swore.

"They are real," the *qujal* said. "They are real."

Vanye forced the reluctant gelding to a steady walk, shouldered into Jhirun's mare by a sudden rebellion of the horse,
and saw Jhirun's eyes, dazed, still fixed upon the horror of
the Gates; her hand was at her throat, where bits of metal
and a white feather and a stone cross offered her what belief
she knew. He spoke her name, sharply, and she tore her gaze
from the hillside and kept by his side.

The camp at the base of the hill was already astir. Shouts
attended their arrival, voices thin and lost in that heaviness of
the air. Men fair-haired and armored gathered to stare at

them: *"Kithan l'Ohtija,"* Vanye heard whispered: he unhooked his sword and rode with it across the saddle as they
rode slowly past pale, gray-eyed faces, forcing a way until the
press grew too thick to do so without violence.

Kithan asked a question of them. It received quick answer;
and Kithan raised his eyes toward the edge of the hill and
reined in that direction. Vanye stayed beside him, Jhirun's
mare at his flank as the hedge of weapons slowly parted, letting them pass. He heard his own name spoken, and
Bydarra's; he saw the sullen, wondering faces, the hateful
looks, the hands that gripped weapons: Bydarra's accused
murderer—he kept his face impassive and kept the horse
moving steadily in Kithan's wake.

Riders came through the crowd, demon-helmed and armored, spreading out, shouldering the crowd aside, spreading
out athwart their path. An order was shouted: and among
them, central amid a hedge of pikemen, rode an all-too-famil-
iar figure, silver-haired, with the beauty of the *qujal* and the
eyes of a man.

Hetharu.

Vanye shouted, ripped the sword free and spurred for him,
into a shielding wall of pikes that shied his horse back, wounded. One of the pikemen fell; Vanye slashed at another,
reined back and back, and whirled on those threatening his
flank. He broke free; Hetharu's folk scattered back, forgetful
of dignity, scale-armored house guards massing in a protective arc before their lord.

Vanye drew breath, flexed his hand on the sword,
measured the weakest man—and heard other riders come in
on his flank. Jhirun cried out; he reined back, risked a glance
in that quarter, beyond Jhirun, beyond Kithan—and saw him
he hoped desperately to see.

Roh. Bow slung across his shoulders, sword across his saddlebow, Roh had reined to a halt. Ohtija and Sotharra gave
back from him, and slowly he rode the black mare into what
had become a vacant space.

Vanye sat the sweating gelding, tight-reining him, who
turned fretfully this way and that, hurt, and trembling when
he stood still.

Another rider moved in; he cast a panicked glance in that
direction: Hetharu, who sat his horse sword in hand.

"Where," Roh asked him, drawing his attention back, "is
Morgaine?"

Vanye shrugged, a listless gesture, though he felt the tension in every muscle.

"Come down from your horse," said Roh.

He wiped the length of the sword on the gelding's black mane, then climbed down, sword still in hand, and gave the reins of the horse to Jhirun. He sheathed the sword then, and waited.

Roh watched him from horseback; and when he had put away the weapon, Roh likewise dismounted and tossed the reins to a companion, hung his sword at his hip and walked forward until they could speak without raising voices.

"Where is she?" Roh asked again.

"I do not know," Vanye said. "I have come for shelter, like these others."

"Ohtij-in is gone," Kithan said suddenly from behind him. "The quake took it, and all inside. The marshlands are on the move; and some of us they hanged. The man Vanye and the Barrows-girl were with me on the road, else I might have died; my own men deserted me."

There was silence. There should have been shock, outcry—some emotion on the faces of the Ohtija *qujal* who surrounded them.

"*Arres*," Hetharu's voice said suddenly; riders moved up, and Vanye turned in alarm.

Two helmless men were beside Hetharu: scale-armored, white-haired, and alike as brothers—shameless in their change of lords.

"Yours," Kithan murmured, and managed an ironical bow. The accustomed drugged distance crept into his voice.

"To protect my brother," Hetharu answered softly, "from his own nature—which is well-known and transparent. You are quite sober, Kithan."

"The news," said Roh, from the other side, "outran you, Nhi Vanye. Now tell me the truth. Where is she?"

He turned and faced Roh, for one terrible moment bereft of all subtleties: he could think of nothing.

"My lord Hetharu," Roh said. "The camp is on the move. Uncomfortable as it is, I think it time to move your forces into position; and yours as well, my lords of Sotharrn and Domen, Marom and Arisith. We will make an orderly passage."

There was a stir within the ranks; orders were passed, and a great part of the gathering began to withdraw—the Sotharra, who were prepared already to move, began to ascend the hill.

But Hetharu did not, not he nor his men.

Roh looked up at him, and at the men that delayed about them. "My lord Hetharu," Roh said, "lord Kithan will go with you, if you have use for him."

Hetharu gave an order. The two house guards rode forward and set themselves on either side of Kithan, whose pale face was set in helpless rage.

"Vanye," Roh said.

Vanye looked at him.

"Once again," Roh said, "I ask you."

"I have been dismissed," Vanye said slowly, the words difficult to speak. "I ask fire and shelter, Chya Roh i Chya."

"On your oath?"

"Yes," he said. His voice trembled. He knelt down, reminding himself that this must be, that his liege's direct order absolved him of the lie and the shame; but it was bitter to do so in the sight of both allies and enemies. He bowed himself to the earth, forehead against the trampled grass. He heard the voices, numb in the Well-cursed air, and was glad in this moment that he could not understand their words of him.

Roh did not bid him rise. Vanye sat back after a moment, staring at the ground, shame burning his face, both for the humiliation and for the lie.

"She has sent you," Roh said, "to kill me."

He looked up.

"I think she has made a mistake," said Roh. "Cousin, I will give you the sheltering you ask, taking your word that you have been dismissed from your service to her. By this evening's fire, elsewhere—a Claiming. I think you are too much Nhi to forswear yourself. But she would not understand that. There is no pity in her, Nhi Vanye."

Vanye came to his feet, a sudden move: blades rasped loose all about him, but he kept his hand from his.

"I will go with you," he said to Roh.

"Not at my back," Roh said. "Not this side of the Wells. Not unsworn." He took back the reins of the black mare, and rose into the saddle—cast a look toward the hill, where row on row of Sotharran forces had marshalled themselves, toward which the first frightened lines of human folk labored.

The lines moved with feverish speed behind: those entering that oppressive air hesitated, pushed forward by the press behind; horses shied, of those forces holding the hill, and had to be restrained.

And of a sudden a tumult arose, downtrail, beyond the

curve of the mountainside. Voices shrieked, thin and distant. Animals bawled in panic.

Roh reined about toward that sound, the least suspicion of something amiss crossing his face as he gazed toward that curving of the hill: the shouting continued, and somewhere high atop the mountain a horn blew, echoing.

Vanye stood still, in his heart a wild, sudden hope—the thing that Roh likewise suspected: he knew it, he knew, and suddenly in the depth of him he cursed in anguish for what Morgaine had done to him, casting him into this, face to face with Roh.

Vanye whirled, sprang for his horse and ripped the reins from Jhirun's offering hand as the *qujal* closed on him; a rake of his spurs shied the gelding up, buying him time to draw. A pike-thrust hit his mailed side, half-throwing him; he hung on with his knees, and the sweep of his sword sent the pikeman screaming backward, that man and another and another.

"*No!*" Roh's voice shouted thinly in his roaring ears; he found himself in ground free of enemies, a breathing space. He backed the gelding, amazed to see part of the force break away: Roh, and his own guard, and all of fifty of the Ohtija, plunging toward the hill, and the Sotharra, and the screaming hordes of men that surged toward the Wells, lines confounded by panicked beasts that scattered, laboring carts, and a horde that pressed them behind. The Sotharra ranks bowed, began to break. Into that chaos Roh and his companions rode.

And the Ohtija that remained surged foward. Vanye spurred into the impact, wove under one pike-thrust, and suddenly saw a man he had not struck topple from the saddle with blood starting from his face. A second fell, and another to his blade; and a second time the Ohtija, facing more than a peasant rabble, fell back in confusion. Air rushed; Vanye blinked, dazed, saw a stone take another of the Ohtija—the house guard that had betrayed Kithan.

Jhirun.

He reined back and back, almost to the cover of the tumbled stones of the hillside; and yet another stone left Jhirun's sling, toppling another man from the saddle and sending the animal shying into others, hastening the Ohtija into retreat, leaving their dead behind them.

Jhirun and Kithan: out of the tail of his eye he saw the halfling still with him, leaking blood from fingers pressed to his sleeve. Jhirun, barefoot and herself with a scrape across the cheek, swung down from her little mare and quickly gathered a handful of stones.

But the Ohtija were not returning. They had headed up, across the slope, where the ranks of the Sotharra had collapsed into utter disorder.

Men, human-folk, poured in increasing numbers up the slope, this way and that, fleeing in terror.

And came others, small men and different, and armed, adding terror to the rout: pitiless they were in their desperation, making no distinction of halfling or human.

"Marshlanders," Jhirun cried in dismay.

The horde swept between them and the Well.

"Up!" Vanye cried at Jhirun, and delayed only the instant, spurred the exhausted gelding toward that slope, beyond thinking whether Jhirun or Kithan understood. Marshlanders recognized him, and cried out in a frenzy, a few attacking, most scattering from the black horse's hooves. Who stood in his way, he overrode, wielded his sword where he must, his arm aching with the effort; he felt the horse falter, and spurred it the harder.

And across the slope he saw her, a flash of Siptah's pale body in a gap she cut through the press: enemies scattered from her path and hapless folk fled screaming, or fell cowering to the ground. Red fire took any that chose to stand.

"*Liyo!*" he shouted, hewed with his sword a man that thrust for him, broke into the clear and headed across the slope on a converging line with her. She saw him; he drove the spurs in mercilessly, and they two swung into a single line, black horse and gray, side by side as they took the slope toward the Wells, enemies breaking from their path in a wide swath.

But at the first of the Ohtija lines, there riders massed, and moved to stop them. Morgaine's fire took some, but the ranks filled, and others swept across the flank of the hill. Arrows flew.

Morgaine turned, swept fire in that direction.

And the Ohtija broke and scattered, all but a handful. Together they rode into that determined mass, toppled three from their saddles. Siptah found a space to run and leaped forward; and Vanye spurred the gelding after.

Suddenly the horse twisted under him, screaming pain—a rush of earth upward and the sure, slow knowledge that he was horseless, lost—before the impact crumpled him upon shoulder and head and flung him stunned against a pile of stones.

Vanye fought to move, to bring himself to his feet, and the first thing that he saw was the black gelding, dying, a broken shaft in its chest. He staggered to his feet leaning against the rocks and bent for his fallen sword, and gazed upslope, blinking clear the sight of opal fires and Siptah's distant shape, Morgaine at the hill's crest.

Enemies were about her. Red laced the opal shimmerings, and the air was numb with the presence of the Gates above them.

And riders came sweeping in toward her, a half a hundred horse crossing that slope. Vanye cursed aloud and thrust himself out from the rocks, trying to climb the slope afoot; pain stabbed up his leg, laming him.

She would not stay for him, could not. He used the sword to aid him and kept climbing.

A horseman rushed up on him from behind; he whirled, seized a pikethrust between arm and body and wrenched, pulled the halfling off, asprawl with him; the horse rushed on, shying from them. Vanye struck with the longsword's pommel, dazed the halfling and staggered free, struggling only to climb, half-deaf to the rider that thundered up behind him.

He saw Morgaine turning back, giving up ground won, casting herself back among enemies. "No!" he shouted, trying to wave her off; the exhausted gray could not carry them, double weight in flight. He saw what Morgaine, intent on reaching him, could not see: the massing of a unit of horse on her flank.

A bay horse rushed past him, a flash of bare legs as he turned, lifting the sword: Jhirun reined in hard and slid down. "Lord!" she cried, thrusting the reins into his hand, and, "Go!" she shouted at him, her voice breaking.

He flung himself for the saddle, felt the surge of the horse as life itself; but he delayed, taut-reined, offered his bloody hand to her.

She stumbled back, hand behind her, the shying horse putting paces between them as she backed away on the corpse-littered slope.

"Go!" she screamed furiously, and cursed him.

Dazed, he reined back; and then he looked upslope, where Morgaine delayed, enemies broken before her. She shouted something at him; he could not hear it, but he knew.

He spurred the mare forward, and Morgaine reined about

and joined with him in the climb. Ohtija forces wavered before them, broke as horses went down under Morgaine's fire. Peasants scattered screaming, confounding the order of cavalry.

They mounted the crest of the hill, toward an enemy that fled their path in disorder, peasants and lords together, entering into that great circle that was the Well of Abarais, where opal lights surged and drifted among the Stones, where a vast blue space yawned bottomlessly before them, drinking in men and halfling riders, seeming at once to hurtle skyward and downward, out of place in the world that beheld it, a burning blue too terrible against Shiuan's graying skies.

Siptah took the leap in one long rush; the bay mare tried to shy off, but Vanye rammed his spurs into her and drove her, cruel in his desperation, as they hurtled up and into that burning, brighter sky.

There was a moment of dark, of twisting bodies, of shadow-shapes, as they fell through the nightmare of Between, the two of them together; and then the horses found ground beneath them again, the two of them still running, dreamlike in their slowness as the legs extended into reality, and then rapidly, cutting a course through frightened folk that had no will to stop them.

None pursued, not yet; the arrows that flew after them were few and ill-aimed; the cries of alarm faded into the distance, until there was only the sound of the horses under them, and the view of open plains about them.

They drew rein and began to walk the exhausted animals. Vanye looked back, where a horde massed at the foot of Gates that still shimmered with power: Roh's to command, those who gathered there, still lost, still bewildered.

About them stretched a land as wide and flat as the eye could reach, a land of grass and plenty. Vanye drew a deep breath of the air, found the winds clean and untainted, and looked at Morgaine, who rode beside him, not looking back.

She would not speak yet. There was a time for speaking. He saw the weariness in her, her unwillingness to reckon with this land. She had run a long course, forcing those she could not lead.

"I needed an army," she said at last, a voice faint and thin. "There was only one that I could manage, that could breach his camp. And it was very good to see thee, Vanye."

"Aye," he said, and thought it enough. There was time for other things.

She drew *Changeling*, by it to take their bearings in this wide land.

BOOK THREE

Chapter Nineteen

The men passed, carts and wagons and what animals could be forced, unwilling, into that terrible void. Jhirun lay between the cooling body of the black horse and the jumble of rocks, and gazed with horror up that hill, at the swirling fires that were the Well, that drank in all that came. Straggling horsemen on frightened mounts; peasants afoot; rank on rank they came, all the host of Shiuan and Hiuaj, women of the Shiua peasants and of the glittering *khal*, men that worked the fields and men that bleached their hair and wore the black robes of priests, fingering their amulets and invoking the blind powers that drank them in. Some came with terror and some few with exaltation; and the howling winds took them, and they passed from view.

Came also the last stragglers of the Aren-folk, women and children and old ones, and a few youths to protect them. She saw one of her tall cousins of Barrows-hold, who moved into the light and vanished, bathed in its shimmering fires. The sun reached its zenith and declined, and still the passage continued, some last few running in exhausted eagerness, or limping with wounds, and some lingered, needing attempt after attempt to gather their courage.

Jhirun wrapped her shawl about her and shivered, leaning her cheek against the rock, watching them, unnoticed, a peasant girl, nothing to those who had their minds set on the Well and the hope beyond it.

At last in the late afternoon the last of them passed, a lame halfling, who spent long in struggling up the trampled slope, past the bodies of the slain. He vanished. Then there was only the unnatural heaviness of the air, and the howling of wind through the Well, the fires that shimmered there against the gray-clouded sky.

She was the last. On stiff and cramped legs she gathered

herself up and walked, conscious of the smallness of herself
as she ascended that slope, into air that seemed too heavy to
breathe, the wind pulling at her skirts. She entered that area
of light, the maelstrom of the fires, stood within the circle of
the Well and shuddered, blinking in terror at the perspective
that gaped before her, blindingly blue. The winds urged at
her.

Her cousins had gone; they had all gone, the Aren-folk, the
Barrowers, Fwar, the lords of Ohtij-in.

This she had set out to find; and Fwar had possessed it instead, he and the Aren-folk. They would shape the dream to
their own desires, seeking what they would have.

She wept, and turned her back on the Well, lacking courage—hugged her shawl about her, and in doing so remembered a thing that she had long carried.

She drew it from between her breasts, the little gull-figure,
and touched the fine work of its wings, her eyes blurring the
details of it. She turned, and hurled it, a shining mote,
through the pillars of the Wells. The winds took it, and it
never fell. It was gone.

He was gone, he at least, into a land that would not so be-
wilder him, where there might be mountains, and plains for
the mare to run.

They would not take him, Fwar and his enemies. She believed that.

She turned and walked away, out of the fires and into the
gray light. Halfway down the hill the winds ceased, and there
was a great silence.

She turned to look; and even as she watched, the fires
seemed to shimmer like the air above the marsh; and they
shredded, and vanished, leaving only the gray daylight between the pillars of the Well, and those pillars only gray and
ordinary stone.

Jhirun blinked, finding difficulty now even to believe that
there had been magics there, for her senses could no longer
hold them. She stared until the tears dried upon her face, and
then she turned and picked her way downhill, pausing now
and again to plunder the dead: from this one a waterflask,
from another a dagger with a golden hilt.

A movement startled her, a ring of harness, a rider that
came upon her from beyond the rocks, slowly: a bay horse
and a man in tattered blue, white-haired and familiar at once.

She stood still, waiting; the *khal*-lord made no haste. He
drew to a halt across her path, his face pale and sober, his

gray eyes clear, stained with shadow. A bloody rag was about his left arm.

"Kithan," she said. She gave him no titles. He ruled nothing. She saw that he had found a sword; strangely she did not fear him.

He moved his foot from the stirrup, held out a slender, fine-boned hand; his face was stern, but the gray eyes were anxious.

He needed her, she thought cynically. He was not prepared to survive in the land. She extended her hand to him, set her foot in the stirrup, surprised that there was such strength in his slender arm, that drew her up.

There were villages; there were fields the water would not reach in their lifetime. There were old ones left, and the timid, and those who had not believed.

The bay horse began to move; she set her arms about Kithan, and rested, yielding to the motion of the horse as they descended the hill. She shut her eyes and resolved not to look back, not until the winding of the road should come between them and the hill.

Thunder rumbled in the heavens. There were the first cold drops of rain.

DAW
C.J. CHERRYH
THE ALLIANCE-UNION UNIVERSE

The Company Wars
- [ ] DOWNBELOW STATION   (UE2431—$4.50)

The Era of Rapprochement
- [ ] SERPENT'S REACH   (UE2088—$3.50)
- [ ] FORTY THOUSAND IN GEHENNA   (UE2429—$4.50)
- [ ] MERCHANTER'S LUCK   (UE2139—$3.50)

The Chanur Novels
- [ ] THE PRIDE OF CHANUR   (UE2292—$3.95)
- [ ] CHANUR'S VENTURE   (UE2293—$3.95)
- [ ] THE KIF STRIKE BACK   (UE2184—$3.50)
- [ ] CHANUR'S HOMECOMING   (UE2177—$3.95)

The Mri Wars
- [ ] THE FADED SUN: KESRITH   (UE2449—$4.50)
- [ ] THE FADED SUN: SHON'JIR   (UE2448—$4.50)
- [ ] THE FADED SUN: KUTATH   (UE2133—$2.95)

Merovingen Nights (Mri Wars Period)
- [ ] ANGEL WITH THE SWORD   (UE2143—$3.50)

Merovingen Nights—Anthologies
- [ ] FESTIVAL MOON (#1)   (UE2192—$3.50)
- [ ] FEVER SEASON (#2)   (UE2224—$3.50)
- [ ] TROUBLED WATERS (#3)   (UE2271—$3.50)
- [ ] SMUGGLER'S GOLD (#4)   (UE2299—$3.50)
- [ ] DIVINE RIGHT (#5)   (UE2380—$3.95)

The Age of Exploration
- [ ] CUCKOO'S EGG   (UE2371—$4.50)
- [ ] VOYAGER IN NIGHT   (UE2107—$2.95)
- [ ] PORT ETERNITY   (UE2206—$2.95)

The Hanan Rebellion
- [ ] BROTHERS OF EARTH   (UE2290—$3.95)
- [ ] HUNTER OF WORLDS   (UE2217—$2.95)

DAW

More Top-Flight Science Fiction and Fantasy from
C.J. CHERRYH

DAW

The first new DARKOVER novel in five years!

THE HEIRS OF HAMMERFELL
Darkover: The Age of the Hundred Kingdoms
by MARION ZIMMER BRADLEY

Set in the age of The Hundred Kingdoms, *The Heirs o Hammerfell* takes place in a time of war and strife when Darkove was divided by border conflicts into numerous small, antago nistic kingdoms. It focuses on a devastating clan feud betweer two of these realms—Hammerfell and Storn—a feud which has seen the land soaked red with blood for countless generations But now Storn has struck what may prove to be Hammerfell' death stroke, setting the ancestral castle ablaze, slaying it lord, and sending its lady fleeing into the night with her twir infant sons, Alastair and Conn.

Conn is separated from his mother and lost to her on tha fateful night, but she and Alastair find sanctuary in Thendar City, among the wealthy and the *laran*-gifted, keeping the mem ory of Hammerfell alive with them in exile. Yet Conn, too survives, rescued by a loyal servant and raised in secret among those who would see the might of Storn overthrown and the banner of Hammerfell flying proudly high once again.

But it is not until Conn's *laran* manifests that the fates of the twins are finally, inextricably linked in a pattern which coulc bring a new beginning or total ruin to Hammerfell and it heirs. . . .

☐ **Hardcover Edition** (UE2395—$18.95